Poetry in Motion

Samantha Wayland

Also by Samantha Wayland

Poetry in Motion

Published by Loch Awe Press
P.O. Box 5481
Wayland, MA 01778

ISBN 978-1-940839-27-1

Edited by Meghan Miller
    & CeCe Carroll
Cover Art by Ben Ellis, Tall Story Designs

Dedication

For Claire, as this is entirely her fault.

Acknowledgements

Not only does Claire get the dedication, but she gets the first acknowledgement, too. The limerick in chapter fifteen of this book is her creation, and is included with her permission. Please see the author's note at the end of the book if you'd like to learn more about the poetry herein.

I must thank my amazing team of beta readers, who were all incredibly quick and kind. Claire (*again!*) for helping Barnaby be as terribly British as I could ever wish. Aven Ellis and Stephanie Kay, who have the dubious honor of keeping me grounded and making sure I don't totally slack off on marketing and my word counts. And finally, AE Wasp, whose encouragement and friendship has been a bright spot for me all through the process of writing this book.

Chapter One

Barnaby had come a very long way to get his PhD—a decision he was giving serious consideration to regretting. Had he known, when he'd packed up all his worldly possessions in London and shipped them to the Arse-End-of-Narnia, Canada, that he'd be faced with *this*, he might well have swallowed his admittedly abundant pride and thrown himself on his parents' mercy.

"But, like, I don't *get* it. Why is she locked in the attic, again?"

Barnaby stopped mid-stride on the path across campus, the student who'd followed him from class stumbling to a halt beside him. He drew a deep breath of the frigid air and let it out slowly, determined to keep his voice even. "Did you read the book?"

The young woman snapped her gum. "You don't have to be a dick about it."

Several responses to that observation clawed up Barnaby's throat, but he choked them back. He was not going to allow his temper to put his TA position in jeopardy. This charming student was but the latest in a long line of underclassmen in Professor Sorenson's 100-level English class who didn't seem to understand that they needed to *work* at university in order to succeed. He gagged on the desire to tell her what he really thought, but the raft of bills stuffed into the messenger bag strapped across his chest weighed him down like the proverbial albatross.

He'd come to Moncton for a fresh start. To leave as much of the past behind as he could. He'd spent the five months since wondering how he'd failed to realize how *cold* Canada was and how fucking *irritating* freshman were. He'd felt lucky when he'd landed the TA position, which only went to show he still harbored the unfortunate streak of wide-eyed optimism he'd sworn not to bring with him to Moncton University. Nevertheless, there weren't enough of these jobs to go around, and he needed all the income he could scrape together.

Some parts of the past weren't so easy to shake loose.

With that in mind, he pasted a smile on his face, answered her question diligently, and resumed walking—even going so far as to thank the young woman whose name he didn't know, nor particularly care to, for walking with him. She probably assumed he had another class to get to, when in fact he was spewing the Cliff Notes of Jayne Eyre while fighting the urge to break into a run toward his car and *freedom*.

By the time they reached the crosswalk to the parking lot, his companion was nodding along to his lecture and they'd picked up another student from the class, who trailed behind them and listened raptly. Or, he certainly appeared to be, given how he was staring at Barnaby with big, moony eyes.

Hello, awkward.

Barnaby was a healthy young man, with a healthy young libido—much to his dismay—but the last thing he needed was to get involved with someone, let alone a student. He was here to study. To learn. To pay off his debts and set himself on the course he'd dreamed of since he'd sat in his own first-year English class back in Oxford. He'd had big plans, and he'd fucked them up royally, but now he had a chance to get back on track and he wasn't going to do anything to jeopardize that.

He concluded his mobile lecture to the satisfaction of his student, who noted the book actually sounded interesting. Tamping down the urge to roll his eyes, he managed to say, somewhat sincerely, that she'd probably enjoy the book if she found the time to read it.

She smiled and trotted off to parts unknown, leaving Barnaby with Kevin.

Unlike the erstwhile Bronte fan, Barnaby knew Kevin's name because he always sat in the front row and stared at Barnaby with those big, moony eyes while Professor Sorenson droned his lessons to the massive lecture hall.

And because Kevin had asked Barnaby to dinner. Twice.

"Can I help you with something, Kevin?" he asked, bracing

for the answer.

Kevin blinked up at him, his cheeks turning pink. Or, more accurately, pinker. The flush of skin exposed to bitterly cold air was a permanent affliction around here. It was only a couple of weeks into the New Year, and Barnaby feared limbs would freeze and fall off before spring brought a thaw.

He tried to remember why he hadn't looked into PhD programs in Morocco. Or Greece. Perhaps Costa Rica.

"Um..." Kevin bit his lip.

"Kevin, do you have a question about class? I'll be holding office hours this week, as scheduled, and the study group on Wednesday night."

He looked painfully young. At eighteen, he *was* painfully young. He might be exactly the look Barnaby usually favored— slim, petite, smooth-skinned, and big-eyed—but he preferred it in someone his own age, which meant Kevin was off the mark by ten years.

Not that it mattered, because when it came to dating, sex, or any kind of intimate relationship, Barnaby was on the wagon. Off the market. On the fucking *shelf.*

Kevin continued to blink up at him.

Barnaby let out a long sigh. "Okay, if you think of what you wanted to ask me—*about class*, that is—you can email me. I'll check my messages later tonight."

He bade Kevin farewell and darted across the street, relieved Kevin didn't follow.

A gust of wind blew across the open expanse of the parking lot, stealing Barnaby's breath and every ounce of warmth he'd managed to accumulate while charging across campus. He burrowed into his parka and yanked his hat down over his ears, cursing the weather, the wind, and Canada.

His thick brown curls were not suited to being shoved under a hat and consistently came out looking like he'd styled them with an eggbeater. Indeed, most days he appeared to have entertained himself before morning lecture by sticking a fork into various electric sockets on the way to class. And while his lips used to be pink, they were now something he called Maritimes Red. It was a vibrant scarlet with little chapped white flecks. He'd had to give up eating salty foods because it hurt too much.

Many men around here grew beards to protect their faces from the cold, but Barnaby was as smooth-cheeked today as he'd been at sixteen. This resulted in the unusual and vastly unattractive condition where his normally pale cheeks now matched his bright red lips. And both were the exact color of the Macalister tartan scarf wrapped around his neck and chin. Just as the bags under his eyes matched his navy peacoat.

Thank goodness he couldn't wear white until summer—it would be far too matchy-matchy with the frostbite on his earlobes.

Diving into his car, he folded his long legs under the steering wheel while slamming the door and turning the key in the ignition. The tiny rust bucket had been sitting in the cold for ten hours, so there'd be no heat for at least five minutes—if he was lucky—and by then he would be home and parked in the shelter of the garage.

On the bright side, the cold would help keep him awake.

He had a huge list of short essays in need of review and grading waiting for him online. His goal for the evening was to get through a quarter of them. It wasn't going to be easy, and not just because for half of them he'd have to take a moment to despair. The real issue was that he'd worked the night before, and while sitting overnight at the front desk of the Moncton Economy Hotel & Suites allowed him to keep up with his own reading and assignments, it meant he was dead tired the next day.

In fact, it probably wasn't all that safe for him to be driving, crossing through the heart of the city while his mind wandered to thoughts of "quick" naps that he knew perfectly well would last until the next morning. He shook his head, forcing that wish aside, and hit the button to open the massive rolling doors that guarded the entrance to his cousin's...unusual home.

He'd traveled thousands of miles from home to start over. To *go it alone.* He'd pictured long hours grading papers in a grim and solitary room that would have made Charles Dickens proud, staring out a rain-streaked window at the endless gray Maritimes being all...Maritimey.

It turned out Barnaby was as good at exiling himself as he was at the rest of adulting.

He'd lasted four months, through countless sleepless nights listening to the neighbors fight and one cockroach infestation, before he'd fled the grim little studio flat just off-campus and moved into the guest suite in the large duplex apartment his cousin shared with his husband and their children. It was on the top two floors of a building that, from the outside, looked like nothing more than a hulking industrial box. Inside, however, was another story.

He took the massive freight lift up from the garage to the top floor, and let himself into the warm, welcoming home that reminded him of Woodcock, his cousin's estate back in England. Only Woodcock had never been so warm, or smelled of chili simmering on the stove, or been filled to the rafters with so much love and affection.

Barnaby dropped his bag and opened his arms.

He caught Oliver mid-air, holding the sturdy seven-year-old with one arm and staggering to the couch to fist-bump Christian, who, at fifteen, was somewhat less exuberant about someone coming through the door. Their father, Barnaby's cousin Rupert, was on the road with the hockey team he managed—a completely bizarre notion Barnaby still couldn't wrap his head around—but Rupert's husband Callum and the kids ensured Barnaby could no longer spend hours brooding out of dull windows in lifeless rooms, even if he could find one in their beautiful and happy home.

Some days Barnaby couldn't decide if that was a good or bad thing.

Most days he didn't think he deserved to have escaped his penance.

Travis hunkered down in his seat on the bus, forcing himself to focus on his laptop and ignore the scenery out the window as they traveled from Rimouski to Fredericton. The frozen landscape was beautiful and familiar, since it had once been home.

They were less than a hundred miles from where he'd grown up. Or, more accurately, where he'd lived as a child. Most of his growing up had taken place on buses like this one, surrounded by a pack of assholes he could, for at least a couple months at a time, call his team.

The Moncton Ice Cats were his current home, and he was grateful for more reasons than the familiar landscape and the usual pack of assholes. Indeed, this pack of assholes, and the people who paid them, were something a little bit unique in the world of hockey.

Hell, in some of the places Travis had played, this team would be a little bit *illegal*.

But that was far away, and right now, in the middle-of-nowhere Canada, the only issue this team had was that they were incredibly fucking *loud* and he had homework to do. He'd already abandoned his usual seat at the back of the bus and moved to sit across the aisle from the team's manager, Rupert Smythe-Morrison. Coaches and trainers surrounded them, some snoozing, others attempting to read or work. Unfortunately, sitting up front with the only people on the bus not shouting at the top of their lungs did little to curb the general volume.

Rupert shot Travis a sympathetic look when the boys launched into an ear-searing rendition of Willie Nelson's immortal classic, "Cowboys are Frequently, Secretly Fond of Each Other." Travis smiled back. He wanted them to shut the fuck up, but you'd have to be made of iron not to be charmed by the Russian contingent attempting a Texas twang.

"How's school going?" Rupert asked over the caterwauling.

Travis shrugged. "It's going," he said, voice neutral.

Rupert frowned. "That doesn't sound great."

Didn't it? Not that Rupert was wrong, but it was a mystery to Travis why Rupert would care. Hell, Travis had been worried about telling Rupert about school at all, given that it was a possible distraction from hockey, but Rupert and the rest of the management team had been nothing but supportive.

Travis scrubbed a hand over his hair and tried to put a positive spin on his current coursework. "It's okay. I'm working on the last of my Gen Ed credits this semester, and the class is tougher than I expected."

"What are you taking?"

"Introduction to Poetry."

Rupert winced.

Travis appreciated the validation. "Yeah, exactly."

He didn't add that he'd foolishly put off taking the Language & Literature requirement until the very end, or that he'd chosen this course with the belief that poetry would be easier to read than a full-length book or two. The only good news was the syllabus required very little in the way of creative output from Travis. Reading poetry was one thing. Writing it?

Nope.

"Is there anything I can do to help?"

Travis tried not to look as bewildered as he felt by Rupert's earnest offer. *Help?* Rupert's primary concern should be how Travis was playing hockey. In fact, that should have been his secondary, tertiary, and *only* concern about Travis.

"That's very nice of you, but I know for a fact you have more than enough to do," he said, looking pointedly at the stack of papers and laptop at Rupert's elbow.

"I can make time," Rupert said.

Travis believed he would, too. "I can't ask that. Anyway, I may be in over my head on this one. I'm considering dropping out."

"No, don't do that," Rupert said quickly.

Travis cocked his head, still confounded that Rupert cared. "It's cool, I can always try again over the summer."

Rupert frowned. Travis had the weirdest urge to thank him. His own mother would have told him to drop out of this class—which was why she, and his dad, didn't know he was taking it.

"Would a tutor help?"

Travis shook his head. "I'm not going to ask you to tutor me with what little free time you've got, boss. If nothing else, your husband would have words for me."

"He would," Rupert agreed, grinning. "But that's not what I'm proposing. I might know someone who could help."

"Really?" Travis asked, warily.

"Yes, really. What would you consider a fair fee?"

Travis wasn't sure where this was going, nor did it feel like a good idea, but he quoted the hourly rate he'd paid the poor slob who'd helped him through his basic math requirement, then added, "But it has to be someone who understands poetry, the college-level coursework, *and* can be flexible about my schedule. It's not easy to find someone who can deal with how some weeks I'm not here at all, and others I'll need to catch up and want extra time."

Rupert nodded enthusiastically. "Let me do some checking, okay?"

Travis should probably say no. He should definitely not drag his team's management into his private shit. And if that weren't a bad enough idea, now it would be embarrassing if he had to bail, or, worse, if he bombed the class.

But Rupert looked so *hopeful*.

"Uh, sure," Travis hedged, making a mental note not to do homework where Rupert could see him for a while. Of course, that would mean sticking to the back of the bus, which would suck, since he'd dare *anyone* to string together two thoughts with a dozen tone-deaf hockey players howling all around him.

Jesus Christ, he liked this team, but he was going to buy them all fucking singing lessons for Christmas next year. If he was still in Moncton. Which, based on past experience—of which he'd had plenty—wasn't going to happen.

Rupert returned to his work with a pleased smile. Travis looked out the window at the fields flying past. A hard white crust covered everything, making it look the same as a lot of places he'd been. Wisconsin. Sweden. Russia. It could be anywhere, but it still felt more like home.

He couldn't help but hope Rupert would sign him to another one-year contract when this season was up. Which he knew, *he knew*, was stupid. It was better not to get his hopes up about anything like that.

He understood his role on the Ice Cats. What Rupert, and the owners, wanted from him. A solid fourth-line center and a veteran presence in the locker room to help settle the young guys when things got tense. As a bonus, he was a guy the rest of the league knew by reputation as someone they did not want to pick a fight with.

And thank god for that, because he honestly didn't know what he'd do if someone *did* want to fight. Whatever it was, it would probably result in a one-way ticket to the next team, wherever the hell that would be. Or maybe he'd be done with hockey forever.

Travis swallowed back the lump of fear lodged in this throat at the idea of another fight, or of losing hockey forever. He was so screwed. He was *paid* to fight, and hockey was all he knew. He fucking loved it.

He took a deep breath and reminded himself he was doing okay. No one was asking for a fight, and he was happy playing hockey in Moncton. He'd asked his agent to reach out to the Ice Cats over the summer and had been thrilled when they'd responded. A lot of guys across a lot of leagues were talking about this team. Some were saying stupid shit, of course, but others were talking, with admiration, about how the Moncton Ice Cats was a place where guys like Travis could be themselves in the locker room and around their team.

He'd known he was gay since about eighteen, and god knew he hadn't dealt with it well at first. That had been a very long time ago, though, and he'd since learned not only how to accept who he was, but to live the sometimes precarious double life of a gay man and a professional hockey player. It hadn't been bad when he'd been on a team outside Vancouver. It had been a terror every minute he'd been in Russia. But still, he'd made it work.

Here, it didn't feel like work at all. He wasn't exactly shouting his exploits to the locker room before morning skate, but he also hadn't hesitated to respond to the man who'd been flirting with him in the bar in Rimouski last night. Nor had he felt anything but delighted when the team had hooted and elbowed each other like a bunch of dorks while he'd escorted his new friend across the room before taking him back to the hotel for a while.

He'd felt younger and dumber than he had in a long time. The blatant, public pick-up was a first, and it had been a rush, so much so he'd ignored the little voice in his head reminding him he was over one-night stands and the mediocre sex that often resulted. It wasn't that he, or the man he was with, was bad in the sack, it just wasn't the same as when he *knew* someone. Even if just for a couple nights. A week. Six terrifying months in Russia.

Maybe he'd get to have something like that in Moncton. Or wherever he ended up next, he reminded himself. It was better to keep his eye on the distinct possibility of his having to move on, so he wouldn't be disappointed when that was exactly what happened.

With a sigh, he focused back on his homework and decided to try something different. He jammed in a pair of ear buds, cranked the volume, and had his computer read him the passage of The Canterbury Tales he'd been trying to make sense of for the past hour.

"Avoi," quod she, "fy on you, hertelees!
Allas," quod she, "for by that God above,
Now han ye lost myn herte and al my love!
I can nat love a coward, by my faith.
For certes, what so any womman saith,
We alle desiren, if it mighte be,

To han housbondes hardy, wise, and free...

His eyes tracked over the words, trying to decipher what the fuck this Chaucer guy was trying to say. Travis couldn't decide if he was relieved or alarmed that the computer wasn't any better at reading this shit than he was. In fact, the computer might be worse.

Desperate, he took a new tack and searched YouTube, elated to discover someone had taken the time to read the Canterbury Tales aloud.

All ten hours of it. *Jesus Fucking Christ.*

It took him a while, but he found the section he was supposed to read, only to discover the diligent YouTube reader wasn't faring much better than Travis or the computer had. Or maybe he was. Maybe he was saying it exactly right, but his thick New York accent wasn't helping. Nor was the low-grade panic building in Travis's gut.

He poked around the internet some more to see if there were translations, but even the cases where people had tried to update the language didn't give him much. Then he found the CliffsNotes, which told him he was reading about angry, and possibly religious, chickens.

What the fuck.

He gave it up as a lost cause long before the bus rolled into Fredericton.

Chapter Two

Barnaby blinked slowly, his eyelids heavy, his head resting in his hand above his elbow planted on the dining room table. He was desperately trying to stay awake long enough to respond to all his emails and eat the dinner Callum was cooking, but he wasn't sure he was going to make it.

He nearly faceplanted into his keyboard when the door flew open and Rupert breezed in from his latest road trip.

Christian leaped up from where he'd been grumbling over his own schoolwork across the table from Barnaby, and bolted to get to his father before either Oliver or Callum. They ended up crashing into Rupert all at once, nearly taking him off his feet.

Most of Barnaby's family—including the bits from which Rupert hailed—would have found this sort of behavior unfathomable. Hell, even after months, Barnaby didn't know what to make of it most of the time. Callum and Rupert's long, sweet kiss, with the kids around them and Eleanor on Callum's hip, would have been *scandalous* in Barnaby's parents' house. And not because it was two men. Well, okay, two men kissing would have blown the doors off the stuffy old pile, but even if it had been some boring, vanilla straight couple—aka, his parents—there would never have been a lingering kiss, let alone the broad palm cupping Rupert's arse.

Barnaby and his sisters had been raised to believe they'd all been brought into the world by way of immaculate conception.

Come to that, he preferred to think so, too.

He tried to recall if, in the very little time he'd spent in his parents' home since he'd been sent off to boarding school at age nine, he'd ever seen any overt affection. He couldn't think of a single instance. Not between his parents. Nor for their children.

It wasn't a wonder his sisters had married the moment they'd left university. Or that he'd gone to London with Robert the day after they'd graduated.

Foolishly, as it turned out.

"Barnsy!" Rupert called once he'd been released.

Barnaby sighed. "Would you *please* not call me that?" He rolled his eyes at the delighted chuckles from the rest of the family. They adored all the stupid nicknames that came with his ridiculous name.

Honestly, a man named *Rupert* ought to know better. Then again, his children had taken to calling him Papa Roo, which made him sound like he ought to be bounding through the woods with Christopher Robin.

Barnaby had plenty of warning before Rupert's hand was messing up his hair, but he didn't duck. He wasn't quite ready to join the run-to-the-door-and-tackle crowd, but he didn't mind Rupert's easy affection. The rest of the family's, too. Oliver was a professional hugger with seemingly boundless affection to share. Eleanor would sometimes nap in Barnaby's arms, and seemed to like when he read to her at night, which he'd taken to doing whenever he had time. And Christian, by far the most reserved of the lot, often did his homework at the table with him and would ask for help, which Barnaby gladly gave.

He was much better at teaching than being touchy-feely. He may have learned to enjoy how much Oliver liked to hang off him or ride on his back, but it wasn't as though Oliver had given Barnaby much choice. Perhaps the others would wear him down as well. Break him in.

It didn't sound terrible, anyway.

"I have a job for you," Rupert announced, yanking Barnaby out of his musings.

"Pardon?"

"A job. How would you feel about being a tutor?"

Barnaby blinked up at his cousin. "Of what?"

"Poetry, as it turns out. Right up your alley. There's a man on the team who is working toward his undergraduate degree online, and he's fallen into the oldest trap in the book."

"He thought poetry would be easier," Barnaby guessed

sourly.

"I'm afraid so," Rupert agreed. "He knows better now, though, and I fear he needs help to survive the semester."

Barnaby tried not to let his panic show on his face as he realized what Rupert was suggesting. He was incredibly grateful to Rupert for giving him a place to live *and* refusing to take money for the rent. How could Barnaby possibly say no if Rupert needed a favor of him? He couldn't. Which meant his already packed schedule would have to make room for another task.

You did this to yourself, he reminded himself. He would just have to suck it up for a semester. He could do it. Maybe the guy would be willing to sit in the lobby of a 3-star hotel at all hours of the night to do his work.

"He's got the same travel schedule I do," Rupert continued, "so it would have to be in fits and starts." Barnaby valiantly did not wince. "And when he is around, he thinks it could be as much as ten hours a week."

"*What?*" Barnaby asked, his voice high and weak, his mounting hysteria leaking through at the idea of trying to stuff ten more hours of work into any week, let alone several. He stared at Rupert, horrified but unable to stop it when his eyes stung and his vision blurred.

Rupert frowned, then his eyes widened. "Oh no. Oh dear, I've explained it in the wrong order, I think." He gripped Barnaby's shoulder. "He's willing to *pay you* for this. This isn't a favor. It's a job. It's a job that will pay more than twice what the hotel does."

A sob lodged in Barnaby's chest. He couldn't have heard that correctly. "*How* much?"

"More than twice what the hotel pays, which means you can make more money in fewer hours and be able to sleep all seven nights a week. I thought it might be better for you," Rupert said, no longer sounding certain. "Wouldn't it?"

Barnaby went a little lightheaded. "Yes," he said. Maybe wheezed. "That would be...that would be much better."

God, so much better. He knew poetry. He knew *a lot* about poetry, even if he'd moved away from it as a focus for his degree.

It would be fun to have an excuse to stick his toes back in those waters, even if just to review the greatest hits covered in those sorts of classes. Even if he had to teach sonnets to some meathead hockey player. It had to be better than sitting at that Formica desk in the hotel lobby, wishing someone would do something stupid to break up the unrelenting monotony.

And he'd make more money. Be able to pay off his debts a bit faster.

He tried to smile at Rupert, but it wobbled badly. At least he managed to croak, "Thank you."

Rupert squeezed his shoulder again. "God, Barn, would you please let us lend you some money? We want to help."

Barnaby shook his head. "No."

"But—"

"*No.* You've done enough. You're doing so much already. Letting me live here rent free makes a huge difference. I can't take anything else." Rupert had argued in the past that Barnaby *wouldn't,* rather than *couldn't, a*nd maybe there was a difference, but Barnaby didn't see it. He'd made his mistakes, been the fool, and he would be the one to pay the price.

"But you will take the job?" Rupert asked.

"Yes. Definitely yes." He didn't care if his new student was a knuckle-dragging, dimwitted homophobe who could barely string three words together. At the price quoted, Barnaby would ensure he passed his poetry class if it killed him.

Rupert smiled. "Yeah? It's not a bad idea?"

"No, it's...it's brilliant. Thank you. Truly. It will be much better than the hotel. I can work around the team's travel schedule and get my grading done while you're on the road to balance things out."

Not that he had any say on when things were due, but whatever—Dr. Sorenson had proven flexible, as long as someone else was doing the work.

"Good," Rupert said with a decisive nod. "I'll let Travis know you're interested and give him your email."

Barnaby agreed, his focus sliding back to his laptop and the pile of work awaiting him. He immediately felt overwhelmed, again, but reminded himself his only goals for tonight were to answer emails and to not fall asleep before dinner.

As it turned out, he only managed one of those on his own, but Callum was kind enough to shake him awake when it was time to eat.

Travis tried to make sense of the words swimming before his eyes before giving up and hitting pause on the computer reading to him. He sat back from the table and sighed.

His friend, Grady McDonnough, sat across the table from him in a quiet corner of the Dipsy Doodle Dangle Coffee House. "You all right there, buddy?"

Grady was slouched in his chair, his long legs stretched under the table, his feet crossed. He cupped a huge porcelain mug in his hands and somehow managed to appear genuinely concerned while smirking. He'd been listening to Travis bitch about his poetry class for two weeks straight.

"I'll manage," Travis grumbled, yanking out his earbud.

Grady was kind enough not to look *too* skeptical.

They'd come as an excuse to get out of their apartments, both in the same converted Victorian a few blocks away. Travis had been planning to wallow in his misery alone at home, but Grady had insisted he needed a change in scenery. Travis couldn't decide if it was weirder to have a friend who actually cared enough to drag him out, or who knew him well enough to be right about him needing to get out of the house. Only Martin had ever known him that well, and they'd been kids when they'd met. The world had seemed infinite then, a hockey season as long as a lifetime, trades to far-flung cities inconceivable.

Now, Travis lived with one foot out the door, always ready to move onto the next team and city. It meant he had an impressive friends list on Facebook, but not the kind of friends who knew him well enough to know when a triple espresso was in order.

Grady was proving an exception. One who was willing to sit with Travis while he banged his head against the proverbial wall while offering Travis silent but steady support.

The bells above the door chimed. Grady's eyes cut across the room and narrowed.

For all that Grady was one of the most easy-going guys Travis had ever known, he was also a member of the Royal Canadian Mounted Police, and there were some interesting quirks that went along with that. Grady might have been lounging like a lazy cat in the quiet coffee shop, but he had an unnerving awareness of their surroundings. It had taken Travis a while to get used to it, but now Travis didn't think before offering up the seat in the corner so Grady could keep his back to a wall. And he certainly wasn't surprised when Grady's eyes darted away in the middle of a conversation because the door had opened.

He even had enough practice reading Grady to know someone interesting had walked through that door.

Travis glanced over his shoulder and his breath caught.

The gorgeous man shaking snow out of his big brown curls and unwinding a huge red plaid scarf from around his neck was...arresting. Unaware he had his audience by the throat, he looked over the cafe, searching for someone or something. His bright blue eyes, pink cheeks, and full red lips left Travis breathless.

No wonder he'd caught Grady's eye. Travis turned to give his friend a ration of shit, but he bit back his needling when he saw Grady's scowl.

"Who is that?" Travis asked.

"No one," Grady said, his eyes still narrowed on the lovely man.

"He a criminal or something?" Because that would be both a crying shame and a perfect testament to Travis's taste in men.

"What?" Grady glanced at Travis. "No."

The bell over the door chimed again and Travis hoped it wasn't the beautiful man leaving. He wanted another look.

He was glad he didn't turn to check, though, or he might have missed the smile that ran across Grady's face, and the way his eyes warmed with interest.

Had Grady not gotten a good look at Hottie McHotterson the first time?

"Gorgeous, right?" Travis said.

"He is," Grady agreed, his voice deep and slow, his eyes dipping in what appeared to be a *thorough* inspection.

Travis had only had a glimpse, but he could picture those long legs in the dark stovepipe cords, the lean hips Travis *knew* would have perfect hipbones to fit under his thumbs. "You know him?" he asked Grady.

Grady nodded. "Yeah, I do. He's a friend."

Travis considered asking for an introduction, but he wasn't going to risk stepping on Grady's toes. He was not, however, above sneaking another peak.

He looked again and found the beautiful man was no longer alone—and he was with someone Travis actually knew. He swiveled his head to look back and forth between Grady and the front of the café.

Oh ho. Grady wasn't looking at the beautiful stranger at all.

Travis bit back his grin. "So...you know Jack Chevalier, huh?"

Grady, the king of cool, flinched. "What?"

"I mean, you said you're friends. And that he's...*gorgeous*, was it?"

A blush washed over Grady's cheeks just as Jack spotted them.

"Grady! Travis?" Jack waved to them.

Every eye in the café turned to Jack, drawn by that smile and the even more stunning face. Jack was probably the prettiest man Travis had ever met. Like, *intimidatingly* pretty. Travis had stared stupidly the first five minutes they'd spent in the same room together, until a sympathetic teammate had whapped him upside the head to shake him out of it.

Jack said something to Hottie McHotterson. Travis willed

him to turn, but he moved to a table in the far corner of the café while Jack strode toward them.

Grady sat up straight. Travis's grin earned him a black look before Grady focused on Jack.

"Hey," Jack said with a big smile. "I didn't know you two knew each other. Small world."

"We're neighbors," Grady said without looking at Travis. In fact, Grady didn't look away from Jack once.

Jack didn't seem to think there was anything out of the ordinary. The guy was probably used to commanding a lot of undivided attention, though it wasn't like Grady to be so focused. Someone could probably walk into the café without Grady noticing.

Which was a shocking thought, actually.

Jack and Grady shot the shit for a few minutes, with very little input required from Travis. He wondered how long it would take either of them to notice if he got up and left.

Not that he would. No way. He was enjoying the show.

He watched them banter back and forth. They were clearly good friends who had known each other a while, but something seemed just one beat off. It was partly that Grady couldn't look away. And partly that Jack couldn't either. But there was something else.

Travis checked to see if Hottie McHotterson was still waiting for Jack in the far corner—he was, and even his profile was gorgeous. When Travis returned his attention to his friends, he was honestly surprised Jack and Grady hadn't leaned closer to each other. They were completely dialed in, but neither did anything to cross the meter between them.

It was a shame the café didn't sell buckets of popcorn. This shit was gold.

Jack gestured over his shoulder. "Well, I'm meeting a friend, so I should get going. Let's get a beer soon."

"That would be great," Grady said. He seemed almost relieved. "It was good to see you."

"You, too," Jack said before turning away.

Travis didn't bother to add anything. He felt like the invisible man.

Grady's eyes trailed Jack across the room.

Travis tried to hold it in, but a snort escaped.

Grady glared. "What?"

"You've got good taste, I'll grant you that."

Grady pinned Travis with his cop eyes. "How do you know Jack?"

"Oh my god, really?" Travis kicked Grady in the shin. "We work together, asshole. If you're his friend, you know this."

Jack was, after all, the Operations Director for the Moncton Arena, and therefore around the team all the time.

"Oh. Right," Grady said, chagrined.

Travis laughed in his face.

"Shut up." Grady glowered.

Travis put up his hands, still laughing. "All right. I should thank you, though. You've unwittingly helped me with my homework."

Grady appeared dubious. "I have?"

"Sure, I didn't know what to write my essay about, but now I think I'll call it, *Some Things Never Change.*"

"Why's that?" Grady asked suspiciously.

"Well, I give you this anonymously penned verse from, like, four hundred years ago."

There is a lady sweet and kind,
Was never face so pleased my mind;
I did but see her passing by,
And yet I love her till I die...

"Ha fucking ha," Grady grumbled. "Also, I assure you, Jack's no fucking *lady.* And neither am I."

Travis cracked up while Grady glared with undiluted disgruntlement.

When Travis could breathe again, he asked, "So, who's the hot guy you were glaring at? The one with Jack."

Grady glanced across the café. "A new friend of Jack's." He frowned. "Maybe a boyfriend. I don't know."

Ah. Travis sighed. "Sorry."

"There's nothing to be sorry about. Jack and I aren't—we're just friends. He's never..." Grady didn't appear inclined to finish that thought.

"But you have."

Grady shrugged. "Doesn't matter. He's not interested."

Travis kept his—admittedly brief—read on Jack's feelings to himself. "Okay."

They fell silent, sipping their coffee while Grady resumed his usual vigilance, with a *few* extra glances toward one particular corner of the café.

"I'll tell you this," Travis said a couple minutes later. "It sure seems like you went into the wrong branch of public safety."

"What are you talking about?"

"You should have been a fireman."

Grady's eyes narrowed. "If you make a flaming joke, I'm going to dump my coffee over your head."

"Nah, man," Travis said with a pointed look toward Jack. "But you sure do like a smoke show."

Grady tried to disguise his snicker as he bounced a wad of napkins off Travis's forehead. "Shut the fuck up."

Chapter Three

Barnaby dashed into the Dipsy Doodle Dangle Coffee House again a week later. He'd begged Jack to take a late lunch and meet him before his first tutoring session that afternoon.

He arrived first, so he ordered their drinks and sandwiches and went to their favorite table in the corner. Jack walked in a few minutes later and sat across from him, taking a moment to savor his coffee and watch Barnaby fidget.

Barnaby tried to eat his lunch and ignore Jack. It wasn't easy, and not just because Jack was hotter than the surface of the sun. Jack had this quality about him, one that when Barnaby had first met him months ago over dinner at Rupert and Callum's house, he'd interpreted as flirting—and maybe to some degree it had been—but now he saw as engaging. Jack was *engaging*, and a good friend. Barnaby's closest friend on this side of the pond—or anywhere, really.

Jack gave in first. "So, what's going on, B?"

"I'm nervous about this tutoring thing," Barnaby admitted.

Jack's eyebrows drew together over his piercing blue eyes. "You like the teaching job you have at the University, don't you?"

"I do."

"And that's in front of hundreds of people sometimes, right?"

"I don't lecture much, just do announcements and assignments. But yes, there are over a hundred students in Dr. Sorenson's class."

"And you're going to be tutoring...what? One guy. You can totally do that," Jack said and took a bite of his sandwich.

Barnaby appreciated Jack's faith in him. "I suppose. It's just...I don't know this man. And I doubt I have a thing in common with him. He's a hockey player, for Christ's sake."

Jack looked up. "He is?"

"Yes. Didn't I tell you that? Rupert connected us."

"You told me about Rupert. You didn't tell me he played. Is he an Ice Cat?"

"He is. His name is Travis Campbell."

Jack blinked. "You're tutoring *Soupy*?"

"What? Who's Soupy?"

"Campbell. Travis. His nickname is Soupy. You know...Campbell..." Jack's hand slashed through the air. "Forget that. Go back. Travis is studying *poetry*?"

Barnaby was not reassured by the incredulity in Jack's tone. "So it would seem."

"Huh." Jack thought about that for a while, an alarmingly sly grin appearing the longer he considered it.

Barnaby eyed Jack. "What?"

"Travis is totally your type."

"Excuse you," Barnaby said tartly. "What do you know about my type?"

Jack laughed. "Handsome. Kind. *And* smart? Seems like a pretty good match to me."

Then why don't you date him?

Barnaby kept that thought to himself. He knew Jack didn't date anyone. Ever. And he'd made it clear he wasn't the least bit interested.

What Barnaby didn't know was *why.*

A legion of men and women expressed their interest to Jack on a daily basis. There had been times it had actually become a nuisance. Jack not only didn't accept those offers, he often didn't seem to recognize most of them for what they were. Or, at least, didn't believe that they were made in earnest.

Jack was the only man Barnaby had ever met who could laugh off a proposition and not leave anyone with hurt feelings. It was strange, but also part of Jack's charm. It certainly had helped Barnaby shut down the crush he might have harbored for Jack, which was lucky, since Barnaby *also* had no interest in dating at the moment.

Yes, his self-imposed celibacy chafed—literally and figuratively—but it was the right thing to do. The way it had to be.

"I'm not going to date a student," Barnaby said coolly, leaving aside the myriad other reasons it was a terrible idea.

Jack rolled his eyes. "Come on, B. He's not some kid on campus. No one is going to care if you do."

"I'd care."

Jack put his hands up. "All right, I hear you," he said, dropping his hands back to the table. An expression Barnaby couldn't decipher crossed Jack's face, then was gone. "He could be spoken for, anyway. I saw him with someone a few days ago."

"Well, good for him. It makes no difference to me. I'm going to teach the man to appreciate great poetry, or at least to be able to fake it, and that's it."

"Fair enough," Jack agreed. "I'll say again, though, Travis is a good guy. If nothing else, I think you two could be friends."

"If you say so. I don't know what I could have in common with a professional hockey player."

Jack arched an eyebrow. "You sound like a snob. And like you don't know a damn thing about hockey players."

"What? No." The accusation stung. "I'm just saying that he's been playing a game his entire life. I respect that he's very good at it, but it's not the same as teaching or an office job or..." Barnaby trailed off at Jack's flat look.

"You're a snob," Jack said. "And you should know better. You *live* with a professional hockey player."

Of course, Jack was right. "But Callum's..."

"What? Handsome? Kind? And smart?"

Barnaby groaned. "Yes, all those things. And possibly the greatest father in the universe, okay? I get it. I'm an arse."

"You *are* an ass," Jack said, but then he smiled. "And I'm going to enjoy watching you learn how wrong you are. You know the last guy I met who was a snob about hockey players and made all kinds of assumptions about their intelligence?"

Barnaby was afraid to ask. "Who?"

"Your dear cousin, Rupert. And look how that turned out."

"Ugh. I'm sure this won't be at all the same."

Jack smirked. "If you say so."

Travis paced around his apartment, telling himself it was too late to bail out. The tutor was supposed to be there any minute, and as the clock ticked closer to his arrival, Travis became more and more convinced that this was a terrible idea.

Rupert's cousin, who was working on his *PhD*, was going to help him through a stupid online poetry class? Travis didn't see a way through this that didn't leave him looking like an idiot to whoever this cousin was, and to Rupert by proxy.

Also, this dude was named Barnaby Birtwistle. Who did that? And what kind of person did someone whose parents hated him that much become? Travis had been imagining every angry English school teacher he'd ever seen on a BBC show. It wasn't pretty.

Could he fire his boss's cousin if he was an uptight and patronizing prick?

Fuck. This was such a bad idea.

He stopped on his next pass through the kitchen to toss the cold pack he'd had strapped on back in the freezer and grab a fresh one. It barely helped his left shoulder, which had been bothering him more and more. As had his right ankle. He supposed he could count his blessings, though, since it had been a couple months since his knee had flared up.

And his head was steady. Or as steady as it had ever been.

He said a silent prayer to the hockey gods so they didn't think he was tempting fate and resumed pacing, reviewing all the reasons he was taking these classes. Why they mattered.

Sadly, the primary reason was because he had no idea what he wanted to be when he grew up. Which was fucking unfortunate, since he was old as shit, and every fucking part of his body hurt, so it was only a matter of time before he'd need to find something to do that wasn't hockey.

But he wasn't kidding himself. He could probably rationalize all that shit away, just like so many teammates had. No, the real reason he took these fucking classes was because his oldest friend, Martin, had made him promise.

Of course, Martin wasn't going to be holding him to those promises. But when they were layered on top of the constant aches and pains, it did prove effective motivation to find something he could do, some way he could occupy his time and make some money once the hockey thing was over.

It could happen sooner than he thought. Sooner than he planned—not that he *had* a plan. Yet. He'd always wanted to be the guy that was still playing at forty, but he was thirty-four and, for a couple years now, he'd had to hope he made it to the end of any given season. Hell, to the end of any given *game*.

So, the risk of feeling stupid with some stranger tutoring him was well within acceptable limits. Right?

He wasn't *actually* stupid—something most of his teachers hadn't been able to figure out. His coaches, on the other hand, had talked about his hockey IQ, his cleverness on the ice, from an early age. They'd made it easy to focus on hockey before school. Encouraged his father to latch onto the idea of his kid being a professional athlete.

He could still hear his dad telling him it wasn't a big deal if he wasn't smart in school. He was smart on the ice. By the time anyone had figured that out Travis was more than capable of succeeding in school with some help, he'd already had one foot out the classroom door and one skate on the ice.

The front door buzzer snapped him back to the present.

Showtime.

Travis hit the button to unlock the door downstairs. Then he wiped his hands on his jeans and told himself to chill the fuck out.

It was clear it hadn't worked when he flinched at the gentle knock on the door. He took a deep breath and opened the door, telling himself he was ready for anything.

He was wrong.

Because there, standing on his stoop and looking delicious, was *Hottie fucking McHotterson*.

Travis could only hope *agape* was a good look on him.

He had no doubt any look was a good one on Hottie— er...Barnaby. His cheeks glowed pink from the cold or the run up the stairs, and his knitted hat barely contained a riot of curls that just screamed to be touched. The same red plaid scarf was wrapped high enough around his neck that Travis couldn't see his sharp jawline and pointed chin, but he could remember it. Clearly.

Maybe he was lost? Maybe Rupert's cousin was out of shape and had to take the stairs really slowly?

"Hi," Travis said. "Can I help you?"

The beautiful boy smiled and Travis's pants were suddenly two sizes smaller. "I'm Barnaby Birtwistle. Are you Travis?"

The accent was a kick in the stomach. It was like Rupert's, but times ten. Crisp and fucking adorable.

Travis choked back a hysterical laugh. "Uh, yeah. That's me."

Barnaby cocked his head, waiting. He was tall, about six feet, but Travis still had a few inches on him, which he liked for some damn reason. Barnaby was a fascinating combination of slim, but broad-shouldered. Overtly masculine in many ways, but still pretty, with long lashes and pink lips. The most captivating part, though, were those deep blue eyes, even as they turned from polite enquiry to confusion.

"Do you still want a tutor?"

"What? Oh, yes. Right. Please." Travis threw his door wide and stepped to the side. "Come on in. I'm sorry about that. I was just..."

Travis had no way of finishing that sentence without being a weirdo or a creep.

Barnaby slid past him and stood looking around the space that encompassed Travis's kitchen, living room, and dining room. Travis had chosen the unit because it was on the top floor of an old Victorian and had been built out with all the strange rooflines and turrets as part of the design. The main room was under the center line of the roof, with high, slanted ceilings and two big windows looking out over the street. The weather was nice, so the room was bright, the light wood floors glowing in the sunlight.

Travis was oddly proud of how the new, dark suede sectional filled the space and made it more welcoming, which was foolish, since he never should have bought it to begin with. What the hell he was going to do with that monster if he got traded tomorrow?

Get a bigger storage unit, that was what he'd have to do. *Foolish.*

"Your home is lovely," Barnaby said.

Travis smiled. "Thank you. Go ahead to the table. We'll be working there, if that works for you?"

Barnaby nodded while still looking around curiously.

Travis went into the kitchen and bit back the offer of a tour. There wasn't much more to see, and he didn't need to show off the other set of huge windows in the bedroom, with his old iron headboard pushed right up against them so he could nap in the afternoon sun.

Barnaby's smooth, pale skin would look amazing against Travis's dark blue sheets with the sun setting him aglow.

Travis mentally smacked himself and yanked open the fridge. "Can I get you a drink? I have water, milk, juice, beer, and cider."

Barnaby appeared adorably bewildered. "It's eleven a.m."

"So, too late for juice?"

Barnaby's wide, toothy smile was heart-stopping.

Another mental smack. "Uh. There's orange, apple, and cranberry juice. I can also do coffee or tea." Travis's nerves were turning him into Martha fucking Stewart, but there was no going back. At least he hadn't put on an apron and offered to bake a soufflé.

"I'll have whatever you're having," Barnaby said.

"Tea, then." Travis turned to start the kettle and opened the cabinet with the teas, immediately dismayed. Now he was going to have to list all the kinds of tea he had.

He jumped when Barnaby spoke from behind him.

"The English Breakfast, please."

Travis almost caused an avalanche of tea boxes when he grabbed for it, but he managed to extract the bright red box, and two teabags from it, and even successfully placed two of his mugs onto the counter without embarrassing himself further.

Go team.

When he turned, he found Barnaby watching him, close enough that Travis could have hooked a finger in one of Barnaby's belt loops and towed his long, lean body closer to tangle those coltish legs with his much thicker ones.

He pressed himself back against the cabinets and gripped the countertop in both hands.

"So, where do you want to start?" Barnaby asked.

Travis pictured himself slowly peeling the clothes from Barnaby's body. "What?"

Barnaby was getting that concerned look again. "What poet are you reading in class?"

Right. "Thomas Wyatt."

Barnaby nodded and went back to the table. "Always a classic, Wyatt."

Travis wondered what that meant. He poured the water, then left the tea to steep and followed Barnaby. "I'm supposed to read a handful of his poems, then pick one and describe what I think it's about."

Barnaby reached out and tapped one long, elegant finger against Travis's laptop. "May I?"

"Please."

Barnaby spun it so he could see the list of poems and the assignment description from the professor, humming thoughtfully.

"If you want to read them, click on the browser tabs. I have them all up," Travis offered. He'd made sure to close the app he used to have the computer read things to him.

"Thank you," Barnaby said, but he didn't look at them, reviewing the assignment page instead.

Travis wondered how this was going to work if he wasn't even going to read over the materials.

Barnaby pushed the laptop away. "Have you had a chance to read them all?"

"Yes." For all the good it did him.

"Have you chosen one you want to write about?"

Travis's stomach twisted. If all this guy was going to do was follow up on the syllabus, there wasn't going to be much point. He could send a copy to his mother and get the same service for free. "No," he said, trying to be patient.

"Why not?"

Travis frowned. *Why not?* What the fuck kind of question was that?

Barnaby's gaze narrowed, presumably at Travis's scowl, but what was he supposed to say? None of them made any *sense*. He didn't know why his brain worked the way it did, but he'd be damned if he was made to feel stupid because of it.

Again.

He gritted out, "I thought that was why I was paying you."

Barnaby blinked, his cheeks growing rosier. Five minutes ago, Travis would have found it attractive. Now, he just wanted to throw the little snot out.

This had been a terrible idea.

"I beg your pardon," Barnaby said stiffly. "But if you somehow got the impression I was going to do your work for you—"

"What? *No.* I didn't mean that. I meant, I thought you were going to explain these things to me," Travis said, gesturing at the computer. "Because I can't make heads or tails of them. And until I do, there isn't any point in choosing one."

The admission hurt, his face hot. *Fuck*, he hated this. He got up and went back to the kitchen, trying to control his frustration. He had no reason to feel stupid, damn it. It didn't matter what this asshole thought.

"I apologize," Barnaby said, and he sounded sincere, though still painfully stiff. Travis wasn't ready to look at him, focusing instead on pulling the bags from the tea and getting out the milk and sugar to give himself time.

When he couldn't avoid it any longer, he returned to the table and placed a mug in front of Barnaby, then he slid into his chair with his mug pressed between his palms.

"Okay, let's look at these together, then," Barnaby said.

Travis pretended not to notice Barnaby watching him out of the corner of his eye. He'd like to think it was because he was devilishly handsome, but he suspected his tutor was aware of how close he was to being tossed out on his ass.

Barnaby scooted his chair closer and turned the laptop so they could both see, then finally clicked through the tabs with the actual material. Scanning the selections, he scrolled through each, looking for god knows what.

Then he stopped. And chuckled.

If he said something droll, Travis was definitely giving him the boot.

Barnaby tapped the screen. "Right, the trick with Wyatt isn't so much that the language is obscure or complicated, I don't think. A few notable exceptions, but mostly he kept it simple."

Travis tended *not* to agree, but nodded, since it was true he hadn't had to look up as many words in these poems as he had for Chaucer. This, of course, wasn't saying much.

"Let's look at *My Lute, Awake!*" Barnaby suggested.

Travis's stomach dropped, because this was where it was going to fall apart. The words on the page were easy for him to read, maybe even understand, but after that...

He tried anyway, silently scanning the poem Barnaby indicated.

My lute, awake! Perform the last
Labor that thou and I shall waste,
And end that I have now begun;
For when this song is sung and past,
My lute, be still, for I have done.

As to be heard where ear is none,
As lead to grave in marble stone,
My song may pierce her heart as soon.
Should we then sigh or sing or moan?
No, no, my lute, for I have done...

Travis gritted his teeth, barely two stanzas into the poem before his frustration began to mount.

"Perhaps," Barnaby said, "it would help if I mentioned that Wyatt was obsessed with women. Or, more accurately, how he appealed, or failed to appeal, to women."

Travis vaguely recalled his professor saying the same thing during the online lecture. He couldn't be sure, since he'd been on a road trip, exhausted, and had fallen asleep, repeatedly. Regardless, he smirked. "If you're hoping I'm going to find some empathy for the guy, you're barking up the wrong tree. I couldn't care less if women find me attractive."

Travis wasn't in the habit of coming out to people he barely knew, but he figured they might as well get it out in the open now. And Barnaby lived with Rupert and Callum, so Travis wasn't taking a towering risk. Probably.

Barnaby met his gaze. His lips twitched. "Nor do I, actually."

Travis smiled. *Well,* then.

"*But,*" Barnaby continued briskly and turned back to the laptop, "I don't think it matters who Wyatt was attracted to, so much as we can empathize with the pain he feels at being rejected, which is what he writes about here and in many of the other pieces you have been assigned."

Travis forced himself to focus. He read the lines again. "So...he's bummed some woman rejected him, and now he's saying his old-fashioned guitar-like thingy won't play music?"

"Yes!" Barnaby said with a pleased smile.

Travis grinned, the warm flush of pride rushing through him. He read the lines again, trying to use every trick he'd learned in school about listening to the words in his head.

Barnaby, who had been reading along silently, let out a little snort of laughter.

"What?" Travis asked.

"Nothing," Barnaby said, waving it away.

"No. No way. If there is something funny about poetry, you have to share." *Please.*

"Well," Barnaby began. "Not everyone agrees, but I always believed Wyatt was using his *lute* as a metaphor..."

Travis squinted at the poem and read it aloud in his head again, and trying to see it in a new light. His stress ratcheted higher as the words failed to mean anything more than he'd already managed to squeeze from them.

Then Barnaby's smirk and the line about *piercing her heart* clicked.

"Wait a minute, is this a poem about his *dick?*"

Barnaby burst into delighted laughter, his cheeks turning pink and his eyes crinkling with his big, toothy smile.

Travis wasn't sure he was going to learn shit about poetry, but for the first time since the semester started, he was maybe, just *possibly,* looking forward to giving it a try.

Chapter Four

A week later, Barnaby knocked on Travis's door at seven o'clock in the morning the day after the Ice Cats had returned from a road trip. It was absurdly early to be visiting anyone, let alone tutoring, but it had been clear in their texts back and forth that Travis was desperate to get together. Barnaby was concerned Travis wouldn't be in the best mindset to learn at this hour. Even the inhumanly energetic Rupert had been flagging badly when he'd staggered through the door last night, happy to lean against his tutting husband's chest while they murmured about four games in six days and traffic on the Confederation Bridge.

Apparently, there was to be another game that night, so the only chance for Travis to carve out a proper chunk of time was at this ghastly hour. Barnaby lifted his hand, ready to pinch color even the frigid cold hadn't been able to restore into his cheeks, but stopped himself in time.

He wasn't here for a date. He was here to *teach*.

So what if his student was a huge, blond, caramel-eyed, broad-shouldered, lean-hipped—

The door jerked open.

—*mummy?*

Barnaby looked Travis over with concern. "Are you all right?"

Travis opened the door wider. "Yeah, I'm fine. I'm just slow to get going in the morning." Travis's voice was rough, perhaps with lack of use—or maybe he'd spent the week shouting?

Barnaby eyed the enormous cold pack strapped to Travis's shoulder. Another was wrapped around his knee. And yet another covered his ribs and waist on one side. All of them were held in place with roughly a mile of sports wrap and elastic bandages. Travis looked like he'd either spent the last week being prepared for burial in ancient Egypt or, as was more likely, having the shit beaten out of him.

Barnaby didn't dare ask him if he'd won, partly because he already knew the Ice Cats had taken most of their games, but also because he wasn't sure if Travis could judge his own balance sheet in the black, given how miserable he looked as he limped toward the kitchen.

Why would anyone do this to themselves?

It was a question Barnaby had asked many times, though in the past it had been about ballet, rather than hockey. He remembered, bitterly, his frustration at how such beauty could tear apart a man's body. A body he'd loved. A man he'd thought loved him back.

Enough of that, he told himself, dropping his bag on a chair at the table and shrugging out of his coat. He was here to talk about poetry, not dwell on the past. Or notice Travis's bare and distressingly vulnerable-looking feet poking out of his faded tartan pajama bottoms.

Those looked uninjured, at least.

Travis also wasn't wearing a shirt, and, though most of his chest was covered, Barnaby couldn't help but check the bare bits for more damage. He needed to know, of course, as the human mind wasn't as capable of learning when it was distracted or in pain. So, it was purely professional interest, really.

"Do you need to see the doctor this morning? Or the trainer?" he asked.

"Oh. No. I'm not injured. Well, not more than usual, anyway," Travis added with a grimace. "Just the usual wear-and-tear for us old guys."

Barnaby squinted. "You can't be more than, what? Thirty-five? Thirty-six?"

"Ouch. Thirty-four, thanks."

"That's hardly *old*."

Travis started to shrug, then apparently thought better of it. "It's pretty old for hockey," he said, carefully lifting and filling the kettle. "English Breakfast again?"

"Please."

"Did you eat?"

Barnaby considered lying, but his stomach would eventually betray him either by making rude noises or forcing him to scavenge for a muesli bar in his bag. "I haven't."

"Allergies?"

"None."

Travis hobbled to the refrigerator.

Barnaby watched, bemused, as Travis pulled out large quantities of fruit, eggs, bacon, juice, and milk. "Are you expecting more company?"

"Nope. I'm just a man with a big appetite."

About forty inappropriate remarks sprang to mind, but Barnaby held his tongue.

When Travis opened a cabinet and reached up for a box of pancake mix, they both winced. Travis, presumably, with pain. Barnaby with guilt.

"You pay me rather too much an hour to be cooking me breakfast. I'd offer to cook for you, but I think we'd all like to live through Shakespeare this morning."

Travis laughed. "I have to cook anyway. I don't mind making extra."

"But, we've work to do, I thought?" Barnaby asked, suddenly unsure. He had the alarming thought that maybe this was the hockey-player version of a date. With ice packs and food for ten and his "date" taking a number of ibuprofen that far exceeded the dosage limitations printed on the bottle.

Should he look up the number for poison control?

"We do have work," Travis said, his broad back to Barnaby.

Barnaby noted the play of muscles under Travis's skin. The morning sun cast mesmerizing shadows that danced as Travis moved. He had two dimples just above the waistband of soft flannel that had been worn so thin it clung to the glorious round arse beneath.

Barnaby realized his mouth was hanging open and snapped it shut. "Right." *Work.*

Travis glanced at him. "Check out my laptop. I think you'll like what's on the screen."

Barnaby slid into the chair in front of Travis's computer, the wood still warm from Travis's huge skater's bum. Barnaby valiantly resisted squirming across its surface to capture more of that heat.

Because that would be wrong, you fecking pervert.

Sitting perfectly still, he traced his finger over the trackpad and brought the screen to life. At first, he couldn't figure out what he was reading. He scrolled up to the title page, blinking in astonishment until he gasped and laughed at the same time—resulting in a hideous snort.

Travis grinned. "Not bad, right? I'll take a B+."

Barnaby was pleased with the grade, but— "Did you really turn in an essay titled *The Lute and Thomas Wyatt's Other Favorite Instrument?*"

"I did," Travis said proudly.

Barnaby laughed. "My god, it's a good thing your professor has a sense of humor. Weren't you worried she'd take points off?"

"Nah," Travis said, with what would have been an easy shrug if it hadn't involved shifting fifteen pounds of cold packs. "That's the best part about going back to school when you're old as shit. Half the professors are your age or younger, and either way, you don't give a shit what they think, as long as they pass you."

"You're not old," Barnaby said, though it was hardly the point. It irked him that Travis kept saying it. Travis wasn't *old*, he was...vital. Fit and strong and, yes, certainly battle scarred, but beautiful for it.

Which was *not* what Barnaby should be thinking about.

"I envy you," Barnaby said, refocusing on more appropriate topics. "I never dared do that when I was at university as an undergraduate. And now, even as an older graduate student, I probably wouldn't."

"Well, yeah, but you care about school," Travis said, coming toward the table with a mug in his hand.

Barnaby jumped up and met him halfway, failing to consider the wisdom of allowing his fingers to slide over Travis's. He could feel the scars that crossed and framed every knuckle. He wanted to inspect them more closely.

Focus.

"Why are you taking classes if you don't care about school?" he asked when his brain finally triumphed over his hormones.

Travis spun on his heel and went back to the kitchen. Barnaby couldn't see much of Travis's shoulders, but he could still tell they'd gone tight.

He slid back into his seat at the table. "I'm sorry. You don't have to answer that, of course. It's none of my business. Did you have any questions for me about the work you had to do on Edmund Spenser this week while you were on the road?"

"No."

Barnaby warmed his hands around his tea. He shouldn't miss the teasing smiles and laughter, let alone wonder how to get them back. He should just move them on to what he was here to do. "This week is Shakespeare, if I recall. Shall we get started?"

Travis's shoulders slumped. "No."

Barnaby frowned, caught off guard by the finality of that single word. He tried not to panic, but if he lost this job because he'd asked one bloody question that hadn't even been that personal, he was going to—hell, he was going to have to go back to working at the hotel. And as much as he'd like to punch Travis in the face for that, he'd probably be too busy crying.

Travis started yanking off the cold packs, his motions jerky, his expression grim. The sight of countless bruises, from fresh black to pale yellow, made Barnaby ache in sympathy, even as his dread grew, a miserable weight in his stomach. Travis slung the packs back into the freezer and slammed the door before they could slither back out.

Barnaby stood, his hand hovering over his coat. If he was going to be fired, he was going to be out the door in thirty seconds or less.

Travis felt stupid, which was a common enough experience, particularly in any setting that had anything to do with school, but it infuriated him anyway. He knew he needed to explain his shit to Barnaby, and he needed to get over his own bullshit hang-ups to do it.

"I care about school," he announced, turning to face Barnaby, who had one hand on his coat, his body turned toward the door.

They stared at one another for a long moment. Neither moved.

"Are you leaving?" Travis asked, confused.

"No." Barnaby dropped his hand. "And I'm sorry. I didn't mean to question your commitment to your schooling."

Travis sighed. "You wouldn't be wrong. To question it. There are days I come so close to withdrawing."

Barnaby opened his mouth, but then closed it again. He looked adorably consternated as he slid back into his seat at the table.

"What?" Travis said. "You can ask."

"To be honest, I don't want to make you angry or upset you. I need this job, and I've enjoyed what we've accomplished so far, so I think I'll keep my opinion to myself." He turned to the computer, navigating to the screen with the current assignment. "Here we are." He looked at Travis. "Are you in the middle of cooking something, or can it wait a moment?"

"It can wait a few minutes," he said, uncertain how to fix the tension he'd created and reassure Barnaby he wasn't about to walked out the door.

"Wonderful," Barnaby said with false cheerfulness. "Shakespeare's sonnets are more accessible than a lot of his writing. Go ahead and read the first few lines of number one hundred and sixteen, and let's see if we can make sense of it."

Travis knew the answer to that, but already felt wrong-footed with Barnaby, so he tried to appear as if just looking at the words on the page didn't send a shiver of panic up his back.

"What is old Bill talking about in this one?" Barnaby asked.

"Old Bill?" Travis tried to smile, failed miserably, then glared at the screen. "It's about love."

"Right. What is he saying about it?"

"He doesn't want to be in love," Travis guessed, wincing when Barnaby started shaking his head. Fortunately, Barnaby didn't seem to notice.

"Okay, let's try it a different way. Shakespeare is sometimes easier to understand when you can hear it."

"You want me to read it aloud?"

"Sure. Go for it."

Travis cleared his throat and leaned in, his shoulder pressed to Barnaby's. Barnaby's breath caught, but Travis was too worried about embarrassing himself to consider what it meant.

He'd just read the words, and listen to the words, and try to understand. No problem.

"Let me not to the marriage of true minds. Admit impediments. Love is not love."

Barnaby held up his hand and Travis stopped. He curled his hands into fists beneath the table and took a careful breath.

"Okay, that wasn't fair of me," Barnaby said. "I should give you more context. It's a passionate piece and that should come through. Also, you have to convince your brain to ignore the line breaks while still adhering to the punctuation."

What?

Travis swallowed, his throat tight. He stood and stepped away from the table—from Barnaby and that fucking poem—before he thought about what he was doing. Not since he'd been in high school had he felt more like crying with pure, unadulterated frustration and fury.

He had no idea what showed on his face, but Barnaby stood, too. "Here, let me."

Barnaby jumped onto his chair and threw an arm in the air. He was stunning, the bright sunlight streaming over him and making him glow, as he read the poem aloud.

Let me not to the marriage of true minds
Admit impediments. Love is not love
Which alters when it alteration finds,
Or bends with the remover to remove:
Oh, no! it is an ever-fixéd mark,
That looks on tempests and is never shaken...

Travis stared, dumbfounded, as Barnaby's resonant voice and crisp accent transformed the words.

When he reached the end, his voice still ringing in the air around them, he glanced down and did a double take. Then he slowly lowered his arm, his cheeks going pink. "Sorry, I thought it might help."

"Do it again," Travis implored. He couldn't take his eyes off Barnaby.

Barnaby started to repeat the poem, but his arm stayed at his side, and his voice was much quieter.

"No, with *passion*. Like you did before," Travis said, poking at Barnaby's leg.

This time he wouldn't be too surprised to hear the words.

Barnaby's cheeks edged to dull red, but he recited the lines again, passionately. Beautifully.

Travis got it. "He's talking about what true love really is. He's saying that if there are impediments, or it can be altered, then it isn't really love."

Barnaby punched the air. "Yes! So it *is* better when you hear it."

Travis scrubbed a hand through his hair, feeling like the asshole he was. "It is. It's not...*shit*...it's not just a Shakespeare thing, either."

Barnaby stepped off the chair and back onto the floor. "I don't understand."

"I wasn't mad at you. Before. When you asked about caring about school. I do care and saying I didn't was bullshit. Like, programming, almost, so I was mad at myself for saying it. It's just..." Travis sighed. He hated talking about this, but Barnaby was here to help. Travis had to trust him. "I have a learning disability—a weird one they took forever to figure out, so I didn't do well in school. Most of my life, people have told me it's not a big deal if I don't like school or don't do well in it, especially because I had hockey and could focus on that. I guess I learned to repeat all that shit, to make the same excuses whether I felt that way or not, which really sucked. Particularly because I *do* like school and I love to learn, but it's fucking hard to do without some help and it's hard to ask for help without sounding like an idiot."

"You are *not* an idiot," Barnaby said with a certainty Travis tried not to be flattered by.

"Thanks."

"No one who can write such a keen evaluation of Thomas Wyatt's lute as a metaphor for his dick, and how either instrument was the key to his ego, is an idiot."

Travis's face went hot but he laughed.

"Now," Barnaby said as he sat at the table again. "Tell me about this learning disability. And for future reference, if anyone who claims to be an educator of *any* sort ever makes you feel stupid because you have a learning disability, then they are worthless scum and you should punch them in the face."

"I'm good at that, at least," Travis joked.

"You're good at learning about poetry, too."

"Oh. Ah, thank you..." he stammered, disproportionately pleased by the compliment. He rubbed his hand over his bare chest, aware, all of a sudden, that he was half naked. Exposed. He glanced toward the kitchen and the shirt he'd left on top of the fridge. When he looked back, he found Barnaby's eyes had wandered to his bare belly and were lingering there.

Huh.

He turned for the kitchen and tried to remember what the

hell they'd been talking about. "My disability is fairly rare," he said, forcing his brain to stay on subject. "There are big, long-winded explanations for it, and I'm sure my mom can dig all the reports and test results out of a box in her attic if you really want the nitty gritty details, but the long and short of it is that I don't learn when I read. The data doesn't get absorbed and interpreted the way it's supposed to."

"You mean, the way it does for most people."

"Yeah, that's what I said," Travis agreed as he cracked eggs into the pan to scramble.

"No, it isn't. Your brain works exactly as it's supposed to. It just does it in a way that doesn't apply to many others."

Travis nodded, not trusting himself to speak, and told himself he wasn't allowed to kiss his tutor. Not at dawn on a game day when he had five sonnets by Shakespeare to learn. No matter how much be wanted to.

Also, this was a *job* for Barnaby. Wandering eyes aside, he had a right to work without being tackled to the floor by his client.

Feeling noble, Travis glanced at his shirt on top of the refrigerator, then discarded the idea of putting it on.

Not *that* noble.

"In any case," Barnaby continued, "tell me more. When you read a book, a work of fiction, can you follow the story?"

"Not easily, no. I can muddle to some extent, but it's painful, slow, and frustrating. Versus if I listen to the audiobook, I do better."

"Ah. So all this poetry?"

"Half the time it might as well be written in hieroglyphics."

Travis peeked over his shoulder to gauge Barnaby's reaction. He appeared thoughtful. He also appeared to be staring at Travis's ass, but that could but be accidental.

Travis turned back to the stove and flexed his glutes, grinning at Barnaby's quietly muttered, *"Good lord."*

Clearing his throat, Barnaby said, "Well, now that I know, I'm sure we can work things better."

Travis nodded, stirring the eggs. It was a relief to have confessed, but he still felt twitchy about it. Not enough practice, probably, which was a sad statement about how much trust he'd put into any number of teachers in the past twenty years.

He was surprised when Barnaby appeared at his side, then slid onto the counter beside the stove. Travis was fascinated by Barnaby's fingers, long and pale, but strong when they gripped the edge of the Formica. In fact, all of Barnaby looked strong. Travis could see the contour of muscles in Barnaby's legs, even through the thick fabric of his pants. He wanted to curl his hand around the lean thigh closest to him and feel the strength beneath his fingers.

"This okay?" Barnaby asked.

Travis pinned his eyes to the stove and stirred the eggs like his life depended on it. "Sure."

He couldn't *actually* feel Barnaby's eyes on him, but his imagination wasn't doing him any favors when he snuck a peek and found Barnaby's eyes tracing over his shoulders.

Travis almost jumped when Barnaby started reciting another poem.

Shall I compare thee to a summer's day?
Thou art more lovely and more temperate:
Rough winds do shake the darling buds of May,
And summer's lease hath all too short a date:
Sometimes too hot the eye of heaven shines,
And often in his gold complexion dimmed;
And every fair from fair sometimes declines,
By chance or nature's changing course untrimmed;
But thy eternal summer shall not fade,
Nor lose possession of that fair thou ow'st;
Nor shall death brag thou wander'st in his shade,
When in eternal lines to time thou grow'st:
So long as men can breathe, or eyes can see,
So long lives this, and this gives life to thee.

Travis wasn't sure he understood half of that, but the parts he did get made his heart beat harder. "What was that?" Travis asked.

"Shakespeare again. Sonnet eighteen."

Travis looked at his laptop, a good fifteen feet away.

"I have it memorized," Barnaby said with a shrug. "And it sprang to mind. I thought perhaps we could talk about it while you prepare us this feast." He eyed the mountain of eggs in the pan. "Are you sure you're not expecting more company?"

"Nope. Growing boy, remember?"

Barnaby's gaze ran over him. "Indeed," he murmured, then sat up straight. "Right. So, any guesses what this one is about?"

"Shall I compare you to a summer's day, right? It's a love poem, too."

"Yes. Excellent."

"I'm not sure why a woman wants to be compared to hot weather, but I can see how it might be romantic."

Barnaby laughed. "Well, what would you have the Bard compare you to, then?"

"A sunny, cold, winter's day. When the snow is blindingly white, and the ponds are frozen so perfectly smooth it's like skating on glass."

Barnaby smiled. "Interesting. I've always liked this one because he doesn't specify the gender of the person he was writing about. Many assume, based on what we know, that it was a woman, but for me, it doesn't have to be. And as someone who loves warm weather, it's nice to imagine someone comparing me to a summer's day."

"Thou art more lovely and more temperate," Travis repeated. "The first part is true, and the second means, what? That you're more even-tempered than summer weather?"

Barnaby stared at him hard. "Yes, that's what he means."

Travis smiled with satisfaction. "And the next part he's saying you're better than the strong winds or hot sun. That summer is too short to do you justice."

"Yes!"

"I'm not as sure about the next part," Travis admitted.

"He's saying weather changes, and summer fades, but her beauty won't, and he'll never tire of it. Of her."

Travis heard the wistful note in Barnaby's voice. "That would be nice. To have someone say that, think that, about you."

"Yes," Barnaby said with a little smile. "Shakespeare has captured the hopes of most people with his flattery. It can be written off as nothing, as a love note or a flirtation, but it can also mean so much more. To compare someone to something as wonderful as a summer's day, and find the summer's day wanting. It's a nice idea."

It was. Travis studied Barnaby while Barnaby gazed across the room. His bright blue eyes looked more than wistful. They looked sad. Travis wished it was any of his business.

He lifted the eggs off the stove and started dishing them onto two plates. "And the end? He's saying that even when she ages, and later when she dies, her beauty will go on because he's written that poem, right?"

"Yes! Very good," Barnaby said.

Travis tried not to glow. He was too old for that shit. "It's very meta," he observed.

Barnaby grinned. "It is. It's a common theme, though. The idea of immortality in writing. Look at us now, four hundred years later, and we know just how lovely he found her."

"And we can wish we were her," Travis agreed. "Only, you know, with dicks."

Barnaby cracked up, his eyes dancing as he hopped off the counter and took his plate from Travis. "Yes. That would have a certain ring to it, wouldn't it? We're as lovely as a summer's day with a dick."

Travis, pleased to see the sadness gone from Barnaby's eyes, thought Barnaby was far, far lovelier than that.

Chapter Five

Barnaby bounded up the stairs to Travis's door, ready to tackle this week's assignments. The Ice Cats had been traveling for a couple of days, and Barnaby had killed himself plowing through his own classwork while keeping up with Dr. Sorenson's insanely needy students.

He wasn't what anyone would call *on top of it*, but he was close. Mostly.

Hell, he still had hours of work to do yet, but none of that seemed to matter at the moment. He was excited to dive into his next session with Travis.

Barnaby came to a jarring halt.

Shit, he was doing it again. Letting his heart and his stupid romantic nature get the better of him. Eager to read poetry to his captive audience. Clinging to the unexpected wonder in Travis's face as he figured out Shakespeare and, in the process, said sweet and funny things. Letting himself yearn for those things.

Barnaby knew nothing good would come of it. His heart should have been well scarred over by this point. It was testament to what an idiot he was that it wasn't.

He was here to teach, he reminded himself sternly. If he and Travis became friends along the way, that would be fine, but he wasn't going to lose sight of his goals. He would not forget *why* he'd dragged himself across an ocean and spent the last two months nearly freezing his knob off. This was his fresh start, which would be pointless if he made the same mistakes he'd made before.

Barnaby knocked briskly, determined to view Travis as a work associate. A colleague, of a sort.

The door swung open and revealed Travis in leggings, very *tight* leggings of the sort runners wore, and not a stitch else. There were bulges everywhere. Arms, shoulders, pecs, abs, and, well... lower, too.

Jesus Christ.

He mentally shook himself. Repeatedly.

This is my work associate. Theirs was a professional relationship. It didn't matter that Barnaby's knees felt weak with the desire to kneel and press his face against Travis's tight stomach, or that his lungs quivered with longing to suck in a deep breath while his nose was buried in the crease where Travis's thigh and body joined.

With a final gulp, Barnaby made very direct eye contact with Travis, whose face appeared to be stuck in a perpetual cringe. He squinted at Barnaby, his mouth in a tight grimace, his complexion an unpleasant and alarming shade of green.

He slumped against the doorframe, the hand hooked over the top of the door the only thing holding him up.

"Are you all right?" Barnaby asked, reaching out, then yanking his hand back when his fingertips grazed warm, bare skin.

Travis closed his eyes. "I'm fine." His voice sounded as though he'd been chewing gravel. "Just a headache."

Barnaby had seen just enough hockey to know it was an endless series of players crashing into each other or into the plexiglass walls around the ice. "Did you hit your head playing? Could you have a concussion?"

"*No*," Travis yelped, standing straight. "No, nothing like that. We went out last night after the team got back into town. It was one of the guys' birthday."

Barnaby's lips twitched. "Did you drink yourself into a sore head?"

"You make it sound far classier, and me feel far stupider, when you say it like that," Travis grumbled, stepping back and letting Barnaby into the apartment.

It was ten o'clock in the morning and the main room, with its huge, uncurtained windows, glowed. Sunlight streaked across the floor and furniture, except the yoga mat tucked behind the couch in what little shade there was to be had.

Travis winced as he moved through a shaft of light en route to the kitchen. "I need some fucking tea."

"You look like you need another couple of hours' sleep and some paracetamol."

Also, clothes.

"I took something when I got out of bed, which was a half hour later than it was supposed to be. That's why I'm not dressed yet."

Barnaby eyed Travis from the back. More interesting bulges. "You sleep in tights?"

Travis grinned over his shoulder. "I sleep naked. I put the leggings on to stretch in the morning."

"Oh. Ah...interesting," Barnaby managed to squeak out while desperately trying not to picture Travis naked and tangled up in his sheets.

He's my coworker. Colleague.

Barnaby slid out of his coat and went to the table, glancing at the laptop. He knew the syllabus, but given that he and Travis met in fits and starts, and Travis tended to do his work the same way while traveling, Barnaby was never sure where they were going to land.

"John Donne today, then?" he asked.

"I guess," Travis muttered as he wrestled with the toaster. His usual dexterity in the kitchen had apparently been left in the bottom of a bottle the night before.

Barnaby scanned the list of poems. "Anything in particular you want to focus on? Shall I start reading them to you?"

Travis came to the table and unloaded jars of jam and marmalade, a sugar bowl, the milk carton, and the butter dish. He squinted at the screen. "I haven't had any time to go through this stuff yet. Is this guy going to be more lovey-dovey crap?"

"Lovey-dovey *crap*?" Barnaby asked, biting back his smile.

Travis's only reply was to grunt and stagger back to the kitchen.

Of course, the reason Travis thought everyone they'd

worked on together so far were all about love poems was probably because those were Barnaby's favorites, and he'd managed to steer them in that direction. He felt a twinge of guilt and decided he would make an effort to provide Travis with more variety. He'd be doing himself a favor, too, if they steered clear of the romantic stuff.

Too bad they were on John Donne. Barnaby was well-familiar with his work, but, of course, most familiar with his romantic pieces, and had always tried to avoid his later work, which tended to be intensely religious.

He scanned the list of poems the professor had included. It seemed she wasn't any great fan of the religious works, either.

Meanwhile, Travis hovered over the toaster with his head resting against the cabinet and his eyes closed. Poor sod.

Barnaby had an idea. "I shall endeavor to expose you to John Donne without any of the lovey-dovey crap."

Travis took a deep breath before he stood properly and returned to the table with a plate heaped with at least a dozen pieces of toast. He plunked it down between them before collapsing into the chair next to Barnaby's. "Will I have to use my brain for this?"

"Generally, that's the recommended method for learning."

"Bummer." Travis shoved the plate at Barnaby. "I made you some, too."

He never knew what to make of Travis's constant, and seemingly reflexive, hospitality. "Thank you."

Travis just squinted at his bright windows as if they offended him.

Barnaby scanned the screen. "Here's a passage that suits you well today," he announced, biting back a snicker. "It's called *The Sun Rising.*"

Busy old fool, unruly sun,
Why dost thou thus,
Through windows and through curtains call on us?

Travis let out a single huff of laughter. "God, I'm feeling that. The sun sucks." He put his head down on the table next to his plate. "I want to die."

Barnaby chose not to view that as an editorial on his poetic recitation skills. He scrolled to another poem and smirked. "How about, then, *The Funeral*?"

For 'tis my outward soul,
Viceroy to that, which then to heaven being gone,
Will leave this to control,
And keep these limbs, her provinces, from dissolution.

Travis grunted into the table. "Now you're just fucking with me."

"I beg your pardon?"

"I have no idea what that meant."

"We'll go back to that one, then."

"Are you trying to make me cry?"

"Oh, let's try *A Valediction: Of Weeping*."

Let me pour forth
My tears before thy face whilst I stay here,
For thy face coins them, and thy stamp they bear,
And by this mintage they are something worth...

Barnaby felt a thrill of victory when Travis smiled against the table. "Okay, you win."

"And what's my prize, then?" Barnaby asked, feeling very proud of himself.

Travis turned his head, his warm brown gaze capturing Barnaby and pinning him on the spot. He was suddenly terrified of what Travis's answer might be. And how weak he would be for whatever was offered.

"I'll make you a deal," Travis said, his voice low and warm. "In exchange for breakfast and tea and your usual rate, you give me fifteen minutes to eat something and try to feel human again. Or at least to make my brain stop hurting."

Honestly, Travis looked like *everything* hurt, his brain being the least of it. With his broad back curled over the table, Barnaby could see a fresh bruise disappearing beneath the waistband of his leggings. He couldn't fathom how one got a bruise there, but he could picture full well how much it would have hurt.

His hand hovered over the dark spot, then he curled it into a fist and pulled away. He grabbed a piece of toast, buttered it, and slid it onto Travis's plate.

"You have a deal," Barnaby said.

The noise Travis made was not an actual word.

Barnaby buttered another slice of bread.

Travis was feeling far more prepared to face the day—and poetry—a half hour later. He may not have met his fifteen-minute goal, but Barnaby didn't seem to mind.

When the last piece of toast had been eaten, Barnaby stood to gather together the jams and butter.

"No, here, let me do that," Travis said, jumping to his feet.

A bolt of pain shot up his leg and he staggered, his thigh catching on the edge of the table before he could steady himself.

"Good god, are you okay?" Barnaby asked, dropping everything back onto the table and grabbing Travis. His normally big blue eyes were enormous.

Travis tried not to think about how good Barnaby's fingers felt curled around his upper arm and his hip. Not because he didn't want them there. Hell, he wanted them *everywhere*, but he was wearing tights, for fuck's sake, and he didn't think his poetry tutor, no matter how gorgeous, needed to know whether or not Travis was circumcised.

"I'm fine," he said, righting himself and taking a deep breath. The skin over Barnaby's high cheek bones looked incredibly smooth and soft. Travis doubted he could grow any sort of beard.

He wanted to rub his lips just there. Over and over.

Yeah, it was definitely time to put on pants.

Unfortunately, when he took a step toward his bedroom, his

knee twinged again. "Fuck," he growled.

"You're *not* all right, are you?" Barnaby asked.

Travis thought if anything would make him feel better, it was the warmth and concern in Barnaby's voice. "No, I'm fine. Just old."

Barnaby's eye twitched, possibly fighting off an eyeroll. "So you say."

"I just need to ice it," Travis said, trying to sound more confident than he felt. "And maybe put it up for a few minutes while I do."

Barnaby bit his lip and scanned the apartment. His gaze lingered on the hallway and the bedroom door beyond before moving on to the couch.

"Can you sit in the sun?" Barnaby asked.

"I'm not going to turn to dust, or sparkle, if that's what you're worried about."

Barnaby laughed. "Fine, then, let's move to the sofa today."

It took some doing to clean up breakfast, most of which Barnaby managed while Travis was limping at half speed behind him. Finally, Travis hobbled across the room with his laptop under his arm and settled onto the couch with his leg propped on the coffee table. He was expecting Barnaby to sit in the chair across from him and start talking about John Donne, but he went to the kitchen and filled the kettle instead.

Travis put his foot back on the ground, girding himself for what he knew was going to be an unpleasant experience when he stood. He couldn't let Barnaby rummage around his kitchen without helping.

Before he could shift forward, though, a cool hand landed on his bare shoulder.

"Stay."

"But—"

Barnaby skirted the end of the couch, his arms full of cold packs in their protective sleeves. Travis arched an eyebrow but didn't protest further while Barnaby propped his leg up on the coffee table—on a pillow this time—and wrapped one of the packs around his knee.

God, that felt good.

Barnaby tapped Travis's shoulder with one finger, motioning for him to sit forward so Barnaby could slip another pack behind him and arrange it right on that fucking awful bruise over his kidney. He settled back with a sigh.

Barnaby was still eyeing him. "I can't remember. Which is the bad shoulder?"

Travis cocked his head. "It depends on the day, but lately it's been the left."

Barnaby pressed the final cold pack into place, tugging one of the bandage rolls Travis kept on top of the fridge for just this purpose from his back pocket and securing the pack with expert ease.

"Better?" Barnaby asked as he surveyed his handiwork.

Travis wondered when and where Barnaby had learned to care for someone this way. It was a very particular skill set, generally reserved for athletic trainers and the long-suffering significant others of athletes.

"Yes. Thank you," he said, trying to decide if he should ask any of the questions running through his head.

Barnaby sighed. "My ex-boyfriend was a ballet dancer."

"What are you, a mind reader?"

Barnaby laughed and sat on the couch next to Travis, one long, lean leg folded under him. He perched the laptop on his bent knee and balanced the other half on Travis's thigh.

"You were looking at me like I was mad. I thought I ought to explain."

Travis noted the way Barnaby's wide, expressive mouth twisted downward at the mention of the ex. "I'm sorry if I've stirred up bad memories."

"Not at all. You thanked me, which was something he rarely managed." Barnaby waved that off. "And in any case, Robert is in the past."

But still haunting Barnaby, clearly. "Sounds like it ended badly."

"Quite. But I'm here, now, and Robert is back in London, no doubt fucking the half of the city he didn't get to while we were together."

Ah. A cheater. Travis leaned into the warmth of Barnaby's body along his side and nudged him with his elbow. "Hey. I'm sorry. Robert is an asshole, and he's an idiot for fucking things up with you."

Barnaby stared at the laptop, his long, dark lashes casting shadows over his incredibly fair cheeks. He drew a deep breath before clearing his throat. "Thank you for saying so."

Travis let it drop and gave them both time to collect their thoughts before he nodded at the laptop. "What's your favorite of these by John Donne?"

"That's not important," Barnaby said. "I can tell you a little about a few of these, and you can tell me which one you'd like to break down first."

"I want to know which one is your favorite."

Barnaby looked at Travis, far too close. "Why?"

Because he was starting to figure Barnaby out and wanted to know more. He wanted to know if it was a coincidence that any number of the poets they'd studied had poems that had nothing to do with love, but Barnaby never spent time on any of them.

"Because those sound the best when you read them to me," Travis said, watching Barnaby.

Color bled into Barnaby's cheeks. He turned back to the computer. "Well, I suppose there are two that stand out for me. *Ecstasy* used to be my favorite, but now I'd say it's *Love's Growth*."

"What's the difference between the two poems?"

"Oh, um..." Barnaby shifted, resettling so their thighs were pressed from hip to knee but his face was harder to see. "*Ecstasy* is about the poet and his love sitting and holding hands and staring into each other's eyes on the river bank. It's about pure love, innocent still, though he uses a lot of metaphor about the body to communicate it. It's very...idealistic, I suppose."

And then Robert fucked with your head and your heart, Travis guessed. He made a mental note to listen to it later if Barnaby didn't end up reading it to him. "And the other? *Love's Growth?*"

The saddest, most wistful smile curled Barnaby's lips. "*Love's Growth* is different. He no longer sees love as pure, but as a mixture of ecstasy and pain. It's not constant and blazing, because then it would have no room to grow, if that makes sense? It's about the fluctuations of love, and how that's okay, too."

"Will you read it to me?" Travis asked.

Barnaby hesitated, then he nodded and scrolled to the poem.

I scarce believe my love to be so pure,
As I had thought it was,
Because it doth endure
Vicissitude, and season, as the grass;
Methinks I lied all winter, when I swore
My love was infinite, if spring make' it more...

Travis listened to the words fall from Barnaby's lips and felt the joy and the pain John Donne had captured centuries before—and the pain Barnaby let slip, no matter how hard he tried to hide it.

When the last stanza was done, they sat in silence. Barnaby's eyes traced over the words on the screen, again and again, as if seeing them for the first time after a long absence. It obviously made him sad.

Travis wished he could do something. "Come to the game tomorrow," he said out of nowhere.

He would be the first to admit he wasn't very good at consoling people.

Barnaby tore his eyes from the poem. "What?"

"Come to the game, and then out afterward. You can meet the guys."

"I know some of the team already," Barnaby said, stalling.

"It'll be a fun way for you to have a break," Travis ventured, going all in. "You said in your texts that you've been working a lot this past week. And I can get you a ticket. If you want."

"I'm rather certain I can get a ticket for myself."

Right. He lived with their manager, and one of the owners, and was friends with Jack.

Which reminded him of something he'd been wondering since he'd first laid eyes on Barnaby. "Are you dating Jack Chevalier?"

Barnaby leaned away from Travis. "I beg your pardon?"

"Sorry. I saw you together once, at the Dipsy Doodle Dangle, and I wondered if..." He dragged a hand through his hair. "You know what? I'm an idiot. Never mind."

And now things were super awkward. *Good job, Travis.*

"I'm not. Dating Jack, that is. I don't think..."

"You don't *think* you're dating Jack?"

Barnaby laughed. "No, I'm very certain I'm not. We're just friends. It's not for me to say, but I don't think he..."

"Is into dudes?" *All class, all the time, that's me.*

"No, that's not it." Barnaby shrugged. "But I don't think Jack is interested in dating anyone."

Travis arched his eyebrows, because he didn't know shit, but he was pretty certain he'd seen interest in Jack's eyes when he'd looked at Grady. "Really?"

"You sound like you don't believe me."

Travis straightened his face out. "No, I do. You seem like a good judge of character."

"I do?"

"Well, you figured out I was an asshole pretty quickly."

Barnaby laughed and nudged Travis with an elbow.

Travis congratulated himself on being the king of awkward. "Anyway, if you wanted to come to the game tomorrow, we could meet up afterward for a drink or something? See if Jack wanted to come, too?"

And maybe if Grady had the night off, he'd want to tag along.

"Okay. I'll, um...see about getting tickets," Barnaby said cautiously. "I think Jack has to work during the games, but I can sit with Callum and the kids, so they can explain what I'm seeing. I've never seen ice hockey played before."

Travis's jaw fell open. "You what now?"

"I've never seen a hockey match. Not in person. And I haven't any idea how it's played. I've heard Rupert and Callum talk about it quite a bit. It sounds like football—what you all call soccer, I mean—but on ice and with a puck instead of a proper ball."

Travis made a noise not unlike being punched in the stomach.

"I suppose it's faster than football," Barnaby continued. "With the skates and all that. And you all crash into each other and the walls quite a bit, right? That looks interesting."

Travis couldn't make words. He was opening and closing his mouth like a landed trout, but no sounds were coming out.

"In any case, perhaps we should get back to your school work so you can be finished in time to take a nap this afternoon. You're looking rather flushed." Barnaby studied his face. "Are you quite all right?"

Chapter Six

Barnaby leaned back against the wall of the lift and eyed Callum. "Why are you smiling?"

Callum tried for a good ten seconds to control his face, then gave up. "I'm just happy that you finally want to come to a game."

Barnaby squinted at him. "No, you've been grinning like an idiot since I mentioned that Travis suggested I come."

Callum shrugged the least innocent-looking shrug possible, which was a neat trick with Eleanor strapped to his chest, smiling cheerfully at everything. "I think it's great you're making friends."

Christian sighed. "*Please.* He's hoping you'll get laid and stop being a miserable git."

"Christian! I can't believe you said that," Barnaby gasped, his face on fire.

Christian looked worried. "Did I not use *git* right?"

How was *that* the issue?

"What does *get laid* mean?" Oliver asked from where he stood in the middle of the lift.

Callum cast Christian a baleful look. "It's a grown-up word."

"It's two words," Oliver pointed out.

Christian and his father exchanged a comical series of expressions over Oliver's head. Christian was in for a lecture later, that was certain. It was equally clear he wasn't particularly concerned about that.

"What?" Christian said defiantly. "I'm not wrong."

"You're not wrong," Callum agreed, "but we don't use adult language around members of our family who aren't yet allowed to use it, which you know perfectly well."

"Wait a minute," Barnaby interrupted. "What do you mean he's not wrong?"

The lift let out a loud *ding* and the doors slid open. Callum took Oliver's hand and practically dove into the brightly lit concourse full of people, the coward. Christian and Barnaby followed them, weaving through the throng past a series of doors on the left and food kiosks on the right.

The arena was bursting with noise and people, easing Barnaby's worry that he was in for a long, dull night. He didn't know a thing about hockey, and based on his experience at football matches in the past, he'd expected, mostly, a long, cold sit.

Callum stopped at a door labeled only with a number. He unlocked it with a key card and ushered them into a small suite with two rows of seats overlooking the lower bowl of the arena. In spite of there being no glass, the room was comfortably warm. There was even a counter, refrigerator, and sink against the back wall.

Oliver led Barnaby to the front row and directed him into a seat, then climbed to sit on his feet in the chair to the right. Christian took Eleanor from his father and took the seat to the left. Callum remained by the door chatting with a seemingly endless stream of people while blocking anyone's view into the room.

Barnaby often forgot Callum was a well-known retired professional hockey player—until moments like this, when he could hear someone asking him to sign something. In fact, Callum was greeting friends as often as he was being introduced to strangers and asked for an autograph. It was strange to think of Callum, who spent most his time raising a family and fawning over his cherry red minivan, as famous.

When the teams burst onto the ice to warm up, Barnaby scanned the Ice Cats to find Travis, but the players were moving too quickly to read the names on the back of their jerseys. He almost asked the boys if they knew Travis's number, but was afraid Callum would overhear and the smirking would start again.

The match, or *game* as Christian corrected, started with some announcements and the anthem. A moment before the singing began, Callum quietly murmured a few more words and stepped into the room with Rupert. They held hands at the railing and looked out over the ice as the whole family sang, including Oliver in a key that was never meant to be applied to *O Canada*.

Barnaby watched, curious, as five members from each team arranged themselves around the center of the ice. He wasn't sure what he was expecting, but it wasn't the sudden clash of sticks and explosion of motion.

Hockey was...exciting. And quick. And very, very confusing.

"Why did the referee blow the whistle?" he asked no one in particular when play suddenly stopped.

Christian was kind enough to explain. Barnaby nodded, but it was hard to concentrate on the answer to his last question when ten more had cropped up in the interim, and it took all his focus to follow the puck as it was slung around the ice, players darting and crashing in every direction.

He finally caught a flash of the name Campbell on the back of a jersey and noted it was above the number 37. His eyes were riveted to Travis as he moved up the ice, caught the puck on his stick, and passed it to another player, all in a matter of seconds. Travis's teammate fired the puck at the goal, eliciting an aborted roar of excitement from the crowd when the goaltender threw up his hand and sent the puck sailing in the other direction.

This seemed to distress Oliver greatly, as he leaped to stand on his seat and bellowed, "Bloody hell, Mike, move your feet! Get back! Get back!"

"Language, Oliver," Callum said mildly, not bothering to hide his smile—it wasn't like Oliver was going to tear his eyes off the ice and see it.

Christian rolled his eyes. "I get a lecture, but everyone thinks *he's* cute for using grown-up words."

Oliver was, in fact, awfully cute.

There was a loud whistle just as Oliver yelled, "Nooo!" and hurled himself onto Barnaby's back. He clung like a limpet and hid his face against Barnaby's shoulder.

Barnaby grabbed onto Oliver's legs to keep them both from pitching to the floor. "What's the matter, Oliver?"

"We're going on the PK," he moaned, as if it were a fate worse than death. "Our PK has been terrible."

Rupert grimaced and Callum patted his back supportively. No one disagreed with Oliver.

Barnaby had no opinion, since he'd didn't have the faintest idea what a PK was. He hadn't a damn clue what was going on, and said as much—less the grown-up word, of course. Christian was kind enough to explain while Oliver clung to Barnaby's back, yelling at the ice as if the players would heed his every word.

Hockey, from the rules, to the players, to the speed, to the crazy fans, was *fascinating.*

Barnaby watched everything Travis did when he was on the ice, and the rest of the time followed Christian's suggestion to watch the team as a whole and see how they moved together. That had seemed impossible at first, but soon he was caught up in the flow of the game. Barnaby was ashamed to recall his assumptions about hockey players, as it was obvious you couldn't excel at this game if you didn't have a good mind. There was a sense of teamwork that often felt haphazard and like barely leashed chaos, and other times looked like the finest choreography.

In many ways, it was exactly like dance. Or no—like a poem. Sometimes choreographed and operating within a set of rules, but the possibilities of what you did within those rules were infinite. Unexpected.

When the clock counted down to zero, a loud buzzer sounded, and Barnaby and Oliver deflated in their shared seat.

"So, this is half-time?" Barnaby asked.

Rupert chuckled. "This is the first intermission. Hockey has three periods."

There would be two more periods like that?

Barnaby was spared from sounding like the ignoramus he was when the door at the back of the suite popped open and Jack came in, followed by a tall, serious-looking man. At almost six and a half feet, he stood a head above most, and even as thin as he was, had a presence that caught Barnaby's attention. Maybe it was the broad shoulders. Or the long-legged stride.

Rupert and Callum said hello, and Barnaby realized this was Jack and Travis's friend, Grady. Jack chatted with them both for a moment, updating Rupert about a delivery that had failed to arrive and might result in a soft pretzel shortage. Barnaby barely contained his impatience until Jack finally turned and made the introductions.

Barnaby held out his hand. "It's a pleasure to meet you, Grady. I've heard many good things."

Grady's dark brown eyes pinned Barnaby on the spot. "It's nice to meet you, too." His easy drawl matched his loping gait. They were both, without a doubt, misleading. "Travis said his poetry tutor would be here tonight. I hadn't realized it was you."

They released each other's hands and Grady turned back to Jack before Barnaby could ask what the hell that meant. Then it didn't matter, because Barnaby saw the transformation that came over Grady when he was focused on Jack. It was like witnessing a magic trick, seeing the cold, almost black stare melt into something gooey and soft and the color of a warm brownie.

Even more amazing was the warm smile on Jack's face. "I have to get going. I'll come find you guys at the end of the game."

Grady's gaze never left Jack's face. "Thanks, Jack. This is great. We'll see you then."

Jack nodded and turned for the door. Barnaby watched, confounded, because unless he was hallucinating, he'd seen, for a fraction of a second, something like attraction flash in Jack's eyes. Then after he'd turned away from Grady, something very like grief.

What is going on there?

Barnaby turned to Grady and saw he was still looking at the closed door.

"So, you a big hockey fan?" Barnaby asked, determined to get to know Grady.

"I'm a fan of the Ice Cats, anyway. And I'm Canadian, so I'm obligated, by law, to like hockey," he said, deadpan.

Barnaby smiled, delighted Grady had a sense of humor, even if the delivery was so dry he needed a drink. "Excellent. Christian is attempting to teach me all he can while we watch. Perhaps you can add your own take."

Grady hesitated, then gave a brief nod. "Sure."

They were back in their seats by the time the game started again, with Grady sitting right next to Barnaby, since Oliver preferred to watch from Barnaby's back. Barnaby was aware of Grady's eyes on him at several points, but he didn't acknowledge it. Barnaby would be flattered if he thought Grady's careful study had anything at all to do with interest—Grady was, after all, a handsome man, and he had a John Wayne thing going on that suited him—but it looked more like Barnaby was a puzzle Grady was trying to solve.

Barnaby was completely unsurprised to learn Grady was a Mountie. He'd probably been one of those cowboy marshals with a tin star pinned to his chest in his last life.

He didn't know why, but he thought that suited Jack perfectly. Barnaby was more into the cat burglar type, himself—Cary Grant rather than John Wayne. Robert's lithe dancer's body had enthralled him, once upon a time. He'd dreamed of it, jerked off to it, and reached for it every chance he could.

Though these days his fantasies had shifted in another direction. Broader shoulders and heavier muscle, and a tight, round ass he wanted to—

Well, that was neither here nor there, as Barnaby wasn't going to be dating anyone, let alone doing miraculous things to their huge, tight bum.

Barnaby watched a certain huge, tight bum race up the ice a few feet behind the Ice Cat who had the puck. They split as they approached the goal and Travis's teammate passed the puck to Travis behind the net. He'd no sooner caught it against the blade of his stick when a massive man on the opposing team crushed him into the boards with enough force that Barnaby wondered how it didn't break every bone in his body, let alone take him off his feet. He cringed, curling back into his seat and Oliver.

Oliver patted his shoulder. "He'll be okay."

Barnaby could picture the bruises forming as Travis skated stiffly back to the bench. He worried, selfishly, that their plans for the evening would be canceled. He'd been concerned it wasn't wise to go out with Travis for a drink, since they were supposed to be colleagues, but he'd had a massive change of heart since seeing Grady and Jack together.

With just a few minutes left in the third period, Rupert slipped out of the suite and Jack slipped back in.

"So, what did you think?" he asked as he took the seat next to Grady.

"I love it," Barnaby confessed. "You were right. I didn't understand this sport at all."

Jack's smile was smug. "Told you."

"Yes, thank you. I just said you're right, there's no need to rub it in."

Jack laughed, and, as always, Barnaby felt a touch of awe. He waited until Jack was absorbed in the end of the game, then on a hunch, snuck a glance to his right, hoping to find Grady gazing at Jack again. Instead, his dark eyes were narrowed on Barnaby.

He did not look happy.

Suddenly, Barnaby recalled Travis asking if he was dating Jack, and wondered if, perhaps, Grady was the reason. He and Jack had been meeting for coffee quite a bit. Maybe to Grady that looked like they were dating.

He arched his eyebrows, silently asking Grady if there was a problem. Grady pursed his lips and ran his tongue over his teeth, returning his attention to the ice.

Barnaby could barely focus on the rest of the game, thanks to his growing anticipation. He was practically gagging on the list of questions he wanted to ask Travis—starting with whether he had dragged Barnaby into an elaborate matchmaking scheme for their mutual friends.

He was still grinning at the thought when the final buzzer

sounded.

Travis raced through his post-game routine, only stopping long enough to listen to a scathing lecture from the coach about their penalty kill. He tried to pay attention, since he was *on* the penalty kill, and since the entire team was being subjected to the shouting on their behalf.

As soon as Coach was done, Travis bolted for the showers and did as quick a rinse as he could get away with and still mingle with civilized people. The shouting in the locker room confirmed that the plan was for the team to head to Quigley's, which was good, since he wasn't sure if Barnaby was ready for Smitty's. For that matter, he wasn't in the mood to have his shoes stuck to the floor all night, either.

He pulled on his coat and grabbed his bag, hightailing it for the door. He almost crashed into Rupert as he came into the room.

"Whoa, sorry about that," he said, taking a step back.

"In a hurry?" Rupert asked.

What was with that smirk?

"Just meeting friends," Travis said. "I convinced Barnaby to come out with the team tonight."

"So I hear."

There was something in Rupert's tone that Travis couldn't begin to unpack. "Don't worry, I'll be sure he gets home safe."

"Or sends a text if he's not coming home at all," Rupert added.

Barnaby didn't strike Travis as the kind of guy who would pick someone up in a bar. He wasn't sure why he thought that, but he did. And he really didn't think Barnaby would cruise in a bar full of guys who worked for his cousin.

Maybe that was his ego talking, though, since in spite of Barnaby's occasionally wandering eyes, he hadn't given Travis any reason to think he'd be open to more than poetry lessons and, as of tonight, a beer with mutual friends.

Rupert was still staring at Travis. With that *smirk*.

A terrible thought clicked into place. Did Rupert think—

Travis froze, doing an excellent deer-in-headlights impersonation. "Uh, yeah, well, I'm just going to head out and meet the guys."

He bolted from the locker room like his ass was on fire, telling himself he'd imagined the entire thing. He jogged along the tunnel beneath the arena until he saw Barnaby, Jack, and Grady in the lobby.

Jack and Grady were speaking animatedly about something, while Barnaby watched like he was at a tennis match, a happy smile on his face. When Travis's shoe squeaked on the concrete floor, Barnaby looked over at him.

His face absolutely lit up when he saw Travis.

Travis was a professional athlete, so he didn't trip over his own feet, but it was a near fucking thing. He hoped everyone watching would think he was winded by the run and not how Barnaby was beaming up at him. Barnaby looked like he'd discovered the most wonderful secret and he was dying to share.

Travis almost asked, but Barnaby cut him off. "I don't know about you, but I'm ready for a drink. Shall we move this to the pub?"

Everyone agreed and they turned for the parking lot.

Jack bumped Grady's arm with his elbow. "If you want, you can ride with me and I can bring you back to your car later."

They all huddled closer when they stepped out into the frigid night air, the wind cutting through their clothes.

"No, that's all right. You should take Barnaby," Grady said, in a painfully neutral voice.

Barnaby widened his eyes at Travis, like he wanted him to do something. Travis had no idea *what*. Did he not want to go with Jack? They were friends, so that didn't make sense. And it was too late either way—there wasn't much he could do at this point that wouldn't make things awkward.

He shrugged helplessly at Barnaby as Jack led him in the

opposite direction and Grady let out a tight, frustrated breath.

Travis studied what little of his face he could see above his scarf. "You want to ride with me?" he asked.

"Nah. I'll take my own car, in case I want to take off," Grady growled before veering away from Travis toward his car.

Travis's feelings might have been hurt if he weren't ninety percent certain Grady's bad mood was due to Barnaby's proximity to Jack. Which, he'd like to point out to his stubborn friend, was entirely *his* doing.

Travis arrived at Quigley's just behind Jack and Barnaby, but there was no sign of Grady. If that fucker didn't show up, Travis was going to go get the big baby and drag his ass back out. They went to the bar to wait.

Jack volunteered to get the first round and was, of course, back in less time than anyone else ever could have been. Jack knew everyone in this damn town, and even if he didn't know this bartender, his face would do the trick well enough, too.

He handed Travis a beer, and Barnaby a dark mixed drink, or possibly a soda.

The rest of the team trickled in and Travis introduced Barnaby to the guys. Every single one of his teammates—*every single one*—gave Travis a significant look when Barnaby wouldn't see. Travis spent so much of the next five minutes shaking his head, it was a miracle he didn't strain his neck.

"Barnaby!" boomed a familiar voice above the din in the bar. "How did you end up with this loser?"

Barnaby spun around and grinned at Rupert and Callum's neighbor—and the Ice Cats' goalie—Alexei Belov. "I'm his tutor, actually."

A number of heads turned at that, but Travis didn't respond. He glared at Alexei. "*You're an asshole*," he said in Russian.

Alexei shrugged. "*You say such mean things to me. And what's this? He's your teacher? What are you studying, Nabokov?*" He emphasized the famous author's name in case Travis missed the obvious Lolita insinuation.

"You're hilarious. And that book may be a national treasure in Russia, but it's about a goddamn pervert. Barnaby is twenty-eight, *and, not that it's any of your business, he's helping me with my poetry class."*

"Poetry!" Alexei exclaimed with delight. *"That's so romantic."* Never before, in Russian or English, had the word romantic contained that many syllables.

A very pointy elbow dug into Travis's ribs. "You speak Russian?" Barnaby asked.

"You don't have to sound so surprised," Travis said.

"No! I didn't mean—"

Travis put a hand on Barnaby's arm. "Hey. I'm kidding. I lived in Russia for a couple years. Alexei's been helping me practice."

Standing far too close, his drink pressed to his chest, Barnaby smiled his big toothy smile. "That's brilliant. I'm terrible with languages. There are a couple of poems I've always suspected were not translated well from the Russian. Could you look at them?"

Travis was acutely aware of their rapt audience. "I'd be happy to, but you'd be better off talking to Alexei about that." He scanned the bar for Grady—*where is that asshole?*—until Alexei poked him in the shoulder. Hard.

"Look how he smiles at you, you fool. Encourage it."

"I will do no such thing," Travis said tersely, then smiled at Barnaby, who clearly didn't understand a word of what was being said. "Ignore him. He's even older than I am, which makes him a relic around here."

Barnaby looked at Alexei, bemused. "Aren't you, like, thirty-six or something?"

Alexei nodded.

Barnaby scowled at Travis. "You have a thing about being old, don't you?"

Alexei smirked.

Travis pointed a finger at his face. *"Do not say the word*

"Daddy" or I swear to god there will be revenge."

Chapter Seven

Barnaby would never understand Travis's insistence that he, and everyone else in their thirties, was old. It was nonsense.

He was about to tell him so, too, but then Jack spoke from behind him.

"You two ready for some food?"

Barnaby spun to find a smiling Jack with Grady standing at his shoulder looking significantly less happy. The bar was getting busier with the arrival of the team and their friends, and Barnaby found himself pressed in the middle of their little group. He tried to step back, but Travis's hand on his waist stilled him just as his ass landed in the cradle of Travis's hips.

Barnaby froze and noted the way Grady's gaze narrowed thoughtfully on Travis's hand.

"Brilliant!" Barnaby said. "Can we get a table?"

Jack scanned the booths surrounding the bar, then turned to the hostess and pointed at one. She smiled and waved. "Sandy says we can sit right there."

Barnaby rolled his eyes. "Of course she does," he said. He decided to test a theory and hooked his arm in Jack's for the walk across the bar. Jack gave him a funny look but didn't shake him off. "Is there anyone in this town you don't know, and who wouldn't bend over backwards for you?" he teased.

Jack disputed that, while Grady and Travis trailed behind them. Barnaby glanced back and it was a wonder he didn't burst into flames from the fire in Grady's glare.

Hypothesis confirmed.

When they reached the booth, Barnaby nudged Jack in one direction and slid into the table on the other side. Barnaby gestured for Travis to come sit on the same side, but Grady smiled grimly and slid in next to him before Travis had a chance.

Shit. Barnaby pressed himself as close to the wall as he

reasonably could without the risk of insulting Grady. Jack hesitated, his face blank but his uncharacteristic inaction telling. Travis took the opportunity to slide into the booth first.

You okay? he mouthed as he settled across from Barnaby.

Barnaby waved off his concern. He'd find another time to talk to Travis about the Jack and Grady thing, and meanwhile, this was just fine.

A waitress appeared and Travis ordered another round of drinks. Barnaby knew he shouldn't have another rum and coke, especially so quickly, but he'd finished his first already and one little indulgence wouldn't hurt too much. He wisely ordered some food to soak it up. It wasn't that he couldn't hold his drink—he was an Englishman, after all—but he was on a tight budget and therefore, perhaps, a *little* out of practice.

They talked about the game and the team over dinner, with Jack and Travis offering funny anecdotes about some of the players. Barnaby had heard enough stories at home to know the Ice Cats had some real characters on the roster, but Rupert and Callum hadn't told him about the practical jokes. Or the singing on the bus.

Or that the team had a reputation as a safe haven for LGBTQ players and staff.

Various members of the team stopped by the table to say hi or defend their honor, if they heard a story being told that involved them. Olle Svensson took particular umbrage to the retelling of the time the team had stolen his underwear on a road trip and replaced them with a package of new shorts that were two sizes too small. Travis was practically in tears trying to describe how Olle walked into the breakfast room at the hotel the next morning, having obviously attempted to wear the too-tight underwear.

Olle rolled his eyes and said something in Swedish. Barnaby didn't have to understand the language to know it had been very rude. Travis laughed and fired something back. Also in Swedish.

How many languages did the man *speak*?

The meal passed too quickly, and Barnaby was surprised

when the waitress came to clear their plates. He didn't remember eating all his food. Nor did he remember finishing his drink, but he must have in order to get this brand-new one in front of him.

Had Travis ordered another round?

Bollocks. Reality came crashing back in with a sickening thud. What was he *doing?* He attempted some frantic maths in his head, but the rum wasn't helping. The sum was the same regardless—three or four mixed drinks and a sandwich were going to add up to too much for his budget no matter what.

He was furiously trying to shuffle his expenses for the next couple of weeks when someone kicked him gently under the table. His head snapped up to find Travis watching him.

"You okay?" Travis asked quietly, while Jack and Grady continued their debate about teams from Toronto versus Montreal. It was amazing, really, that Grady could still look so fond of Jack while calling his favorite team a bunch of dirty assholes.

Which was quite an image, now that Barnaby thought about it.

Travis kicked him again.

"I'm fine," Barnaby said. He was, wasn't he? He could offset the cost of his drinks by finally dropping the international plan on his phone. He'd not be able to call home, but he never did anyway. Skype kept him in touch with his family, and he'd avoided his supposed friends long enough that they'd given up trying.

That should have been more of a relief than it was. It also should have taken longer than it had, so at least he could take solace that he'd been correct in thinking that they hadn't cared that much anyway.

Oh dear. He was getting maudlin.

Another kick.

"*What?*"

Jack and Travis looked at him, startled.

Travis looked pointedly at Barnaby's hands. Barnaby followed his gaze and found a pile of shredded napkins on the table in front of him. He dropped the last pieces still clutched in his fingers and pushed the whole mess toward the center of the table.

"Sorry."

Travis's eyes narrowed. "What's going on?"

Barnaby wasn't so drunk he was going to answer that question. Instead, he tried to stand up.

It didn't go well, what with being on the inside seat of a booth, but Grady was kind enough not to say anything—though the look spoke volumes—and to get up so Barnaby could free himself.

"Just a run to the loo," he said, breezily, before diving into the crowd at the bar.

He thought he heard Travis say, "Excuse me," but didn't look back. If he had, he would have seen Travis catching up and not been startled when he clamped a hand on Barnaby's shoulder.

"The *loo* is this way," he muttered, steering Barnaby in the opposite direction.

He allowed Travis to guide him, fully intending to hide in a stall until he was sure he was alone, but when he went to step through the door, Travis nudged him further down the hallway to where there had once been a payphone of some sort.

"What's going on?" Travis asked.

Barnaby spun around, determined to ask for a moment's peace, and stumbled.

Travis caught his elbow. "Hey there, you okay?"

"I used to be able to hold my drink," Barnaby said. Well, perhaps he whinged it, but he was entitled to a little self-pity. Look how far he'd fallen.

Travis's smile was sweet, and maybe just a shade indulgent. God, he was handsome. It was the eyes. They were intelligent and kind. Direct. Not like Robert's, which had always slid away when they were this close.

"I'm skint," Barnaby blurted.

Travis took a quick step back. "You're going to puke?"

It took Barnaby longer than it should have to work out how those two things were related. Only they weren't. "What?"

"What did you say?" Travis asked.

"I'm skint. I'm broke. I can't afford to drink anymore. I can't afford to be drinking the drinks I've drunk, really."

Travis chuckled. "Drunk being the operative word."

"Shut it. I'm not that far gone."

"Debatable."

"Grady is in love with Jack," Barnaby said, trying hard not to sound wistful about it and failing miserably. "It's nice."

"Wow, I just got whiplash. What does that have to do with you being short on money?"

"Nothing. Why would those two things have anything in common?"

Travis smiled at Barnaby, so close. It would only take a step to press himself to Travis's chest, to nudge their thighs together. Travis would be warm. Barnaby was sure of it.

That would be so nice.

Travis blinked and licked his lips. "You've had too much to drink."

That was patently obvious, so Barnaby didn't know why Travis sounded like he was trying to convince himself of it.

"Do you actually need to use the bathroom?" Travis asked.

"No."

"Then how about we get you some water?"

Barnaby agreed, mostly because water was the only drink he could still afford. He walked beside Travis back down the hallway. The second time he bounced off the wall, Travis's arm curled around his shoulders and pulled him close.

He was just as warm as Barnaby had expected. Barnaby pressed closer.

They waded into the crowd and to the bar, and Barnaby

downed the water Travis pressed into his hand. When a couple of the Ice Cats around them toasted something in a language Barnaby couldn't identify, but of course made Travis laugh because he was some sort of linguistical savant, Barnaby lifted his glass, too, and added,

Drink of this cup; — you'll find there's a spell in
It's every drop 'gainst the ills of morality;
Talk of the cordial that sparked for Helen;
Her cup was fiction, but this is reality.

Travis shook his head, his smile wide. "A poem for every occasion, right?"

"Thomas Moore knew rather more about the evils of drink than most, so I thought it was appropriate."

"Of course you did," he said, warmly, and pulled Barnaby close again for the walk back to the table.

Travis was earning his fucking spot in heaven tonight. Barnaby was loaded, and adorable, and had looked so fresh and hopeful reciting old poetry in a bar packed with drunk hockey players, that Travis wanted to steal him away so they could be alone together.

He contented himself, though, with an arm around his shoulders, guiding him through the crowd.

They were almost back to their table when Barnaby stumbled to a halt. Jack and Grady had been watching their progress with amusement and Barnaby waved at them cheerily before turning to Travis.

He looped his arm around Barnaby's waist to steady him and they ended up bumping together at various points from chest to knee. Barnaby leaned in closer, and it took Travis a moment to realize Barnaby wanted to whisper into his ear.

Fucking sainthood was a fought-off erection away.

"I think we should go home," Barnaby said, his lips catching on the shell of Travis's ear.

"What?" Travis asked, his arm tightening and his heart tripping into a gallop. Christ, was Barnaby actually propositioning him?

"We have to go. Home. To our homes. Because I want to leave Jack and Grady together. Alone."

"Why?"

"Grady's been attempting to cockblock me all evening. I think Grady thinks we're dating."

"You and I?"

Barnaby giggled. "Don't be ridiculous. Me and Jack."

Why was that ridiculous? It stuck in his head a little, that the answer had been so quick and sure.

Barnaby was staring at him as if awaiting an answer.

Travis shook his head. "What about you and Jack?"

Barnaby looked at the table and his hip brushed Travis's dick. Their friends were watching them like they were the entertainment for the evening.

Barnaby huffed and turned away from their grins. "Maybe I should tell Grady I have no interest in Jack. That the path is clear."

"I'm not sure that's a good idea." Travis wasn't sure of anything, at this point, but he was pretty sure about that, actually. It wasn't that Grady didn't need to know—he did. But Travis was worried what else might fall out of Barnaby's mouth, as he was clearly prone to over-sharing when he was drunk. Also, touching. There was a lot of touching.

"Why not?" Barnaby asked, peering at Travis from far too close.

God, his eyes were *pretty*.

They disappeared, though, when he yawned right in Travis's face. "Sorry. I'm bloody knackered."

"You're very British when you're drunk," Travis observed.

Barnaby frowned. "I'm just as British now as I was when I was sober."

That wasn't an argument Travis could win, so he turned to the table, dragging Barnaby along and ignoring Jack's raised eyebrows and Grady's concerned gaze. He pulled out his wallet and dropped enough cash for both of them. "You mind handling the bill?" he asked Jack. "I'm going to take this one home."

"Yeah, I got it," Jack said with a grin for Barnaby.

"I'm not a child," Barnaby snapped.

"I never thought you were," Travis said honestly.

He didn't need any encouragement to see Barnaby as a full-grown man. Every day it was harder not to think about lean hips and wide shoulders and long legs that Travis wanted wrapped around him so badly he was practically shaking with it now.

He glanced at Barnaby and smiled at how the booze had put a flush on his face, the same one he sometimes got when he was pleased about something. And since alcohol seemed to completely erase Barnaby's basic understanding of personal space, he leaned against Travis, barely moving away when Travis reached for their coats, pressing close again when he stood straight.

Travis could only hope no one noticed his quick adjustment while he juggled their coats.

He handed Barnaby his and tried not to laugh as he struggled with it. Taking pity, he pulled the scarf out of the sleeve so Barnaby's arm would fit. He didn't think before looping the scarf around Barnaby's neck, or pulling the gloves from his pockets while he was zipping up. Barnaby took them with a smile, then turned back to the table.

"I hope you won't end your night on my account. I'm terribly sorry to be dashing off like this."

Even Grady was starting to look charmed, which was impressive, since Barnaby was absolutely correct that Grady had been cockblocking him and Jack all night.

Travis said goodnight and tugged Barnaby toward the door before Barnaby could say *cheerio* or whatever other incredibly British thing he could come up with. The cold night air bursting into Travis's lungs as they stepped outside cleared his head of the lingering effect of his beers. He hoped it would do the same for Barnaby.

They turned toward Barnaby's house. Or building. It wasn't really a house so much as a *ware*house with inexplicably nice homes hidden inside it. Travis had only been there once, for the team holiday party, but it was hard to forget.

Fortunately, it was only a few blocks away.

He let go of Barnaby's arm, but Barnaby immediately threaded them together again, so they walked down the street arm in arm. Travis didn't mind.

"Did you see it?" Barnaby asked out of nowhere.

Travis looked at the street around them. "See what?"

"The way Grady looks at Jack."

Travis chuckled. "Yeah. I saw it. I'm pretty sure you can see that from space, if you're paying attention."

"He's in love with Jack," Barnaby said.

"You sound sad about that."

"What? No. Well, maybe. I suppose I'm a bit...worried. I think Jack is interested in Grady, too."

"And that worries you? That sounds like good news for our friends."

"No, but Jack is hiding it from Grady. From everyone. I only saw it because he didn't know I was observing him." Barnaby sighed. "That means it may not matter how strongly Grady feels for him."

Which *was* sad. Travis pulled Barnaby a little closer. "Grady is pretty tough," he said.

"It doesn't matter, though, does it? Strong, weak, ready for it, or utterly blindsided. A broken heart bloody hurts, doesn't it?"

The voice of experience, again, Travis thought grimly. "Yeah, I suppose it does."

"Have you had your heart broken?"

Travis thought of Martin, but shoved that away. "Not by someone I was in a relationship with, no."

If Barnaby picked up on the odd wording, he didn't ask. "It's awful. Even when you know the love is fading, or maybe even dead, there's a terrible moment when you realize it's over—or worse, that you've been betrayed—and it *hurts*. I was foolish enough to have read all those poems and not realize it actually hurt. In your chest. That that's why it was called heartbreak."

"I'm sorry. That he hurt you." They both knew who he was talking about.

"I'm glad you've never experienced it," Barnaby replied.

Travis wasn't so sure he was grateful for that.

"Though I'm surprised you haven't experienced it even once, at your advanced age," Barnaby added, his lips curling.

Travis laughed. "I *am* old."

"Always leave them first, then, is it?"

Travis sighed as they came to a halt at the door to Barnaby's building. "Yeah."

Barnaby took a step away. "Oh."

"Not like you're thinking," Travis added, fighting the urge to pull Barnaby back. He followed him inside, not willing to see him off at the garage level. He'd been in the ramshackle old elevator in this place and he wasn't sending Barnaby into that thing alone while he was drunk.

Also, he wasn't ready for the night to end. At the very least, he needed to explain.

"I've lived in seventeen cities in the last sixteen years. I've changed teams almost every season. Sometimes two teams in a season, once three." He laughed, but it came out brittle. "I can't promise I'll be here next week, though I think Rupert is happy enough with me for now. So, maybe? But I don't know."

Barnaby stepped into the old freight elevator and waited for Travis before closing the doors. The damn thing started upward with a horrible shudder. "I don't understand. Rupert likes you quite a bit."

Travis shrugged. "That's nice, but it doesn't matter. The right deal comes along and he'll trade me."

"He wouldn't!"

Travis appreciated the indignation, even if it was misplaced. "He would. He *should*. If some team needs a guy like me and they have a guy that can fill a hole on the Cats, then I'm gone. That's how it goes in this business. I'll have to leave within hours, usually, and the next day I'll have a new team. A new home." He shrugged, trying to be philosophical about it. Somewhere along the line, moving on had stopped being an adventure he looked forward to. "I try to make that clear to anyone I get involved with. I'm a bad bet, relationship-wise. Strictly for temporary purposes, you know?"

"No," Barnaby said, bewildered.

"No, I don't suppose you do," Travis agreed, stepping forward to haul the elevator open when they arrived on the fourth floor.

"But—"

Travis waved off whatever Barnaby was about to say. "It's cool. I just didn't want you to think I was a serial heartbreaker. I haven't—I *wouldn't.*"

Barnaby nodded just as the door to his apartment popped open and Callum appeared.

"You're home early," he observed, eyeing Travis before giving Barnaby's flushed face a closer inspection.

"I'm trolleyed," Barnaby announced, in case Callum had somehow missed the slight weaving.

Callum's lips twitched. "So I see."

"I'm also going to bed," Barnaby said before turning to Travis and falling into his arms.

Travis caught him, then hugged him when he realized that was what Barnaby wanted. He kept it brief, setting Barnaby on his feet and stepping back. Barnaby waved and disappeared through the door.

Callum stood staring at Travis, his arms crossed over his chest, an eyebrow arched high.

Travis bolted back into the elevator.

Chapter Eight

Barnaby stood at Travis's door at ten o'clock the next morning with his proverbial hat in his hand. Actually, he literally had his hat clutched in his cold fingers while he waited for Travis to answer the door.

He felt awful, for many reasons, but none more than having gotten drunk and, worse, behaved inappropriately while out last night. He'd embarrassed himself utterly and now had to repair any damage done.

He knocked again, wondering if Travis might leave him standing on the doorstep. He'd probably deserve it, but he didn't believe Travis would be so mean. Or judgmental, for that matter.

He finally heard footsteps approaching and braced himself.

Travis threw open the door. "Good morning!" he said, cheerful and *far* too loud. He was, of course, shirtless, with a cold pack on his troublesome shoulder.

"Good morning," Barnaby mumbled back, which was a lie.

He'd passed out last night as soon as he'd landed in bed, and slept for a solid eight hours, only waking when Callum had come to make sure he was still breathing and to remind him he had a tutoring session. He should have felt rejuvenated after so much sleep—more than he'd had in months—but the rum and cokes had installed the hammer currently working on the back of his skull.

Travis looked sympathetic. "Come on in," he said, softly this time.

Barnaby followed him, pausing to kick off his shoes and hang his coat. Travis kept walking toward the kitchen, and Barnaby noted the low rise of his jeans did magnificent things to frame the swell of his bum, and that he had a huge bruise along his ribs from the game.

He fought the urge to reach out and touch the mottled

purple spots. He'd done quite enough of that sort of thing last night. It was lucky Travis didn't seem bothered by it. That didn't mean there wasn't an apology due. At the very least, Barnaby needed to do it to remind himself where the lines were drawn.

He stopped when he saw the table laden with eggs and sausage and...was that french toast?

"I hope you haven't eaten. I made my favorite hangover foods." Travis eyed Barnaby. "I had a hunch they'd be needed."

Barnaby's shoulders slumped and his bag fell to the wood floor with a loud thunk. "I am so sorry."

Travis took a quick step back. "Are you going to puke?"

The laughter was unexpected—and *god* it hurt his head—but he couldn't stop it. "You're always on guard for that, aren't you?"

"Comes with the job," Travis said, a tentative smile on his lips.

"I'm not going to be sick," Barnaby said, so Travis would stop hovering so far away, "And you have a very strange job."

Travis nudged him to the table. "I suppose I do. I love it, though."

"You're very good at it. I'm not sure if I told you that last night. I enjoyed watching the game. Very much. And from what I learned, you acquitted yourself well."

Barnaby had the singular pleasure of watching Travis's cheeks go pink. "Thank you." He fidgeted with the bottle of maple syrup and butter dish. "You're uh...you're good at teaching poetry, too. Like, really good."

Barnaby sighed. "Thank you. I don't feel very good at it this morning. I woke up horribly embarrassed by my behavior. It wasn't very professional of me."

Travis looked confused. "What are you talking about?"

When Barnaby opened his mouth to explain, Travis held up a hand.

"Wait. First, please sit and eat something. Before it gets cold." He grimaced. "God, I hate it when I sound like my mother."

Barnaby chuckled and slid gratefully into a chair. Travis grabbed a few more things from the kitchen, then sat. It was instinct for Barnaby to help wrap bandages around Travis's arm and neck to hold the gel pack against his shoulder, then place another behind his back so he could lean against it where the fresh constellation of bruises had formed.

Once settled, Travis loaded a plate with far too much food and set it in front of Barnaby, then heaped even more on a second for himself.

They dug in for a couple of minutes before Travis gestured with his fork. "Okay, so what's this bullshit about you not being professional?"

Barnaby's bite of food went down like a lump of concrete when he swallowed. "I drank more than I should have, and then I was too..." He cast about for the right word and finally landed on, "...friendly."

Travis smiled. "You mean when you were acting like personal space was something you've only read about in books."

"Indeed." Barnaby glared at the french toast he speared on his fork. "And blathering on incessantly while I was at it. It was very bad form."

"I thought your form was excellent, actually. Even the East German judge gave you a ten."

Barnaby's face heated. "You were kind to invite me out, but you didn't ask me to hang all over you and talk your ear off. I didn't realize how low my tolerance for alcohol has become since moving here—not that it's an excuse for my behavior," he added quickly.

"There's no excuse needed."

"That's not true. We work together."

Travis put down his fork and sat back. "Is that really how you see me? Just some guy you work with?"

Barnaby considered his answer carefully. "No," he admitted. "Though I probably should."

"Well, I see you as a friend," Travis said.

Barnaby felt a foolish burst of happiness. "Thank you. That's...I'd like to be your friend."

"You are. I assure you, my math tutor never helped me ice my bruises. Nor did he try to matchmake our mutual friends—not that we had any."

Barnaby rolled his eyes. "I was a bit much last night. I hope Jack and Grady didn't overhear any of that."

"They didn't."

"You seem sure," Barnaby said.

"I'm your *friend*," Travis reiterated, picking up his fork and gesturing with it. "I wouldn't let you embarrass yourself—*or* them—if I could prevent it. You were fine."

"I was far from fine. And I hardly escaped the evening without embarrassing myself."

Travis grinned. "If you're talking about the flirting again, you have nothing to worry about. I liked it. And you may have noticed, I flirted back."

He had noticed, but had written it off as drunken stupidity on both their parts. "I thought we were friends."

"We are. That doesn't mean we can't flirt."

"It doesn't?"

"Nope," Travis said, popping the P. "Do you remember what we talked about on the way home? About how I might be gone tomorrow? Friends is the best I can do in a relationship. Sometimes there are benefits, sometimes not. But if I'm thousands of miles away by the end of the week, we will still be friends."

Barnaby didn't know what to do with that. He stuffed a big bite of breakfast into his mouth and chewed slowly, thinking about what Travis had said.

And what it could mean between them. He wondered if it was weird that one of the most attractive things about Travis was how he *didn't* want a relationship. At least, not by the definition Barnaby had always used.

No, that wasn't exactly right. What was so attractive was that he was *honest* about it. Totally upfront about his limitations.

That was something to think about.

As was the fact that Travis liked it when Barnaby flirted with him.

Travis could see Barnaby's big brain working and left him to it. He leaned back into the cold pack Barnaby had positioned against that fucking bruise and watched the color come back to Barnaby's face as the sugar and caffeine from breakfast worked into his system.

Travis could probably sit and watch Barnaby for an embarrassingly long time. He was beautiful, certainly, and probably a really, *really* awful poker player. His emotions ran across his face in little frowns and pinched brows, quirked lips and slow blinks. Travis wasn't psychic, so he didn't know if Barnaby was thinking about his favorite blue cheese or recalling the last time he gave head, but it was fun to watch anyway.

He was struck again by how much he wanted Barnaby. How much more he wanted to learn about him. What *was* his favorite blue cheese? Did he like giving head? What would his face look like when he was close to orgasm? Did he get that same earnest, serious expression when he was focused on his pleasure? What if he was focused on *Travis's* pleasure?

A shiver worked up Travis's spine, goosebumps lifting on his arms and neck, obvious given he wasn't wearing a shirt. Barnaby watched them, curious, his lip caught between his teeth.

Barnaby could probably have his pick of men. He was handsome, classically so, with his huge blue eyes and high cheekbones. Add on the silky curls, and—let's be honest—the accent, and Travis didn't know what man could resist. God knew Barnaby could have had Travis any way he wanted him last night, had he been a little more sober.

Travis had lain in bed recalling how Barnaby had pressed up against him, how sweet and strong his body had felt cradled close, until he couldn't stand it anymore and thrust his hand beneath the sheets and wrapped it around his dick.

He'd slept with a smile on his face, he swore to god.

But, as fun as it was to imagine what they could do together, there were a lot of miles between Barnaby flirting with him and actually wanting to do anything about it. Out of respect for Barnaby's professional position as his tutor, and because he had an epic hangover, Travis didn't push. He'd explained his situation, and Barnaby was a smart dude. That would have to be enough for now.

Once they were done eating they focused on Travis's classwork. Barnaby suggested they move to the couch and went to grab new cold packs himself. Travis wondered what the third one was for while Barnaby helped him with his shoulder and back, then chuckled when Barnaby collapsed onto the couch next to him, crossed his feet on the coffee table, and propped the last cold pack behind his own head and neck.

It was comfortable, the two of them slouched on his couch with the sun pouring in and a laptop perched on Barnaby's legs. Travis liked it. More than he should, since he knew better than to get attached to anything that could remotely be filed under "domestic". Home today, gone tomorrow, he reminded himself firmly.

He was back on the road later this week, so he and Barnaby looked ahead on the syllabus, which was novel for Travis, since he had always felt so *behind* when he took classes. Barnaby read him the half-dozen poems, and Travis closed his eyes, listening as Barnaby's voice wove through the words. None of them were love poems, but Travis didn't enjoy listening to Barnaby read them any less.

Unlike previous weeks, each of the poems was from a different poet, and the professor had included short biographies for each. To this point in their tutoring, Barnaby had always focused on the poems themselves, but today he asked, "Do you need me to read you these?"

Travis hesitated. "No, you don't have to."

Barnaby gave him a long look through narrow eyes. "But you'll do better if you hear the material instead of read it." It wasn't a question.

"My computer can read it to me, though. It's not like the poems, where the computer doesn't know what to do with all the weird line breaks and punctuation."

"What if I said I *want* to read these to you?" Barnaby asked.

What a stupid reason for his heart to skip a beat. "Oh, well that's...that would be nice. Better than the computer," he admitted. "Thank you."

Barnaby nodded, then read him a short biography on Robert Herrick. He pulled up the next, but before reading it, he turned to look at Travis again. "Can I ask you something completely unrelated?"

"Sure," he agreed, hoping he didn't regret it.

"How many languages do you speak?"

Travis laughed and wondered how long Barnaby had been chewing on that. "I'm only fluent in English, and I guess I'm close in French."

"I heard you hold conversations in at least two other languages last night."

"Russian and Swedish. I'm pretty good at those, since I lived in both places, but it's been a while, so I'm rusty. The boys let me practice."

"You like working on them? Languages, that is."

"I do. It's like a puzzle, and sometimes I forget some of the pieces, but if I hear it again for a while, some of them come back to me."

Barnaby shook his head. "That's brilliant. I'm the opposite. I hated learning French and Latin in school. And there was nothing I hated more than being asked to speak them aloud. I knew I would make mistakes, so I would panic and freeze up."

"A lot of people are like that. I don't know why I'm not. I used to freeze up in school when I was asked about something we'd just read. I *hated* how stupid I felt. I think the language thing is different for me because I spent the early years of my career on various teams in Canada and the US, playing with a *lot* of guys from all over the world who struggled with English. I never thought they were dumb because of it, so I guess it gave me a different perspective."

"I never thought of it that way. I've always admired anyone who attempts a new language, particularly English, but never gave myself the same benefit. Still, I'm impressed you've got three in addition to English that you practice."

Travis scratched the back of his head and shrugged. "Some languages are harder than others, and some I have more exposure to. I can speak a bunch of Swiss German, but I never get to practice that. Same with Norwegian. And I took Spanish in school, but absolutely suck at it because I haven't come across many Spanish speakers in hockey. My school Spanish did help with some of the Portuguese I've picked up. Most of those guys were bilingual Canadians, though, so they only taught me how to swear and say incredibly rude things to our opponents."

"That's the first thing everyone learns in a foreign language, isn't it? The swear words?"

"Especially in the locker room. And you can't believe a word those assholes say. Thanks to believing my teammates were actually trying to help me learn the language, I ended up asking my landlord in Stockholm where I could find a dick sandwich. Those idiots laughed for days."

Barnaby laughed, too. Travis liked to see him like this, happy and loose. If he had to guess, he'd say the drugs and the cold pack had taken effect, his eyes brighter and his mouth no longer pinched.

Barnaby turned back to the laptop, but before he began reading the next biography, he said, "Next time someone makes you feel stupid while learning anything, you should tell them to kindly fuck themselves sideways in at least four languages."

Something bright and happy expanded in Travis's chest. "Maybe I will," he finally managed.

Barnaby nodded once, then read to him about Thomas Carew. When they finished with the biographies, Barnaby read the poems again, this time stopping so they could parse out the meaning of the more obscure passages as they went. The theme of most of the poems was religion or domestic life, which would have been intensely boring without Barnaby's explanations and insight into the poet's lives.

Mindful of his practice that afternoon, Travis glanced at the clock. He needed to see the trainer, too, but he wasn't willing to stop working with Barnaby, so he'd calculated exactly how long they could stay pressed together on the couch and set an alarm on his phone to make sure he didn't forget.

Barnaby was finishing a poem called *Inviting a Friend to Supper* by Ben Johnson when a couple lines stood out to Travis.

Nor shall our cups make any guilty men;
But, at our parting we will be as when
We innocently met. No simple word
That shall be uttered at our mirthful board,
Shall make us sad next morning or affright
The liberty that we'll enjoy tonight.

"Wait," Travis said. "Can you read those last lines again?"

Barnaby did.

"Right. And what does it mean?" Travis asked in the exact tone Barnaby always used.

Barnaby blinked. "Pardon?"

"Go on. What does it mean?"

Barnaby turned back to the computer, his eyes running over the poem again. His lips twitch before he scowled. "It's not my job to tell you what these things mean," he said tartly.

"Try again, hot shot."

"It says a good night out means that no matter how much we drink and what stupid things we say, we should have no regrets in the morning," Barnaby admitted.

Travis hooted with laughter. "How about that! There *is* a poem for every occasion."

"There's no need to be smug."

"Oh, I disagree." Travis cracked up at Barnaby's offended

huff, dissolving into outright cackling when Barnaby dug his elbows into Travis's ribs in retribution, their feet coming off the coffee table and tangling together as they shoved at one another.

Jesus, those elbows were sharp. Travis squirmed, nearly upsetting the laptop before he could shove it onto the coffee table. Barnaby's laugh was breathless as he exacted his revenge.

When his fingers dug into the sensitive skin below Travis's arm pit, Travis had no choice. He *hated* being tickled, and years of wrestling in locker rooms, hotel rooms, living rooms, and on the ice had trained him well.

"Oh, no you don't!" he shouted as he grabbed Barnaby's arm and clamped his other hand around a knee. Barnaby's eyes widened, realization dawning a moment before Travis dumped Barnaby onto the floor, shoving the coffee table a foot away in the process.

The astonished expression on Barnaby's face made Travis laugh so hard he wheezed, until Barnaby's face pinched and he said, quietly. "Ow."

Oh shit. Travis was reaching for him without a thought, without hesitation, so he wasn't prepared for Barnaby to grab his wrist and sweep his feet out from under him. Travis tried to catch himself but ended up landing mostly on top of Barnaby, nearly taking a hip to the dick before flopping onto his back with an undignified grunt.

Barnaby was up on his knees, straddling him, his strong hands holding Travis's forearms to the floor, his feet hooked over Travis's legs, pinning him to the floor.

"You little shit," Travis said with admiration. He could, probably, use his additional height and weight to throw Barnaby off, but since that was exactly what he *didn't* want, he lay still.

Barnaby's grin was triumphant. "I wrestled in school until I figured out *why* I liked rolling around on the mats with the other boys and the stupid singlet became my enemy."

Travis snorted with laughter. "And people say hockey is homo-erotic."

"Do they?" Barnaby asked, clearly intrigued. "You'll have to tell me more about that."

Abruptly, the atmosphere changed from playful to something a whole hell of a lot more intimate. "I'd be happy to," Travis said.

Barnaby cocked his head, studying Travis. "I promised myself I wouldn't date anyone until I completed my doctorate."

Travis had a few questions about that policy, like *why*, but none worth asking. "I can't date anyone. It wouldn't be fair."

"But we can flirt."

"We can."

"Can we kiss?"

Heart tripping, Travis let his eyes trace over Barnaby's wide mouth. Just thinking about those ripe, pink lips on his sent blood surging through his veins. "We can," he said, his voice scratching from his throat.

Barnaby licked his lips and Travis's stomach tightened with a heady mix of anticipation and arousal. He trembled with the desire to thrust his fingers into Barnaby's soft curls and yank him closer, but he was still pinned.

Maybe it was better this way—the decision entirely Barnaby's. Though if he dropped his butt even an inch closer to Travis, he'd feel how much the anticipation alone affected him.

"Whatever you want," Travis whispered, dying to be put out of his misery.

Barnaby released his arms and slid a hand behind Travis's neck, tilting his chin up. A thumb brushed over the pulse pounding in Travis's throat.

The urge to capture Barnaby's lips and grab hold of him with both hands was fierce, but he held still as Barnaby drew closer. He watched Barnaby's eyes flutter shut and let his own eyes slide closed.

The press of warm, full lips was gentle, at first. Barely more than a brush of fragile skin and shared breaths. When Barnaby drew back, Travis skimmed his tongue over his own lips to taste what wasn't there. Yet.

His eyes popped open when Barnaby's fingers fluttered over his cheek. Barnaby's dark blue gaze scanned his face, the tip of his finger traced over the long, shallow scar above his top lip, long ago split and sewn closed.

"I could feel that," Barnaby murmured.

Travis blinked up at him, at a loss for words.

A pleased smile curled Barnaby's lips and he ducked in closer, quicker this time, pulling his fingers away a moment before he kissed Travis again. His lips lingered, nibbling at the point where the scar bisected his lip. Travis kissed him back, clinging. He cupped the back of Barnaby's head in his hand, silky curls wrapping around his fingers.

Barnaby made a happy noise, and it felt like a blow to Travis's chest. He craned his neck, trying to press closer, and was rewarded with a flick of tongue.

Now *Travis* was making happy noises. He opened his lips, meeting Barnaby's tongue with his own, tangling them together. Barnaby sucked in a breath through his nose, his hand tight on the back of Travis's neck, his tongue quick and agile.

Blood raced, hot and swift through Travis's veins, his heart pounding. He wrapped his free arm around Barnaby's ribs, pressing his palm over his spine and holding on without towing him closer. Need and aching arousal coursed through him, and he writhed against the floor, his back arching to get closer to Barnaby.

Barnaby licked into his mouth, possessing it completely.

Travis groaned, twitching, his fingers curling into a desperate fist in Barnaby's hair. His cock throbbed, full and hot, his thighs and ass quivering with the desire to thrust his hips up against Barnaby.

Barnaby spread his legs and let his weight push Travis to the floor, rolling his hips to press their cocks together, making Travis gasp into their kiss. Barnaby's legs freed his and Travis arched up, his hand skimming down Barnaby's back until it was cradled in the dip of his spine, his pinky barely reaching the swell of Barnaby's ass as he held on for the ride. Barnaby's narrow hips swiveled in such a perfect, dirty grind that their kiss fell apart. Travis's head dropped to the floor with a solid thunk while Barnaby's tilted back, his neck stretched taut.

Travis wanted to leave his mark on every inch of that pale, perfect skin. *Fuck.*

The blood pounded so loudly in his ears that he could barely hear the muted strum of guitar strings coming from his pocket.

Barnaby froze. "Not that the vibrations aren't a welcome addition," he said with a breathless laugh, "but I think someone is trying to call you."

It took an embarrassingly long time for Travis to realize what was happening.

He slumped onto the floor, boneless. "Fuck, that's my alarm."

Barnaby knelt above him, then reached into his fucking pocket and grabbed his phone. Travis whimpered helplessly as the denim shifted over his cock. He couldn't decide what was hotter—Barnaby's hand that close to his dick, or the utter fucking chutzpah it took to just reach into another man's pocket like it was nothing.

Barnaby yanked the phone free and pressed STOP.

"I cannot fucking believe I have to go," Travis said, trying really hard not to whine. He wasn't *close* to being done. And he didn't just mean orgasm-wise. Though that was still a pressing issue. He shifted carefully, trying to get his cock to stand down. He was going to change out of these horrible jeans and into a nice pair of stretchy sweatpants for the rest of the day, damn it.

He was also going to jerk off the *second* he had a chance. Which, technically, given the time, might not be for hours, some of which he would spend in a cup.

Yup, that did the trick. Deflation achieved.

Barnaby smirked, then rose to his feet above Travis as if he could actually feel his legs, which Travis absolutely could not. "Well, then, I'll be off."

Travis opened his mouth to say a hundred things, including *I can't wait that long, have dinner with me, how can you be so goddamn calm?,* and *get back down here because I'd rather retire than not blow you right now.*

He didn't actually manage to say anything, but just lay there, a boneless wreck, while Barnaby pulled on his coat, grabbed his bag, and left him with a wink.

Chapter Nine

Barnaby entered the arena via the employee and player entrance alongside Rupert. The game wouldn't start for an hour, but Rupert needed to be here, and Barnaby hadn't wanted to drive his own car. It would be better if he had to go home with Rupert at the end of the night, and not be tempted to go...anywhere else.

He'd told Callum and Rupert that he wanted to watch the game because he found hockey intriguing. Rupert had managed to only look skeptical—Callum had laughed in his face. They thought he was only here because of Travis, but Travis didn't even know he was coming, and Barnaby wouldn't see him before the game. He didn't know much about hockey, but he well remembered how Robert had been before a performance, and he had no desire to inject himself into Travis's pre-game routine and risk throwing him off kilter.

He'd said as much while attempting to defend his decision to come out tonight, and Callum had conceded that Barnaby was probably correct about that, at least.

Barnaby intended to put the next hour—and, perhaps, the intermissions—to good use. He had his laptop in his bag and, thanks to Rupert, the arena's WiFi password in his pocket. He would work on marking up the essays handed in this week while he had the suite to himself and Rupert was off doing whatever he needed to do.

Barnaby was disappointed Christian and Oliver weren't able to join him tonight, but they had school tomorrow. That meant Callum would also be absent. Barnaby had texted Jack to let him know he'd be there, and received word that Jack had a lot to do that night, but he would come find Barnaby when he could.

So, really, this was just a chance to do his work somewhere new, catch up with a good friend, and watch a hockey game.

It all made perfect sense.

Rupert brought him up to the suite and Barnaby paid more attention this time, so he'd be able to find the elevator and the suite without a chaperone in the future. Just in case he decided to come to more games. As it was, he felt guilty when Rupert ushered him into the suite and immediately left, passing him the key card on his way out.

Barnaby wouldn't see him again until the end of the first period. He did get through a few essays before the teams came out on the ice for their warm-ups, and snuck in one more when they disappeared back down the tunnels to their locker rooms.

His laptop was forgotten, though, once the anthem began to play. Then he couldn't tear his eyes away from the game.

He still had a *lot* to learn. Icing, offsides, the various penalties that all seemed to have the same hand signals from the referees. He was beginning to get the hang of some of it, but it was tricky when everything moved so fast. When *Travis* moved so fast.

For a man who considered himself old, Travis looked as vital and adept as anyone else on the team. He tore up and down the ice, crashing into people and the boards, hurling himself on and off the bench as if his knee, and his shoulder, and the bruises on his back and ribs and hip and calf, didn't hurt him at all. It was exhilarating to watch, to better understand the dedication it took, and to recall the look on Travis's face when he'd said he loved his job.

Barnaby was on his feet, cheering with the rest of the crowd, when Travis's linemate caught a pass from Travis and tore up the ice on a breakaway. He wished he were closer to the ice, so he might be able to catch a puck when it was deflected into the crowd. So that he could have the crowd around him and see Travis's face as he skated past. He looked very serious from up here, but he also appeared to be shouting, and sometimes the call of voices would ring out above the crowd noise and cheers. Would he be able to hear what they were saying if he were closer?

Of course, if he sat in the stands, he wouldn't be able to work. Not that he was getting anything done right then, but he swore he would at intermission. He was in Moncton to succeed. To focus on his studies and get his life back on track.

The pang of guilt hit him hard. University was going well enough, but he could be at home, working his way through all the essays. Reading his assignments, or even re-reading his own work. He had a meeting with his advisor next week, and he hadn't yet finished preparing for it. There was plenty to be done, but here he was, at a *hockey game.*

Barnaby sat slowly, his eyes still on the game, but his heart no longer in it.

What was he doing? He'd left London, left England and the opportunities his former professors had sworn were still available for him, left his *life*, to come to Canada and start over. He was to be a student and a teacher, and eventually receive the doctorate he should have begun working on years before, had he not let himself believe that Robert, and love, and his hopeful heart would sustain him.

It hadn't. Not any of it. He'd maxed out his credit cards and been working in a windowless office within months, spending evenings doing more work, or attending Robert's performances, or just trying to do the bloody washing up so their flat didn't deteriorate into such a revolting state that they'd be too embarrassed to have anyone by.

Robert had liked to entertain. No, that wasn't fair. Barnaby had enjoyed it, too. He'd felt less isolated when they were with their friends, though most of them he'd only known through Robert. But they'd been funny and full of life, and he'd believed they were kind.

He wondered if any of them looked back on those nights and felt even a drop of guilt that at least two of them had been or would soon be sleeping with Robert. Or that all of them would know of it, and the numerous others, but not one of them would tell Barnaby.

Christ, he'd been a fool, and he'd come to Moncton to *stop* being a fool. *Not to watch hockey.* His degree program was very good, and they'd offered him the TA position and hope for future teaching opportunities. But what had really mattered were the thousands of miles it put between Barnaby and home. No, not home. London. His parents' house. Those places weren't home. Not any longer.

Now he lived in the guest suite at Rupert and Callum's, and, if he were honest with himself, he felt more comfortable there than he had anywhere since he'd left the dormitories, and Callum and Rupert were becoming something more to him than just cousins or friends.

But that did not change the fact that he was supposed to keep his head down. He wasn't here to have fun. There was to be no fucking about—literally or figuratively—until all the credit cards were paid off. Not until he could open his mail, just once, and not see the legacy of his attempts to keep Robert happy for what had turned out to be no good reason.

The door opening startled Barnaby, and he turned to see Jack enter. He smiled at Barnaby, and Barnaby smiled back automatically, some of his anxiety slipping away.

Jack was a good friend. *His* friend.

"You okay?" Jack asked, slapping him on the shoulder and dropping into the seat next to him.

Barnaby waved it off. "It's nothing. Woolgathering."

"You sure?" Jack asked, smile in place, but his eyes scanning Barnaby's face.

"Yes, I was just considering what it is I'm doing here."

"So, we're not going to admit it's a booty call?"

"I beg your pardon." Barnaby glared at Jack's wide grin. "What makes you think that Travis and I have any interest in each other's booties?"

In hindsight, he rather wished he'd found another way to phrase that.

Jack cracked up, his laughter cutting off abruptly when Travis got tangled up with one of the opponent's defensemen and went awkwardly into the boards.

Barnaby gripped the rail, not breathing for the seconds it

took for Travis to get back to his feet. The other man was not as lucky, curled up on the ice and protecting one of his arms against his chest. The Snow Dogs' trainer was jogging toward the fallen player while everyone hovered.

Travis looked concerned, but then the Snow Dogs' other defenseman grabbed him by the collar and spun him around.

"Oh shit," Jack muttered, jumping to his feet.

The Snow Dog released Travis, but only long enough to shake off his gloves.

"What? What's happening?" Barnaby asked.

Jack leaned forward. "Fight."

Barnaby had heard, of course, that fights were fairly common in hockey. He hadn't seen one yet, though, and he couldn't imagine Travis engaging in one. Travis did, however, shake off his gloves, which Barnaby gathered was akin to throwing down the proverbial gauntlet. "Does Travis fight often?"

"He's supposed to," Jack muttered as Travis and the other man circled each other, both grabbing the other's jersey with one hand, keeping them an arm's length apart.

"What do you mean, *he's supposed to*?"

"That's one of the reasons Rupert brought him on board. He's a good fighter, and he protects his team. If someone pulls a shitty hit on one of our guys, Travis is supposed to be the deterrent."

Travis and the Snow Dog circled again, each trying to get in a jab but neither connecting. It was another form of dance, and a far less elegant one.

Barnaby's stomach churned. "You keep saying *supposed to*. What does that mean?"

Jack didn't answer, his eyes riveted on Travis as he dodged a series of blows, then yanked his opponent closer. They went over backwards, Travis landing on his back with the other man on top of him.

The referees immediately pulled them apart and pushed

them toward the penalty boxes.

Jack winced. "Shit."

"What? Was that not good?" Barnaby asked.

"No, it's fine. But Travis isn't fooling anyone," Jack said with a frown.

"What do you mean?"

"He did that on purpose—taking them both to the ice. He's avoiding the fight."

"And that's bad?"

"Once in a while? No. When it's what you were brought here to do? Yes."

Barnaby sat slowly, digesting that. He would have asked Jack more questions, but at that moment, Rupert came into the suite. He made a face at Jack that confirmed he'd seen the fight, too, and had drawn the same conclusions.

All Barnaby could hear was Travis's blithe promise that he could be traded tomorrow.

Travis had a fantastic fucking game, even scoring a goal in the third to put them ahead by two. He was a fourth line guy, so goals were few and far between, but every one of them was gold. And even without that goal, his game had been strong. The Dogs hadn't been able to get to the net, let alone score, anytime he'd been on the ice.

Too bad it probably wasn't going to make a difference.

He'd been lucky so far this season, his reputation alone enough to keep most of their opponents from picking a fight— but he knew what his role was. He knew why Rupert had brought him here. What the coach needed him to do. And somehow he'd made it this far into the season without having to make it clear that not only did he not *want* to fight, he couldn't even bring himself to try.

Well, he had tried, tonight. He'd gone round and round, dodging more jabs than he'd had to all year, but as soon as the first blow had landed, just above his ear, he'd dropped them both to the ice.

He had *zero* expectation that it hadn't been obvious to everyone. His coach yelling, "What the fuck was that?" when he got back to the bench after five minutes dwelling on his choices in the penalty box had been confirmation enough.

Fuck, where was he going to end up next? And what would that team do when they figured out their enforcer couldn't fight?

Travis sat on the bench in front of his locker, his elbows on his knees, his game-day dress shirt sticking to skin still damp from the showers. Coach was ranting about the penalty kill again, but they'd done much better tonight on that front, so Travis only gave it half an ear. Instead, he stared at his hands and knew this was what it felt like to watch your career slip through your fingers.

Worse was knowing he didn't have a choice. Not in careers—that ship had sailed long ago—and not in how he was going to kill that career, one non-fight at a time.

Was it the good news or the bad news that it probably wouldn't take a whole lot of them before it was over?

He closed his eyes and took a deep breath, releasing it out slowly and letting Coach's curse-laden tirade wash over him, familiar and comforting. He was still here. He was still playing. For now, that had to be enough.

He tried to remember how he'd felt coming into the game tonight, tapping back into the energy that had buzzed beneath his skin. Hell, he'd been wired for sound since kissing Barnaby. Or maybe it was more accurate to say since Barnaby had kissed him.

Goddamn, that had been good. Better than good.

The two orgasms he'd tugged out since hadn't been bad, either. Not nearly *enough*, but not bad.

With another deep, steadying breath, Travis sat up and opened his eyes. Of course, the first person he saw was Rupert, leaning against the doorway to listen to Coach's colorfully described suggestions, but with his eyes pinned to Travis.

Travis looked back. He'd been around way too long, and

seen way too much shit, to bother with the pretense of innocence or confusion. Rupert always came down after the game, usually sometime around the Coach's talk and after they'd showered. When he'd first come to Moncton, Travis had wondered if that was on purpose. Did Rupert, because he was gay, think he had to give everyone a chance to shower and change before he showed up? But then Travis had spent a few days in the locker room, and with the team, and realized that probably wasn't the case. There were a few openly gay or bi guys on the team, and, if Travis had to guess, another handful besides who weren't out.

He eyed Tim and Chris where they sat practically in each other's laps across the room and smothered a snort.

Coach went on, and Rupert kept watching Travis, which was fucking unnerving. He didn't look mad, so much as thoughtful. Maybe even concerned, which would be just like him. He cared about the men on his team as individuals, and as a whole.

That didn't mean he wouldn't trade Travis in a red-hot minute.

Coach wrapped up with a final suggestion that might not, in fact, be anatomically possible, a reminder they had practice tomorrow afternoon right before they got on the bus to Edwardston, and an instruction to get some fucking sleep.

Somehow it still made sense when he ended with, "Good game!"

As soon as everyone started talking, Rupert came straight to Travis.

Oh, shit. Here we go.

Travis stood, not sure what to do with his hands. He ended up jamming them into his pockets.

"Good goal," Rupert said, his voice pitched low so only Travis could hear him.

Travis shifted, uncomfortable with the way Rupert wasn't just looking at him, but studying him, his head cocked as if he was trying to work something out.

"Thanks," Travis mumbled. What the fuck else was he going

to say? He sure as shit wasn't going to be the one to bring up the elephant in the room.

"What did you think of the Dogs' new center? Number eight?"

The question was so far from what Travis had been expecting, it took a good ten seconds for him to make sense of it. "What?"

"The Wagner kid. He's only nineteen, but he's fast."

Travis forced his brain back to the game. He'd been matched up with the kid a few times. "His skating is strong. He could use more practice with the puck, but he's defensively responsible. Hits like a freight train. I'd guess he'll pack on another fifteen or twenty pounds in the next two years, if he keeps up with his conditioning."

Rupert nodded. "I thought the same." He smiled, a quick and unexpected flash. "There's someone here to see you."

Travis blinked and wondered if conversational whiplash was a genetic trait. "There is?"

"He's in the hallway. He seems to have a new-found interest in hockey. I suggest, if you'd like a moment to chat before we have to head home, you go see him quickly."

"Okay," Travis said stupidly. Rupert couldn't know. It was one kiss. They were all adults. *Shit.* The knowing, if slightly unimpressed, expression on Rupert's face was enough to stop the trickle of excitement working down his spine. "Thank you."

Rupert hummed. "I have a few people to speak with here. I should be about fifteen minutes. Tell him I'll text when I'm ready to go."

Travis nodded, and Rupert turned away. Travis waited the span of a heartbeat, then ran across the locker room and blew through the door.

Chapter Ten

Barnaby had been hanging out in the corridor for ten minutes, increasingly feeling like one of the creeps who tried to catch a glimpse into the women's changing room at Marks & Spencer. Rupert had warned him it might be a while before they was able to leave, and, in hindsight, Barnaby wondered why he hadn't asked to sit somewhere he could work.

Probably because he was the creep standing outside the *men's* changing room, hoping to catch a glimpse. Though he didn't want to see just any man, but one in particular.

Did that make him more or less creepy?

He jumped when the door swung open, ready to tell whoever it was that he was waiting for Rupert and could be left right where he was. He'd already shooed along all manner of support and training staff, feeling increasingly foolish.

But this wasn't just anyone. It was Travis, who smiled widely upon seeing Barnaby. Travis put out his hand, perhaps to curl around his arm or put on his hip, but drew up short at the last moment.

"Hi." He looked almost nervous, and devastatingly handsome in his game-day suit.

Barnaby smiled, charmed to find Travis could be as awkward and dorky as anyone. "Hello," he murmured back. He caught his lower lip between his teeth and watched Travis's eyes drop to his mouth.

Barnaby had less restraint than Travis, his fingers skimming over Travis's hip until the scuff of a shoe on the concrete floor from just down the corridor forced him to keep his hands to himself.

"Travis." The older woman walked past them with a polite nod and what Barnaby feared was a knowing look.

Travis smiled. "Hi, Sheila."

As soon as she disappeared around the bend of the long oval corridor, Travis grasped Barnaby's hand and towed him in the other direction.

"Where are we going?" Barnaby asked, his bag bouncing off his hip as Travis picked up speed.

Travis didn't answer except to mutter, "Fifteen minutes."

They'd gone a few yards down the hall when Travis grasped the handle of an unlabeled door and shoved it open, yanking Barnaby in after him.

"What—" Barnaby tried, but then Travis's mouth was on his, their chests bumping and feet tangling as they slammed the door and came up hard against it.

Every thought drained from Barnaby's head. His bag fell from his shoulder and he shook the strap off his arm and kicked it away. He grabbed for Travis, blind in the pitch-dark room that smelled vaguely of bleach. His fingers dug into Travis's hips, pulling him closer, demanding he pin Barnaby against the door harder while their mouths opened in gasps and tongues tangled between them.

God, he'd been thinking of almost nothing else since he'd left Travis on his floor. Every time he'd closed his eyes, he'd pictured how the arousal had stained Travis's cheeks red. The slack-jawed shock on his face when Barnaby had stood up and walked away with a wink.

Never had a departure been more fun. Or more difficult. His hands had shaken as he'd stumbled down the stairs, every cell in his body screaming at him to go back and peel those jeans off Travis, leaving him not wanting but panting and wrecked.

But if Travis had needed to set an alarm, then their time was up, and he'd hoped a little anticipation might bring them to this very point.

Travis rocked their hips together and Barnaby opened his legs, giving their cocks room to rub and press. He hooked a foot behind Travis's calf and met his thrusts, tilting his head to kiss Travis more deeply, his hand threading into Travis's hair and holding him close.

He sucked Travis's tongue into his mouth and ate the groan that slipped from his throat. For a man who had quite ably pinned another to the door, Travis seemed equally responsive when Barnaby was taking charge. The give and take of it was brain numbingly arousing. As was the notion that Barnaby might happily take control of Travis, who was so much stronger and larger than he.

Lust seared through his brain and he feared he, or Travis, would ruin their trousers if they didn't find another way to channel their energies.

He ended their kiss and reveled in Travis's wounded gasp, the way he pressed forward again, seeking Barnaby's mouth.

Barnaby turned his head to the side. "I'm not going home in the car with Rupert with my pants full of spunk," he groaned as Travis turned his attention to his jaw and down his neck.

Teeth dug into the muscle beneath his ear and Barnaby hummed. He felt Travis shaking and realized he was laughing, even with Barnaby's flesh caught in his bite.

"You laugh, but that's not an indignity I care to experience." He imagined Callum's reaction and almost lost his erection.

"I'll drive you home," Travis murmured, nuzzling behind Barnaby's ear.

"In your soiled trousers?"

Travis laughed, his lips leaving Barnaby's neck at last. Barnaby assumed Travis was looking down at him, but unless Travis had the eyes of a cat, he wasn't going to see Barnaby's amused exasperation.

Travis's hands slid under Barnaby's untucked shirt, circling his waist and sliding to his back, holding him close. "What would you like to do, then? Go home like this?"

Barnaby shuddered. "No," he said quickly. "God, no. I nearly killed myself getting home from your flat last time and I didn't have an audience. Thank god, too, because I very nearly pulled over to have a wank."

Travis laughed. "I never made it off my floor."

The simple statement stole Barnaby's breath. He considered apologizing for having left Travis in such a bad way, but there was no point in lying.

He gripped Travis's face in his hands and tugged him down for another kiss. This one sweeter than the ones before. No less arousing, but gentler. Barnaby was thanking Travis for telling him. Perhaps Travis was thanking Barnaby for leaving him hanging.

It was something else to consider. Another time.

When they separated, Travis pressed their foreheads together and skimmed the backs of his hands over Barnaby's belly. Barnaby shivered, his breath catching when Travis dipped the tips of his fingers beneath Barnaby's waistband.

"Yes?" Travis asked, tugging a little.

"Please. God, yes, *please*, you can—"

Barnaby's pleading cut off when Travis began to sink to his knees. His better instincts made him grab Travis, stopping his descent. "No."

Travis's agile fingers froze, though the button still slipped free, offering not nearly enough relief. "No? Did I—"

Barnaby kissed him again, hoping to dispel the uncertainty in his voice. "Your knees," he explained between slick licks and biting nibbles. "The floor is concrete," he added, in case Travis was feeling as incapable of higher brain function as Barnaby.

Barnaby didn't know what to think when Travis groaned and attacked the fastenings of Barnaby's trousers like a man possessed. The moment the zip was down, Travis shoved his hand into Barnaby's pants. Strong, callused fingers wrapped around his shaft.

Barnaby released a startled cry.

"Ssshhh," Travis murmured, capturing Barnaby's lips.

Barnaby heard voices outside in the corridor and gurgled helplessly. Chuckling evilly, Travis tugged his hand up Barnaby's cock, then slid back down again with a little twist. On the second pass, he paused to draw his fingertips up over the head.

"Not circumcised," he said with obvious delight.

Barnaby made an inarticulate noise of inquiry that Travis would hopefully understand. It was hard to make words when Travis was sliding his foreskin gently up and over the head of his cock and back, his fingers tracing its path, as if to feel it peel away from Barnaby's achingly sensitive crown.

"I like that you're not cut. I never knew what that looked like, what it really meant, until Russia." He gently pinched Barnaby's foreskin in his fingers, making his knees weak and proving he'd learned plenty since then. "You'll have to tell me what you like. Show me with your own hands."

Barnaby groaned. Was Travis trying to kill him?

"I want you in my mouth," Travis whispered, abandoning the head for the shaft again, working him over in a tight grip. "I want to stretch you out in the patch of sunlight on my bed one afternoon and look at every inch of you. I want to see your face when you come."

Barnaby whimpered. Not just because of the scorchingly hot things Travis was making him picture, but because there would be more surprises for Travis than he knew. "Yes, please."

"So polite," Travis said with a soft chuckle.

"Yes *fucking* please," Barnaby growled as Travis's hand picked up speed.

Travis laughed and captured Barnaby's mouth. Barnaby held on for dear life, a fist in Travis's hair and another in his shirt as the tension crawled up his spine and tightened the muscles in his ass. His climax hovered just out of reach, drawing his balls up tight, pulling him onto his toes.

The rubber bands coiling inside Barnaby snapped and he cried out, frantic, as his climax rushed through him. Their kiss muffled his cry and Travis's cupped palm caught Barnaby's come as his hips jerked and shuddered.

God, it had been *ages* since he'd had an orgasm that hadn't been brought on by his own hand, let alone one that made his knees give out and his eyes roll back in his head. He saw spots in the pitch dark room when he managed to roll them forward again.

For a long moment, the only sound was Barnaby's harsh breathing, the only movement the heaving of his chest. Travis eased back, moving slowly to protect Barnaby's clothing from his handful of spunk. Their legs stayed tangled, hips close, otherwise Barnaby would have slithered into a heap on the floor.

He couldn't see a thing, but he felt Travis dig in one of his trouser pockets.

"Good thing I carry a handkerchief when I wear a suit," Travis said in a teasing voice.

Barnaby laughed, delighted and not even a little bit sorry he would be adding to Travis's laundry.

When Barnaby was certain Travis was done cleaning up, he gripped the front of Travis's shirt and spun them. A loud *ooof* burst from Travis's chest when his back hit the door with more zeal, perhaps, than Barnaby intended. He didn't bother with an apology, his legs folding beneath him, his hands scrambling at Travis's trousers.

And from there, it was very clear Travis didn't need one.

His fingers tangled with Barnaby's, trying to help, so Barnaby let him undo his own clothing, leaning close, waiting until he heard the purr of a zip before grasping the fabric at what he guessed to be thigh-height, and yanking down.

He and Travis both gasped when his cock sprang free and smacked Barnaby on the face.

"Jesus Christ," Travis growled, his hand clamping on Barnaby's shoulder, his body curling over and around Barnaby. Barnaby turned his head, letting the smooth, hot crown of Travis's cock rub over his cheek and catch at the corner of his mouth, teasing with one quick flick of his tongue before turning the other way and letting the silky shaft run over his other cheek.

"God, Barnaby," Travis whispered. A hand cupped Barnaby's cheek, his thumb pressing to his lips so his cock smoothed over both.

Barnaby wrapped his hand around Travis's shaft, shivering at how thick and hot it was, and rolled the head over his tongue.

Travis made a desperate, almost frightened noise, and jerked back, pulling his cock from Barnaby's mouth.

The moment he popped free, the first hot stripe of come landed on Barnaby's face.

"Oh my god," Travis whispered in horror.

His guilt and embarrassment at having come so quickly, and with no warning, weren't at all assuaged by Barnaby's joyful laugh.

"I am so sorry," Travis said, dragging his thumb from Barnaby's lips, only to have it smear through his come on Barnaby's cheek, making a bigger mess.

No amount of horror made that less hot.

Travis would give his left nut to have a goddamn light in this room. He shivered thinking of what Barnaby must look like, kneeling at his feet, covered in his come.

Barnaby grasped his wrist before he could pull his hand away, so Travis rubbed his thumb over Barnaby's cheekbone again. Barnaby's pleased hum made him smile.

"I wish I could see you," he said when he felt sure he could speak without his voice cracking.

Lovers don't reveal all their secrets,
though in private they may count each other's moles,
hidden in shy places

Barnaby's voice vibrated against Travis's hand and he recognized the tone.

"Are you...are you quoting *poetry*?"

Travis could feel Barnaby smile by the shape of his cheek against his palm. "I am, though not one likely to be covered in your course. It's by a gentleman named Hafiz."

"Too modern for class?"

"Too erotic. And that piece is over six hundred years old."

"Some things truly never change," Travis observed.

"Thank goodness," Barnaby murmured, then slid his hand up Travis's thigh. "May I?"

Travis had no clue what he was asking to do, but that didn't change the answer. "Yes."

Barnaby tucked his hand into Travis's pocket and pulled out his phone. "We're going to need some light. Rupert will be looking for me soon, and I'm sure as hell not walking out of here like this."

Travis took the phone and turned on the flashlight, careful to keep the light away from their eyes. Even the indirect light made him squint. The view set his brain on fire. Barnaby's huge eyes stared up at him, his cheek and lips shiny with spit and come.

"Jesus Christ, you're gorgeous," Travis growled.

A slow smile curved Barnaby's lips. He carefully tucked Travis back into his clothes—making Travis wish he were a younger man with a younger man's refractory period—and rose to his feet with more grace than Travis could ever manage.

He swung the light around to see where the hell they were. Fortunately, it was a linen and supply closet. He wished he'd known that before trashing his handkerchief—not that it hadn't been one hundred percent worth it. This time, though, he plucked a towel from the stack on the shelf, and carefully wiped the remains of his orgasm from Barnaby's face.

"I am sorry," he said with a wry smile.

Barnaby's fingers trailed over his hot cheek. "You're embarrassed."

"I'm totally embarrassed. I came on your face like a teenager with zero control."

"It was absurdly hot," Barnaby said in a way that made Travis believe him, even if it didn't leech the heat from his cheeks. Barnaby was still running his fingers over them. "Thank you for not coming in my mouth. We've jumped into things without some conversations we probably ought to have."

"Including you telling me what we're jumping into, exactly," Travis observed.

He was disappointed when the fingers fell away from his face.

"I thought we were friends," Barnaby said.

"We are," Travis said firmly.

"And friends can flirt." It wasn't quite a question.

"Correct."

"And have benefits?" Barnaby asked, sounding decidedly less certain of himself.

"If you want," Travis agreed.

Barnaby cocked his head. "Do you want?"

"Since the first time I laid eyes on you from across the Dipsy Doodle Dangle."

"What?"

"I saw you having coffee with Jack a couple weeks before we met. He came over to say hello to me and Grady."

"I remember that day. I didn't see you."

"No, you never looked our way. But I saw you. I could see the blue of your eyes from across the room."

"Oh," Barnaby said, casting those eyes down. It was too dim to be sure, but Travis thought it might be Barnaby's turn to turn pink. "And you noticed me with Jack?"

"Forget Jack. I noticed you the moment you walked through the door."

Barnaby leaned in and pressed a kiss to Travis's lips. "I'm sorry I didn't meet you then."

"What would you have done if I'd hit on you?"

Barnaby laughed. "I would have told you to fuck right off."

"Then I'm glad we didn't meet. I like this better."

Barnaby smiled. "Me, too."

A chime came from the floor a few feet away from them in the darkness.

"Oh shit, my phone," Barnaby said.

Travis angled the light so Barnaby could find his bag and see to pull out his phone. "Rupert is wondering where I am." He laughed. "I don't suppose I should tell him I'm in the linen closet."

"Let's hope he's not standing right outside the door, then."

"Oh, god, you don't think—"

"I'll tell you what, you stay here and I'll step out and see if the coast is clear."

"Thank you," Barnaby said, hefting his bag back onto his shoulder.

Travis was about to pull the door open when Barnaby's hand on his arm stopped him. He looked back.

"For what it's worth, there's nothing on my side of things that prevents you from coming in my mouth next time. Or vice versa."

Travis's knees honest-to-god went weak. And his dick, god bless it, twitched. "Good to know. Nothing on my side either. I can get you some test results, if you want. The team tests us regularly."

"I could do the same, though it would take a few days."

Travis smiled slowly. "I'm on the road for the next five days, anyway. Not that there's any pressure. Or any hurry."

"Speak for yourself," Barnaby said, nudging him toward the door. He waited until Travis was about to slip through it before very quietly adding, "There's no way I'm going to give up seeing my come sliding from your body and down your thighs if I don't have to."

Travis practically fell into the corridor, his brain wiped clean but for the filthy image Barnaby had planted. He blinked stupidly until the pointed sound of Barnaby clearing his throat penetrated—er, got through to him.

"All clear," he croaked.

Barnaby slipped into the hallway, his hand trailing over Travis's ass. "Goodnight," he said in a low voice.

Travis was incapable of responding. He just stood there like an idiot, listening to Barnaby's laughter fade as he disappeared around the corner.

Chapter Eleven

Barnaby ran the two blocks from his car to the Dipsy Doodle Dangle. He cursed the snow, both for taking up valuable space that could have meant parking closer to the café, and for creating a slick white pack under his feet on the sidewalk. It was a miracle he didn't slip and crack his head open, but there was no way he was walking, let alone carefully picking his way down the street, when it was -4 degrees out and the wind was blowing hard enough to rip through his clothing.

He had managed to get to the ripe old age of twenty-eight without realizing it could be so cold it hurt to breathe. It was never this cold in Oxford. There was never snow up to his arse in Oxford, either. Though, to be fair, the parking was absolute shit over there, so Moncton had a leg up on that.

The bells above the door jangled when he fell into the welcoming warmth of the coffee shop. He shut the door quickly to avoid dirty looks from those foolish enough to sit nearby and take their coats off. Barnaby wasn't sure he was ever going to be able to remove his own, as his hands were frozen, his fingers stiff and useless. He needed better gloves.

He made a beeline for the counter, hopeful that a latte would thaw him, inside and out. He'd just given his order when the door bells pealed again and Jack walked in.

The barista trailed off halfway through reciting Barnaby's order back to him, her mouth hanging open. Jack did look particularly delicious in the heavy-knit cream fisherman's jumper and an old pair of jeans. The fucking lunatic wasn't even wearing a coat.

Jack smiled at Barnaby and came toward him, his cheeks red from the cold, his hair wild when he pulled off his hat. At least half the people in the cafe were watching Jack, but unlike whatever lascivious thoughts they were having, Barnaby was wondering if Travis had that same kind of sweater, as it would suit him as well, given his coloring. Then he wondered when Travis's birthday was. Then he wondered what the fuck was the matter with him.

Friends with benefits, he reminded himself. Though he supposed friends bought each other birthday gifts. Didn't they?

"You all right?" Jack asked.

Barnaby shook himself out of his ridiculous thoughts. "Of course. Why do you ask?"

"You looked like your brain hurt."

"Barn baby!" cried the barista.

Barnaby rolled his eyes. "Is my name really that hard?"

"It's weird," Jack said, ever helpful, before turning to give his order. He was damn lucky his name was so easy, based on the dazed expression on the barista's face while Jack flirted with her.

Barnaby paid for their drinks and went to the table in the corner. He looked across the café and wondered where Grady and Travis had been sitting the day Travis had first seen him. He'd been dead flattered that Travis had noticed him, particularly since he'd been with Jack. Barnaby often thought he could burst into song—with appropriate dramatic hand gestures—while standing next to Jack, and no one would notice him.

Jack joined him and they chatted about school and work, Jack sipping his coffee while Barnaby clung to his until he felt sufficiently thawed to take off his coat, hat, and scarf.

"So, how are things going with Travis?" Jack asked.

The image of Travis standing above him in the dimly lit closet, blushing a furious dark red while his spunk slid down Barnaby's cheek, assailed him. *Oh god.* He shook his head, trying to clear it of the obscene pictures flashing through it like a personal peep show, while Jack looked at him with growing concern.

Say something, you berk.

"Um...good. Things are—things are just smashing. With me. And Travis."

Jack blinked, his coffee halfway to his lips, his eyebrows going way up.

Barnaby felt the urge to squirm.

A slow smile creased Jack's face, his eyes crinkling. "Anything you want to share with the class?"

God, he was an idiot. "No, there is not."

Jack waggled his eyebrows, which should have made even him look ridiculous. "Nothing at all?"

"Nothing that would fall under the heading of any of your business."

"Oh, snarky," Jack observed slyly. "And defensive."

"I am not defensive!"

Jack laughed in his face.

Barnaby glared at his so-called friend. "Are you quite finished?"

Jack was still laughing, the arsehole. "God, no," he said. "But when I am, I'm going to have to say I told you so."

"How about we consider that done, then?"

"If you insist." Jack made a show of wiping his eyes.

Determined to move the conversation along, Barnaby offered, "Travis is a very quick learner."

Jack snorted, inhaling his sip of coffee.

"Of poetry," Barnaby added, loudly, over Jack's coughing. "*Poetry*, Jack. Good god, man, pull yourself together."

With a last gasping wheeze, Jack waved his hand and nodded, which Barnaby chose to interpret as concession.

"Thank you."

"For now," Jack croaked.

That didn't sound ominous or anything. "The *tutoring* is going very well," Barnaby plowed on, eyeing Jack.

"Yeah?" Jack asked.

"He's incredibly smart. Very thoughtful and focused. Wants to be a good student, which I assure you is far rarer than one would imagine from an entirely voluntary student body."

"I'm not surprised," Jack said. "Now that you've seen some games, maybe it will make sense when I say his hockey IQ is pretty high. And he's a great influence in the locker room. Calm and helpful when the younger players need it, passionate and driven when the team needs it."

"I'm not sure what *hockey IQ* means, exactly, but I'm not surprised by any of that. He's a passionate student, too. Though I bet he wouldn't admit as much. He claims he doesn't care as much as younger students do, but it's not about his studies. He's just less interested in his professor's opinions of him. I envy him that."

Jack cocked his head, studying Barnaby

He lasted thirty seconds before breaking. "What?"

"You really like him," Jack said.

"I do. He's a good friend."

"Friend or *boyfriend*?" Jack asked.

"No. Just a friend."

"As simple as that?"

Barnaby shrugged. "Yes, it's that simple. I can't be involved with anyone right now. And Travis says he could be traded at a moment's notice, so there's not much point in him investing in anything long term. It works out well—I can focus on my studies, and Travis won't feel guilty if he ends up in Russia, or Wisconsin, or Vancouver, by the end of the week."

Jack frowned. "That's pretty unlikely, though."

"Is it? I'm not about to ask Rupert about it, since I don't want to draw further attention, but you yourself said Travis is avoiding fights, which even I know is a problem."

"Okay, that might be true, but if you really like him—"

Barnaby cut him off there. "I do really like him, but we're not going to *date*. As I've said before, that's not in the cards for me at the moment. Travis and I are friends. With benefits, as you've clearly sussed out, which isn't something I had considered before, but suits me fine."

"Why can't you date?" Jack asked. Barnaby frowned and Jack held up his hand. "No judgment, and not about Travis in particular. You've been saying since we met that you can't date anyone. Until Travis, you wouldn't even give anyone a second look."

"That's not entirely true. I gave *you* a second look," he said, laughing when Jack appeared horrified.

"Oh, that's...you did?"

Barnaby sagged back in his chair, shaking his head. "Yes, I did. I knew as soon as we met that I liked you, and that we'd be friends." Then he grinned, the devil winning out after all. "And you're terribly handsome."

Jack grimaced. "Thanks."

"Yes, well, I got over it. But even if I hadn't, I wouldn't have said or done anything, because I'm still in university, and will be for some time."

"And that matters because...?"

"Because I can't fall in love while I'm working on my degree. I'll become distracted. I need to finish this."

"I'm no authority, but I'm pretty sure lots of graduate students are in love or fall in love while they're in school," Jack pointed out.

"Which is fine for them," Barnaby said, "but not for me. I was to begin my doctorate studies the year after I graduated, and I threw that away to follow Robert to London." He really wanted Jack to understand, but he didn't know how to describe how disappointed he'd been in himself. He settled for saying, "It's not a mistake I'm willing to repeat. I put too much time and energy and *faith* into my last relationship, and it cost me dearly."

"But you've learned from that," Jack pointed out. "Now you know better."

Barnaby shook his head. "I can't risk it. I don't—I don't trust myself not to give too much." It was not easy to admit the brutal truth. "I don't trust myself not to get lost."

"I don't think you give yourself enough credit," Jack said.

"Perhaps, but this is the least penance I deserve for being such a fool."

"Is that how you see Moncton? A penance?"

Barnaby knew thin ice, especially when he'd run right out onto it like a complete knob. "No. I don't. Not at all," he said, backpedaling like mad.

"But you did."

"I think we've long established I was both a snob and an idiot. I hope I've learned better and improved. If it helps, you may gloat, at length, over having dispelled, completely, my misconceptions about the Maritimes, hockey, and hockey players."

Jack rocked his head back and forth, his lips pursed, as if considering. "Okay. I accept that offer."

"I'm overwhelmed by your generosity," Barnaby said, deadpan.

Jack chuckled. "You asked for it. Literally."

And so he had. He couldn't regret it, though. Nor could he regret having flung himself across the ocean in what amounted to, in hindsight, a semi-adult version of throwing a massive wobbly. He was extraordinarily lucky it had turned out as it had.

Jack was still smiling at him. "For what it's worth, B, and despite your best intentions, you deserve to be happy."

"And I am. I love what I'm doing now, and in two or three years, I'll be ready to consider a relationship. Maybe."

Jack nodded and Barnaby appreciated both his kindness and that he let it go there.

They sipped their drinks and Barnaby surreptitiously studied Jack, wondering if he dared tread on what he'd considered, to this point, sacred ground. They'd already gone into a few topics they hadn't touched in the past. Would he have a better opportunity than now?

"You know, Jack, you deserve to be happy, too," Barnaby said.

Jack's head jerked up, but otherwise, he appeared as

unflappable as ever. His smile was, perhaps, a touch wooden. "Thanks."

Not *I'm happy.* But *thanks.*

Barnaby decided he did dare, after all. "Do you date?" he asked.

Jack took a sip of his coffee, his focus there. "No."

"Do you want to?"

Jack's eyes lifted to him. "What?"

"Ha. Not with me, to clarify. I meant, only, would you like to date someone, someday. Would you like to have a relationship?"

Jack opened his mouth to answer, then closed it again. Twice. Barnaby watched, dismayed, as the color bled from his cheeks and his face went still as stone. Jack, his confident, gregarious friend, was almost unrecognizable, his gaze flat and eyes dead.

Barnaby sat forward, unsure what to do. He regretted having pushed, though he'd never imagined it would upset Jack to such a degree.

"Yes," Jack blurted, startling Barnaby. He looked a little better once he got the word out, as if he'd released some pressure he'd kept locked inside.

The next question on Barnaby's tongue was if he had someone in mind, but Barnaby suspected he knew the answer. Either way, he couldn't bring himself to ask. Not right then, anyway.

He put his hand over Jack's fist where it rested on the table. They weren't very tactile, normally, but he was pleased when Jack smiled at him, albeit weakly. He squeezed Jack's hand with a small smile in return and let go to take a desperately casual sip of his coffee.

Jack took a deep breath and let it out slowly before picking up his coffee and slouching back in his chair. He appeared thoughtful, and Barnaby thought he might address whatever the hell had just happened until he turned a speculative look on Barnaby.

"So, does this mean you're going to become an Ice Cats fan?"

Barnaby laughed, please to see the gleam back in his friend's eye. "Jumping in with the first *I told you so* already, are you?"

Jack grinned. "Oh, my friend, the first of many."

Travis didn't see much of Rupert the first two days of the road trip.

Traveling with a team was always far more intimate than most people would guess. A whole lot of proximity was demanded of them on a regular day in the locker room and on the ice, then add in long bus rides and the time spent in hotels and it felt like the team lived in each other's pockets.

That was why Travis went down to breakfast early the morning after their game, hoping to linger over his food in relative quiet. He refused to be disappointed to find the hotel dining room wasn't empty, but he was relieved it was just Rupert, some guy he vaguely recognized but hadn't been introduced to, and two players he liked a lot, Alexei and his best friend Mike.

Rupert and the man Travis didn't know stood just inside the door, huddled at one end of the buffet. If Travis had to guess, neither was very happy with the other.

Travis skirted around them and went to the end of the buffet. He was only halfway through when Rupert's voice rose above a furious whisper.

"Bob, I asked you for a scouting report. It's not difficult. It's literally your job."

Travis veered away from the waffle station like it was on fire. He could do fruit next.

"He's not gay. What do you care?" Bob said loudly.

Travis stopped mid-stride and turned around. Mike and Alexei put down their forks.

Rupert arched his eyebrows at Bob. "Because he's a good goalie with an eager agent?" he said, making it clear this was obvious.

136

Bob scoffed. "I didn't bother writing anything up once I heard he had a girlfriend. You think I don't know what you're doing? You want me to chase around every queer kid on skates so you can hang a fucking rainbow flag on the team bus. It's bullshit."

Rupert narrowed his gaze on Bob, who clearly wasn't that bright, because any semi-intelligent man would have taken a step back. "I asked for a scouting report, and I expect to get one," Rupert said, his accent clipped. "If you have a problem with that, Bob, then you have a problem performing the most basic functions of your job."

"This is no way to build a hockey team," Bob snapped. "It's fucking ridiculous."

Rupert just continued to stare at him, in silence, and let the tension build until Bob's face was red, his hands curling into fists.

He let out a sound of pure rage and yelled, "I fucking quit!"

No one moved as he stormed out of the room. Then Travis very quietly finished loading his plate and went to Mike and Alexei's table.

"Mind if I sit here?"

Alexei gestured at an empty chair with his fork.

Travis barely had his ass in the chair before Rupert plunked down a plate and collapsed into the seat across from Travis.

"That sucked." Rupert sighed and smiled sourly at the rest of them. Travis thought he would apologize. Or maybe explain. Though neither was needed. Rupert sighed again. "Well, since I don't have that goddamn scouting report, do any of *you* want to tell me what you think about John Murphy?"

"I hear he has a girlfriend," Travis volunteered.

Everyone laughed, even Rupert, though it looked like it hurt. "I heard that, too. And in case you're wondering, apparently, that means he's straight."

"Yeah? Weird."

Rupert nodded, then looked around the table expectantly.

Alexei shrugged. Travis wondered if this was going to get awkward, since Murphy was a goalie, and could be considered a replacement for Alexei, but Alexei seemed unbothered by it.

"He's good," Alexei allowed. "Young."

Everyone nodded, even Mike who was only a year or two older. The rules were different for goalies. "He crosschecks like a son of a bitch if you get close to the blue paint," Mike said. "I'll have a bruise from shoulder to shoulder tomorrow."

Travis winced. Alexei looked concerned.

Rupert made a note on his iPad, which he'd set up beside his plate, then he looked at Travis and waited.

Right. My turn. "So, ah...he's good," Travis started, mentally flipping through what he knew and games he'd played. "Stays in position, doesn't go down too soon, doesn't try anything very fancy."

Rupert chewed thoughtfully. "Anything else?"

"He does better when he's busier. The fewer shots he faces, the more likely he is to let one in."

"That's what Callum said."

Given Callum had been a goalie in the NHL, that felt like a compliment.

The conversation moved onto other players, both on the Sea Dogs and elsewhere, and Travis shared his thoughts where he could, which was pretty often, actually. He'd played with or against a ton of guys over the years, so he knew their habits and attitudes, not just their playing style. More than that, he knew their types. Embellishers, whiners, trash-talkers, leaders, locker room disruptors. No two players were the same, but there were parallels that could be drawn, and when Mike, Alexei, and Rupert seemed interested, Travis went ahead and threw that shit out there, too.

"I thought the Wagner kid looked better last night than he did in the last game," Travis offered when they got around to the Sea Dogs again, since Rupert had asked about him a couple days ago.

Rupert looked up from his breakfast. "How so?"

"He's using his speed more. He still needs more puck work, but some of that is going to be on Craig, and not on the kid."

"Craig? Craig Belmare, the coach?" Rupert asked.

"Yeah, he's a good guy. I played for him in...shit, where was that? In Quebec. He was pretty green back then, but his style looks the same to me. Very defensively focused, not the least bit interested in anything fancy, or, as he likes to call it, *cute*. That's how Wagner is playing. He's young, and he might be focused on adopting his team's system and impressing the coach instead of finding his own style. It would be interesting to see what he looks like outside this arena."

Rupert smiled. "Wouldn't it?" His phone buzzed and he glanced down at it. "Well, I'm off. I'll see you on the bus in a bit."

Travis nodded, surprised when Rupert flipped his iPad closed and left without another word.

Barely eight in the morning and already the day was a weird one. Though he couldn't say he was sorry he'd missed out on the solitary breakfast he'd been hoping for. He was used to guys who could do little more than grunt until their fifth cup of coffee, so Mike, Alexei, and Rupert had made for a nice change.

He chatted a while longer, but had to excuse himself to finish his packing before the team moved out.

The bus ride to Halifax was a choice between stunning views out the windows, or joining the singalong inside the bus. Different teams had different cultures, but never had there been a hockey team that liked to sing more with, collectively, less talent, than the Ice Cats.

The game in Halifax was a shit show from start to finish. Thankfully, no one tried to get Travis to fight, though there were some skirmishes. During one of those, some asshole called Jamie a homophobic slur, and Travis discovered he *was* willing to overcome his aversion to fighting for special occasions. Before he could do anything, though, Olle had his gloves off and the guy's lip busted open.

Fortunately, the refs had heard the whole thing, so while

Olle got five minutes in the penalty box, the asshole was handed a game misconduct and tossed off the ice for the rest of the night.

My, how times have changed. Travis could remember his midget coach calling literally every kid on his team, the other teams, the refs, and some of the parents that same word. And, at the time, that had seemed *normal.*

They got on the bus right after the game, opting for a late night arrival in St. John so they'd have time for a practice the next morning. If Travis had his way, they'd spend as little time as possible in St. John and with the memories that city held. He couldn't even look up at the rafters in that fucking arena.

Sighing, he walked all the way down the aisle of the bus, laughing at the boys heckling each other and taking his own share of the abuse good-naturedly.

"Oh no! Are we in trouble?" Tim asked. "Dad is sitting in the back of the bus!"

Travis laughed. "Shut the fuck up. I sit back here all the time."

"Not since the New Year you haven't," Chris observed.

Travis hadn't told anyone about his school stuff, so he just shrugged. "Well, now I'm back."

He took the bench in the last row. Most guys avoided it, since it meant you were the de facto bathroom monitor, but he liked being able to stretch out his knee, and he knew the trainers would have an ice pack for him once they were on the road.

He was shoving his bag under the seat in front of him when the back of the bus went eerily silent.

"Oh shit, Dad *is* sitting in the back of the bus," someone whispered.

Travis picked his head up to see Rupert coming toward him.

"I heard that, Timothy," Rupert said as he passed that row. He stopped at the bathroom door, and, for a moment, Travis thought Rupert had decided to take the world's most awkward shit.

"Is this seat taken?"

Travis didn't let his surprise show, but it was close. "No. Please, sit." He slid into the corner by the window and waved at the empty space beside him.

Rupert settled into a seat with his phone in hand and his briefcase at his feet. Travis sat beside him like he had a very large and uncomfortable stick up his ass. He didn't think Rupert would lecture him, or, worse, *trade* him on the team bus, but he couldn't figure out why the hell else he'd be back there.

By the time the bus started moving, Rupert was immersed in whatever he was working on, which was somehow both a relief and anticlimactic.

Travis forced himself to unclench. He smiled gratefully at the trainer when he wandered back with an ice pack. "You ready for this?"

Travis reached for the ice pack, twisting to straighten his leg as best he could in the limited space. Rupert crossed his legs to one side to give him more room but otherwise ignored him.

This was going to be the longest four hours of his *life* at this rate, made a zillion times more annoying because they would be *driving through Moncton* to get from one city to the next. He'd give his right arm for them to stop for the night so he could sleep in his own bed.

Maybe even invite Barnaby to join him.

Was *that* what this was about? He eyed Rupert, who seemed content to ignore Travis. He didn't think Rupert had an issue with his friendship with Barnaby. He'd set up the whole tutoring thing to begin with, and he'd sent Travis out into the hallway to see him just last week.

Travis looked out the window, unable to see anything but his own reflection in the glass. He looked tired. And old. And like he'd forgotten to comb his hair after his post-game shower.

He wasn't really surprised. Even thinking about St. John made him nervy, and going there was worse. He was physically tired but his brain was stuck in overdrive. He tried to play something on his phone but gave up when he couldn't focus.

Then, out of nowhere, Rupert said, "Can I ask you

something?"

Travis jumped so hard he almost dropped his phone.

Rupert let out a quick, quiet laugh. "Sorry. I didn't mean to startle you."

Travis didn't bother to mention it wasn't Rupert's fault he was wound tighter than a spring. That came with explanations he wasn't in the mood to make. "No, that's fine. What did you want to ask?"

"What do you think of our D pairs?"

"What? Like, all of them?"

Rupert nodded, turning back to whatever he'd been working on and worrying his lip between his teeth. Travis looked around, confirming everyone in the back of the bus was sacked out. Even if they hadn't been, the roar of the engines and the tires on the pavement were enough to keep a conversation private back here.

So he answered, as diplomatically as he could. When he finished, Rupert sat, eyebrows up, and waited. Travis lowered his voice and answered more honestly and a lot less diplomatically.

Rupert listened, nodding at points, bouncing his head back and forth at others as if considering Travis's opinions but not necessarily agreeing. He asked a lot of questions—about their guys, about guys on other teams, about what sorts of players and skills they needed as a team, and where Travis thought the league was going.

It was breakfast the other day all over again, but this time he wasn't joking with the guys. That didn't make the conversation any less interesting, though. In fact, Travis was surprised when they pulled off the highway into St. John.

Where the hell had the time gone?

While Rupert packed up his work, Travis looked out the window, jarred by the familiar scenery. There wasn't a street in St. John he didn't know. He'd played here for almost two seasons, twenty years ago, and they had been some of the best years of his life. This place had felt like home before he'd realized how far and how many places his career would take him. Before there was Sweden or Russia, before he'd realized his aptitude for languages, or his ability to make friends wherever he went, there had been St. John.

And Martin.

Thankfully, it was late, so Travis could grab his room key and disappear without a word for anyone as soon as they arrived at the hotel.

He was happy to see a seat available at the table with Rupert, Mike, and Alexei at breakfast the next morning. He'd take whatever distraction he could find.

He was halfway through his waffles when he noticed how Rupert's elegant fingers rested atop his phone on the table. He had the random, horrible thought that Rupert might be sticking close so he'd know where Travis was when the call came in to trade him.

The thought made breakfast sit like a rock in his stomach, but he told himself he was being paranoid. He'd sat with Rupert this morning, not the other way around. And even if he was right, there was nothing he could do.

The day crawled by after that and by the end of the game Travis was tapped. He listened to coach's talk, pleased the penalty kill had escaped his notice for the first time in weeks, then ducked into the showers. He stayed there until he wondered if someone would come make sure he hadn't drowned.

Dragging his feet, he knotted a towel around his waist and stood at the mirror to give himself a close and thorough shave. He liked to keep a scruff sometimes, especially in the coldest months, but Barnaby's skin was so pale, it wouldn't take much to leave beard burn all over him. And while that had a certain appeal when he considered Barnaby's thighs and the sweet round cheeks of his ass, Travis had no desire to send the poor man back to Rupert and Callum with a fiery red face.

When he'd dawdled for as long as possible, and then some more, he trudged back into the locker room, expecting to have it to himself. The team bus to the hotel would be long gone by now. His plan was to torture himself with a walk around town, then head back to the hotel alone.

He stuttered to a stop when he found Rupert sitting in front of his locker.

Fuck.

"Travis," he said, hardly looking up from his phone.

Travis's stomach fell. *Please don't let this be what I think it is.*

Forcing himself to move, he went to his locker and reached over Rupert for his clothes. Rupert slid down the bench to give him more room and kept his eyes on his phone when Travis pulled off his towel, chucked it in the hamper across the room, and began to dress.

"I noticed you weren't on the bus, so I wanted to make sure everything was okay," Rupert said, looking up and tucking his phone into the inside pocket of his suit coat as Travis pulled on his shirt.

He managed a nonchalant shrug. "Sure. Just primping too long."

"How like you," Rupert observed dryly.

What the fuck was he supposed to say to that? It wasn't like Rupert was wrong.

"Do you need me for something?" he asked, hoping like hell he wasn't asking to be told about his own trade, but unable to figure out why else Rupert would still be there.

"Nope. I thought I might walk back to the hotel with you, if you don't mind the company."

Travis felt a rush of relief, while being no less confused. "Oh, ah...sure. Yeah. Just give me a minute."

Rupert nodded, studying him while he pulled on the rest of his clothes. He felt an itch between his shoulder blades, waiting for Rupert to say *something.*

As harassed as he'd felt by Rupert's company, their talks had been great. Travis always had a lot of thoughts about hockey, whether it was the game, the players, or the league. Rupert seemed to have an infinite capacity to listen to that shit—and he was funny, with his own ideas to share. He had a way of taking in what Travis was saying and then picking it apart, to either strengthen or destroy the argument, that made Travis want to keep digging in.

In other words, Travis really liked him.

He promised himself he wouldn't be mad when Rupert traded him. They could remain friends after he was gone, though it was hard to imagine Rupert on social media.

"You played here, didn't you?"

Travis hesitated, then pulled on his coat. "Yeah. Long time ago."

"You were friends with Martin Leduc."

Travis stopped what he was doing. Just froze, one arm still half out of his coat sleeve, his scarf hanging from his hand. "Yeah, he was my best friend."

"A long time ago?"

"And every day since."

Rupert didn't say anything for a long time, and Travis couldn't bring himself to look at the other man. He was picturing Martin's number, retired now, hanging above the ice.

"I'm sorry," Rupert said at last.

Travis closed his eyes and took a deep, steadying breath. "Yeah, me, too." He shrugged his heavy wool coat over his shoulders and finished preparing for the bitter cold outside.

Rupert pulled on his own winter gear, which ran more to a beautiful cashmere coat and leather gloves. He would be frozen solid by the time they reached the hotel.

Hefting his bag, Travis led the way out of the arena, thankful for Rupert's silence. And, if he were honest, his steady presence.

His plan, though he hadn't admitted it fully even to himself, had been to visit Martin's grave, which seemed foolish the minute they stepped outside. Martin would have smacked him upside the head for even considering anything so tragic. Instead, Travis let Rupert pull him into a quiet bar about halfway back to the hotel and order them each a scotch. Rupert talked about his children and his husband and Travis laughed at the appropriate times, and maybe ached a little with longing.

It was late by the time they got back to the hotel. Rupert said goodnight and headed straight to his room. Travis watched him walk away, grateful to work for such a good man.

His own room was warm and dark, but he wasn't tired. He pulled out his phone, having ignored his messages all night, and opened his on-going conversation with Barnaby.

Generally, they kept it light. Barnaby congratulating or consoling him on his games. Travis trying to talk Barnaby off the ledge when one of his students was being particularly ridiculous. Tonight, though, Barnaby had sent a series of messages.

I was looking at the syllabus, and I see there are some longer pieces this week. How's that going?

After an hour, when Travis hadn't answered, Barnaby had written again.

Well, just in case, here you go...

Six audio files followed.

Travis stripped down and crawled into bed with his phone. He tucked his earbuds into place, and listened to each of the poems, not bothering to read along. Not bothering to do anything more than close his eyes, let the covers warm around him, and listen to Barnaby's voice.

They are all gone into the world of light!
And I alone sit lingering here;
Their very memory is fair and bright,
And my sad thoughts doth clear...

Chapter Twelve

Travis had left home in high school to live with a billet family and play for a team that traveled so much they'd done more than half their schoolwork on the road. Homework hadn't been a priority, but not failing out of school had been a requirement, so he'd done what he'd had to, confident he'd be making at least a million dollars a year playing hockey by the time he was twenty.

Needless to say, things hadn't worked out exactly as he'd planned, but he didn't have any complaints. There were times he wondered what it would have been like to stay in school like a typical student. Maybe even go on to college. What would it have been like to join study groups for long hours in the library? Doing his high school algebra homework in a Holiday Inn somewhere in Quebec with five other guys lying half on top of him and copying his answers had never felt like the genuine experience.

Curled up on his couch, shirtless, his legs tangled with Barnaby's, his poor dick semi-erect for most of the last two hours, probably wasn't the genuine experience, either, but he still had no complaints.

Barnaby started petting his thigh. Travis wasn't sure he was aware he was doing it, but it forced Travis to shift around, trying to find room in his jeans.

Okay. So, maybe he had *one* complaint.

"You all right there?" Barnaby asked with a knowing smile.

"You'd think listening to Alexander Pope go on and on would be enough to kill anyone's boner."

Barnaby snorted. "Am I boring you?"

"No! Not at all. And it's not like you chose what we have to work with."

"Indeed, not," Barnaby agreed, frowning at the laptop.

"What would you pick, if you had a choice?"

"From Alexander Pope?"

"From any of these guys. Dryden. Vaughan. Pope. Marvell."

Barnaby shrugged. "Some of the same, because you do have to read the classics." He laughed at the look on Travis's face. "You do," he said, nudging Travis with his foot. "But I'd mix it up with some lesser-known works that are more relevant to today's student than treatises on the Bible and an ode to Horatio."

"Yeah? I think I'd like that class." And not just because he could sit and watch Barnaby get fired up about poetry all day. "You should teach it."

Barnaby hummed. "Maybe, one day."

"Teach me something now."

"Isn't that what we've been doing for the past hour?"

"No—I mean, *yes*, but I want you to pick a poem you think I would like."

Barnaby gave him a long look, his hand stroking the length of Travis's denim-clad thigh, over and over, as he considered Travis's challenge

Travis pressed his hand over Barnaby's to hold it still.

It had been a long road trip, with far too much alone time spent thinking about the things he wanted to do to Barnaby that he hadn't done in a dark storage closet before he'd left. Hell, he'd spent too much time thinking about doing what they *had* done in that closet and when he might be able to do them again.

Barnaby looked at their hands, then dragged his eyes up further to the vicinity of Travis's cock. The damn thing perked up hopefully.

Bright blue eyes dragged up his bare torso, detouring to admire his shoulders, lingering on his neck, then catching his eyes. "I know just the poem."

"Yeah?"

Barnaby slid his hand up Travis's leg. "I do. It's by Andrew Marvell."

"One of the guys I'm studying this week."

"Indeed. And he wrote a wonderful poem called *To His Coy Mistress*. Guess what it's about?"

"Love?" Travis ventured, pinned by Barnaby's gaze.

He was certain he'd never seen a sexier smile.

Barnaby shoved the laptop onto the coffee table and crawled over Travis, straddling his lap. "Nope."

Travis's pulse picked up, his body humming with anticipation. Barnaby's knees dug into the couch and he leaned in close. Travis tipped his chin for a kiss, but Barnaby ducked to the side, teeth nibbling along his jaw while hot breath tickled his ear and neck. Travis clutched Barnaby's hips, trying to anchor himself against the storm.

The tip of Barnaby's nose dipped into his ear, then wet lips sucked his earlobe into the heat of Barnaby's mouth. Travis shuddered. Another minute of this and he would melt into a puddle. As it was, Barnaby could have whatever the hell he wanted.

What had they been talking about?

Right. School work. Poetry.

"Tell me," Travis gasped.

Barnaby was so close his words were hot in Travis's ear. "It's about how he will worship her body. How it will take him years to do it properly." His hand slid down Travis's chest, brushing over his cock where it pressed against his jeans.

My vegetable love would grow
Vaster than empires, and more slow...

"He's talking about his eggplant, right?" Travis gasped.

Barnaby shook with silent laughter. "By modern emoji standards—yes, he is." His hand rubbed Travis's erection, making him squirm, then traveled back up his body.

An hundred years should go to praise
Thine eyes, and on thy forehead gaze;

Two hundred to adore each breast,
But thirty thousand to the rest;
An age at least to every part,
And the last age should show your heart.

Travis thrust his hand into Barnaby's hair and dragged him down into a kiss. Their tongues slid against one another, the heat that had been building between them boiling over. He drew Barnaby down onto his lap with a hand on his hip, his weight on Travis's cock a relief and torture.

He wanted exactly what Andrew Marvell had wanted three hundred years ago, so Barnaby had been right, that poem did feel really fucking relevant.

And unlike that night in the arena, today they had time. A day off for Travis, and no classes for Barnaby to attend or teach. It was the middle of the afternoon, the sun bright and high outside his living room windows, but he knew his bedroom would be even better.

"Come on," he gasped, pushing Barnaby off him and climbing to his feet.

"Where are we going?"

Travis threaded his fingers through Barnaby's and towed him across the room. "To bed."

Barnaby stumbled behind him, drawing him up short.

He turned around slowly. "Or not. That's okay."

"The fuck it is," Barnaby said with a bark of laughter. "But before you sweep me off to your lair, I have something for you."

"My *lair?*"

Barnaby shook his hand free and dashed to his bag. He came back with a single sheet of paper and handed it to Travis.

Travis's brain failed to register what he was looking at for a moment. Then he grinned.

"You should know," Barnaby said, very seriously, "that those tests were the most intimate relations I've ever had with a woman. And, in related news, I'm never going to be one of those men who likes to have things shoved up their penis."

Travis laughed while Barnaby shuddered dramatically.

"So noted." He towed Barnaby in and gave him a long kiss. "Thank you for being so brave."

Barnaby rolled his eyes while Travis pulled out his phone and found an email from the training staff. He showed Barnaby the test results from his last physical. "I can print these out for you."

"Not at all necessary." Barnaby handed the phone back. "Well, now that we've been responsible adults, where were we?"

"You were about to tell me all the things you *do* like, I think."

"I was?" Barnaby asked.

"And I was going to spend an age, at least, on every part of your body, per Andrew Marvell's suggestion."

Barnaby's eyes fell to half-mast. "I think you're in for a surprise or two."

"*Really*?" Travis drawled. Beyond intrigued and completely out of patience, he bent and put Barnaby over his shoulder.

Barnaby let out a squawk of outrage. "What are you doing?"

"Carrying you off to my lair," Travis said with a laugh as he went down the hallway.

Two hands cupped his ass and squeezed it. "All right, then."

Travis strode through his bedroom door and tossed Barnaby on the bed. He landed in the bright pool of sunlight, bouncing hard enough to make the metal headboard knock against the high windowsills. The room had been designed so the bed should sit against the opposite wall, but Travis had pushed his right up against it as soon as he realized he'd be able to sleep in the sun for his pre-game naps.

He'd also painted the walls dark blue, so the room had the feeling of a sunny, cozy cave.

"This is lovely," Barnaby observed, looking around curiously.

Travis didn't take his eyes off Barnaby as he crawled up on the bed. "So are you."

He'd guessed Barnaby's fair skin would look amazing in the sun and against the dark sheets and comforter, but imagination hadn't done him justice. He drew his hands up Barnaby's long legs, pausing at the tops of his thighs and plucking at his jeans. "Can I take these off?"

"Yes, please. Take anything off. All of it."

He unfastened Barnaby's button and fly and tugged the jeans down. Barnaby twisted and arched to help. His cock pressed up under his impossibly sexy tight black boxer briefs, but Travis made himself wait, drawing his hands down strong, firm legs. His knees and ankles were smooth beneath Travis's palms.

Barnaby propped himself up on his elbows, his lips wet and bitten red, and watched as Travis tried to learn everything he could. The hint of blue veins beneath ivory skin was fascinating, the bright light making Barnaby glow. What little hair he had was coarse against Travis's palms when he ran them back up Barnaby's thighs, a study in contrasting textures with the smooth skin beneath.

He rubbed over Barnaby's hips, smiling when the shift of cotton made Barnaby hiss, then grasped the tails of his shirt and began to slowly unbutton from the bottom up. He didn't part the fabric. Not yet. Teasing himself as much as Barnaby. The back of his fingers could feel how firm Barnaby's belly was and how his breath shook. When he got to the top button, Barnaby stroked a hand over Travis's cheek and scratched into his hair. Travis ducked in for a kiss before sitting back and parting the edges of the shirt.

He'd expected to feast his eyes on the expanse of pale skin stretched over lean muscle. He'd figured, given how little hair was on his legs, that Barnaby's chest would be hairless, or close to it. But he hadn't dreamed of the two bright flashes of color, startling in contrast to Barnaby's ivory skin.

"What is this?" he murmured, drawing the tip of his index finger over the line of blue...*scales*?...that curled around Barnaby's waist, then draped over the jut of his hip before narrowing down to circle his navel.

His other hand slid up Barnaby's chest until he could draw another finger along the ribbon of dark pink, almost red, that appeared over Barnaby's shoulder, slithered beneath his collar bone as if underlining it, then ended in a curl tucked into the divot at the base of his neck.

Was that a tongue? A *forked* tongue?

He lifted his eyes to Barnaby's face and found him staring back.

Barnaby had been with Robert long enough—and not with anyone since—that he'd forgotten how odd this moment could be. Even at sixteen, he'd had the good sense to get his ink where no one could see it unless he wanted them to, but he hadn't anticipated that he'd have to go through a series of unveilings from that day forward. Some men loved it, others had found it off-putting, and one man, when he'd been in his first year at Oxford, had gotten up and left after telling Barnaby he "clearly wasn't who he pretended to be."

To this day, Barnaby had no clue what the fuck that had meant and didn't regret having called the man a snotty prick as he'd tugged his pants back on.

"Would you like to see the rest?" he asked, confident Travis wasn't about to do anything so foolish.

"Yes, please," he rasped.

"If you pull my boxers off, you'll be able to see it all," Barnaby added.

Travis laughed. "I bet you say that to all the boys."

"Far fewer than you would imagine," he admitted as he arched his hips and helped Travis peel his shorts down his legs. He was so hard that his cock slapped his belly when it sprung free. Travis froze, his fingers and the elastic waistband digging into Barnaby's thighs, his eyes hungry.

Barnaby nudged Travis's leg. "Don't get distracted now."

"Fuck you, I'm drooling here," Travis groaned.

A shiver worked down Barnaby's back, his legs squirming to

get free of his underwear. He didn't care what they did next, but it was becoming painfully necessary for them to do *something*. His cock throbbed under Travis's stare. Barnaby curled his hand around it, running it up and down, peeling the foreskin back from the head and drawing it back up. Shocks of pleasure raced over him. He was far too primed already.

Travis watched, mesmerized, the color high on his cheeks, his eyes wide and glassy. He shuddered, then shook his whole body. Much like a dog would after getting out of water. "Right, I'm going to blow you to next Tuesday, but first I want to see what's on your back."

A helpless whine escaped Barnaby's throat. "You can't say something like that and expect me not to beg for you to skip directly to the blowing."

Travis laughed. "Over." He tapped Barnaby's hip. "I'll work my way back around, don't you worry. Right now, I want to see every inch of you so I can decide where I'm going to start."

Travis ran his hands over Barnaby's skin, nudging him to roll over, his palms skimming over hip and waist. Barnaby shed his shirt and stretched out on his stomach, his elbows planted on the bed, his legs spread so Travis could kneel between them and look down at his back.

Travis gripped Barnaby's hips, his thumbs digging into his ass. "Jesus fucking Christ."

Not for the first time, Barnaby wished for a mirror, or an Exorcist neck, so he could see Travis's face. His reaction.

The curse sounded good. Maybe even flattering. Though there was no mistaking the surprise.

A broad, warm palm ran from his left hip to the top of his arse, then up over his spine and curled over his right shoulder. Barnaby knew Travis was tracing the long, sinuous line of the blue and green scaled dragon whose tail looped around his bellybutton, and whose tongue slid over his shoulder to end at the base of his throat.

"This is beautiful work," Travis said, following the dragon with his hands again.

"Thank you."

"I never would have guessed."

Barnaby sucked in a deep breath, recalling all the people who'd had the gall to see his ink and tell him who he was or wasn't, and what was expected of someone "like him".

"But it suits you," Travis added.

Barnaby twisted to see Travis over his shoulder. "It does?"

"Yes, definitely," he said before his lips skimmed over his shoulder, his tongue tracing the dragon's.

Barnaby settled onto his chest and stretched his neck to the side, encouraging Travis's exploration. "No one ever says that," he admitted.

"People are stupid." His tongue slid down, a kiss pressed to the spot Barnaby knew to be the tip of the dragon's nose. "And you're beautiful."

Barnaby's breath caught, trapped behind an unexpected lump in his throat. Travis drew his fingertips along the dragon, as if he could feel the scales. Barnaby knew they were incredibly detailed and life-like, had seen pictures from a thousand angles and distances, but he still wished he could see it himself just once. He'd managed to gift himself with something he cherished, was proud of, and felt was an intrinsic part of who he was, and it was always just out of reach.

"It must have taken hours," Travis observed as he dropped kisses along the ridged spine of the dragon, from Barnaby's shoulder blade to his ass.

Barnaby hummed, happy and turned on. He let his eyes flutter closed so he could focus on the sensations Travis evoked. "Almost fifteen."

Travis froze. "Fifteen *hours*?"

Barnaby let out a huff of laughter, wanting to beg Travis not to stop. "Yes. I had to break it up into nine sessions, which didn't help."

"Why so many?"

Barnaby shivered with pleasure when Travis started

touching him again, his hands drifting down and cupping Barnaby's arse. His fingers dug in, lifting Barnaby's cheeks to his lips as he peppered kisses along the dragon's tail from the top of his ass to his hip.

"I was sneaking out of school to do it. I only had so much time before I had to be back. And I could only go on days I'd not regret being sore for days afterward."

Travis stopped just as his tongue spread over the dimple at the base of Barnaby's spine, then it was gone. "You were sneaking out of school?"

"I was sixteen."

"You got this tattoo when you were sixteen," Travis repeated, not so much a question as to make himself believe it. "That's..."

"Not entirely legal, as I was well aware."

"I was going to go with insane."

"It was that, too. But I found an artist in London who was willing to do the work, for a small fortune, and there wasn't anything that was going to stop me. By the time the school figured out what I had done, I was healed and they were in a difficult position, having failed to keep proper track of me. They never told my parents."

Travis's finger traced over one particular spot. "Is this Japanese?"

"It is."

"What does it say?"

Barnaby sighed, letting the memories come. "Ryu Haruto."

"Will you tell me what it means?"

Barnaby appreciated that Travis understood it was special. And private. "It's a name. He was my best friend at school, and when we were fourteen we figured out we shared more than just the same taste in video games and movies."

"He was your first love."

"He was," Barnaby agreed with a smile.

"And then?" Travis asked, his finger still tracing the name.

"Then one day he was gone. He told his parents he loved me, and they felt very strongly that we should no longer be in the same school, let alone roommates. They shipped him off to some dreadful place in the States that would teach him *Christian values*, which was bloody rich, given his parents were from Japan and he'd been raised a Buddhist. He'd been so sure they would understand, that they would accept us, that he didn't warn me he intended to tell them."

"I'm sorry."

"Yes, well, the worst part may be that they'll never forgive themselves. He drowned at that godawful school, struck in the head during *sailing class* of all things. Then, at his funeral, his parents *apologized* to me. They regretted what they'd done, not just to poor Ryu, but to me as well. Can you imagine? I went and found the tattoo artist that afternoon. Paid in full up front. There was to be no stopping me."

He took a deep breath, having long ago accepted that the grief would never fade completely, then let it out slowly.

Travis kissed his shoulder, his chest warm against Barnaby's back, the tattoo pressed between them. "He was lucky to have you. To have loved you."

"And I him," Barnaby agreed softly, moved that rather than dwell on condolences and pity, Travis had recognized the thing Barnaby thought most important. They'd been lucky to have each other.

Travis sat up, his jeans coarse against Barnaby's bare thighs, and traced the dragon with his fingers again. "Is it weird if I keep touching it? It's incredibly sexy."

"That wasn't my intent, but I'm glad you think so," Barnaby admitted.

"What *was* your intent?"

Barnaby laughed, rolling his eyes at himself. "Drama, I think."

"What does that mean?" Travis asked with a quiet laugh, touching each line of ink again.

"It means I'm rather prone to grand romantic gestures. It's a failing of mine."

"That doesn't sound like a failing."

An observation that should not have made Barnaby as happy as it did. He laughed again, forcing the thought away. "Well, one can only get enormous tattoos so many times before one runs out of canvas. As you can see, I decided this was a one-and-done thing."

"Your first and last grand gesture?"

"Hardly, but I've done enough to kill the mood already, so perhaps we'll save further tales of my foolishness for later."

"Oh, I don't know about that," Travis said, curling forward and pressing his mouth to the back of Barnaby's neck. His teeth captured the knob of one vertebra.

Barnaby shuddered. "No? You want to hear them now?"

Travis's hot breath tickled as he laughed silently, his lips working across the sensitive skin there. "No. I don't think we've lost the mood."

The things Travis was doing to him were certainly going a long way to restoring it, anyway. Barnaby arched his back, pressing up against Travis.

Travis groaned. "Have you seen how your muscles play under the dragon when you do that? It's gorgeous."

He hadn't, and no one had ever said anything to him before. "I always wish I could see it better."

"It's stunning. You're stunning," Travis whispered, running both hands up his back.

Barnaby whimpered. "Travis, *please.*" He couldn't still the roll of his hips, his cock leaking between his belly and Travis's soft duvet.

Travis moved back and helped Barnaby roll over. Barnaby reached for him, but his arms went weak and he collapsed back onto the bed the moment Travis's hand wrapped around his cock.

Travis's hand was hot, his callouses rough as they drew up

his shaft. Barnaby's eyes fluttered, trying to roll back in his head, but he was determined to see.

Travis bent over him and paused. Warm brown eyes traveled up his body and caught his gaze. "Can I?"

"God, please. Anything you want."

Travis's gaze made the return trip to Barnaby's cock, and it was impossible not to be flattered. Barnaby wanted to thank him, which seemed foolish, but it had been far too long since anyone had looked at him with such appreciation.

Travis hummed when he got to Barnaby's cock, and Barnaby's stomach tightened in anticipation. Travis seemed fascinated by the fact he wasn't circumcised. He drew his hand up slowly, urging the foreskin over the sensitive crown and sending shivers down Barnaby's legs and up his back over and over. Travis watched, his caramel eyes hot and avid, until Barnaby's legs quivered and his cock ached. A pearl of pre-come bloomed from the tip, and Travis licked his lips, making a happy, almost eager sound before he ducked his head and sucked Barnaby's cock into his mouth.

A shout tore from Barnaby, the moist heat all-consuming, the tight suction perfect. Travis took him deep, his lips bumping his hand where it was still wrapped around the shaft, then eased back to lavish his attention on the tip. The cold air was shocking where Barnaby slid free of Travis's mouth, the stroke of soft, wet lips and agile tongue exquisite. Keeping his hips still was almost impossible. He couldn't tear his eyes off Travis's face and the apparent pleasure he took from driving Barnaby out of his mind.

He drew off and Barnaby whimpered. "Please, Travis."

A hand cupped his balls and tugged, making Barnaby jerk but helping stave off the orgasm he could feel clawing its way free. His cock leaked more pre-come and Travis whisked it away with his tongue before tilting his head, as if considering Barnaby's cock thoughtfully. A hysterical laugh bubbled up in Barnaby's throat. God, he wished he could read what was going through Travis's mind.

Then he didn't have to wonder any longer because Travis

slid his tongue between the achingly fragile foreskin and the head of Barnaby's cock.

Barnaby let loose a string of curses, losing his battle to keep watching in favor of grinding his head against the bed. Travis stilled Barnaby's thrashing legs with a hand, then pressed them open so he could kneel between them while he licked Barnaby's brains out through his cock. Barnaby planted his feet on the bed and let his knees fall open, happily granting access to any part of his body Travis wanted. He was rewarded with a pleased moan that shivered right up his shaft and echoed through his body, and that calloused palm returning to his balls, rolling them gently.

Not that Travis wouldn't be able to guess by how tight they were, but Barnaby tried to warn him anyway. "I'm going to come. Travis, I'm going to come."

Travis's tongue slid out of the hood of foreskin and he sucked, hard, at just the tip of Barnaby's cock, like a long, perfect kiss that ended with an obscenely slick noise. "So come."

Barnaby clenched all the muscles from his navel to his knees. "No, goddamn it. I'm going to get you naked this time."

Travis sat up, his hand holding Barnaby's cock up for his inspection. He tilted his head, appearing thoughtful, before he said, simply, "Nope," and dove back in, pulling the foreskin up over Barnaby's engorged crown and swirling his tongue into it.

"I'll have my turn," Travis murmured between sweet sucks and agonizing licks. "For now, I'm having lots of fun, I promise." To punctuate that point, the hand around Barnaby's balls tightened, Travis's thumb and forefinger making a ring and forcing Barnaby's climax back again.

Barnaby made a choking sound, like his orgasm was trapped in his throat. He gasped for air, each desperate breath filling his chest and barely able to escape, his head spinning. He threaded his fingers into Travis's hair, desperate to feel him, to know he was there when Barnaby's eyes were squeezed shut and his ears were ringing with the blood singing through his veins.

Travis moaned around Barnaby's cock, driving harder. Barnaby's altruistic plans blew away, his hips canting and thrusting his cock farther into Travis's mouth.

He gasped, horrified, but Travis groaned in pleasure.

"Sorry. I'm sorry," Barnaby gasped anyway, because it was rude until it was something Travis asked for. He pressed his hips to the bed and Travis followed him down, sucking hard, his hand moving faster, bumping his own lips. The rasp of his tongue was quick and constant, each lash a zap of electricity straight to Barnaby's nervous system.

A stream of helpless, desperate noises bled from his throat as his balls tried to draw up tighter, stymied by Travis's grip.

And then that grip was gone.

Barnaby's orgasm slammed into him. He cried out Travis's name, each pulse tearing the word from his throat again and again. Travis was relentless, sucking, swallowing, riding out the storm of Barnaby's climax.

Barnaby trembled all over, then collapsed on the bed and patted gently at Travis's head, nudging him away from his oversensitive cock.

"Bloody hell," he gasped, staring sightlessly at the ceiling. He couldn't feel his extremities, so he lay motionless, trying to gather his scattered wits.

Travis crawled up over him. "Come here," he murmured, drawing Barnaby up the bed until he lay with his head on a pillow, Travis beside him, both stretched out in the bright sunlight coming in through the windows. It felt decadent to be so warm, to feel the sun on his skin after months of winter. His eyes fluttered, and he fought to keep them open.

"No, go ahead," Travis said, kissing his eyelids and guiding Barnaby to rest his head on Travis's shoulder.

The moment Travis's arm curled around Barnaby's back, he was out.

Chapter Thirteen

Travis stroked his hand down Barnaby's long, pale body. His palm fit perfectly over the swell of Barnaby's hip, his thumb tracing the scaly blue tail.

He'd have to ask if Barnaby was in the habit of passing out after he orgasmed, as that would be good to know for future planning. He smiled, enjoying the idea of teasing Barnaby about it. Then again, last time he'd blown all over Barnaby's face before he'd had a chance to do anything, so he wasn't in much of a position to make fun.

He ran a fingertip along the dark fringe of Barnaby's lashes, eyelids so pale and thin he could see the tracery of veins within. He looked achingly vulnerable like this, which was all the sweeter because Travis knew he wasn't anything of the sort. Smart, funny, strong. Surprisingly demanding and utterly comfortable with his body while rolling around naked in bed. It was a dangerously sexy combination.

Bright blue eyes eased open, then blinked in confusion a few times before going wide.

"Oh my god, I fell asleep."

"You did," Travis said.

His heart skipped a beat or four when all of a sudden Barnaby was above him, straddling his hips, his hands on Travis's pecs.

"*Holy shit*, do you always wake up this fast?"

"It was just a nap," Barnaby said with a shrug. "And I've been rather neglectful, so there's no time to waste."

"Oh yeah?" Travis asked, laughing as Barnaby's nimble fingers undid his jeans and pulled, scooting down the bed to draw the denim down his thighs and yank it free from his feet. Barnaby's hands ran right back up Travis's legs, stopping mid-thigh with a huff of laughter.

"I can't decide what to ask about first—the jockstrap or the unusual body hair arrangements you have going on."

Travis stacked his hands behind his head and grinned up at Barnaby. He could spend days like this, with Barnaby naked in the sunlight above him, laughter in his eyes. He shivered when Barnaby dragged the pads of two fingers along the strip of bare skin in the middle of his thigh.

"Okay, I've decided," Barnaby announced. "How often do you wear a jockstrap?"

"Pretty much every day. It's the job."

Barnaby poked at his ribs, making him laugh. "I mean when you're off the ice."

"I don't know, how often do you *want* me to wear a jockstrap off the ice?"

Laser-beam blue eyes pinned him in place. "All the time."

Travis's cock plumped up, just like that. Barnaby eyed it with a pleased smile that only sped the flow of blood into Travis's dick. By the time Barnaby dragged a finger down from the center of the jock to the point between his legs where the straps split, Travis was hard as rock and wondering if it was healthy for a man his age to get there that fast.

Not that he was complaining.

Jockstraps every day sounded just fine to him. "Done," he said, his voice hoarse.

Barnaby dipped that damn finger lower, teasing the skin behind Travis's balls with the barest of touches. "I like how much access I can have with this," Barnaby murmured before pulling his hand away. "But today, I want it off so I can see what you've done to yourself."

Travis lifted his ass off the bed so Barnaby could hook his fingers in the wide band of the jock and pull it off.

He stared at Travis's junk for a long moment. "You look like someone attacked you with a hedge trimmer."

Travis burst out laughing, the sound choking off when Barnaby started tracing all the spots missing the coarse blond hair that was otherwise thick around his cock and sparser along his thighs. He shuddered, his breathing cut off altogether, when Barnaby pressed his lips to the bare spot in the middle of his treasure trail.

Barnaby sat up and looked him over again. "Please explain. Is this some alternative to tattooing? Topiary pubes?"

"God no," Travis said with another laugh. "Some of it I shaved so that various pieces of tape won't tear it clean out. And the rest were because some damn piece of tape tore it clean out."

Barnaby winced. "That sounds dreadful."

"It is," Travis agreed, shuddering at the recollection of some of those free wax jobs. "One price you pay for playing hockey this long."

"Well, I shall kiss it and make it better, then," Barnaby said with a mischievous smile.

Travis held his breath as Barnaby leaned in and ran his tongue along bare skin, rubbing the flat of it back and forth on the wider spots and tickling with just the tip in the narrowest parts. It was amazing how sensitive the skin was, particularly the bits that had most recently been torn away. Travis sprawled across the bed, shivering, his cock rock hard but neglected except to be moved aside so Barnaby's lips could explore. By the time he'd done a complete investigation, a drop of pre-come had pooled in one of the bare spots.

Barnaby kissed it away, nuzzling his lips just there.

Travis ran his fingers through Barnaby's soft brown curls. Beyond the thrill of desire and the promise of release, it was nice to have someone so close. There was a warmth that came with being pressed against another naked body that couldn't be replicated any other way. A warmth he missed just as much on the hottest August day as any night in winter. A warmth he'd experienced far too infrequently in his life.

He didn't think he'd ever been so relieved to discover it again.

Barnaby lifted his head. "What do you want?"

"You."

It felt too honest, and inadequate, but the smile he got as reward was worth it.

"What do *you* want?" Travis asked. At this point, he was feeling pretty flexible. Mostly, his goal was not to come on Barnaby's face in under a minute. He'd set the bar low for himself.

"I wanted you to worship every inch of my tattoo, then blow me into next Tuesday. And since we've already done that, it's your turn."

Travis laughed, the sound embarrassingly breathless because Barnaby was nuzzling his way up Travis's chest, lulling him with soft lips until the sting of teeth would zap through him, making him shudder until Barnaby soothed him with his lips and tongue again.

He forgot the question when Barnaby set his teeth to one nipple.

He knew the answer when Barnaby started to suck.

"Can I fuck you?" Travis asked, his voice cracking mid-sentence.

Suddenly, Barnaby's lips and hands were gone. He sat up, his legs folded beneath him by Travis's hip, his hands in his lap. He gnawed on the corner of his lower lip before saying, "No."

Travis nodded. "Okay, then, how about—"

"Wait. I think we should talk about that for a second," Barnaby said, his hand sliding onto Travis's thigh and rubbing.

Travis settled back against the pillows and stroked a finger from Barnaby's shoulder to his elbow, needing a connection, too. "Sure. You know I'm not upset or anything, right?"

"No, I didn't think you were. You're not an arse."

"Well, not about this, anyway," Travis said. "I'm sure I have my moments."

Barnaby smiled and nudged his thigh with a knee. "But I'm curious. And I don't want to make you uncomfortable."

Travis shrugged. "Most things, honestly."

"So, you're vers?"

It wasn't a label he'd ever applied to himself, but only because no one had ever asked. "I like feeling good, and, for me, that can happen a lot of ways. So, yes. And you?"

"Same, but it's not a fifty-fifty thing, which it sounds like it might be for you. I'm definitely more of a top."

Travis looked up at Barnaby and let that sink in. It shouldn't have been a surprise, but somehow he was kind of thrown.

"I'm guessing by your expression that perhaps you're not as vers as I suggested?"

"What?" Travis asked, his brain kicking back into gear. "No. I am. I'm just…"

"Not into it?" Barnaby guessed.

"No, that's not it at all. I'm just surprised, I think."

"I don't read as very toppy to you?" Barnaby asked with a sharp smile that warned Travis that a nerve was dangerously close to being struck.

"Actually, you do. I think the surprise is more about me," Travis said, picking his way through the thoughts crowding his mind.

"How so?"

Travis scratched his fingers through his hair. "Usually, the men I've been with have…I don't know, assumed I wanted to top? Or that I only top? Or maybe I've accidentally tended to end up with men who don't top?"

Barnaby arched a dubious eyebrow. "Is that somehow different than you preferring men who bottom?"

"Actually, it is. Maybe it's my size, or my profession, or the insanely stupid bro company I often keep, but I think I've been giving off the wrong vibe. Or not the *wrong* one. Just not the right one." In hindsight, he was feeling pretty dumb.

Barnaby thought about that. "So…you're okay bottoming?" He didn't sound certain, which was fair since Travis was doing a horrible job of explaining himself.

"Yes," he said firmly. The more he thought about it, the more certain he became, his imagination offering up a host of promising possibilities. "That was the surprise. Not that I want it, but how hot the idea of you preferring to top is." He shivered. "So, yes, I want you to fuck me. Often. And hard. Hell, I want you to fuck me straight through the mattress and into the floor."

"I'm fairly certain Grady wouldn't appreciate that much," Barnaby said, a smile growing.

Travis laughed, dizzy at the promise of what they could do. *Would* do.

Barnaby pulled his spiraling attention back with a stroke of his hand along Travis's thigh. "And you'll tell me if you don't want to do something?"

"Always."

"Okay," Barnaby said, and he finally looked convinced. He reached for Travis.

"But not today," Travis added.

Barnaby's hand folded back into his lap. "What?"

"We can't today. Have sex. Well, we can have sex, obviously, but you can't fuck me, no matter how much I want you to." Just saying it made him want to roll over and stick his ass in the air, which was a new and welcome feeling.

"Why not?" Barnaby asked, admirably free of whine.

"I have a game in less than twenty-four hours, and I can't be sore." Barnaby happened to trace his fingers over the remnants of a nasty bruise on Travis's thigh. "Well, more sore than usual. And in new places."

"So, what's the rule here? More than twenty-four hours?"

Travis made a face. "It's more of a guideline than a rule. And I'd say it's closer to forty-eight hours."

Barnaby smiled. "I can work with that." He leaned in and stole a kiss, surprising Travis, who eagerly tipped his chin and pulled him closer. It started out sweetly enough, but soon tongues and hands and hips were involved, and Travis was hauling Barnaby closer. He hummed when Barnaby crawled on top of him, their cocks trapped between them. It was both amusing and arousing to feel Barnaby getting hard again. God, to be in his twenties again. Though he would happily take advantage of being with someone whose refractory period was so blessedly short.

Goddamn, he wanted Barnaby to fuck him.

The more he thought about it, the more the idea burrowed deep in his brain and made a home there. He liked sex. He liked being with a confident and capable man. Barnaby was all that and more.

He was also cautious. Travis liked that Barnaby was so thoughtful about sex, and so thorough, his hands stroking Travis's sides, his lips and tongue devouring, pausing before exploring new places, giving Travis ample opportunity to agree, or deflect, or encourage.

He spread his legs and Barnaby settled between them, moving to nibble up Travis's jaw.

"Tell me if I do something that breaks the rules," Barnaby murmured as he nuzzled in behind Travis's ear.

Travis's toes curled. "Guidelines. They're guidelines," he gasped. He ran his hands down Barnaby's back, pressing him closer, feeling how the muscles shifted as he took up a slow and dirty grind.

Barnaby chuckled breathlessly. "I'm going to memorize your game schedule," he promised in a thick voice. "I'll know when you'll be home with enough time for me to take you apart."

Travis arched up against him, his spine curling. "God. Yes."

"I want to give you a proper seeing to. I'll need to do it more than once. There won't be that many chances."

Travis whimpered. "There's always the summer."

Barnaby slithered down Travis's body, his smooth skin rubbing along his cock, his mouth leaving a cool trail until it latched onto a nipple and sent a zing straight to Travis's balls. Barnaby released him with a rude pop. "The summer?"

"I grew up near here, so I come back to the area in the off season." He shrugged, trying to make it seem like not a big deal, though it kind of was. He was making this shit up as he went.

"Even if I get shipped out tomorrow, I'll keep this place until the fall rather than pack it all up. Most of it lives in a storage unit near here anyway."

Barnaby hummed thoughtfully, his finger stroking over the damp nipple. It was damn distracting. When he didn't say anything, Travis realized he'd made a few assumptions.

"That is, if you'll be here? We can keep doing this if you're here, and you want to," he added, dangerously close to babbling.

"I'll be here," Barnaby said, ending Travis's verbal diarrhea with a wave of relief he wasn't going to study too closely.

Barnaby kissed him again, then said, against his lips, "And I do want to."

Barnaby coasted his lips across Travis's cheek and jaw, enjoying the coarse rasp of his stubble, the smell of his skin and soap. He could spend hours learning Travis's curves and textures, and was relieved he had time to do exactly that.

He wasn't certain when he had decided he wouldn't go back to the UK for at least part of the summer, but he feared it was in the last three minutes. Though, to be fair, he hadn't planned to go for more than a few weeks, and he had been wondering for a while where, exactly, he thought to spend the time. He couldn't abide to stay with his parents for more than a few days. There would be bloodshed. And while he loved his sisters, and they him, he wouldn't impose on them for longer than a day or two. He had a few friends from school he'd like to grab a pint with, but not so much that he needed to fly a couple of thousand miles he could scarcely afford to fly.

And then there was London, where once he'd had a life and friends. The longer he was in Moncton, though, the less London seemed to matter.

He'd given himself a fresh start. With new friends. Friends who wouldn't cover up for a cheating boyfriend. Who wouldn't *sleep* with the lying bastard, for fuck's sake.

Travis gasped as Barnaby's teeth sank into the thick muscles running up his neck from his shoulder. He eased back immediately, guilt nipping at him until Travis arched his neck and pressed closer.

Ah. Well, if that was how he *wanted* it...

He nipped his way down Travis's neck, closing his eyes and letting the stroke of Travis's fingers through his hair and over his shoulders soothe and guide him. He sucked one nipple, then the other, pleased by Travis's murmured encouragement, delighted by Travis being ticklish along the ribs.

Watching Travis writhe beneath him was a heady thing. His powerfully built body was mesmerizing, particularly when it was Barnaby's hands and lips that made it move so sinuously. He could imagine Travis arching as Barnaby's cock slid home. The way he'd use all that strength to move against him.

Why had he thought he had to give this up? Eighteen months of celibacy, and for what purpose? Self-torture, and a lot of self-abuse, hadn't brought him anything. What a stupid idea, that he could repent for his past mistakes by depriving himself of this.

His lips were pressed to Travis's sternum when he started to laugh. God, he'd been such a fool.

Travis lifted his head. "What?"

"Sorry. Sorry. You've gotten me in the terrible habit of thinking of poems at the most ridiculous moments."

"Really? You're going to pretend that's my fault?"

Barnaby licked down the center of Travis's torso and wiggled his tongue into his navel as punishment. He was rubbing his face along the flat panes of Travis's tight stomach when Travis asked, "Well, are you going to tell me?"

"Tell you what?"

"The poem?"

Barnaby smiled and kissed one hipbone.

But I hate to be cheated, and never will buy
Long years of repentance for moments of joy...

He kissed the other hipbone.

Travis carded his hand through Barnaby's hair. "Smart guy who wrote that."

"Smart lady," Barnaby corrected, curling his hand around Travis's cock and listening to the air leave his lungs in a long hiss. "Lady Mary Wortley Montagu. It's called *The Lover: A Ballad*. I'll read you the whole thing." He licked across the shiny, bright pink head. "Later."

Travis spread his legs, his thighs twitching with each brush of Barnaby's tongue. "Normally, I don't like it when men talk about a woman when they're blowing me."

Barnaby laughed, the tip of Travis's cock balanced on his lower lip. "Another rule?"

"Guideline," he groaned as Barnaby slid him into his mouth.

All thought of poetry, and repentance, drained from Barnaby's head, focused instead on giving Travis as much pleasure as he'd given Barnaby. He wrapped his hand around the base of Travis's shaft and stroked up and back, bumping his lips with his fist. Men often did what they themselves enjoyed, and it would seem it was true for Travis, too. He barked out an inarticulate noise that still managed to convey just how much he liked what Barnaby was doing.

Travis was circumcised, though, so the rub of Barnaby's dry hand, if held too tightly, made him wince.

Barnaby pulled off with a swirl of his tongue. "Lube?"

Travis flung an arm in the general direction of the bedside table.

Barnaby reached inside, shoving aside a few interesting items to find a small bottle. He tucked that under Travis's hip to warm and sat up on his knees between Travis's wide-spread legs.

Travis reached for him and Barnaby caught one of his hands, drawing two fingers into his mouth and running them along his tongue before pulling them back out and kissing his palm.

"How often do you fuck yourself?"

Travis's eyes popped open. "What?"

Barnaby's meaningful glance at the bedside table was enough for Travis to understand why he asked.

Travis smiled. "How do you think I figured out the forty-eight-hour thing?"

"That often?"

"God, no. I wish. It's a lot of work, and sometimes with my shoulder..." He shrugged the body part in question.

Barnaby slicked up his hands. "My shoulders feel great, just so you know. No pain at all."

"Is that so?" Travis asked, watching.

"Indeed." He wrapped a slick hand around Travis's cock, running it up and making a tight ring of his index finger and thumb to tug on the frenulum until the crown popped free.

Travis's mouth fell open, his gaze locked on his cock. Barnaby ran his other hand over Travis's balls, rubbing and tugging, trying to gauge Travis's reaction to everything he tried. It wasn't easy, given that Travis seemed to have lost the ability to speak, thrusting his hips up into Barnaby's grasp in time with his motions. Barnaby was making a bit of a mess, which Travis didn't seem to mind.

"Too much lube?" he asked, just to be sure.

"God, no. It feels..." Travis trailed off, his eyes losing focus as a trickle slid down his perineum.

Barnaby hazarded a guess. "Good?"

"Filthy," Travis gasped. "I like it." His skin shone as Barnaby rubbed and tugged and added more slick to his hands. Travis's cock was a fiery pink. The head, exposed and a few shades darker, seemed so vulnerable to Barnaby. He stopped to rub little circles into the rough divot beneath it with his thumb while he slid the pad of one finger along the seam of skin running from behind Travis's balls to his hole, skimming over the pucker of muscles.

They gave easily. Gorgeously. Barnaby's cock twitched with anticipation, a shiver working up his spine.

Travis's arse was gorgeous, thick and round with the

muscles he needed to skate as often and as hard as he did. The powerful cheeks clenched around Barnaby's hand and he could imagine how they would feel, firm against his belly as he sank into Travis.

If he weren't so delightfully occupied, he'd be scrambling for his phone to determine when the Ice Cats next had two days between home games.

For now, though, his concern was that he needed more space than Travis's giant arse allowed in this position. Without stopping the shuttle of his hand over Travis's cock, or the tease of his fingers over his hole, Barnaby pressed a kiss to the inside of Travis's bent knee. "Can you hold this leg?"

Travis pulled up until it was pressed to his chest. Barnaby slid one finger past barely resistant muscles and into Travis. He shuddered as he felt the silky inside, imagining how it would stretch to let him in, then surround him with the same heat.

"Oh god," Travis groaned. "That's good."

Barnaby pumped his finger in and out of Travis's hole, the muscles clinging but clearly not tested. Barnaby wanted to ask when Travis had last fucked himself. Wanted a real answer of how often, because Barnaby felt like he could open him up in a matter of minutes.

Hips rolling in rhythmic, almost clockwork circles, Travis worked Barnaby's finger in and out. His chest shone with perspiration, flushed from the corded muscles in his neck to his nipples. His breathing was ragged.

Barnaby's cock was rigid, the foreskin gathered beneath the exposed head where it lay on his thigh. He wished desperately for another arm, for a third hand, because he wasn't going to take either of his off Travis.

"God, you're fucking gorgeous like this," he murmured, mesmerized by the ridges of Travis's abdomen, pronounced as he rocked his hips.

Travis whimpered, his neck arching.

Barnaby tucked in a second finger and thrust deep.

"Fuck, like that—do it like that," Travis shouted, reaching for his other leg.

Barnaby stopped him, throwing his leg over Travis's to keep it on the bed. "No, that's your bad shoulder."

Travis laughed, though it was breathless. "Who cares?"

"I do," Barnaby said, spreading his knees and settling lower. His balls grazed the furred skin of Travis's thigh. His breath skittered, the delicate sensation sizzling through him. He pumped his fingers faster, matching the speed to the hand jacking Travis's cock.

Travis writhed against the bed, his breath coming in fast pants, his eyes sightless. "Fuck, how are you—what—why hasn't anyone done this before?"

Why, indeed. It was a fucking shame that no one had taken care of Travis like this. That no one had bothered to learn this man well enough to feed his desires in this way. He obviously loved it. His cock leaked a drop of pre-come that Barnaby regretted not being able to lick away, but the taste of lube was among Barnaby's least favorite things.

Unlike watching Travis's pink flushed cheeks edging to red.

Barnaby spread his fingers in Travis's arse, groaning when the muscles gave, his ears ringing with Travis's hoarse shout. God, he wanted to shove his cock in there so badly he shook with it, but as that was off the table, he wasn't sure what would be allowed.

Travis answered the question by shouting, "*More!*"

"I thought there was a rule?" Barnaby asked, even as he wedged his third finger in beside the others and pressed forward.

Fucking hell, now *that* was tight.

"It's a guideline," Travis gasped as his body gave, letting Barnaby in. "It's just a fucking *guideline.*"

Barnaby laughed and twisted his wrist, going deeper, opening Travis up. His own cock leaked onto his thigh, his balls drawn up. Travis was absolutely stunning, one arm flung across the bed with a fistful of sheets clenched in his fingers, his head thrown back, his hips still moving.

"That's it," he gasped. "That's it. That's..."

Barnaby swore when Travis's muscles clamped down around his fingers. He stroked his hand over Travis's cock faster, focusing on the head, driving Travis higher and harder until he cried out and come shot from his cock. It landed in long streaks on his belly, his mouth hanging open and desperate little *ahs* bursting from his throat, the pulses shaking him with every muscle in his body tight and quivering.

With a last cry, he went boneless, melting into the bed.

Barnaby released Travis's cock and grabbed his own, scolding himself to be careful in the removal of his fingers from Travis's still-twitching hole. He let out a shout at the grip of his own hand that almost drowned out Travis's whimper.

Barnaby wasn't going to do himself proud today, but Travis wouldn't hold it against him. He hoped Travis understood that Barnaby's climax crawling up his back and tightening his thighs and rushing through him in a matter of seconds was a compliment.

His hand was a blur, slick with lube that was still warm from Travis's body. He fell forward, catching himself on one arm, the elbow locked, as the first dizzying pulse thrummed through him. He bit his tongue and whined as his come mixed with Travis's all over his belly. He'd not even finished before Travis's big hand was dragging through it and rubbing it into his skin.

With a last shudder, Barnaby's elbow gave out and he landed on Travis. Slippery hands searched for purchase while their mouths met and tongue tangled. The kiss was messy, half laughter, as Barnaby slid off Travis's slick belly and landed on the bed beside him.

Chapter Fourteen

The friends with benefits thing really worked for Barnaby. It had only been a month since the first time he'd kissed Travis, but they'd spent a lot of it together. Well, as much as they could, which meant with Travis's travel schedule and Barnaby's work and studies, their calendars tended to align in fits and starts.

This past week had been a long one with Travis on the road, which was why Barnaby was vibrating in the booth at Quigley's, looking over his shoulder at the door every few minutes. Only a few of the Ice Cats had straggled in so far.

Travis had been traveling for almost a week, and all day Barnaby had been high with the anticipation of seeing him again. He'd gone to tonight's game with Grady and they'd met up with Jack before coming here. The two of them sat across from Barnaby, chatting about the goals Jack had missed while he'd been seeing to his various duties.

Barnaby could probably jump up and down in his seat and Grady wouldn't notice. He had stopped glowering at Barnaby as soon as Travis had told him about their little arrangement, and since then, Barnaby had been given the genuine pleasure of getting to know Grady. He understood completely why Travis and Jack liked him so much.

And more than that, Barnaby *really* liked him for Jack. Jack was more animated around Grady. More open.

Barnaby hadn't dared bring it up since that moment in the café, but he watched, and he waited, and for Jack's sake, he hoped.

So, he was more than happy to let them zone out on each other and therefore, hopefully, fail to notice Barnaby dithering with his drink, and his napkin, and his straw, his straw wrapper, his scarf, and whatever else came to hand between quick looks at the door.

Fucking hell, he hadn't been this horny since...well, not since before he'd met Robert his second year at Oxford, and he'd had the excuse of being nineteen years old at the time. His cock no longer seemed to recognize the interim decade, which was unexpected—and sometimes inconvenient. It didn't help that there hadn't yet been a long enough stretch of time for Barnaby to be able to fuck Travis. Though if Travis were willing to squint at the calendar a certain way, they might be able to stay within the rules—pardon, *guidelines*—tonight.

The anticipation was killing him, but it wasn't only about the sex. He'd *missed* Travis, which was a scary thought, but one which he'd spent most of the last week chewing on and had decided was perfectly understandable.

Travis had become one of his closest friends. The best friend he'd ever had, as an adult. Of course he missed him, given that. And given that the days Travis was away were far more dull than the ones when he was home. Barnaby enjoyed helping Travis with his class, but even more, he'd gotten in the habit of going to Travis's apartment just so they could sit together and work on their separate assignments. When Travis had to review game tape and read reports on the teams he'd be facing next, Barnaby would grade papers. If Travis had to stretch, Barnaby could help, leaning on his legs or gently tugging his arms further than Travis could take them, all while they talked or watched a game on TV.

Barnaby had become quite a hockey fanatic, which almost everyone he knew in Moncton liked to rub in his face—though none more than Jack.

He did another quick scan over his shoulder, his face lighting up when he saw Travis coming through the door. He looked...angry. No, sad. No, wait, there was a smile, turned up to full wattage for whatever Alexei was saying to him before swatting his ass and steering him toward their table.

Travis waved when he saw them and Barnaby waved back. Travis was grinning when he slid his coat off and Barnaby got a look at the bold white lettering on the black t-shirt clinging to his broad chest.

School is important, but hockey is importanter.

Barnaby towed Travis into his side of the booth. "Where on earth did you find that shirt?"

He had to tell himself to let go of Travis's hand once he was settled.

"I found it on this road trip. I thought it was perfect."

Barnaby laughed while rolling his eyes and shaking his head. When Travis greeted Jack and Grady, Barnaby took a sip of his beer to settle himself. He'd not sported wood from the mere sight of a man since he was thirteen and he wasn't about to start again now.

"So, do you like it?"

Barnaby realized he was asking about the shirt. "It's somehow both awful and perfect," he admitted.

"Good, because I got you one, too." Travis passed him the bag he'd been carrying.

"You...what?" Barnaby looked into the bag and found the identical shirt, only his was long-sleeved.

"I thought you'd like the warmer version," Travis said. "I know you're still getting used to real winter."

Barnaby held the shirt up by its shoulders, refusing to be drawn into the argument about the hell-season they called winter around here. He rarely wore something so casual, but he would wear this with a pair of jeans to campus tomorrow. He expected office hours might prove entertaining.

"I absolutely love it," he announced, folding it back into the bag and smiling at Travis. "Thank you."

They stared at each other, Barnaby fighting the urge to lean in and kiss Travis, and wondering if Travis was having the same difficulty.

Grady cleared his throat, waited a beat, and said, "Good game."

Travis's smile faded, something far less happy and more self-deprecating taking its place as he faced their friends. "Not really."

Barnaby's hand twitched in his lap, almost reaching out

before he quelled the urge. "I thought you played well. You got an assist."

"Thanks. I wish that was enough."

Barnaby opened his mouth to ask why it wasn't, but was interrupted by the arrival of several of Travis's teammates, eager to tell of the prank they'd played on Travis while on the road.

It *was* a pretty funny story, but Barnaby couldn't help but notice Travis's smile didn't quite reach his eyes. His laughter was a little quieter than usual.

"Yeah, yeah, thanks to you assholes, I had to go shopping on our day off. At least I found this awesome shirt while I was at it."

The guys cracked on him about that, too. Barnaby looked across the table and found Jack watching Travis, his eyes narrowed. Grady, though, was watching Barnaby, a decidedly unsettling discovery. Grady had a way of looking at a person that made them feel *seen*. Possibly *seen through*.

Travis's teammates wandered off to get another round at the bar. Grady didn't waste any time. He turned to Travis. "You okay?"

Travis tried to offer a smile, but it fell away. He sighed. "Not really."

"You want to talk about it?"

"Nope. Just hoping I won't be packing tomorrow."

"What?" Barnaby yelped, immediately embarrassed by his outburst.

"Have you been traded?" Jack asked. "I haven't heard anything and I normally do."

"Nah, not yet. But let's face it, it's only a matter of time. Or really, only a matter of how long it takes Rupert to find a team willing to have me. That could be a while. I suppose he could just buy out my contract."

That pronouncement seemed to sit particularly heavy on everyone who understood what the fuck it meant.

"Is this about the fight you almost got into?" Barnaby asked.

"Operative word being *almost*," Jack said, eyeing Travis.

Travis winced and took a long drink from his beer. A very long drink.

Barnaby's dreams of negotiating his way around the forty-eight hour rule went out the window, which was fine because he was far more concerned about Travis's state of mind and how to help him than about anything else.

"Can you explain to me what's wrong?" Barnaby asked. "I don't know enough to understand."

Travis stared at his beer, one hand around the pint glass, the other curled into a fist in his lap. "It's my head."

Jack's shoulders slumped.

Grady whispered, "*Aw, shit.*"

The oily slick of nerves roiled in Barnaby's stomach, even if he still didn't really understand.

"Your head?"

"I've had a lot of concussions," Travis explained, and Barnaby's stomach got greasier.

"How many is a lot?"

"Eleven on record."

The number seemed to hang in the air above the table. "Eleven," Barnaby repeated. He'd seen the articles, read about the research. The era of pretending even a single head trauma couldn't have long-term repercussions was long past. And several...

He couldn't fathom *eleven*. And what did *on record* mean?

"Yeah. I mean, they weren't all bad ones. A couple were just me getting my bell rung. But, you know, it adds up, and there are probably a few from when I was a kid that aren't in the count, so..." Travis said, bringing his glass to his mouth. He hesitated, then only took a sip before putting his glass back down. "It's why I generally don't drink a lot."

"Drinking can bring on symptoms?" Barnaby asked.

"No. I mean, I don't think so? But I don't want to be dizzy. Or clumsy." Another sip. "And the headaches the next day scare me," he added quietly.

Barnaby slid his hand over Travis's in his lap, his heart jerking in his chest when Travis threaded their fingers together and clung tight.

"Have you been having symptoms?" Jack asked, his expression serious. "Because you have to tell the trainers, Travis. You know that."

"No, I haven't. I swear." He took a deep breath. "But last season was rough. I got in a couple fights, and the last one..." He shook his head. "He got me good, you know? Then we fell onto the ice and my helmet was off. I'm not sure what did it, to be honest."

"Were you out long?" Grady asked.

"Couple weeks. Not that bad, really." It sounded fucking awful to Barnaby. "I missed three months a couple seasons before that. And both times I didn't rush to get back on the ice. All the symptoms were gone for a full week before I went back out."

A week? Barnaby couldn't comprehend any of this. He rubbed his thumb over Travis's hand and desperately tried to come up with something, *anything* that would help. But there was nothing.

"Anyway," Travis went on, "I felt fine at the end of last season." He looked at Jack. "I swear, I was at a hundred percent when I signed with the Ice Cats."

Jack frowned. "I don't give a shit about that, Travis. Come on."

"Yeah, well, I do," Travis murmured, looking at the table again. "I feel bad I'm not holding up my end of the bargain, you know? Rupert hired me to, among other things, *fight.*"

"What changed your mind?" Grady asked. "About the fighting."

Travis sighed. "I had a headache this summer. Pretty bad. Out of the blue. Scared the crap out of me."

"One headache?" Grady asked.

"It lasted three weeks."

"Why on earth do you still play?" Barnaby asked, the question out before he could think better of it.

He recognized his mistake when Jack and Grady cringed.

Travis shrugged, like Barnaby's question wasn't a big deal. Like Barnaby wasn't actually asking why Travis was putting his life at risk for a fucking *game*.

"I love it. I love playing hockey. And it's the only thing I know how to do."

"Rubbish," Barnaby snapped.

Travis scowled at him. "No, really, it's the only thing I know how to do."

"You're a keen student. You can learn anything you set your mind to."

"With a tutor."

"And I say, again, rubbish. I wasn't with you all week, and you completed your assignment with no input from me. And it wasn't a simple one at all. You wrote a haiku!"

Travis snorted derisively. "I'm sure employers will line up around the corner when they see that on my resume."

Barnaby swatted Travis's arm. "It's not the poetry that matters, it's that you work hard and learn quickly."

"An old dog who can still do new tricks."

"Oh my god with the bloody *old* thing again. You're not old," Barnaby said, seeing the light in Travis's eye spark back to life. If bickering about this ridiculous subject did that, then Barnaby was willing.

Also, thirty-four *was not old*.

"Wait a minute," Grady said, smile hovering like he didn't quite believe his ears. "You wrote poetry?"

Travis suddenly looked horrified. "Uh, not really. It's just a haiku."

"Just a haiku." Barnaby sniffed. "They are very difficult. I'm terrible at them. So few words to impart so much meaning."

"You're assuming mine didn't suck," Travis said with a laugh.

"You know I didn't get the syllable counts right."

Barnaby glowered at him. "We've already discussed this. It's a *guideline*, not a rule."

Travis's lips twitched, his hand squeezing Barnaby's under the table. "So you've said. Still..."

"Let's hear it, then." Barnaby waved between them, calling the words forth. "You've not shared it with me, for some reason. Let's have it."

"I don't have it with me," Travis said.

"It's...what? Twenty words total? Probably less?"

"Twelve."

Grady poked his arm across the table. "If you know how many words are in it, you fucking know what the words are."

Travis sighed with resignation and recited his haiku.

Cupped like a palm,
Over my junk, my pride and joy,
Ever vigilant.

There was a long pause, during which Travis's cheeks got increasingly red. He looked between the three of them and then longingly toward the door.

Barnaby kept moving his lips, but he couldn't find the words. "You...that..."

"Dude, you wrote a poem to your *jockstrap*?" Jack asked incredulously.

These words seemed to break something in Grady. He slumped over the table with a snort, shaking with laughter until all that was left was a thin wheeze when he ran out of breath.

Jack whapped him on the back—his face *was* turning a color that would make anyone wonder if he was asphyxiating—and grinned at Travis. "That's fucking awesome."

Travis rolled his eyes. "Thanks."

"I cannot *believe* you handed that in as your assignment," Barnaby finally managed to gasp.

Travis laughed. "You said a haiku was supposed to be about a small, intimate thing in our lives that touches us and offers us more meaning than we expect."

Grady wheezed again. Jack's big smile and bright eyes as he laughed drew the attention of half the room.

Barnaby dropped his face into his hand, his elbow propped on the table. "Oh my god, you certainly did that. I cannot imagine what your professor thought."

"She gave me an A."

Barnaby's head snapped up. "What?"

Travis's proud grin did things to Barnaby's insides. "I got an A. She said, and I quote, that it was *perfect.*"

Barnaby squeezed Travis's hand hard. "That's amazing. I *told you.* You're bloody brilliant."

Travis basked in Barnaby's obvious delight and tried not to squirm with embarrassment. He'd waited his whole life for his parents, or *anyone,* to say something like that to him, let alone for an academic achievement, and now that it had happened he felt exposed. Raw.

"Thanks," he said, trying to keep his voice light and his smile in place when all he wanted to do was snatch Barnaby away to somewhere private and ask him to hold Travis as hard as he could and say it again.

Maybe that would be enough to erase the memory of one of his teammates coming up to him in the locker room after the game and telling him to *do his fucking job* in a voice everyone could hear.

Including Rupert, who'd been just a few feet away.

He'd been regretting having arranged a night out after the game, but in the months he'd known Grady, he'd never once seen him laugh this hard. Grady was a funny bastard, his humor often running to the sly and dry, but he also had a seriousness that never left him.

Except, apparently, when Travis dazzled him with his

poetry.

Travis may not have been in the mood to socialize, but that made it worth it.

He sat back and listened as Barnaby answered questions about what, exactly, was a haiku, and smiled at his passionate response, his arm waving in the air even as the other was still tucked beneath the table, gripping Travis's hand.

Jack and Grady were fond of Barnaby, that much was obvious. As was Travis, though he wasn't going to dwell on that. He'd be gone soon enough.

It was just...he didn't want to leave Moncton. This city, his apartment, *these people*, felt more like a home than anywhere had in a long time.

Which was foolish. It was a mistake to feel this way. Not that it wasn't true, but he knew better than to allow himself to think that, because underlying that thought was hope. Hope he had no right to cling to.

He visualized leaving, really working to picture it, to make it real, and his heart ached. Like maybe he'd broken it before he even got around to giving it away.

"Earth to Travis," Barnaby said, giving his hand a shake.

"What? Sorry." Travis sighed. "I'm wiped."

"Let's get you home and to bed, then," Barnaby said, nudging him toward the end of the booth.

Travis didn't argue. He said goodnight to Jack and Grady, who didn't seem bothered by the early departure. In fact, Grady looked distinctly amused, but Travis wasn't going to acknowledge that.

They made their way through the bar, Travis taking a lot of ribbing about being old and having to leave early from his teammates. He enjoyed Barnaby's outrage, but he let out a sigh of relief when they hit the sidewalk. The silence, the cool air, and Barnaby at his side were all welcome. They walked in silence the few blocks to the warehouse, and Travis wondered if Barnaby might rather call it a night and head up to his place—it wasn't like Travis was much fun tonight—but Barnaby unlocked the door, reached inside to grab a small duffel bag and his messenger bag stuffed with schoolwork, and let the door swing shut again.

This wasn't the first time Barnaby had spent the night, but it was the first time they'd planned it well in advance. They were leaving Barnaby's car at the warehouse and they didn't have anywhere to be the following morning. Travis was both nervous and excited at the prospect. He knew perfectly well he should be neither.

They chatted about their weeks on the way home, and Travis appreciated that Barnaby wasn't digging into the whole concussion thing. Barnaby was smart, well-read, and curious—there was no way he didn't have questions. But since Travis didn't have answers, at least not ones he was prepared to offer, he was happy not to have to talk about it.

Travis breathed another sigh of relief when his door was closed behind them. It was good to be back on his turf. He'd only been here long enough to unpack the groceries he'd purchased on the way home from the arena after the bus pulled in this morning, and to empty his rank laundry into the machine. He left Barnaby to his own devices while he tossed his clothes into the dryer, then wandered aimlessly, wondering if he should offer to make tea, or ask if Barnaby wanted to watch a movie, or just give in to what he really wanted and strip naked and beg Barnaby to do whatever he pleased.

God, he needed to get out of his own fucking head.

He startled when Barnaby touched his shoulder.

"Come here," Barnaby murmured, towing him in and pressing a gentle, lingering kiss to his lips. Travis didn't open his eyes when Barnaby pulled back, clinging to the moment his brain stopped thinking about anything but the taste of Barnaby's lips. Barnaby kissed him again, longer, deeper. Their tongues moved in a slow dance between their mouths, without urgency, and it was all Travis needed. He dug his fingers into Barnaby's hips but didn't pull him closer. Barnaby was his anchor.

When this kiss ended, it was Barnaby who sighed. Travis's

eyes fluttered open and his heart skipped a beat to see the sweet smile on Barnaby's face.

Without a word, Barnaby walked to the bedroom, towing Travis with a hand curled loosely around his wrist, no pressure needed for Travis to follow him anywhere.

Travis stood where Barnaby left him at the foot of the bed, watching Barnaby strip off his clothes before turning to take Travis's off as well. He helped, barely, but mostly focused on the brush of Barnaby's hands. Their clothes ended up in a heap on the chair in the corner, the jockstrap he'd worn for Barnaby perched on top, all but forgotten as they climbed into the bed and reached for each other.

Barnaby rolled them, pressing Travis's back to the cool sheets. The width of Barnaby's shoulders blocked out the rest of the world, the dragon on his back a shield, his long legs tangling with Travis's so they could be still. Travis drew a deep breath and let it out slowly. Barnaby kissed him again, licking into his mouth, pulling his scattered focus down to one thing. One kiss. One man.

This was what he'd thought about all week. What he'd needed when he'd been on the road and frustrated about every damn thing. Haikus and hockey games and the ever-increasing pile of data that told him he shouldn't take another hit to the head. That told him he shouldn't have taken the last ten.

Here, his body worked just as he wanted it to. As it was supposed to. His cock, pressed between them, filled with blood as they rubbed against each other, subtle shifts brought on by their chins tilting and necks stretching to reach for kiss after kiss.

He opened his knees and Barnaby's narrow hips slotted between his thighs, pressing Travis into the bed as their erections slid together, but it still wasn't enough. It didn't feel like they were close *enough.*

He thrust his hands into Barnaby's hair and wrapped his legs around Barnaby's waist, his ankles hooked together, trapping Barnaby against him. It felt greedy and needy, but he didn't care.

Barnaby sure as hell didn't mind, his hips rolling, his mouth ravenous.

Travis tugged on Barnaby's hair, but rather than pull back, he changed his focus to Travis's jaw, his neck, working his way back to his ear.

Barnaby had learned a lot about how Travis's body worked over the weeks, and he happily exploited all his weaknesses. His lips skimming the shell of Travis's ear made him shiver.

"I want you to fuck me."

"I want that, too," Barnaby murmured, his breath hot on Travis's neck. He rocked his hips and Travis moaned.

This. This this this this. It was all that ran through Travis's head now, the urgency escalating as his need turned fierce. There wasn't a molecule of space between them, but Travis clung harder, his thighs aching. Barnaby wasn't trying to move away. Hadn't paused in his careful exploration of the space behind Travis's ear.

Travis tilted his head. Pressed his skin to Barnaby's lips. "There's enough time." *Barely. Sort of.*

"Not tonight."

Disappointment curled in his stomach, a cold ache, even as Barnaby's lips cruised down his neck, under his chin, making his entire body throb. Travis arched his back, pressed closer, and Barnaby slid a hand under his spine, his palm nestling into the dip at the very base, urging Travis's hips to match the rhythm he set.

Travis stuttered at first, out of sorts, not sure what he wanted. What he needed.

"I've got you. Just let go," Barnaby murmured.

Travis screwed his eyes shut and clung to Barnaby, a hand in his hair and the other wrapped over his strong shoulders.

"Just let go," Barnaby whispered again, his lips close to Travis's ear. The words barely had to take form in order to sink into his brain. "I'll be here. No matter what happens, I'll be here."

And Travis didn't even know what that meant. This

summer? If he was traded?

But god, the words felt amazing against his skin.

He was weightless.

Safe.

A tear slid from the corner of his eye to his temple and down into his hair. Then another. He wasn't sure where they came from, because he wasn't sad. For the first time in a week, his chest wasn't tight with worry. There was only this. The rub of his cock along Barnaby's smooth belly, the sound of his breath rasping past his open lips.

His orgasm, when it came, surprised him, welling up and out of him from the same place as the tears. The only warning was three quick gasps as his spine went tight and his toes cramped. Barnaby caught the last gasp in his mouth, kissing him fiercely as the waves pulsed through him, slicking the space between their bodies and easing the friction of their skin.

Barnaby made a sound in his throat, and Travis smiled because he sounded so *pleased*, as if he'd done what he'd set out to accomplish. And maybe he had. Maybe making Travis feel good, making him come, making him *forget* for five fucking minutes, was his goal and his reward.

Whatever it was, Barnaby's hips lost their rhythm and their kiss became messy, coordination lost until Barnaby's own climax struck and he cried out against Travis's mouth, his body still but for the fine tremors racing over him.

Travis held him, feeling oddly protective and grateful.

And so, so tired.

Barnaby went limp, sliding to Travis's side, still holding him. Travis's mind was blank. His chest loose. His eyes heavy.

He was vaguely aware of Barnaby leaving the bed, startled back out of sleep when a damp cloth was run over his belly and cock. He reached for Barnaby, dragging him back into the bed. Barnaby's laughter was sweet and quiet and Travis smiled. He tucked Barnaby close and curled around him, Barnaby's ass in his lap and both his arms wrapped around Barnaby's chest.

"This is nice," Barnaby murmured, burrowing closer.

"Hmmm..." It was the best Travis could do.

"I do rather have to breathe, though, at some point this evening."

Travis loosened his grip a fraction, and Barnaby took a deep breath. They were both asleep by the time he finished letting it out.

Chapter Fifteen

Barnaby lounged on Travis's couch two weeks later, stretched out in the morning sun and wallowing in it. He'd moved twice already, shifting with the light, sure to get as much as possible on the black cotton of his *Hockey is Importanter* shirt. That, the heavy flannel pajama bottoms he'd annexed from Travis, along with these wondrous things called SmartWool socks he'd been given by Rupert, and he was feeling nice and warm. By no stretch of the imagination could one say he was *enjoying* the winter here, but he'd found ways to cope that he did enjoy.

He shifted again, this time landing against Travis, who was slouched at one end of the couch with his legs stretched out on the coffee table. Barnaby folded his legs beneath him, leaning into Travis more.

"You're like a damn cat," Travis said with a laugh, reaching up to stroke Barnaby's hair.

If Barnaby could purr, he would. As it was, he ducked his head against Travis's palm, helping his fingers scrub through Barnaby's curls.

He'd woken up with Travis half on top of him this morning, his erection pressed to the bed, Travis's pressed to his bum. He still wasn't sure if Travis had been completely awake by the time Barnaby had brought them both to orgasm.

No complaints had been filed, though.

He thought he might like to go again, and that Travis might be ready as well. For all his grousing about being old, he seemed more than able to keep up with Barnaby.

He closed his eyes, steeped in the pleasure of Travis's slow, steady scratch against his scalp. Maybe he'd do this for a while longer, then get a cold pack for Travis's shoulder, since Barnaby was making him hold his arm at an odd angle. That sounded good, too.

His phone buzzed on the table and he ignored it.

Travis leaned forward, forcing Barnaby to shift with him as he reached for Barnaby's phone. Barnaby frowned and pressed closer.

"Definitely like a cat." Travis laughed. "And your call is from an international number. You should probably answer it."

Barnaby hummed, refusing to open his eyes. "Then you do it."

"What?"

"Go ahead. Answer it if you must, but I have no intention of doing so."

Travis laughed, then the git said, "Hello?"

Barnaby's eyes popped open.

"Hello?" a confused voice said. "Is that you, Barnsy?"

Long distance and over speakerphone or not, Barnaby knew that voice. "Hello, Robert. This is unexpected."

Travis jolted at the name, his hand freezing in Barnaby's hair. Barnaby considered grabbing his phone and making the call private, but he didn't want to give Robert even that much effort.

"How are you, darling?" Robert asked. "It's so good to hear your voice."

Barnaby blinked, wondering if he was hallucinating. "It is?"

"Don't be ridiculous, of course it is. How are you? Tell me what you've been doing."

Barnaby shook his head in some combination of wonder and dismay. Travis's arm dropped around his shoulders and pulled him in tight, pressing his lips to Barnaby's hair.

Barnaby's throat tightened up even as his spine firmed with resolve. "I'm well. I'm enjoying being back at university very much."

"University? Darling, where are you? Back at Oxford?"

Did literally none of their mutual acquaintances tell him anything? Had he even asked? Barnaby was still on social media with some of them, for fuck's sake. And none of that was nearly

194

so damning as Robert's obvious surprise that Barnaby had resumed his studies. It had always been his dream.

Barnaby cleared his throat and kept his voice even. "I'm in New Brunswick, actually. Moncton."

"I beg your pardon?"

"That's in Canada," Barnaby added, turning enough to see Travis's lips twitch. The last of his shock dissipated and Barnaby recognized this was very likely a waste of their time. They could be doing far more interesting things. "Robert, why have you called?"

"Don't be like that, darling," Robert cajoled, and Barnaby wondered if Robert had always been so whiny. Barnaby feared the answer was yes. He'd been a terrible idiot. "I wanted to catch up. I miss you."

Travis met Barnaby's eyes, transparently concerned for Barnaby. He needn't be. Barnaby felt remarkably little, save embarrassment. He didn't love Robert. Not anymore. And at some point in the last couple months, even the sadness over having given over so much of his life and love to this man for so many years had faded.

Listening to Robert's wheedling, Barnaby realized quite suddenly that, somehow, after all that Robert had done, perhaps *because* of it, Barnaby had ended up where he was supposed to be.

"You miss me?" he repeated, because it was frankly absurd and bore repeating. He didn't bother to keep his skepticism from his face or his tone.

Travis's concern faded, replaced with cautious amusement.

"Of course I do. We had so many good years together, Barnsy, and I know I ruined everything. I've been thinking about it a lot recently. I made so many huge mistakes."

Barnaby rolled his eyes, pleased when Travis smiled. Barnaby knew Robert well enough to know he wanted something—Barnaby didn't know or care what. He had the shocking notion it might be reconciliation Robert was after, but the very idea made Barnaby want to laugh. He didn't even know what to say.

He decided on the truth. "You did make a lot of mistakes, Robert."

"I know, baby. I'm sorry. I'm sure I can't even remember them all, but I'm sorry for each one."

"I can help you remember, if you'd like. There was Bryan. And Michael. Robbie, which particularly stung, given he and I worked together. Oh, and never let us forget Joel. I seem to recall you saying he was hung like a bull, isn't that right? How could you possibly have said no? You actually asked me that. Does that jog the memory?"

A snort escaped Travis, then he looked appalled with himself.

Robert had the gall to be indignant. "There's no reason to be bitchy, Barnaby. You know they meant nothing to me."

"Nor, it seems, did I."

"No!" Robert cried. "I love you. I just got lost. It was so stressful, making the company, the performances every night. But now I see I've ruined everything. It was all better when you were here."

"I'm sure it was. I paid the rent, had dinner on the table, cleaned up after you—"

"God, you're so *angry*," Robert said. "You need to let that go. It will eat you up inside."

Now Barnaby did laugh, both at Robert's ridiculousness and the look of outrage on Travis's face.

"I appreciate your concern," Barnaby said dryly. "If you want to help, you could always help pay off the massive debt I foolishly accumulated while trying to help you launch your career, and to which you have not yet contributed a penny."

"I'm not responsible for your choices, Barnaby," Robert said. Scolded, really.

"*Unbelievable*," Travis muttered.

"What was that?" Robert snapped. "Is someone there with you?"

Barnaby pressed a finger to Travis's lips, then smothered his laughter when Travis caught his wrist and tried to lick him.

"Robert," he said as sternly as he could manage, "I forgive you."

Travis froze.

"You do?" Robert asked, and to his credit, he sounded bewildered.

"Yes. You're weak, and remarkably lazy, and selfish to boot. I knew that and chose to ignore it. That's on me. The cheating, however, is on you, and I shan't forgive it. I'm not angry, and nothing is eating me up." He suppressed his snort when Travis dropped his eyes to Barnaby's cock and waggled his eyebrows. "But unless you've suddenly become the sort of reasonable and responsible adult who can see he ought to be helping me pay off my debts, I haven't a lot to say."

"I have become no such thing," Robert announced.

"I didn't believe it for a moment," Barnaby assured him. "Do take care, Robert. Send my best to your friends who I once thought were also mine. You can tell them I've learned better, and that I'm happier for it."

Robert was still spluttering when Barnaby tapped the red button on his screen.

Travis couldn't *not* kiss Barnaby the second he hung up on Robert. It was hard to believe anyone as sweet, and thoughtful, and brilliant as Barnaby would ever give a twat like that the time of day.

The kiss was lingering but still mostly sweet. Travis didn't think now was the time to start anything, but he'd wanted to express, somehow, how proud he was of Barnaby.

Of course, words worked too, but they were so *hard*.

"You're amazing," he said when they broke apart, because it was never too late to grow as a human being.

"Thank you," Barnaby said, bemused. "Why?"

"Because that can't have been nearly as easy as you made it

sound. You were a lot nicer than he deserves. I want to find that guy and punch him in the face."

Barnaby grinned up at Travis. "Well, I hope you never have the chance, as that would likely mean my path had crossed Robert's, and I have no desire to ever see him again."

"I don't blame you. He sounds like an..." It occurred to Travis too late that perhaps this was an opinion he should keep to himself.

"He's an arse. You can say it," Barnaby said with a shrug.

"I'm not going to argue." Travis shook his head recalling Robert's behavior, consigning it and him to hell. There was some other stuff that had come up, though, that Travis wanted to ask about.

"I can see you practically gagging to say something." Barnaby poked him with a pointy elbow. "Out with it."

"Barnsy?" he asked with a smirk.

Barnaby rolled his eyes. "Please, he used to call me Nubsy in bed. Those are only two of a long list of horrible nicknames for Barnaby."

Nubsy, Travis mouthed, bewildered. He didn't let go, his arms still tight around Barnaby, his eyes searching Barnaby's face.

"Go on. You can ask," Barnaby said, nudging him more gently.

"Your friends. Did they all choose Robert's side when you split or something? I mean, he's the one who cheated."

"They chose his side long before that. Most of them knew about the other men. Some of them *were* the other men. And not one of them told me. A coworker caught Robert out with someone else and had the courage to tell me."

"That takes some stones," Travis observed.

"It does. I'll always be grateful to her. Then I started asking, and it was embarrassingly easy to uncover the truth, which ended up being far worse than I anticipated. I reckon I still don't know the full extent. By the time I had a list of five names, I was more concerned about packing my things and getting tested for everything under the sun than I was about the details."

Travis could imagine the fear. "And your friends?"

"They weren't, were they? They weren't my friends. Robert was careful, thank god, but they didn't know that, had no way to be certain, and let me be put at terrible risk—*repeatedly*—never mind the humiliation of them all knowing. So I left. Not just Robert, but the whole damn lot of them."

Travis pressed his lips to Barnaby's hair. "I'm sorry." It was totally inadequate.

Barnaby sighed, but it didn't sound sad. More like relief. "You're not like that. Like them."

"I'm not," he vowed.

"And Jack isn't either. Nor Grady."

"No. You're right. They're loyal by nature, and they care a great deal about you, so they're protective, too."

"That's nice to hear," Barnaby admitted. He picked up his phone from Travis's thigh and fiddled with it, pausing when the screen lit up. He sighed again. "I have to get going. I need to run home before I hold office hours this evening."

Travis nodded, holding Barnaby close for another minute before forcing himself to let go. He stayed where he was and watched Barnaby pack up before he disappeared into the bedroom. He reappeared a couple minutes later in his own clothes. He'd taken to leaving the t-shirt Travis had given him folded on the chair in the bedroom with the pajama bottoms he favored. Travis never touched them, unless it was to toss them in the laundry with his clothes, and then he'd fold them and put them back.

He refused to dwell on why it made him happy to do so.

Barnaby came back to the couch and Travis hauled himself to his feet to pull Barnaby in for a long, slow kiss. Barnaby returned it eagerly, cupping the back of Travis's head and leaning in close.

"I'll miss you," Barnaby said when he took a step back.

Travis felt something give in his chest—a fist he hadn't realized had been lodged beneath his ribs his entire adult life. Whatever it released spread through his body, warming him from the inside out and setting down roots.

"I'll be back before you know it," he said, and felt stupid because what he wanted to say was *I'll miss you, too.* But he couldn't. He shouldn't.

But, holy shit, he *wanted to.*

Barnaby didn't appear to think anything of his cowardly answer, smiling happily as he pulled on his winter gear and threw his bags over his shoulder.

With a final wave, he was gone.

Travis stood in the middle of this living room, dithering like a complete idiot for a solid ten minutes before his exasperation won and he threw himself into cleaning his apartment. He tried to watch the video package his coach had sent out, but he couldn't sit still, so he focused on packing for his road trip, which took a sum total of ten minutes.

Fuck, why was he so fidgety? His apartment felt empty, his skin twitchy.

A soft thump issued from below his feet and inspiration struck. He had his coat on and was out the door before considering that calling ahead would be the polite thing to do.

Fuck it.

He knocked on Grady's door. A lot.

Grady called out, "Hold your damn horses!"

Maybe he'd been a little enthusiastic. Travis tucked his hands in his pockets while he waited. When the door flew open, he blinked at a shirtless Grady. His skin shone with perspiration, highlighting every ridge and muscle in his chest. There were a lot of them to see, particularly because his basketball shorts barely clung to his narrow hips.

"Goddamn, dude. You're *ripped.*"

Grady rolled his eyes. "Look who's talking, Mr. Professional Athlete."

"Yeah, but you can see how hot I am even when I have clothes on."

Grady laughed. "Asshole. I'm plenty hot with or without clothes. Wanna see?"

Travis slumped. "Would you take it personally if I said no?"

"Is there a reason you look sad about that?"

Travis thought about how to answer, then chickened out and asked, "You want to get an early dinner?"

Grady eyed him, no doubt seeing right through Travis's nerviness. "Sure."

Travis waited on the couch while Grady put away the free weights he'd been working with and excused himself to shower and change.

They decided on Chinese food and the House of Lau by shouting at each other through the bedroom door while Grady got dressed. It wasn't like the upstairs neighbor was going to complain, and since the downstairs neighbor was either never home or never *left* home and had never been heard from once, Travis wasn't much worried about him either.

The walk to the restaurant was short and they walked quickly, their faces buried in their coats. Travis could picture the gasp of outrage Barnaby would have given when he stepped outside earlier and he was grateful his scarf hid his face so he didn't have to explain his smile to Grady.

God, he was a mess.

House of Lau was a welcome distraction from his thoughts. They settled into a booth and ordered, then chatted with the owner, a friend of Grady's named Brian.

"You're almost as bad as Jack," Travis teased once they were alone. "Between the two of you, you know everyone in this city."

"Hardly," Grady said, turning his dark, serious eyes on Travis. "But I know you."

"Yeah?" Travis said nervously.

"What's wrong?"

"Nothing." He said it way too quickly to be convincing.

201

Grady arched an eyebrow. "Is it school?"

"No, school is good. I mean, I'm not flunking so I'm doing better than I probably should."

Grady rolled his eyes. "Shut up. You kicked ass with that haiku."

Travis had tried to forget that he'd recited the damn thing to his friends. "Oh. Uh...thanks. It wasn't that hard."

Grady sat back and eyed Travis. "You're a pretty clever guy," he observed.

"What? No, come on. I—"

"Write haikus that get As and impress beautiful men."

Travis's mouth hung open for a second before he snapped it shut, because he couldn't refute any of that, but that didn't stop him from wanting to wave it away. "It was one poem," he muttered.

"I bet you could write another if you needed to."

Grady's confidence was flattering, but he was uncomfortably close to a truth Travis hadn't shared with anyone. "Yeah, maybe that's my savant skill. Poems about jockstraps."

Grady laughed, then circled his hand in the air, as if to say *go ahead.*

"What?" Travis asked with a nervous laugh.

"Do it. Tell me, what rhymes with *athletic supporter?*"

The answer was *nothing good*, which Travis knew because he had taken to noodling out little limericks to his fucking jockstrap. Goddamn Barnaby for making what had once been an innocuous piece of equipment into something so sexually charged. He still had to wear the damn things for work, and god knew he wasn't going to play hockey with an erection, but there were times he could barely control his errant thoughts.

The poems were less about that, though, and more about thinking up ways to make Barnaby smile. He couldn't forget the proud and happy look on Barnaby's face when he'd heard that stupid haiku.

It may come as a bit of a shock
If given a choice of a helmet or jock
I'd choose that fantastic
Small piece of plastic
That stops pucks from hitting my cock

Travis hadn't intentionally waited until Grady was drinking tea before reciting his stupid limerick, but he wasn't sorry when it almost came back out his friend's nose.

Grady coughed to clear his sinuses, then cracked up. "Oh my god, that's amazing."

"Like I said, my savant skill. In all other things, I'm a fucking idiot."

Travis was spared a response by the delivery of their appetizers. He focused on his soup, thinking about ways to change the subject since he was pretty sure they'd managed all the awkward either of them could take.

When he looked up, Grady was ignoring his dumplings and watching Travis.

"You know," Grady began, painfully serious, "your intelligence has never once been in doubt, even when I've called you a fucking idiot. And Barnaby is a smart guy, too, so if he says you're a good student, I believe him. No amount of poems about your dick or adjacent equipment is going to fool anyone who knows you."

"Oh. Uh. Okay," Travis said.

"So maybe you could stop pretending you don't enjoy school and that you're not good at it. Give your friends the benefit of the doubt."

Travis swallowed hard. "Yeah. I can do that."

"Good," Grady said with a nod before picking up a dumpling with his chopsticks.

Travis went back to his soup, thinking about what Grady had said. Something about it wouldn't sit right, and he couldn't let it go. It took him a while to figure out what it was, though. And when he did, he mostly felt angry with himself for falling into the same old trap.

"It's not you," he said.

Grady finished chewing. "What's not me?"

"It wasn't about faith in you or Barnaby or Jack. The jokes about school, especially. I never thought I'd go back to school, let alone like it. I think maybe I'm still having a hard time convincing myself it's true."

"You've been taking classes for a couple years now, haven't you?"

"I have, and I'm lucky I got this far."

Grady glared at him. "Did we not just cover this?"

"No, I mean, I'm lucky I stuck with it, since I didn't have any faith in *myself* about school. Not before."

"But now you do?"

Travis smiled. "I do."

"I bet I know the answer to this, but what's changed?" Grady asked before taking a bite of dumpling.

Travis gave the simplest answer he could come up with. "Poetry."

Grady's eyes widened with surprise. "The stuff really speaks to you, huh?"

Travis laughed. "No, actually." Though that wasn't strictly true. When Barnaby read it to him, his voice passionate and his eyes alive with the excitement he felt for the words, it spoke to Travis in ways he could barely wrap his head around. "This class is fucking hard, and half the time I still don't know what the hell I'm reading or doing."

"So how does poetry mean you believe you're into school?"

"Because if I wasn't, this class would have made me quit." Travis laughed, shaking his head. "Seriously, I'm dazed and confused by this shit half the time, but I still like learning about it. It's different, and interesting, even if it's not going to be my life's work. Or, hell, have a single damn thing to do with what I do with my life."

The standard flutter of nerves kicked off in his chest at the mere allusion to the future.

Grady smirked. "So, it doesn't have anything to do with your insanely hot tutor?"

"He's definitely helped," Travis agreed.

Grady threw his head back and laughed. "My bedroom is right under yours, bud. You don't need to tell me about all the help you give each other."

The idea was horrifying, but he also knew Grady was kidding. Or, at least he was pretty sure. *God*, he hoped so. Travis still kicked him under the table for form's sake. "I don't just mean because we're...you know, friends with benefits. He comes over to do his schoolwork a lot when I'm not on the road, even when I don't need him to tutor me. It's been great. I had a really hard time in school when I was kid, but sitting there with Barnaby, I get how, for a lot of kids, homework was normal. Even fun, sometimes, when it was an excuse to hang out with friends. For me, it was a constant nightmare I had to get through before I went out on the ice again. But he always calls it my homework when I'm watching the video packages for the team, and I get it. I've been doing homework and studying for hockey most of my life, and now I'm doing it for school, and not dreading every second of it. I think he's been really good for me."

The x-ray stare was back, and this time Travis couldn't meet it.

"I think he's been good for you, too," Grady observed, his gentle voice making Travis want to hide under the table. "But, dude? That shit doesn't sound like friends with benefits."

"It is. It has to be."

"Are you sure?"

If anyone had asked him that before the last month, he would have said *definitely yes*. But now?

He put his spoon down on the table, his appetite lost. "I'm so fucked."

"You want to talk about it?"

"No."

Grady accepted this with a nod, returning to his dumplings and letting the silence gather around them. It felt like it was pressing down on Travis, forcing the words up out of him.

"I've got *feelings*," Travis blurted, appalled with himself but unable to stop, "and they're just as fucking terrible and amazing as everyone always said they were, but there's nothing I can do except swallow them down and pretend they don't exist."

Silence hung heavy around them once Travis finally stopped spewing out the horrifying truth.

Grady wore a sad, sympathetic smile. "I get it."

Travis blinked, because never once had Grady hinted at what Barnaby and Travis suspected.

He took a chance and asked, "Jack?"

Grady's eyes dropped to his food and he focused on picking up the next dumpling before he nodded, once.

Before Travis could come up with any kind of response—not that he had any fucking idea what he was going to say—the food arrived and Grady saved them both by inviting Brian Lau to sit with them for a drink.

Chapter Sixteen

O my luve's like a red, red rose,
That's newly sprung in June;
O my luve's like the melodie
That's sweetly played in tune...

Travis sat tucked in the corner of his row of seats on the bus, happily alone for the ride home. It had been a hectic couple of days on the road and he hadn't gotten much in the way of schoolwork done. He wasn't behind, but he was still hoping to get some work done before he got home.

Tomorrow he had a day off, and no practice until the following afternoon. Breaks like this were rare in the season, and this was the last one. Travis intended to spend as much of that time as possible with Barnaby. The endless possibilities of *how* they could spend that time stretched out before him, and he was determined to have schoolwork distract them as little as possible.

Barnaby might have been feeling the same way, since the recordings of the poems they were reviewing that week arrived via text shortly after the bus had departed Moncton. In hindsight, Travis wished he'd listened to them sooner. Robert Burns was a bitch to read, but he could listen to Barnaby recite these poems all day. He'd actually sent two recordings of each one: one in his usual accent, and one in a Scottish accent Barnaby said would help explain how and why Burns had chosen the words he had.

Travis did like the sound of the Scottish accent, and it did help Burns' spelling make sense, but he didn't think there was much explanation needed when it came to the actual poems. He'd been listening to *A Red, Red Rose*, over and over, and he got it.

Oh boy, did he get it.

He hit play again and stared out the window, watching the

snowy fields fly by. He was startled when someone cleared their throat behind him. Travis yanked out his earbuds and turned to see Rupert standing in the aisle.

He held out an envelope. "Barnaby asked me to pass this along to you once we were on the way home."

Travis shrugged, took the envelope, ripped it open, and tugged out the card. He got an impression of flowers and hearts before he finally got it turned around and could read the fancy script emblazoned across the front of the greeting card.

THE HONOR OF YOUR PRESENCE IS REQUESTED IN MY PANTS.

Travis slapped the card against his chest and a hysterical laugh gurgled out.

Rupert looked *deeply* unimpressed.

"Uh...thanks. For giving me this," Travis blurted, still clutching the card to his sternum like a strand of pearls. He hoped like hell Rupert hadn't seen *any* of it.

"You're welcome," Rupert said, though he looked like he regretted it as he went back to his seat a few rows ahead of Travis.

Travis took a few deep breaths, trying to get his heart rate back to normal before peeling the card off his chest and grinning down at it.

Wondering what possible message could be inside, he flipped it open. He caught the picture as it slid from the card, then his heart rate, and his breathing, were shot to hell again.

Jesus fucking Christ, Barnaby was crazy. He was also *naked*, sprawled on Travis's bed in the sunlight, his cock in hand, the dark pink head peeking out from the foreskin and Barnaby's fingers. He was fucking stunning, his skin like alabaster in the bright light, but it was his smile, wicked and knowing, that absolutely killed Travis.

On the inside of the card, he'd written, *Hurry home.*

It felt like a punch to the gut, seeing Barnaby stretched out across the bed they'd shared so many times over the past weeks, and knowing he was there, waiting for Travis to come home.

Home.

For the first time since he'd left his parents' house almost twenty years before, Travis thought he knew what that meant. What it *could* mean. If only he wasn't...him.

But he was, and feeling sorry for himself because he got to do his most favorite thing in the world and be paid for it was fucking ridiculous. Particularly when he had a truly beautiful man waiting for him to come and join him.

Hurry home. Fucking hell, if Travis could toss the driver out of his seat and take over, he would. He'd break every speed limit between there and Moncton to get there faster.

He shifted in his seat, willing his cock to stand down as the miles ticked slowly by. He was achingly conscious of his jockstrap—bright blue cotton with black elastic, worn in anticipation of seeing Barnaby—and how it cupped his burgeoning erection. He couldn't stop looking at the card. And the picture. After the first dozen times, though, he started laughing. God, Barnaby was such an asshole. He had to know what kind of torture this would be, and to have *Rupert* give him the card? Travis hadn't appreciated before just how devious Barnaby was.

It was the longest two hours of his *life* getting back to the Moncton Arena. He climbed over teammates and friends to get off the bus as quickly as possible, jogging to his car with a wave over his shoulder to those asking if they'd see him at Quigley's that night.

Not fucking likely.

He drove to his apartment on auto-pilot, and he wasn't going to win any awards for the half-assed parking job he did out front. He was bounding up the stairs and digging out his keys before he thought to wonder if he'd locked the car. Or closed the car door, for that matter.

None of which slowed him down.

He walked directly from his front door—which he *did* make sure was locked—toward the bedroom, dropping his bag and shedding his clothes as he went. He arrived naked, except for his jockstrap, which barely managed to contain his erection. He stumbled to a halt at the door and found Barnaby propped up in bed, just as bare as he'd been in the picture. Same smile, same gorgeous pink cockhead peeking out from his fingers.

Barnaby gave him a long look, eyes dropping all the way to Travis's feet before dragging back up again, with extra attention paid to his straining jockstrap. Based on how Barnaby's fingers tightened around his cock, he liked what he saw.

"I got your card," Travis said. He felt lightheaded with anticipation, and something like relief.

This was where he was supposed to be. The only place he wanted to be.

Barnaby held out his hand. "Come here."

Travis didn't run to the bed, but it was a near thing, and he definitely jumped onto the mattress hard enough to make Barnaby bounce—and laugh.

Travis swallowed the sound with a kiss.

He was in no mood to ease into things. Warm-ups were over. Hell, warm-ups had been going on for *weeks* and now it was game time. He knew what he wanted, and he was going to ask for it.

Just as soon as he took his tongue out of Barnaby's mouth.

Barnaby beat him to it. "Can we, tonight? Is there time?" He drew Travis back in for another long, hot kiss, and Travis shivered when Barnaby's palm skimmed over his bare ass. "I want to be inside of you. So much."

Travis nodded, wrapped his hands around both sides of Barnaby's head, and plunging his tongue into every corner of his mouth. Travis had to screw his eyes shut and remind himself to breathe through the swell of happiness.

He was doing a lousy job of hiding the emotions driving him, but he couldn't stop touching Barnaby. Kissing Barnaby. He'd just have to hope Barnaby would attribute it all to nerves or eagerness, because those were true, too.

The kiss ended with a mutual gasp, and Barnaby shoved at Travis, pushing him down on the bed and kneeling above him. His smile was wicked and fierce, distracting Travis so he wasn't prepared for those long, hot fingers to curl around his cock.

"I love that you're wearing this," Barnaby said, hooking a finger in the elastic of the jockstrap and tugging.

Travis had been wearing one more often than not since Barnaby had told him that was what he wanted. But in case Barnaby didn't know, Travis said, "For you."

Travis was rewarded with a gentle stroke of those fingers along his cock, maddeningly separated from Barnaby's touch by the cotton, except where the head poked out. When Barnaby circled his palm over that exposed flesh, Travis shuddered and realized the extra layer was probably for the best.

His eyes fluttered shut, rolling back in his head as Barnaby teased him, again and again, with the rub of his palm. That was it. Just four square inches of flesh, total, touching each other and Travis was ready to blow.

He jumped, his eyes flashing open, when Barnaby tapped his hip.

"Up."

Travis sat up. "Where am I going?"

"Over," Barnaby added with a smile.

Travis flipped onto his knees. He didn't ask what Barnaby meant. Didn't feel one ounce of concern or regret or shame as he laid his chest on the bed and left his ass in the air.

Barnaby slid his hand under the pillow and came up with a fresh bottle of lube, then crawled behind Travis, a hand pressed to his back to steady them both.

They'd spent a whole lot of the past month with Barnaby's fingers in Travis's butt, which had been a revelation to Travis, because if he'd been asked before this winter if he was into being fingered, he'd probably have shrugged and said it was okay.

It was way fucking better than okay. It was amazing. All it

took was Barnaby pointing out something on his laptop screen, and Travis would flash back to when he'd come screaming from little more than two of those long, magnificent fingers manipulating his prostate like it was their calling.

He swallowed back a moan when a single finger dragged over his hole. He was prepared to beg to move things along. Barnaby was always so careful with him, always sure to use plenty of lube, so until he took up the bottle still on the bed next to Travis's knee, Barnaby was just going to *tease*.

Or not.

The warm, wet swipe of Barnaby's tongue over his hole stopped Travis's heart.

Oh god. They'd never done this before. *No one* had done this before.

Barnaby swirled his tongue over Travis's hole, teasing the thousands of nerve endings to attention and sending Travis's mind spinning. A string of kisses, some sweet, some with a nip of teeth, worked their way along his perineum until Barnaby's lips were pushing aside his jock and nestled behind his balls.

When Barnaby pulled back, Travis wanted to scream with need.

"This okay?"

"Yes," Travis gasped. "God, yes. Please. That feels amazing. I didn't—"

Barnaby's fingers dug into his ass, spreading him open to run his lips up the seam of skin from Travis's balls to his hole. Every hair on Travis's body stood on end.

"You didn't what?" Barnaby murmured against the slope of one cheek.

"I didn't *know*," Travis said, his voice trailing to an embarrassing whine. "I didn't know it would feel like this."

As if to prove his point, Barnaby returned his devoted attention to Travis's rim, licking over it, getting it wet and warm. There was something so inherently naughty and delicious about the act that it made Travis's belly quiver and his legs spread wider on the bed. He clenched his muscles against the press of lips and tongue, and it was Barnaby moaning, his fingers digging into the flesh of Travis's ass, keeping him open.

"Your arse is fucking magnificent. How is it so..."

"Big?" Travis said with a breathless laugh. "It's the skating."

"I could eat it for days."

Travis smashed his face to the bed, no idea what to say to that. *Yes, please?*

It seemed he didn't have to say anything. Barnaby lavished attention on Travis's body. From the base of his balls to the divots at the small of his back, no inch of skin was left untended, no nerve-ending left dormant. Kisses, licks, and bites tantalized and sensitized, and with each pass, Barnaby focused longer on the tight pucker of muscles, until Barnaby was stabbing his tongue into Travis and Travis was shouting Barnaby's name, certain the ferocious pounding of his heart could be heard for miles.

Barnaby's tongue retreated, to be replaced immediately by a finger.

"Fucking hell," Travis growled. "More. I want more." He'd learned, with Barnaby's help, that he liked the stretch of multiple fingers, two or even three. One just wasn't enough.

The very tip of a second finger wedged in next to the first, but no farther. "This is all I can do without lube," Barnaby said, licking around his fingers and dipping his tongue between them.

Travis hummed. The little licks making him shiver, the stretch sending a zing straight up his spine. "Then use the lube."

Barnaby didn't answer, too busy driving Travis out of his mind.

His cock leaked into the soft cotton of the jockstrap, his balls drawn up. Arousal consumed him, made his thoughts slow and his body ache. He wanted to come, so much, but he didn't want to do it until Barnaby was inside him.

On a particularly deft stab of tongue, Travis went against every instinct screaming at him to shove himself back and fell forward onto the bed instead. He grunted when Barnaby's fingers and tongue slipped out of him.

"Are you okay?" Barnaby asked, climbing over him to peer down at his face with concern.

Travis took a couple deep breaths, waiting to answer until he could hear his breathing over his heartbeat.

"I'm okay. But I was close, and I didn't want to come."

"No?"

Travis rolled over onto his back. "Unless you've changed your mind about fucking me?"

"Never," Barnaby said with a smile, carding his fingers into Travis's hair and pushing it back from his forehead.

Travis's heart twisted painfully in his chest. He wished, stupidly, for a camera to capture what Barnaby looked like at this moment, so he could take the image with him everywhere he went once he left Moncton.

Maybe it was indelibly burned into his memories even without a picture.

He wrapped an arm around Barnaby, pulling him closer. Just before they kissed, he whispered, "Get the fucking lube and open me up. Please."

The kiss was messy, mostly because Travis was laughing at Barnaby patting down the bed—flailing, really—to find the bottle. The tension leaked out of Travis's shoulders and back, the ache in his chest easing, with Barnaby curled over him and laughter pressed into every kiss.

He hadn't done this in a long time, but by god, he wanted to. More than he wanted anything. And he wanted it to be with Barnaby.

Barnaby clowned around a little, delighting in Travis's laughter while he searched for the lube, noting how it brightened Travis's eyes and eased the rigidity in his shoulders.

Then he got down to the very serious business of fucking Travis.

He wasn't going to rush, in spite of the urgency that rode him hard, but he also wasn't going to tease. Not any longer. Travis wanted it, Barnaby wanted it, and he had come to know Travis's body as well as his own over the last weeks.

That was why he slid two lube-coated fingers into Travis, thrusting them deep, without any hesitation.

Travis arched against the bed, his shout happy and hoarse. The huge muscles of his gigantic skater's bum clamped around Barnaby's fingers, but the pucker of smaller muscles let him in willingly, clinging as he thrust slowly, unfailingly, in and out.

He feasted on the stubbled skin along Travis's jawline, loving his smell under the unfamiliar scent of soap from the arena he'd left earlier that day. Travis tilted his head back, a silent request for more and Barnaby happily obliged, working his way to the point of his chin and down until he could set his teeth around Travis's Adam's apple.

Travis groaned, his body loose and warm against Barnaby. He hated to have to pull away, but he managed to add more lube in a heartbeat before returning to lavish attention to each of Travis's nipples. In the middle of his journey between one and the other, he slipped a third finger inside Travis.

"Please, B," he whined.

Barnaby smiled at the nickname. Travis had tried *Nubsy* exactly twice, then decided he wanted to have sex with Barnaby, *ever*, more than he wanted to amuse himself with dreadful nicknames.

Ignoring Travis's plea was easy, but Barnaby refused to be rushed, even if his arm shook with the desire to thrust further, faster. Travis could take it. Travis *would* take it, cheerfully, as they'd proven time and again. A twist of the wrist and a crook of the fingers, and Barnaby could get him to the point where his cock leaked constantly, the veins pronounced, the crown flushed from pink to red. From there, it took hardly a brush of his lips to make Travis come.

But not tonight.

Tonight, he pushed his fingers in, nice and deep, and then

spread them open.

Travis clutched Barnaby's back as he rode out the stretch. There was a dark spot on the bright blue cotton of his underwear already, so Barnaby was careful not to hit his prostate. Not yet.

He eased his fingers back out and watched Travis's chest deflate, a long breath released slowly. Then he pushed them in again to see Travis's spine arch, his toes curl, his mouth drop open. He was fucking stunning like this, and he gazed up at Barnaby like he was wondrous.

It made Barnaby a little crazy. "I'm so glad to be here. To be here with you," he said, gazing at Travis sprawled out across the bed, wrecked.

"Me, too," Travis gasped. "I'm glad you're here, too." Barnaby couldn't help but grin, which made Travis roll his eyes. "And not just because you're awfully fucking good at this."

His body had already given into Barnaby's demands, opening for him beautifully, but Barnaby was determined to keep going.

Travis's hand cupping his cheek stilled him. "Now."

Barnaby opened his mouth and found he had not one argument. He wanted to be in Travis more than he wanted to draw his next breath. He wanted to be connected with this man in the most intimate way he could think of.

He eased his fingers free of Travis's body and nudged his hip. "Over, again."

Travis sat up, bringing their faces close. Barnaby couldn't stop himself from kissing Travis. Not just now, either. It was a constant battle.

When they broke apart, Travis hesitated.

"What's wrong?" Barnaby asked gently.

"Nothing's wrong. I just like looking at you." He smiled, a sweet and self-deprecating thing.

Barnaby drew in a long, steadying breath even as his heart cracked in two and attempted to fall from his chest into Travis's hands. He kissed Travis again to give himself a moment.

And because he wanted to.

When he pulled back, Travis's smile was far cockier. He rolled onto his hands and knees, wriggling his delicious backside at Barnaby.

"Tart," Barnaby said affectionately, running his hands over all that glorious skin and muscle. When Travis wiggled again, Barnaby snapped one of the elastics. "Behave."

Travis laughed, the sound choking off when Barnaby slid two fingers back in. Travis felt just as ready as he had before, but Barnaby told himself he had to check, not that he was hesitating. Not that he was afraid of how what came next would affect him. He'd never wanted something more, but he wasn't foolish enough to pretend it wasn't going to have a cost, too.

One, it seemed, he was infinitely willing to pay.

He knee-walked over the covers, his hand on Travis's hip, steadying him as they sorted out legs and feet and knees in the universal dance between lovers. Barnaby couldn't stop running his hand over every inch of bare skin he could reach, soothing himself as much as Travis. He ran his palm up the trench of Travis's spine.

Travis bent his elbows and pressed his face to the bedding. "*Please.*"

"Yes," Barnaby murmured, slicking his cock with lube, grateful it was cold, as even the touch of his own hand was too much right then. He held his shaft and settled the other hand over the twin dimples at the base of Travis's spine, pressing down gently. Travis's knees slid across the mattress, canting his hips and lowering his ass without question. Barnaby's head spun at the sight of Travis spreading himself open. At the trust.

He rubbed the head of his cock over the pucker of muscles, spreading the lube around, and watched Travis clench. Then relax.

Barnaby pressed forward.

"*Fuuuuck,*" Travis groaned, his shoulders rounding as he pulled his arms beneath him and tipped his ass up farther.

Barnaby bit his tongue as the puckered skin smoothed out,

the muscles giving beneath, and Travis opened to him.

The crown of Barnaby's cock wedged into unfathomably tight heat, the grip almost painful, but he pushed on. Pushed forward until the head popped into Travis and the ring of muscle clamped around Barnaby's shaft.

They both froze. Panting. Barnaby noted how his hand trembled as he drew it away from his cock and curled his fingers around Travis's hip.

"You okay?" Travis asked, his head turned, his face smashed to the sheets, his eyes closed.

He's asking me? Then again, maybe he had the right of it, as Barnaby couldn't seem to string together even the most basic of sentences.

It took a couple of tries before he managed to say, "I'm fine."

The one eyebrow Barnaby could see arched. "Fine?"

Barnaby curled over Travis's back, wanting to be closer. To feel the warmth of his skin as he gently rocked his hips forward, making them both gasp.

"God, I'm good. This is good," he groaned, nudging his hips forward.

"*Good?*" Travis asked, indignant.

Laughter bubbled up. Barnaby pressed his smile against Travis's skin and pushed, forcing more of his cock into Travis. He was so fucking tight it was a fight for every inch, a battle Barnaby didn't know if he would survive. He very nearly choked on his own tongue when his cock sank farther into Travis.

Still, he kept his voice bland. "This is very nice."

"*NICE?*"

Barnaby's smile grew. "Shall I compare thee to a summer's day?"

It was hard to tell if the groan was due to the poetry or because Barnaby had managed to ease even farther into Travis as he'd spoken the words. He rolled his hips again, setting a rhythm that took him deeper each time.

God, Travis was letting him in. Quicker with every press.

"Thou art more lovely and more temperate," he murmured against Travis's back, running his hands up and down Travis's sides. He might have forgotten to breathe altogether were it not for Shakespeare.

"Temperate," Travis gasped. "That doesn't sound like me." His voice cracked at the end.

Barnaby scrambled for another adjective, but his brain was derailed, focused on one thing only. "Tight?" he asked, adding power to his next thrust. "Is that better?"

"Ungh. More accurate," Travis cried as Barnaby withdrew, Travis's knuckles going white when he clutched at the sheets.

It was Barnaby's only warning before Travis shoved himself back.

Barnaby made a sound that was maybe a laugh. Or a sob. "Eager? Would that work?" He met Travis's next push with one of his own. "Thou art more lovely and more eager?"

Shakespeare was very likely rolling in his grave. Barnaby feared he'd be going to his own soon enough with the way his heart was pounding.

"God, yes," Travis shouted, and it was unclear to Barnaby if that was in reaction to the terrible poetry or the way Barnaby was stretching him open, the wider base of his cock wedging into Travis relentlessly.

Barnaby thrust harder as more adjectives burst into his brain. "Fuck. Hot. Beautiful." With a last, desperate shove, Barnaby seated his cock fully. "*Perfect.*"

He wrapped his arms around Travis's chest, holding him tight as they both panted.

"Fucking hell," Barnaby mumbled, trying to reign in the chaos of his mind and body.

"I'm sure Shakespeare never said *that.*"

Barnaby laughed and even the minute shifts of his cock made Travis groan and Barnaby's head spin. "Well, he never wrote it down, anyway. Are you okay?"

"Yeah. God, *yes.*" He reached back and ran a calloused hand over Barnaby's hip, making him shiver.

"You seem sure," Barnaby teased breathlessly, shifting on purpose this time—just a tiny grind that made Travis's mouth fall open.

"Fuck, do that again."

Far be it for Barnaby to deny Travis anything. He swiveled his hips slowly, luxuriating in the velvety heat pressed all around his cock, in the electric shocks firing from his balls to his toes and out to his fingers.

"God, Barnaby. You have to move."

"I *am* moving," Barnaby said with a roll of his hips that might have been more devastating to him than to Travis, though it sounded like it was a close thing. He peeled himself away from the comfort and warmth of Travis's back, his head clearing marginally from the cool air on his overheated skin.

Travis was flushed beneath him, the sheen of perspiration giving his long, muscular frame a glow.

Shall I compare thee, indeed.

Barnaby curled his hands around Travis's hips, getting a good grip as he spread his knees and planted himself more firmly on the bed. Then he hauled Travis back and thrust his hips forward, their bodies meeting with a firm smack.

"Better?" he asked—needlessly, as Travis's shout of pleasure was ringing in his ears.

He dragged his cock from Travis, slowly, holding his hips still when he tried to speed things up, then pulled them together again.

"Barnaby, please. *Please*," Travis pleaded.

A tremor worked down from the top of Barnaby's head to his balls. Fucking hell.

He didn't try to contain Travis's need to move on the next withdrawal. He didn't try to contain himself either. Their timing was off, the bump of hips uncoordinated and frustrating for the first few thrusts, but then Travis was shoving back and Barnaby was arching forward, and their bodies met with an impact that made them both cry out.

From there, they found their rhythm.

Barnaby held onto Travis's hips and squeezed his eyes shut. The sight of his cock disappearing into Travis's ass, his rim smooth and pink, would be the death of him. The muscles in his back and thighs shook, his balls drawing up. Travis was tight and hot, his cries needy, and the combination was a firestorm in Barnaby's brain.

That was the only excuse he had for what came out of his mouth.

"Rough winds do shake the darling buds of May," he gasped, pulling his knees closer together, changing the angle. "And summer's lease hath all too short a date."

"What?" Travis cried, throwing himself back on Barnaby's cock again, body quaking when the head of Barnaby's cock bumped directly over his prostate.

"Sometimes too hot the eyes of heaven shines," Barnaby groaned.

"I'm not going to last long, either," Travis said.

Barnaby laughed helplessly. Fucking *Shakespeare.* What was he doing?

Sometimes poetry said what he could not. Sometimes it was better if he just used his own words.

"I want it to last longer," he admitted, hips pistoning, hands clutching bruises into Travis's hips. "I don't want to stop. But..."

"If you don't come you're going to die?" Travis asked, a noise that sounded something like laughter dissolving into a gurgle.

"God, yes. That exactly."

Travis's groan seemed to be some kind of agreement. Barnaby wondered if he'd been doing something wrong for the better part of the last decade that he hadn't laughed so much during sex once. He hadn't teased and been teased. God, he'd probably been rather dramatic and *romantic* about the whole thing, but this was much better.

And, perhaps, more romantic, in its way.

He took a deep breath, collecting himself and shaking off strange thoughts that were better saved for later. He pulled almost all the way out of Travis, watching his pink rim cling to his shaft, shivering at the drag over his cock.

Barnaby pushed forward and Travis held himself still, letting out a loud and joyous noise as Barnaby's cock bounced over his prostate. Barnaby wanted to bottle the pleasure in that sound, but the best he could do was make Travis do it again. And again. It never got old, even when it tilted to a higher pitch, almost a whine.

Barnaby slid his hand from Travis's hip to cup his cock, still trapped in the stretched cotton of his jockstrap. He traced his fingers over a huge damp spot.

Travis whimpered, then shocked Barnaby and fell into his climax the next time Barnaby thrust into him. Barnaby thrust his fingers beneath the cotton and slicked his fingers in Travis's come before curling them around his rigid shaft and dragging a tight fist along its length.

Travis cried out, the muscles in his ass clamping down on Barnaby's cock and locking him inside his body. Barnaby's head swam, his cock swelling and his balls hard and tight to his body.

"Bloody hell," he barked, shoving forward, trying to get every last millimeter of his cock into Travis as his orgasm tore through him. He shook, spots forming before his eyes, holding onto Travis for all he was worth.

When the last pulse ebbed away, he eased back.

"Glurgh," Travis grunted, pitching forward and curling up on his side.

Barnaby had a moment of concern that he'd hurt Travis, that Travis was having regrets, then a long arm hooked him behind the neck and towed him down until he lay facing Travis on the bed.

Travis smiled, his eyes still closed. "That was...thank you."

Saying *you're welcome* seemed stupid and selfish, so Barnaby just brushed the back of his fingers over Travis's still-flushed cheek, and settled on "You're amazing," instead.

The hand cupped behind his neck towed him closer and their mouths met. It started as a gentle kiss, but Barnaby couldn't resist nipping at Travis's lips. Travis opened to him, humming contentedly while Barnaby explored his mouth and ran his fingers through his hair and down his neck.

Travis wriggled closer and slid his leg over Barnaby's hip. "I can feel you leaking out of me."

Barnaby's cock made an honest, if futile, bid toward another erection. He dragged his hand down Travis's body, felt the curve of Travis's smile against his lips as he skimmed the tips of his fingers into the very top of the valley of Travis's ass.

"May I?" Barnaby murmured between more kisses.

Travis nodded, the motion stilling, his breath stuttering, when Barnaby slipped two fingers into the slick mess coating Travis's hole, feeling the swollen rim and dipping inside.

Travis shuddered and pressed his face into the crook of Barnaby's neck, his breathing getting deeper and more even as Barnaby held him with one arm, and ever-so-gently fucked him with the other hand.

Something big and painful grew in Barnaby's chest as Travis fell asleep so trustingly in his arms. Something that should frighten him, but only made him feel light. And happy.

Chapter Seventeen

Barnaby, Jack, and Grady sat in the owner's suite, beers in hand, laughing over one of Barnaby's student's antics.

"Then I said to him, 'Charlie, these are office hours for your English course. I think you might have me confused with the student health center'."

Jack guffawed. "What did he say?"

"He just looked at me, completely bewildered, and asked, 'So, you don't have any condoms?'"

Barnaby grinned, pleased to make Grady and Jack laugh. Grady had started coming to more games, and Jack—not coincidentally, Barnaby supposed—was spending more time in the suite during games. Barnaby was happy to have their company, particularly on the school nights, when the boys couldn't come. Rupert was all well and good, but he was working, so Barnaby left him alone while the game was on.

Tonight, Rupert was on the phone at the end of the row, scoffing over what he clearly considered to be a ridiculous offer. Barnaby could only hope it wasn't for Travis and forced back a pang of panic the mere thought sparked in his chest.

He focused on the game, which was going very well for the Ice Cats. They were up by two goals with only a few minutes left in the second. Their opponents, the Halifax Bears, were getting increasingly frustrated, taking penalties that only made it worse for themselves.

Barnaby leaned forward when Travis's line jumped the boards and flew onto the ice. They picked up the puck in the neutral zone and turned toward the net, with Travis catching it on his stick. The puck bobbled, and Travis looked down to settle it just as a huge man slammed into him from behind, his stick planted across the numbers on Travis's back sending him crashing, head-first, into the boards.

Jack jumped to his feet. Grady went unnaturally still.

"No," Barnaby whispered when Travis crumpled to the ice, his hands holding his helmet.

The sound of the referee's whistle rent the air, the crowd roaring their rage. No one cheered when the asshole was sent to the penalty box because all eyes were on Travis. Who was still on the ice, unmoving.

"No," Barnaby said again, standing.

The Ice Cats' trainer jogged across the ice toward Travis, escorted by two of the players in case he slipped. When he knelt, Travis tilted his head a little, maybe to see him, or to hear him better, and Barnaby felt faint with relief to know he was conscious.

Barnaby heard Rupert snap, "I have to call you back," but didn't look at his cousin. He couldn't tear his eyes away from Travis as he slowly got up on his hands and knees. The trainer appeared to be speaking non-stop, then frowned and looked up at the players around him, gesturing to Travis.

Two teammates hooked Travis under the arms and lifted him onto his skates, moving aside to allow the trainer to walk beside him as he slowly made his way toward the bench.

Barnaby told himself to breathe. To take some nice, deep breaths and relax, because Travis was tough. He was going to be *fine*.

Travis was still five feet from the door when his legs wobbled, nearly going out from under him, his torso listing drunkenly out of the trainer's grip.

Mike Erdo caught him as several members of the team's staff darted onto the ice to drag Travis to the door. He disappeared down the tunnel surrounded by grim-faced escorts.

Barnaby thought he might be sick. He barely felt it when Grady tugged his beer out of his hand and set it aside. He was surprised when he finally turned away from the ice to find Rupert standing next to him.

"Jack," Rupert began without taking his eyes off Barnaby's face, "I'd like to go check on Travis."

"Can I come?" Barnaby asked.

"I was going to ask Jack to stay here with you, but I think, perhaps, it will be better if you come. You're as white as a sheet."

Barnaby nodded. It was like he was one step removed from his own emotions. Not numb—god, nothing like numb—but his brain couldn't get past the fear, and the need to get to Travis, long enough to allow him any emotion like gratitude or embarrassment.

"Thank you," he murmured.

It was an effort not to run for the door. Not to scream *hurry up*. Grady came with them, and Barnaby didn't have the wherewithal to wonder why or if he should or if it was weird.

His legs felt wooden, which, in combination with the way his heart rate kept accelerating the closer they got to Travis, was disorienting. They followed Rupert through the tunnels under the arena. At some point, Grady pressed his hand to Barnaby's shoulder and he leaned into it gratefully.

Barnaby almost ran into Rupert's back when he came to a stop.

"I'm going to step inside and speak with the trainer. You have to stay here."

A protest lodged in Barnaby's throat. Jack stepped in front of him. "Let Rupert do his job before he breaks any rules, okay? You're not supposed to be down here at all."

"What do the wives do?" Barnaby asked, embarrassed to even tangentially imply he was on par with someone's spouse.

"What?"

"What do the wives and girlfriends do? When their player gets hurt?"

"Oh," Jack said, glancing up at Grady. "There's a family room. They wait there for word or for someone to come and get them."

"Should I do that?"

Jack shrugged helplessly. "I think Travis would have to put your name on a list for you to be allowed. I mean, I'm sure Rupert could do it, but..."

"No, that's okay." Barnaby was aware he was putting Jack in

a difficult position, forcing him to remind Barnaby that he wasn't the boyfriend.

Just friends, remember? Friends with benefits.

Barnaby was pretty sure he'd fucked that up thoroughly. The fear, the ache in his chest, the way he'd held Travis and looked right into his eyes as he'd made him come last night, were all outside the parameters of friends with benefits. Barnaby knew that.

And worse, he didn't care. Or care to stop. Not yet.

His head snapped up when the door to the trainer's room opened. Rupert slipped out and closed it again quickly. Barnaby's intestines attempted to tie themselves in knots.

Rupert didn't bother to look at anyone but Barnaby. "I spoke with Travis, briefly, and he gave me permission to tell you what's happening. He's in the dark room."

Barnaby could tell by Jack's grimace and the fall of Grady's shoulders that it wasn't good. "What does that mean?"

"He has a concussion."

The words hung in the air of the hallway, grim. Barnaby could tell Jack and Grady were also thinking about Travis's history and what this could mean. He wondered how much Rupert knew.

Rupert cleared his throat and went on. "They're going to send him for some scans this evening, then he'll probably be allowed to go home. Barring any..." Rupert waved his hand uselessly, as if saying it might jinx them. "I'm sure he'll be released tonight, but we'll have to figure out where he'll go. He shouldn't be alone."

Barnaby was so focused on thoughts of getting through the door to Travis, it took him a while to notice the consternated expression on Rupert's face.

"I, ah..." Rupert grimaced. "In hindsight, I realize I should have asked you first, but I offered him the guest room at our house." He glanced at Jack and Grady, then back at Barnaby. "I thought you might not mind if he were to share the space," Rupert finished, somehow making his attempt at arranging

Barnaby's cohabitation sound prim.

"That would be fine," Barnaby managed.

"Yes, well, I'm happy to hear I've not offended you, but your friend is tryingly stubborn. He turned me down flat. Insists he wants to go home."

Barnaby nodded, not surprised, though frustrated. Having Callum and Rupert, even Christian, to help look after Travis would have been ideal. Barnaby had a moment where he thought, *I can do it all myself,* but that would mean missing classes and office hours and generally fucking up school.

That was what the old Barnaby might have done. A grand gesture. He wasn't that foolish any longer. Nor would Travis want him to be.

He looked at the three men watching him. "I'll look after him, this evening. And as much as possible, but I can't do it alone."

"I'll help," Grady said.

"I will, too," Jack added.

Rupert nodded. "I'll speak with Travis about giving the medical staff permission to speak with each of you if you have questions."

Once they'd agreed on a plan, Rupert allowed them into the trainer's office. They got a long and detailed lecture from the team doctor about concussions and what they should look for, who they should call if they saw something, and what to expect. Barnaby's mouth went dry, the bile rising in his throat as he was trained on the litany of concussion symptoms, both short and long term.

It wasn't that this was new information to Barnaby. He'd been reading quite a bit about concussions in the past few weeks, unable to stop himself from learning more. And as was the case then, too, he was left with one thought. One nagging question.

Why would Travis put himself at so much risk?

When they were finally allowed to see Travis, it was one at a time. Jack and Grady surprised Barnaby by deciding they'd hold off until they were back at Travis's flat. Barnaby was halfway through the door into the fabled dark room when he heard Grady offer to have Jack crash at his place that night.

And Jack's quick, albeit polite, refusal.

Barnaby shut the door behind him and took a moment to let his eyes adjust to the dark.

Travis was frighteningly still, curled up on his side on a gurney, his eyes closed.

Was he asleep? If so, Barnaby would step out again and speak with Rupert about retrieving some of his belongings from the warehouse.

"Travis?" Barnaby said quietly.

Travis's head started to come up, then subsided with a painful grunt.

"No," Barnaby whispered, crossing the small room in two strides and putting a hand on Travis's shoulder. "No, don't move."

"Don't worry. It's not exactly an option right now," Travis said, his voice hoarse.

Barnaby took a seat on the stool, pulling it closer without allowing the legs to scrape the floor, and noted the bucket by Travis's head. It was clean, at least, but the stale air told him Travis had been sick.

He sighed, beating back the instinct to ask if Travis was okay. Barnaby knew the answer. He ran the tips of his fingers through the hair above Travis's ear without thinking, then yanked his hand away.

"No, don't stop," Travis murmured.

Barnaby resumed petting Travis, watching his eyes slide shut again. He didn't look peaceful. He looked terrified.

"Jack, Grady, and I are going to look after you," Barnaby said softly, still stroking. "Don't argue, you won't win."

"I might."

"I intend to conduct my entire side of the argument by quoting obscure religious poems."

Something akin to a smile curled Travis's lips. "Okay, you win."

Barnaby let out a breath he'd been holding. He'd been prepared for a battle, so he felt a little at sea. Maybe that was why he said, "You're going to be okay."

"You don't know that," Travis said, his voice barely more than a scratch.

Barnaby wanted to argue, but he fucking well *didn't* know that.

It was horrible, to feel so helpless.

Travis's eyes squeezed shut, and Barnaby reached for the bucket, his hand freezing mid-air when a tear slid over the bridge of Travis's nose and landed on the table.

"Oh, baby," Barnaby whispered, carding his hands carefully into Travis's hair and holding his stubborn, broken head. He curled over and around Travis and wished with all his heart he could offer better shelter than this.

The next three days were some of the grimmest of Travis's life.

The good news was that the nausea, after the first night, wasn't bad at all. He got queasy, sometimes, but didn't actually get sick, and was able to eat regularly enough that he didn't drop weight. He'd been through one round of this shit where he hadn't been able to keep anything down for weeks. In hindsight, he had no idea how he'd been able to get back on the ice once he'd been cleared, having failed to gain even a pound of it back. All he could remember was being determined to play. To prove he was okay.

That was the worst part, now. Not the headache, or the sensitivity to light and noise, not the restrictions on movement and entertainment, not his inability to focus on his school work no matter how much Barnaby tried to help. The worst part was knowing he *wasn't* okay.

There was a constant creeping dread, a voice in his head saying it wouldn't ever end, that he'd be sitting in this dark room with his friends whispering around him for the rest of his life—

or, until the friends couldn't take it anymore and he was sitting in silence, in the dark, alone.

Another voice, one that often sounded a lot like Barnaby, but sometimes sounded like Martin, would tell him to stop thinking that way. To keep fighting.

He didn't know what to believe, and he didn't tell anyone any of these thoughts, silently brooding over them every minute he was awake.

Needless to say, he wasn't great company.

His friends, though, didn't give up easily.

By the time Barnaby had brought him home from the hospital that first night, Jack and Grady had already been at the apartment for hours, taping tinfoil over the gigantic windows above his bed to black out his bedroom. Travis had thanked them and passed out, but not before recognizing that renting a place with as many windows and as much light at this place had been the worst sort of optimism.

Since that night, at least one of the three of them had been with Travis. Often more than one. Barnaby slept beside him at night, so careful not to move and disturb Travis that Travis was ready to scream and insist Barnaby jump up and down on the bed. The days weren't much better, with Travis stuck in his bedroom while Barnaby, Jack, and Grady were in and out, always whispering, always willing to sit in the dark with him.

He was able to sit up in bed today. And have a light on. No screens, yet. And he didn't want to read, so mostly he sat and thought. It didn't do much for his mood, that was for sure, and he was practically twitching with the need to walk around his apartment, *at least*, by mid-day. He made himself wait until the sun set, and let Barnaby go first and lower all the lights for him.

In spite of planting himself in the only chair in the living room, sending out the clear message that he just wanted to be alone, the Three Musketeers of Moncton were there in the dim light with him. Worse, Jack and Grady were listening to Barnaby read this week's poetry homework out loud.

It felt too intimate. Barnaby's voice wove around Travis,

burrowing into his chest, making it tight and achy. It didn't feel right to have other people there to hear it.

Even worse, it was a seriously long-ass poem called *Intimations of Immortality*—of all fucking things—by William Wordsworth, and Travis was sure it would piss him off if he could focus on it long enough. Well, if he could stop sulking long enough to focus on it—it probably wasn't *just* the concussion at play here.

He tried to tune into Barnaby's voice—the words, at least, if not the passion he couldn't help but infuse into them.

Whither is fled the visionary gleam?
Where is it now, the glory and the dream?

"Stop."

Barnaby fell silent. In fact, it felt like everyone had stopped breathing.

"Is something wrong?" Barnaby asked from his perch on one end of the couch. Jack had a shoulder propped against the wall by the windows, but he turned away from the view outside to frown at Travis.

Travis *hated* that look. Hated the hesitance in Barnaby's voice. Guilt burned through him because he *knew* he'd been a colossal asshole for the past three days. Worse, he knew he wasn't going to get much better anytime soon. And not just on the asshole front.

He knew what his answer should be. *Nothing is wrong.*

Only if he didn't count brain damage, anyway.

Was that something that didn't count? Ever?

"Yes."

Barnaby made to get up. Travis put his hand out, stilling him.

"Are you feeling sick?" Barnaby asked.

"I don't know."

"You don't know?" Grady asked calmly.

Travis looked at his friend, sitting next to Barnaby on the

couch. Grady put a hand on Barnaby's knee, as he looked ready to spring to his feet at the least provocation. The worry in Barnaby's gaze made everything worse.

Travis focused on Grady. "I'm nauseous, and I have a headache, and even this much light hurts my eyes." They knew all this, but it still took that hand on Barnaby's knee to keep Barnaby still. "And I don't even know if it's my fucking head," Travis spit out, his voice getting louder, even though it made the headache worse. It all made the fucking headache worse. "I can't tell if it's the concussion or the fear or the stress half the time. I can't stop *thinking*, and I can't distract myself."

He saw Barnaby open his mouth and cut him off with a slash of his hand. "*You* can't distract me either. I appreciate that you keep trying, that you're even attempting to help me keep up in school, but it feels futile."

"You're frustrated," Grady said.

His calm voice was the only thing Travis was willing to listen to through the noise in his head. "Yes, goddamn it. I'm fucking frustrated. And I'm terrified, okay? I'm fucking terrified and I don't know what to do with that."

For a long moment, nobody spoke. Travis stared hard at his knees, mortified by his own behavior, which only made him worry more. Was he losing control?

"Are you afraid you won't get better?" Grady asked at last.

"No. Yes." Travis heaved a sigh. "I don't think I'll be sitting in the dark for the rest of my life. Or feeling nauseous if I stand up too quickly." Barnaby's eyes narrowed. Yeah, so, Travis hadn't actually told him about that. "I've been through this before and can tell already that I could be better within the week. Maybe two."

"Then what terrifies you?" Grady asked in an even voice that was still warm, somehow. He had missed his calling as a shrink.

"My head."

"Your head?"

"I'm sure you've noticed I've been moody."

"It's been noted." God bless Grady, because he was the only person who could make Travis laugh right then. "It doesn't seem unreasonable, considering what you're going through."

That was generous, but Travis let it go. "But what if it's not that? What if it's my head playing tricks on me? Sending the wrong messages at the wrong time."

"I don't understand," Barnaby said.

"When I was sixteen, I moved out of my parents' house and went to live with a billet family in St. John."

Barnaby blinked at the radical shift in subject, but no one interrupted Travis.

"Within a week of moving in with the Leduc family, their son, Martin, was my best friend. We were the same age, on the same team, had the same interests. Martin was the first person I told that I was gay, and he just thanked me for telling him and started pointing out the boys he thought would be good for me." Travis smiled at the memory, his heart breaking all over again.

"We played on the same team until we were eighteen, then I was picked up by St. John, and Martin was drafted and sent off to Quebec. I continued to live with his family, mostly so I could spend as much time with Martin as possible when he came home. When I was traded, I still came back as much as I could. I was there when he buried his mom, and a decade later, his dad. As far as I was concerned, I was burying my own parents, too. That's how I saw it, and that's how Martin saw it."

Travis glanced up. Barnaby and Grady watched him steadily while Jack stared out the dark window, listening.

"Martin made it to the show, spent some time in Montreal, then Minnesota. We were all so proud of him. But he kept getting injured. He kept getting *concussions*. We used to joke that we had targets on our heads because while I wasn't keeping up, I'd started to rack up a bunch of concussions, too. God, we used to joke..." His voice shook.

He took a deep breath. *Just spit it out.* "He retired at thirty, with over fifteen concussions, not counting the ones we'd ignored as a kids, or had shitty trainers ignore. He'd bounced back and forth between the big show and the minors a bunch, made some money. He was married, but it was falling apart and him being home all the time didn't help. She said he was crazy. Out of control. I knew he was drinking too much, but I didn't understand what was happening, and I guess maybe Martin didn't either. He ended up moving in with his sister, who said he was like a stranger. She made him go to the doctor. Lots of doctors. They explained the damage to his brain was significant enough that he couldn't regulate his emotions. That it might not ever get better."

He took another deep breath. And another. Until the air could move in and out of his lungs without a hitch.

"I was in Russia when I got the call. He'd been doing awesome, you know? Really up, not drinking. He was working out and talking about coaching a kid's team. The day before, he'd gone out with his sister to see some cousins, no headache, no mood swings. The next day, he woke up, went to the basement, and hanged himself."

Travis made himself ignore the wounded noise Barnaby made from the couch.

"His brain, you know? His stupid fucked-up brain just sent that signal that day, I guess. Like a switch had been flipped."

Jack whispered, "Jesus," but didn't look away from the window.

Barnaby and Grady still watched Travis steadily. He thought that if Grady took his hand off Barnaby's knee, he'd be in Travis's lap in a heartbeat. He almost wanted that. To bury his face against Barnaby's neck and hide. But he supposed if he'd dragged them all this far into his darkness, he might as well finish it.

"So, that's what I think about—if the switch is going to flip in me, too. Am I moody because this is a shit situation and that's perfectly understandable, or is it my head doing its own thing?"

His friends did him the courtesy of not leaping to his defense or into denial.

"Travis," Barnaby said, then paused and took a deep breath,

clearly thinking about what he wanted to say. "We've spent a lot of time together recently, yeah?"

Travis nodded.

"And with the exception of your behavior while watching Toronto games, I've never once thought your emotional responses were unexpected or odd, let alone extreme."

It did make Travis feel better to hear it. And the thing about Toronto was probably fair.

"I know that's not a solution," Barnaby continued.

"No, it helps," Travis admitted.

"Okay," Barnaby said, and then he just looked sad. "I'm sorry about Martin, Travis. That's a terrible loss."

"Thanks. I keep thinking the grief will get better, but it's still right there, you know? It haunts me that I wasn't even in the country."

"You can't blame yourself. That would be like me wishing I'd secretly switched to Ryu's school so I could fish him out of the lake before it was too late. It doesn't work like that."

Travis studied Barnaby's face. "How long did it take you to accept that?"

"A hell of a long time, I'm sorry to say. But I was much younger. Maybe you'll have better luck."

At Grady's curious look, Barnaby explained, briefly, about his childhood sweetheart. Travis looked forward to the moment their friends saw that crazy tattoo—which Barnaby did not mention.

Grady nodded. "Grief is a funny thing. It doesn't ever end."

"It doesn't," Barnaby agreed. "I think about Ryu every day, but I like that I do. I think it's important I remember him, and fondly. We had many joyous moments, and I think about those a lot."

Travis had certainly had many of those with Martin, too. He forced himself to recall one, right then, and almost smiled as the image of Martin's bare ass running down Somerset Street in St. John popped into his head.

Maybe Barnaby had a point.

"You speak from experience, don't you?" Barnaby asked Grady gently.

Grady sighed, his face grim. "I'm a member of the RCMP in Moncton. I woke one perfectly normal Wednesday and went to work. By the end of the day, three of us were dead, and another two wounded. " Just hearing the words was like a punch to Travis's gut. He knew about the Moncton shooting, of course, but he'd never connected the dots with Grady.

"I'm so sorry," Barnaby said before anyone else could speak. "We heard about it, even over in the UK. And the manhunt after."

Grady nodded, seeming to steal himself before glancing over at Jack. Maybe he was trying to gauge Jack's reaction, but whatever Jack was feeling was locked behind a carefully blank mask. His eyes were frighteningly flat, devoid of any emotion.

He didn't stop staring out the window. He didn't so much as blink when he said, "I went to prison at twenty-two, a naive kid, with a face like this. I know a thing or two about grief."

No one said a word. What could they possibly say? Jack's blank visage was haunting next to the horror on Barnaby's face and the devastation on Grady's. Barnaby gripped Grady's hand on his knee so hard their skin turned white.

Travis's head throbbed, his stomach churned, and for the first time in days, he didn't have to question the cause.

Chapter Eighteen

I wandered lonely as a cloud
That floats on high o'er vales and hills,
When all at once I saw a crowd,
A host, of golden daffodils;
Beside the lake, beneath the trees,
Fluttering and dancing in the breeze...

Travis grunted. "Wordsworth was really into flowers, is that it?"

"What?" Barnaby asked, distracted. He was currently taking multi-tasking to a whole new level, and it wasn't easy. He and Travis had moved the coffee table to one side so Travis could do his stretches and Barnaby could help. It wasn't easy to recite poetry, from memory, while pressing a considerable portion of your weight on another man's leg and bending it to his chest.

"He's talking about daffodils. I feel like poets are really into daffodils."

Barnaby eased off, then leaned in again. "They're the first flower of spring, so they're a sign of hope. Of resilience."

With a final groan, Travis tapped Barnaby's hip, and he released the leg. Travis shook it out on the mat beside where Barnaby knelt. "Goddamn, that leg is tight."

A week of little activity would do that. It had been almost two since the concussion, and as Travis had predicted, he'd been feeling quite well again for the better part of the last five days. Barnaby was getting a crash course in how quickly an athlete's body could deteriorate with inactivity, and was trying to help any way he could while keeping a careful eye on Travis to make sure he didn't overdo it.

Travis wasn't far behind in school, but Barnaby was pushing to get him caught up. It could probably wait, but Barnaby needed something, *anything*, to keep him from thinking too much about *why* they were getting Travis back into shape.

Travis sat up to work through some stretches on his own, so Barnaby scooted back to give him room.

His body was beautiful, and already Barnaby could see the difference from a few days back. Travis had been allowed to resume normal activity in the gym that morning, while Barnaby had pretended to work in his office on campus. His attention span would rival that of a gnat, at this point.

They'd met here for lunch, and Barnaby had stayed with the hope of chipping away at some schoolwork. And because there wasn't anywhere else he'd rather be. Travis had practice that afternoon, which Barnaby was diligently not thinking about. It would be the first time Travis was allowed back on the ice, and even with no contact allowed, Travis had glowed with happiness when he'd mentioned it.

Barnaby frowned and watched Travis bend himself in half. "What classes are you going to take next?"

Travis looked up over his feet. "I don't know."

"Do you have an idea of what you'd like to study? My feelings won't be hurt if it has nothing to do with poetry."

Travis repositioned his legs and bent into another stretch. "No, it won't be poetry. With all due respect to your work, I don't think a degree in poetry will help me find a job someday."

Barnaby couldn't really argue. Short of writing the stuff or teaching, there wasn't a lot of call for poetry degrees. Barnaby tackled the question from another angle. "Do you have something—or some things—in mind?"

"For school?"

"For work. Jobs that might interest you?"

"Nope. Do you want to watch the Toronto game tonight?"

"Sure. What did you want to be when you were in school?"

"Hockey player."

Barnaby manfully refrained from rolling his eyes. "How about when you were really little?"

"Hockey player."

"You never wanted to be a teacher?"

"God, no. That's your gig, and you're good at it. The only kids I like are the ones who love me back."

Chuckling, Barnaby anchored one of Travis's feet to the mat while he stretched his back. Barnaby let his gaze linger.

It seemed he had a thing for men in tights. Running tights, dancing tights, base-layer of hockey tights. It all worked for Barnaby.

Travis turned the other way. "I don't know what I would be good at," he admitted. "I keep taking classes, waiting for inspiration, or at least something I want to try more than once and see, but so far I've come up blank."

They shifted positions again, only this time Barnaby skimmed a hand over Travis's ribs, eliciting a shiver in reaction. "What about the trades?"

"The only trades I know about are in hockey."

This record was starting to sound broken. Barnaby bit back his impatience. "I mean like being a plumber or an electrician."

Travis paused, appearing to give it genuine thought. Then, "Nope."

Barnaby sighed.

Travis patted his knee consolingly. "Do you know if Grady is working tonight? Maybe he'll come up to watch the game with us."

"Travis…"

"I don't know, okay? I don't fucking *know* what I'm going to do when I grow up. Can you leave it alone? I know one thing. *Hockey.* And that's what I do for a living."

Barnaby took a deep breath and let it out slowly, knowing Travis wasn't actually mad at him so much as frustrated at himself. Travis looked apologetic before Barnaby was even done with his breathing exercise.

He'd never say it to Travis, but he felt sorry for him. His whole life had been one thing. He wasn't well-rounded, he didn't have broad interests. He was the product of a school system and

241

parents who had thought letting him escape into hockey would be a blessing. And in many ways, it had been. It still was. But it had also left Travis here.

It occurred to Barnaby that maybe hockey *was* the answer. Or, at least, part of it.

"What about physical therapy? Or sports training?"

Travis actually shuddered. "Have you seen the animals on my team? I do *not* want to be the one to have to tape them up."

Barnaby barked out a laugh. "I had no idea you were so prudish."

"It's not being a prude!" Travis exclaimed. "It's just I have a sense of *smell,* for Christ's sake. And you've seen what they've done to me. What did you call this?" He gestured at his groin. "Topiary pubes? I don't want that job. And gay or not, I do not need to see the hairy ball sac of even one of those jerks."

"I'm not sure the practice of physical therapy involves what you think it does. And I'm suddenly feeling a great deal of pity for your trainer."

"You should," Travis agreed with another shudder.

"What about team management?"

Travis rocked his head back and forth. "Maybe."

Barnaby barely suppressed the urge to leap to his feet and cheer. A *maybe* was better than all the *nopes* that had come before.

"So, maybe you could take a couple of classes about that?"

"We'll see," Travis hedged. "Vague interest and being any good at it are miles apart."

Barnaby had heard enough of *that* bullshit. He tackled Travis onto the mat, a hand behind his head to protect it, but otherwise letting his full weight knock Travis to the floor.

"*Stop it.*"

Travis laughed, his hands settling on Barnaby's hips. "What?"

"You act like everyone knows what they want. Like it's been

written in stone for them all their lives."

Travis arched a brow. "When did you figure out you wanted to be a teacher?"

He'd been eight. But that wasn't the point. "How long did I spend sitting in a cubicle hating my life?" he shot back.

Travis nodded, begrudgingly.

"Lots of people change paths in the course of their lives, some more than once. You can, too."

Travis sighed. "The question is, in what direction? And will it put food on the table?"

"You can be a barista at the Dipsy Doodle Dangle until you figure it out."

"Not with my knee."

Barnaby rolled his eyes, but he noted Travis looked more thoughtful than frightened, for once. He'd take that as a win, for now. "You know what I mean. You have options. We can find you a job." He dragged his eyes over Travis with a lascivious look. "Fitness models make a lot of money, right?"

Travis laughed, as Barnaby had intended, and dragged him down for a kiss.

Travis knew Barnaby was trying to help.

He seemed innately programmed to be supportive, incapable of not trying to find solutions to problems Travis couldn't even fucking articulate without blind panic taking over his brain and his mouth. And he knew he was being stubborn and that the only person he was hurting was himself.

That didn't stop him from doing it, though.

As much as kissing Barnaby seemed like a fine way to pass the morning, Travis was a grown up, with a job, so he indulged himself in a few last nibbles and eased back.

Barnaby pouted, but he climbed off Travis. He did it by rubbing the length of his thigh over Travis's cock, the asshole, but he did it.

Travis rearranged his stretching routine so he'd be in a position that allowed Barnaby to ogle the bulge he'd helped to create.

"What do you want to teach?" he asked.

Barnaby's eyes were glued to Travis's abdomen. And lower. "Sorry...what?"

He whapped Barnaby's leg with the back of his hand. "What do you want to teach? Middle schoolers? University?"

"University."

"In England?" Travis asked, being careful to keep his voice neutral. It wasn't like the answer should matter to him. He'd be gone himself when the season was over. He'd probably escaped a trade this year just by being injured when the deadline rolled around later this week.

"Yes, that was in England."

Travis huffed out a laugh. "No, do you want to go back and teach there?"

"Oh, I..." Barnaby looked away. "I suppose that was the plan, when I arrived here."

Travis's heart gave a foolish leap. "And now?"

Barnaby smiled at Travis. "And now it's not. I'm not saying I wouldn't go back. I may have to, as I'm not a citizen here, but I wouldn't mind staying."

It was hardly a ringing endorsement, but for some stupid reason, Travis felt better.

At least until Barnaby added, "Moncton is growing on me. Rather like a fungus."

This time it was Travis who tackled Barnaby, his heart stuttering at the cocky grin lighting up Barnaby's face. "Smart ass."

"That's smart arse to you."

How could he not kiss him after that?

Barnaby kissed him back, running a hand down his spine until the fingers dug into his ass cheeks.

With a final peck and a huff of exasperation at his own weak will, Travis tore himself away.

It took a satisfying couple minutes for Barnaby to regroup. Travis rolled his eyes at both of them. This had to be the singularly most ridiculous workout session ever.

Barnaby knelt beside him and resumed watching him like a hawk, sometimes with worry, sometimes with blatant interest. Travis ignored the first and basked in the latter.

"The thing about teaching positions," Barnaby said, returning to their previous discussion, "is that it's a little like hockey. When it's time to look for a job, I'll have to see what's out there, and who is interested in me, if anyone. Regardless of where I want to go, I might have to go where they'll have me. If I write the most boring dissertation ever, I'll be the one to take a position as a barista at the Dipsy Doodle Dangle."

"I doubt that will happen," Travis said, rolling onto his stomach and popping up into a plank.

"Are you trying to torture me?" Barnaby asked.

"You're the one who wanted to talk about the future," Travis said.

Travis managed to maintain his position when Barnaby slapped him on the ass. "I don't mean about that," Barnaby said with a laugh. "I mean *this*."

A single finger traced the band of elastic cupping his ass on the right side.

"What?" Travis said innocently.

"You're wearing a jockstrap." Barnaby managed to make it sound like an accusation.

"I had to stretch. And now I'm doing exercises."

Barnaby snorted. "Yeah, right. I'm *sure* that's the reason."

It wasn't, but Travis wasn't going to admit it. He was glad Barnaby couldn't see his grin.

For the first time since he'd taken that fucking dirty hit, he believed he'd come all the way back. Again. He couldn't dwell on what it would have meant if it hadn't happened this time.

Instead, he wanted to revel in it.

He dropped to the mat and rolled, catching Barnaby unaware and wrapping his arms and legs around him to bring their bodies flush.

Barnaby laughed, the sound muffled by their kiss, which he fell into enthusiastically. Travis arched against him, his cock filling, Barnaby's pressing back.

This. This was what he needed to heal.

He was drowning in how good it felt when Barnaby flipped them, pushing Travis onto his back and sitting up on his cock.

Travis spread his arms and smiled. Barnaby's bright blue gaze was hot under his heavy lids, promising Travis would get just what was coming to him.

Thank god.

Barnaby shoved his hand between the cushion and the arm of the couch beside him. Travis cracked up when Barnaby's hand reappeared clutching a bottle of lube.

"Did you have big plans for when I'm napping later?"

"Hardly, Mr. Jockstrap. I could tell you were feeling better."

"Yeah, I'm definitely feeling better." He gripped Barnaby's ass and ground them together, making them both gasp.

Travis was going to be late to practice and he did not give a shit. Some steps in his recovery couldn't wait.

Chapter Nineteen

Barnaby managed to have a viable excuse to miss the first three home games Travis was back on the ice. He told himself he needed time to get used to seeing Travis being hit again. That he could come to terms with the risks, and enjoy the atmosphere and the competitive spirit as he once had, even if he couldn't feel the same degree of anticipation at seeing Travis on the ice.

Then the first playoff game arrived, and he had no excuse readily available. Not one sufficient for a Saturday game. Not when it was Christian and Oliver begging him to come with them, practically vibrating with excitement. Not when Rupert and Callum looked equal parts proud and determined about the team and their ability to make it deep into the playoffs. Maybe all the way to win the championship.

Barnaby regained some of his enthusiasm as they entered the arena and got swept up in the bustle and noise of the crowd. The suite was laden with food and drinks, and crowded with people. Barnaby was introduced to Reese Lamont, another of the team's owners, and Reese's partners—plural—who couldn't seem to take their eyes off him. Barnaby also met Gabriel Santangelo, who ran a local youth and family shelter, and with whom he swapped emails in order to learn more about volunteering. There were at least five other people whose names he could barely remember as the team came out for warm-ups and his attention was drawn to the ice. To Travis.

This part he could watch easily—the flow of men gliding over the smooth surface almost hypnotic. The power in their strides, the grace in their movements.

After warm-ups, Barnaby found Grady standing at the back of the suite, doing the thing where he appeared almost bored, but his eyes never stopped moving, taking in all the details.

Barnaby practically flung himself at Grady, he was so relieved to see him. Grady laughed and didn't comment when

Barnaby suggested two seats in the back row, rather than where they'd always sat before, up near the boys, who were waving him over.

The anthem played, the players lined up, and Barnaby forced himself to sit in his seat as the first puck was dropped. It had never occurred to him that this game wouldn't be anything like the ones he'd been to before.

The hits were brutal, the battles against the boards vicious. Every time the referees had their backs turned, Barnaby caught a slash, a trip, a cross-check. His stomach rolled, waiting for Travis's line to take the ice. The whole box gasped and twitched as the action unfolded before them.

"What the hell is happening?" he asked weakly.

Grady chuckled until he saw Barnaby's face. "This is playoff hockey. Didn't anyone warn you?"

"No." Barnaby wasn't sure he managed to say it audibly.

Grady searched his face. "Barnaby—"

Travis's line jumped into the play and Barnaby lifted a hand, stalling whatever Grady was going to say. He didn't breathe the entire minute Travis was on the ice, his eyes glued to Travis. Every possible awful scenario ran through his head. A hit. A fight. Travis twitching on the ice. Unconscious.

By the time Travis was back on the bench, Barnaby felt dizzy.

He jumped to his feet and swayed. "I'm going to get something to eat." The idea of food made him gag, but he made a beeline to the counter and picked up a plate, determined to act normal instead of throwing himself at his cousin's feet and begging him to pull Travis from the game.

That would be awkward. Especially since Barnaby was just a friend with benefits.

A very, very *stupid* friend with benefits.

When Jack came into the suite a few minutes before the first intermission, he didn't seem surprised to find Barnaby practically cowering against the back wall. He'd been pretending to eat the same lump of risotto for the better part of forty minutes, under the watchful eye of Callum and Grady, both of whom looked back every few minutes to check if he was still there.

He thought maybe he could last the whole game like this, particularly when Reese's spectacularly built boyfriend stood just behind Reese's chair, blocking Barnaby's view of the ice and replacing it with a view of David's frankly *outstanding* arse instead.

"You doing okay?" Jack asked.

Barnaby both appreciated and hated the sympathy in his eyes. "I'm fine."

Jack was kind enough not to call him a liar. A look passed between Grady and Jack that told Barnaby they'd probably been texting about him.

Jack focused on Barnaby again. "You going to tell him?" Jack asked.

"What, that I can't stand the sight of him doing the one and only thing he's convinced he was born to do?"

"No, are you going to tell him *why* you can't stand it?"

Barnaby shook his head. "It's not my place. We're just friends. With benefits, but still just friends. I ought to simply support him."

And focus on his own studies. He needed to keep things in perspective, and to keep his focus, even if it killed him a little. He was doing great so far, enjoying university and preparing for the end of term. Professor Sorenson was already asking about him taking the TA position next year, which Barnaby would gladly accept.

"Everything is *fine*," Barnaby said emphatically, as if saying it aloud would make it true.

Jack sighed. Barnaby appreciated Jack's concern, just as he appreciated Jack standing at the back of the room with Barnaby until the intermission, and checking on him periodically for the rest of the night.

By some miracle, Barnaby made it through the game without having to hide in his car, so he patted himself on the back and didn't pretend to be anything short of eager to get downstairs to wait for Travis. He forced himself to say goodnight, even managing to say he looked forward to seeing Reese and his partners at the next game in two days' time. It wasn't a lie, exactly—they were nice people and he was certain that if he could get to the point of sitting in one of the chairs, maybe during intermission at least, they'd be lovely company.

It wasn't their fault that this innocuous and luxurious little suite was crushing his soul.

Travis was shaking when he came off the ice after the third period. He'd been in plenty of playoff games in his career, but he couldn't remember if the adrenaline had ever hit him this hard. Not when he and Martin had made it to the first round when they were eighteen, and not when he'd made it to the finals in Russia five years ago.

He kept telling himself it was normal, but he knew it wasn't. The hits had been just as hard, and just as painful, as they'd ever been. The pace as grueling. He used to be fucking chill about that. Hell, that was his *job*. The veteran presence who helped the kids stay calm in the face of the storm.

Instead, he could barely get his gear off, and had to clench his fists or hide his shaking hands in his lap more than once when someone stopped to talk to him. He could fake it. He *had* to fake it.

One glance at Rupert told him all he needed to know about how successful he was.

There was nothing he could do about that. Not right now. His focus needed to be on going through his post-game routine, which he managed to accomplish in record time, and then getting the hell out of there.

He was practically running by the time he plowed through the locker room door and out into the hallway. The guys weren't going out tonight, thank god. No one would be going out until this series was over, one way or the other. If they won, they'd celebrate for a night before knuckling down for the next round. If they lost, they'd lick their wounds in a collective drunken stupor.

He stopped mid-stride when his traitorous heart leaped at the idea of being done.

Jesus Christ, what was the matter with him?

He shook his head to clear it of fucking ridiculous thoughts and resumed his jog toward the exit. It had been a long season and he was still a little fucked up about that last concussion. And the one before. Not his head—that was clear. No headaches. No light sensitivity. All good. He just needed more time to shake it off, which he wasn't going to get during the playoffs.

God, he needed food and sleep and—

"Travis!"

Barnaby ran toward him and Travis dropped his bag without thinking, or wondering why he was rushing forward to catch Barnaby against his chest and squeeze him until he was certain neither of them could breathe.

But Barnaby was holding on just as hard, so...

He caught sight of Jack and Grady hovering a few yards away and reality reinserted itself. He let Barnaby go and stepped back, though he didn't stop touching his arm. His elbow. He expected his friends to laugh at him. To roll their eyes. *Something.* He didn't know what to make of their serious expressions.

"You did great," Barnaby said.

He hadn't, actually. It hadn't been his worst game, but he hadn't done enough. He wanted to ask Barnaby if he'd been at the same game, but Barnaby wasn't actually making eye contact. And Travis didn't want to talk about it.

Next game he'd go all in. It was what he was being paid to do.

He ducked his head closer to Barnaby's. "Come home with me. Please?"

Barnaby finally made eye contact, and the heat in his eyes was all Travis needed to know.

They said goodnight to their friends, finally eliciting the knowing smirks Travis had been waiting for, and tore out of the arena. He didn't think they'd been rude, but hell, he didn't care.

He dragged Barnaby to his car, promising to bring him back for his own later. Or tomorrow. He could barely remember the details, too focused on getting them home.

It felt like a thousand pounds were lifted from his shoulders when they stepped through his door and shut it behind them. Maybe that was why he went a little crazy.

Barnaby seemed to be suffering from the same affliction, because the moment Travis's hands landed on his body, intent on towing him close and kissing him until they were both staggering from it, Barnaby's hands were everywhere, slamming their mouths together and practically climbing Travis like a fucking tree.

"Yes. God, yes," Travis gasped between hot, wet kisses. He clutched at Barnaby's thigh and back, hauling him higher. Closer.

Barnaby yanked his head back with a fist in his hair, the pain to his scalp like a cleansing fire. He wanted Barnaby to make him feel everything again for the first time. Pain. Pleasure. Fear.

Happiness.

And he got those and more while Barnaby hovered above him, his long legs clamped around Travis's waist, his kiss dominating Travis's every thought.

Then Barnaby was gone, springing free and landing on his feet, his hands shoving Travis's coat off his shoulders.

"Off. *Off.*"

Clothing flew in all directions as they tried to strip each other simultaneously, then realized it was fucking impossible with arms and legs and shirts and pants tangling, so they turned their attention to themselves. Travis was a seasoned professional when it came to stripping down in record time, thanks to years in the locker room, but Barnaby kept pace, his boxer briefs sailing to parts unknown as Travis finally stood naked before him.

"Come here," Barnaby growled, his fingers in Travis's hair,

yanking, his legs wrapping around his ribs again. Travis lifted his face, his mouth, his entire fucking *being* to Barnaby's kiss and held on tight. By muscle memory and luck alone, he managed to walk from the front hall to his bedroom with his eyes closed, and his blood pumping, and his entire body at Barnaby's command. He staggered at the doorway, leaning against the wall just inside and letting himself forget the rest.

There was no longer a game in two days. No practice tomorrow. No fresh bruise on his back. His knees didn't hurt. His shoulder didn't ache.

He gave himself over to Barnaby and felt healthy and strong. He let Barnaby take care of him and he felt safe to ask for what he needed.

"Fuck me."

Barnaby groaned, as if he agreed. That was good enough for Travis.

He stood away from the wall and took the three steps to the bed, tipping them onto the mattress. They bounced and he reached for the lube that had taken up permanent residence under his pillow.

He shoved it into Barnaby's hand. "Hurry."

Barnaby blinked at him, confused. "What?"

"Fuck me. Come on. *Please.*" He was more than willing to beg. Hell, it made him hot to consider it—him on his knees, pleading with Barnaby to fuck him. Though that would have to be saved for a night he had an ounce of patience left in his body.

"We can't." At least Barnaby sounded upset about that.

Travis growled. "We *can.*" They *had to.* It felt like he'd shatter into a million pieces if they didn't. He snatched the lube back from Barnaby and slathered it on his own fingers. He knelt, ignoring the painful objection from his bad knee, and reached behind himself to shove two fingers into his ass.

Shit. That was *tight.*

He couldn't quite suppress a whimper, which made Barnaby look alarmed. Travis thrust his fingers deep, the sound leaking from him again. It wasn't the stretch that sucked. He and Barnaby had been playing often enough, for long enough, that two fingers weren't unmanageable. It was that they were his own fingers. It didn't feel the same. The angle was all wrong, the dueling sensations sucked.

God fucking damn it, why wasn't Barnaby helping him?

Strong fingers clamped around his wrist, stilling his frantic thrusts. "Stop it."

Travis's eyes fluttered open. He'd never heard Barnaby use that tone with anyone. He thought, vaguely, it was his stern teacher voice.

"I'm not helping you because I don't understand what you need. What you want," Barnaby said.

Travis realized he must have asked for help aloud, and even as his cheeks went hot, the truth poured out of him. "I want you to fuck me. Please, Barnaby."

"You have a playoff game in less than forty-eight hours. Are you sure?"

"I'm sure. I need this. I need *you*."

Barnaby's bright blue gaze searched Travis's face. He had no idea what Barnaby found there, but eventually he nodded. "Okay."

Travis practically melted with relief, sliding down onto the bed with Barnaby's hands guiding him, wiping his hand on the bed before wrapping both arms around Barnaby and pulling him close.

He let go a deep sigh when Barnaby slid two slick fingers back into him.

Yes, he thought. *This is what I need.*

Barnaby didn't waste any time, adding lube and a finger while they exchanged long, drugging kisses. Travis's brain was a blissful blank slate by the time Barnaby rolled away, but he wasn't so out of it that he didn't know what he wanted. Needed.

He reached for Barnaby, pulling him back, pulling him over Travis.

"Like this."

Barnaby kissed his lips sweetly. Then he touched Travis's face. The new bruise on his hip. His bad knee and stupid shoulder. The touches didn't heal him, but it felt like it. Barnaby's smile and the heat in his eyes and the gentle brush of his fingers felt like renewal. Like a release.

Travis wrapped his legs around Barnaby. "Please."

Barnaby nodded and his cock was there, pressing against Travis's hole, stretching him open. The angle was weird, the prep too short, but it felt perfect. Travis willed his body to open, to let Barnaby in.

The crown popped past straining muscles and Travis gasped, but at some point Barnaby must have come to understand what Travis needed, what he'd been asking for, because he pushed forward relentlessly, filling him up, the stretch bordering on burn, the ache finally soothed.

"God, Travis," Barnaby gasped against his lips, his hips working relentlessly. "*God*."

Maybe. Maybe God had something to do with it, if you believed. But all Travis could think about, could *feel*, was Barnaby. Each thrust a benediction. Each kiss a baptism.

If given a choice, he might have stayed like that forever. No more hockey. No more school. Nothing but this. But his body wasn't having any of that. Not when Barnaby was whispering how beautiful he was. How good it felt. Not when he felt speared through the heart with every word. His orgasm hovered just out of reach, but he didn't care if he never came if he meant he could draw this out.

Barnaby freed his lips and pressed their foreheads together. "I'm going to come." He sounded almost sorry. Travis understood.

Before he could assure Barnaby it was fine, *he* was fine, Barnaby pushed himself up on an arm and one hand slithered between their bellies. The moment those long, clever fingers curled around Travis's cock, Barnaby's hips thrust into him and ground in a tight circle.

"Jesus fuck," Travis cried out, his system swamped as his orgasm went from hover to dive bomb, bursting through him. His aching ass clenched and clenched around Barnaby as he painted warm, white stripes up his belly and chest. He knew when Barnaby came, because the clockwork circle of his hips ceased mid-motion, his mouth falling open, his eyes fluttering shut. Travis imagined he could feel Barnaby filling him up, and it made his cock pulse again, the muscles stretched around Barnaby's cock clamping down again and sore for it.

The distance between how he'd felt coming off the ice and how he felt in this moment was so great it was hard to fathom. He was suddenly exhausted. Wrung out and limp against the bed.

"Shhh…" The whisper of Barnaby's lips against his eye lids encouraged him to keep them closed. "You're so good. *So good*," he murmured, pressing a kiss to each lid.

Travis smiled. Or he thought he did.

"So beautiful." Two more kisses, to his temples this time.

His lips. "Smart."

His chin. "Kind."

Travis drifted, wondering what was real and what was a dream. Wondering if it were possible for it to be both.

A final kiss was pressed to the center of his forehead, and he was sure he heard poetry.

Thanks to the human heart by which we live,
Thanks to its tenderness, its joys, and fears,
To the meanest flower that blows can give
Thought that do often lie too deep for tears.

Chapter Twenty

Barnaby wasn't at the arena when it happened. It was only game five of the first round of the playoffs, and while he'd somehow managed to hide in the back of the suite for game two, he'd happily demurred when Jack and Grady asked if he wanted to take a road trip to see the away games in nearby Fredericton. He had responsibilities at the university, after all. They understood.

Perhaps better than he wished.

Tonight he was missing the game because Professor Sorenson had requested Barnaby lead an evening study group to help their students prepare for their exam. That Barnaby had chosen tonight would be his secret.

He hadn't even felt bad about it until the texts started coming in.

Travis is hurt, Jack wrote.

Barnaby read the text, then quickly flipped his phone back over and tried to listen to one of his students attempt to answer a sample question. His heart was beating loud in his ears, but he had a job to do, and goddamn it, he was going to do it.

His phone buzzed again. Twice.

It looks bad. It's his head.

What do you want us to do?

Barnaby's stomach roiled, his mouth dry. Why were they asking *him*? He was just another friend. The one who had nursed Travis back to health just a few weeks ago. The one who spent all his time with Travis. The one who cared more than he should.

He rubbed his chest, the ache pushing up and out, making it hard to swallow. Hard to breathe.

He stood without warning and abruptly apologized to his students for having to leave early. He shoved his things into his bag and told himself he could take comfort that the students had each other and he'd set them on the right course. He ran down the stairs and out the front door of the library in time to empty his stomach into the bushes just off the stairs.

And they were asking *him* what should be done?

He considered calling Rupert to ask what the hell was going on, but he didn't trust himself not to say something he'd regret. Travis was a grown man who made his own decisions. Rupert couldn't possibly know the full extent of Travis's concern for his concussion history and the state of his health unless he had told Rupert and the team, which Barnaby knew for a fact he hadn't.

He knew a lot of fucking things for a fact, and none of them were going to help him, or Travis, tonight.

He drove to the arena on autopilot and found his way to the trainer's office by memory.

He saw the concerned looks from Rupert and Callum. He saw the worry on Jack and Grady's faces. It was the frustration, though, on the trainer's face, that spoke to him. With a nod from Rupert, Barnaby was allowed to enter the dark room.

He paused outside the door, his hand on the knob, and told himself he needed to be calm. He was Travis's friend, and Travis needed help.

The Florence Nightingale of Moncton. That was him.

He opened the door and the acrid stench of vomit assailed him. Instinct took over, pushing him forward to make sure the bucket was where Travis needed it. He pressed a hand to Travis's back to steady him. He was supposed to press the emergency button if he felt sick, but of course he hadn't.

Of fucking course.

Barnaby did it for him, and he was certain Travis would have shot him a dirty look if he could have stopped retching long enough.

Score one for Florence Nightingale, then.

The trainer and team doctor came in and didn't bother to push Barnaby out. He tucked himself into the corner and listened as they discussed what scans would have to be done. They decided it was best to send Travis by ambulance, at which point they went to speak with Rupert and Callum in the hallway, leaving Barnaby and Travis alone again.

"I'm sorry," Travis murmured, his stomach having either settled or just given up by this point.

Barnaby thought about asking what he was sorry for, but he wasn't sure Travis knew. And Barnaby wasn't sure he wanted to.

Logistics, then. "I'm going to go to your place and take care of things there. Let me know if you want me to pick you up when you're done at the hospital or if you have a ride."

Travis blinked up at him blearily. "Okay."

Leaving felt like the thing he was supposed to do next, but Barnaby hovered there while Travis lay on the gurney and looked up at him. Everything felt off. *Wrong.* He was distantly aware of the throb of his heart at all times, and he couldn't stop rubbing his fingertips together where they felt slightly numb.

He wondered if he needed a doctor himself, but discarded that. He wasn't sick. He was *terrified.*

He stepped forward, and Travis reached for him at the same moment, pulling him in. Barnaby folded himself over Travis, trying to make a shell around him, his face buried in Travis's hair, his arms curled around Travis's shoulders and ribs. Surrounding him, and feeling all the more useless for it.

Barnaby couldn't protect Travis from what was hurting him.

He took deep breaths, willing back the sting in his eyes, forcing the air to move in and out of his chest without a hitch.

"I'm sorry," Travis said again and it tore at Barnaby.

A thousand words crowded to the tip of his tongue, but he didn't say any of them. Not *it's going to be all right,* because it wasn't true. Not *I understand,* because he didn't. Not *you have nothing to be sorry for,* because that somehow felt like the worst lie of all. Maybe that wasn't right, and it certainly wasn't fair, but he couldn't bring himself to feel anything else.

Logistics, he reminded himself. That was...safe. "I'm going to go take care of everything at home, okay? You just rest and let the doctors take a look."

Travis nodded once, his shoulders going tight from the tiny motion. Then he was shoving Barnaby away and heaving nothing but bile into the bucket on the floor beside him.

Rather than press the button again, Barnaby opened the door and let the sound of Travis being sick inform the trainer and doctor of what they needed to know. He stepped out of the way to let them into the room, then walked on shaky legs to the hallway.

He wasn't in the mood to be hugged, but Callum caught him off guard. Barnaby sucked in a single breath, let it hitch once, then pushed Callum away.

"I have to get going. I need to black out Travis's bedroom."

"Barnaby, you're as pale as a ghost," Callum said, clearly worried.

Barnaby didn't have the emotional or mental capacity to make anyone, even himself, feel better. "Can you please get his things from his locker?"

Callum hesitated, then nodded. "Yeah."

"I'll bring them home," Grady said.

Barnaby tried a quick smile. "Thanks."

He was sure there was more that needed to be said, but he was in no condition to say it, so he turned and walked out of the arena without another word. He heard Rupert ask if it was safe for him to drive, but he didn't pause on his way out the door.

It took hours to do what needed to be done. He taped aluminum foil up over the huge windows in the bedroom, changed the sheets, and put buckets on both sides of the bed. He went to the store for Travis's favorite flavors of Gatorade and juice, and picked up two weeks' of the bland foods Travis had been forced to live on for the days before his stomach settled last time. When he got home and had everything put away, he made certain there was plenty of water in the fridge and a pitcher beside the bed. Then he did the dishes. Folded the laundry. Grady stopped by, and Barnaby took the huge gear bag from him with a nod and a thanks, then dumped it out and put everything that could be washed into the washing machine.

Travis still wasn't home by the time the laundry had dried, been folded, and stacked on top of the machines.

Barnaby checked his phone regularly, knowing someone would tell him if Travis had to spend the night in the hospital. He'd received messages from Rupert, Callum, and Jack. He hadn't written any of them back.

He just waited.

It was almost two in the morning when the trainer helped Travis to his apartment door. Barnaby turned off all the lights but the one over the stove and watched as Travis made slow but steady progress across his apartment toward his bedroom. It was a relief to see he was on his own feet, at least. And he wasn't vomiting, which was nice.

Barnaby listened to the lecture from the trainer, again, and nodded along. It was the same as last time, so he was well-versed in the protocols.

Once he'd locked the door behind the trainer, Barnaby went into the bedroom, his heart pounding louder with every step. He stopped in the doorway and saw Travis was stripped down to his boxers, lying on the bed. His eyes were open and focused on the blank wall a few feet away.

"Do you not want to get under the covers?"

"I was waiting for you," Travis said with a little shrug. "I'm feeling much better than I was at the arena," he added.

Barnaby nodded and came into the bedroom, closing the door behind him. It took a minute for his eyes to adjust to the dark. While they did, he toed off his shoes and stripped down to his underwear.

It was a relief, a *huge* one, to know Travis was already doing much better. That was a good sign that this time around could pass quickly.

He'd read a lot about concussions online, at odd moments when no one would see him, like his curiosity was a dirty little secret. He didn't want to upset Travis. He didn't want to tip off Rupert and betray Travis. He didn't want to offend Callum—

because he'd spent a lot of time reading about the lawsuits and the research that the hockey establishment was working hard to brush under the carpet, and he didn't know where Callum, after his long career on the ice and more-recent position as a team owner, stood on it all.

So while it was a relief Travis was already doing better, the absence of fear letting Barnaby's stomach unclench and his hands go steady, there was plenty of rage to take its place.

He climbed into bed and pulled the covers over them before lying down and pressing his chest to Travis's back. They could have fit on a twin bed like this, given Travis's need to be near the edge of the bed, and Barnaby's desire to see he didn't fall out of it in the middle of the night. He curled his arm around Travis's waist and pressed a kiss to the back of his neck.

It was a routine. One they'd already had a chance to perfect in their relatively brief relationship.

Travis slipped into sleep soon after that, which was good because he needed to heal. Barnaby wouldn't sleep for hours, and even then, it was fitful.

He didn't wake up so much as give up on sleep for the day and crawl out of bed. He made himself breakfast, then some toast for Travis and went back into the bedroom.

He was surprised to find Travis sitting up in the dark. "What are you doing?"

Travis smiled tentatively. "Feeling better?"

Was that a question? "Are you hungry?"

Travis started to answer, then leaned over the bed and heaved.

Barnaby sighed. "Okay, I guess that's a no."

"Sorry."

"Don't—" Barnaby stopped himself. "I'll put it back in the kitchen if the smell is bothering you and you don't think you'll want it."

"No, leave it beside the bed. I might feel up for it in a bit. I think I sat up too fast, is all."

Barnaby skirted the bed and put down the plate, keeping a careful eye on Travis. The only light was coming from the hallway through the door Barnaby had left cracked.

He jumped when Travis took his hand, but stopped and gave him his full attention.

Travis cleared his throat. Twice. "So, I know this isn't a great time to bring this up, but I'm hoping you—that we…" Travis swallowed, his eyes never leaving Barnaby's. "I'm really grateful for all you've done for me, and I don't want you to think this is about that."

"I have no idea what this is," Barnaby said slowly. He told his rioting brain and hopeful heart to simmer the fuck down.

"What I mean to say is, you take really good care of me. Better than I deserve. And I guess I'm hoping that's because I'm, you know, more to you than just another friend with benefits, you know? I mean, I haven't thought of you as a friend with benefits for a while, to be honest."

Despite his best intentions, Barnaby's heart did something painfully happy and full of hope in this chest. "Me, neither."

"So, I was hoping you might…you know…"

"Be your boyfriend?"

"God, I feel too old for that word."

"Shut up," Barnaby said, unable to contain his grin. "You look just right for that word to me."

A big smile transformed Travis's face, and Barnaby saw all the hope and happiness he was feeling reflected in Travis's eyes for one perfect moment—then Travis winced, just a quick tightening of the skin between his eyes, and blinked.

"God, what are we doing?" Barnaby asked, exasperated with them both. "You need to lie down. You need to get better." So he could be Barnaby's boyfriend. So they could start to build something together. "Come on, lie down," he said, helping Travis get settled back on the bed. "Why were you sitting up anyway?"

"I just wanted to see how it went."

Well, he had his answer. Barnaby rubbed his shoulder.

"Don't rush things. You know it takes time."

"I know," Travis agreed, and for a moment Barnaby thought it might be that simple. "But it's playoffs and they need me out there."

Hope and happiness winked out, a candle snuffed in a gale-force wind.

Barnaby took a slow step back, his hand slipping off Travis's shoulder. "What?"

"Playoffs are a big deal," Travis said, his eyes pleading with Barnaby to understand. "And I'll never get a contract next year if I don't get back out there for a few games."

"Next year?" Barnaby repeated numbly.

Travis settled back against the pillows Barnaby had mounded behind him to protect and support his head. The head he was going to take back out on the ice at the earliest opportunity.

Something in Barnaby broke, his denial coming out as a hoarse whisper. "*No.*"

"No?"

"You—you can't. You can't mean that."

"Mean what?"

"You're going to play again? This season?"

Travis looked confused. "Yeah. Of course. If I can."

"You *can't.*" Barnaby's stomach pitched, and he knew, he *knew* he had no right to say anything, or tell Travis what he should and shouldn't do. But his knees went weak, his fingertips numb, again, at the idea of Travis going back out on the ice.

"I have to. What the fuck are you talking about? I can't *not play.*"

Barnaby shook his head, trying to ward off the images flashing through his brain. Of Travis down on the ice and not getting up. Of him sitting, just like this, in a dark room that reeked of stomach bile, and not being able to get out. Not being able to get up and *live his life* the way he wanted to.

Suddenly Barnaby could feel his fingertips just fine. Just as he could feel the heat searing his cheeks, and the rage boiling through him.

He took a quick step closer to the bed and glared down at Travis. "You're killing yourself," he snapped, his voice too loud, his anger too huge to be contained. He couldn't care that Travis paled, stark white against the sheets. "And what's worse," he ground on, "what's fucking *worse,* is that you know it and you ignore it."

Travis struggled to push himself up on the bed. "Fuck you," he shouted, then had to steady himself.

"Look at you!" Barnaby cried.

"Yeah, fucking look at me. I'm a *hockey player,* Barnaby. That's what I do. That's *what I am.*"

"You are. You *were.* And I get it. Goddamn you, and Rupert, and Callum, you made me fall in love with the sport. It's noble and beautiful and fun, and I admire all of you for the work you've done. But *god,* I hate it, too, when I see what it's doing to you. You've had enough, Travis. Traveled enough miles. Taken enough blows." Barnaby sucked in a breath and blinked furiously, unable to stop the tears from escaping. Not bothering to wipe them away. "It's time to move onto the next part of your life. It's time to be sure you *have* a life. You've got this big, beautiful brain and you put it at risk, *damage it,* with every concussion. And you *know* that's what is happening. I don't have to ask you if you've read about post-concussion syndrome and CTE. I know you have. I know you did years ago."

"And how do you know that?" Travis snapped furiously.

"Because that's who you are. You loved Martin and you would have wanted to help. To *know.*"

Barnaby hadn't thought it possible for Travis to go any paler, but he'd been wrong. The mention of his dead friend drained every drop of color from his face. "Fuck you," he growled. "What do you know? You sit in your ivory tower and judge, you don't have any clue what it's like to not have any future. To not know what you're going to do with your life."

"That doesn't mean you shouldn't fight to *have* that life," Barnaby cried. "And fuck you right back for that ivory tower shite. Every time you get hurt, I hurt. Every time you're sitting in a dark room with your head practically cracked open, I die a little, too. Everyone who loves you dies a little more."

Travis looked stricken, his eyes wide.

"I know. I know I don't have any right to tell you what to do, or even to ask you to stop. It feels wrong even as I'm saying it, but what kind of person would I be if I didn't say *something*? How would either of us live with ourselves if I kept pretending this was okay? I mean, maybe if we'd managed to nail that friends with benefits thing, but I knew I'd fucked that up weeks ago. God, I fell in love with you. It was so easy I didn't see it coming until it was too late. And I wouldn't have stopped it if I had. I'm *in* love with you, Travis Campbell, and I want to be your boyfriend, your partner, your future, but I don't know how to do that. How do I give my life to someone who doesn't look after their own properly?"

"Barnaby," Travis whispered, and he sounded as sad and desperate as Barnaby felt.

"Tell me, damn it. Tell me how this can all make sense. Tell me what our happily ever after looks like two concussions from now. Or maybe six. Tell me that, Travis."

Travis lay on the bed, his head throbbing so painfully he could barely keep his eyes open, but he couldn't possibly tear them away from Barnaby, either. Barnaby, who was in love with him, confessing it like a sin as he scrubbed away the tears coursing down his cheeks.

Barnaby loved him, but it wasn't enough to overcome the panic. He couldn't give up hockey. Not yet. Not this season, with the playoffs in full swing. Not next season, either, while he continued to save and go to school. He hadn't had enough time yet. He wouldn't have anything to *offer* to Barnaby.

Which was basically what Barnaby was saying, too. They just saw it from different angles.

At least they agreed, Travis thought bleakly.

"I told you I was a bad bet," he croaked.

Barnaby dropped his hands to his sides. "What?"

He was beautiful, even tear-streaked and red-eyed. Even with his heart in his eyes and with it so clearly already broken. Travis wanted to pull him into his arms and soothe him, but that wasn't what Barnaby needed.

"I'm a bad bet," he repeated. "I knew it going in. And now you know it, too."

"Travis—"

"No. No, don't say it." He didn't know what Barnaby had been going to say, but he didn't want to hear it. He just wanted silence. He wanted the headache, the heartbreak, to end. He drank in what he could see of Barnaby in the dark room, then he pulled the plug.

"I think you should go."

Barnaby blinked at him, like he couldn't understand the words.

"Just go. Please. It's better if you go."

For the longest, most painful minute of Travis's life to date, Barnaby stood and stared at him. Then he did just as he'd been asked.

He left.

Travis pulled the covers up over his head and cried his fucking heart out.

At some point he passed out, and when he woke up he found Grady sitting in the chair in the corner of the room, his face blank. He stood and tested Travis's eyes with a penlight, then asked if he wanted anything to eat or drink. Travis declined politely. Grady nodded and left the room.

The next three days were a blur of dark rooms and frequent, albeit brief, visits from Jack and Grady. Barnaby had clearly sent them, just as someone had told the trainers they should check in more often as well. Travis didn't question it. It hurt too much to look at, let alone give it a poke.

It sucked to have so many people through his place, but it wasn't nearly as painful as the void left by the one person who wasn't there. Travis broke the no-screens rule and picked up his phone a thousand times to send a text. To beg. But he still had nothing to offer, and he loved Barnaby too much to ask for him to come back and suffer for nothing in return.

It was a hell of a thing, figuring out what that funny feeling in his chest was, the feeling that had been growing since the first time he'd laid eyes on Barnaby in the coffee shop.

Maybe that was why, when there wasn't anyone around, Travis spent an embarrassing amount of time crying. He'd felt like this the first weeks after Martin had died, and he knew it boiled down to the same thing.

Grief.

When he couldn't stand his own company, or the stench, any longer, he hauled his ass out of bed and stripped it to the mattress. He almost brained himself on the washing machine when he bent to load it, but powered on, ignoring his shaking hands and heaving stomach as he remade the bed.

Then he got out the huge bottle of Maker's Mark he'd been saving for the end of the season, plunked it down on the coffee table, and sat in the chair. It was only ten o'clock and the night stretched out before him endlessly. He'd give anything, *do* anything, to shut off his brain for some of it.

He was still sitting there when Grady came in. He paused halfway across the room, his eyes moving between Travis and the bottle a few times, before he sat on the couch across from Travis, the bottle between them.

"You trying to kill yourself?"

"That's what Barnaby thinks."

Grady looked surprised. "He knows about the Terrible Bourbon Idea you have going here?"

"No. And I haven't drunk any."

"Why not?" Grady asked.

"Because I don't want to die."

Grady stared at him for a long time, his lips pressed flat.

"I told Barnaby to leave," Travis said at last.

"I know. He arranged for me and Jack to take over."

He nodded. He'd figured that right. "It was the right thing to do. Sending him away."

"Why is that?"

Travis lamented Grady's ability to be so fucking unreadable. "He shouldn't have to take care of me. Not now, or when the long-term effects of the concussions rear their ugly head."

"That what Barnaby said?"

"More or less."

Grady looked him right in the eye. "You can bullshit yourself, but you're not going to bullshit me, Travis."

"Fuck you."

"I'd say fuck you back, but why bother? You've done such a good job of it all by yourself."

Travis reared back as if the slap to the face had been more than just metaphorical.

"That man loves you," Grady went on, his voice soft even if each word was like a blow to Travis. "That's not something someone with a heart as big as Barnaby's will get over any time soon. So how about you?"

"What about me?"

"You going to keep fucking up?"

"I don't have any choices, Grady. I just don't."

Grady sighed. "You're a stubborn bastard."

"I'm not. I'm realistic. Barnaby is better off without me. Next season I'll be gone. God knows where. The long-distance thing would have sucked anyway. This way he can find someone else."

His stomach turned just saying it.

"Yeah, he probably will," Grady said agreeably. "I bet he could have someone doting on him soon enough. Just picture it. Picture another man kissing him, touching his body, rolling him under—"

The sound of the Maker's Mark bottle shattering against the wall obscured whatever Grady said next. It was followed by a profound silence.

"Yeah," Grady said as he rose to his feet, "that's what I thought."

Travis put up a hand when Grady came toward him.

Grady sighed. "I'll clean up this mess, but you're going back to bed. You need sleep. I've been listening to you pace all damn day, which is why I came up here to begin with."

Travis slumped, defeated. "Yeah, okay."

He let Grady shuffle him off to his room, recalling his manners long enough to thank him for his help and for coming by.

Grady snorted. "You're welcome. I'll be on your couch tonight if you need anything," he said, closing the bedroom door in Travis's face before he could respond.

Apparently, Grady thought he needed a keeper. He was probably right.

The bed felt as empty tonight as it had since Barnaby left, his back cold and heart aching. His last recovery had been so much smoother. Quicker. And he knew why. Barnaby. He'd never had anyone take care of him like that. He'd had coaches and teammates and trainers come and go, but not someone who had been...*his*.

And he'd fucked it up. For what?

Desperate to turn off the voices in his head, terrified of what they meant, he pulled his phone out of the bedside drawer and opened his text message string with Barnaby.

As with all the times before, he closed it, and instead tucked his earbuds into place and pulled the covers over his head like a naughty child. He'd turned the brightness all the way down and made it a point to only look long enough to hit play on what had already been cued up.

Barnaby's voice spilled out of the earphones and into Travis's broken head.

Samantha Wayland

When we two parted
In silence and tears,
Half broken-hearted
To sever for years,
Pale grew thy cheek and cold,
Colder thy kiss;
Truly that hour foretold
Sorrow to this...

That Lord Byron knew his shit.

Chapter Twenty-One

The irony did not escape Barnaby that he spent the first couple of days after leaving Travis's flat shut away in his room with the shades drawn. He stayed on top of his emails and his work, but otherwise, he was curled up in a ball in the dark, hoping that Travis was doing the same, that he was healing, even while Barnaby was cursing his name.

On the third day, Barnaby had to suck it up and drag himself to campus. He didn't consider stinting on his obligations there, no matter how much he wished he could take more time to lick his wounds. Imploding his own life wasn't going to help anything, and he would never forgive himself.

He knew better, damn it. He'd learned.

That was also why he'd left a voicemail for his manager at the Moncton Quality Hotel & Suites, asking if he could have his old job back. Letting him know he might be able to do even more hours over the summer.

The first time he staggered into the living room, all activity ceased as the family turned to watch him. He paused, daunted, then kept going until he was out the door and could pretend he hadn't seen the long look Callum and Rupert had exchanged, or the worry in Christian's and Oliver's eyes.

Eleanor, at least, had simply appeared happy to see him. Tonight, he'd ask if he could read her bedtime stories. He clung to that idea to get through the long day on campus.

The moment he finished reading *Goodnight Moon*, though, he tucked Eleanor into her crib and slipped back into his room, locking the door behind him.

It became the routine, the only change being that Rupert had to go on the road, the playoffs moving between Moncton and their opponent's arena. Callum was a master at keeping the household running smoothly—he and his trusty minivan carting the children to their schools and activities. He wasn't subtle in how he watched Barnaby traipse through the house between his room and the front door, but he didn't stop him. And he didn't make him *talk*.

Barnaby wasn't ready for that, and he was grateful that Callum was willing to give him some space. He returned to sitting with the family for dinner and doing work with Christian at the table if there was time. He was happy to go over whatever Christian needed help with, but otherwise, he remained mostly silent.

It wasn't bad, though it got dicey when the conversation turned to the team. Barnaby kept his head down and his face blank, retreating to his room as quickly as possible.

While Callum and Rupert proved to be incredibly patient, it ended up being *Jack* who got tired of waiting, after a week of Barnaby barely returning his texts and refusing to make any plans.

Barnaby was already in bed, listening to the sounds of the family coming home from another game. The Ice Cats were still in the playoffs, with more games to come, and Barnaby couldn't stop thinking about what that might mean. He wouldn't ask, though. He swore he didn't want to know.

He was in nothing more than his boxer shorts when there was a firm knock on his door. He sat up. "Yes?"

"Open up."

"*Jack?*"

"No, it's your mother. *Open up.*"

Barnaby huffed and jumped out of bed, yanking on a pair of pajama bottoms and stumbling to the door. He'd barely unlocked it when it swung open, nearly taking his nose off.

Jack stepped into the room and shut the door behind him. "Jesus Christ, those two are like a couple of guard dogs."

"Who?"

"Rupert and Callum. Though I'm pretty sure Christian and Oliver would have tackled me to the floor and dragged me out onto the street if they'd thought I was a threat."

Barnaby chuckled. "You have to watch out for Oliver. He's little but he's crafty."

"I have no doubt," Jack said, but it sounded rote, the natural conclusion to their banter, while his focus was on Barnaby's face, searching for who knew what. "How are you doing?"

Barnaby honestly didn't know, but his manners made him say, "Fine."

"You're pale. And you've been hiding from me."

"No, not you," Barnaby said, touching Jack's arm. "I needed a little time to myself, I guess. I—it—he…" He was frustrated by the tears welling in his eyes. "I'm a bit of a mess, frankly."

Jack frowned and studied him. Then he sighed. "I don't suppose this is going to help, but Travis asked me to give this to you."

Barnaby took an instinctive step back, putting up a hand to ward off the envelope Jack held out.

Neither moved, Barnaby's eyes locked on the envelope, Jack's on Barnaby's face. "Come on, B. You can do this."

Jack's confidence more than any desire to know what was in the envelope, pushed Barnaby to take it from him and tear it open. Inside was a wad of cash and a note.

Barnaby,
This is what I would have paid you for the rest of the semester, which only seems fair.

I'm sorry.
T.

Barnaby's hand shook and he crushed the note and the cash in his fist. His eyes burned.

He turned toward his bed to give himself a moment to pull it together.

Jack gasped. "*What the fuck.*"

Barnaby froze, though he was happy for the distraction. "Oh. Ha, yes. So, I have a tattoo," he said weakly.

"No shit," Jack said, then a warm hand pressed to Barnaby's back.

Barnaby held still. Jack didn't often initiate physical contact. He could flirt a person into submission in the blink of an eye, but rarely touched them.

Jack's warm fingers traced the same path over the dragon's body that Travis's had months ago, and many times since, but it was completely different. It wasn't sexual, though it was intimate in a way he didn't think Jack often allowed.

When Jack's hand got to his shoulder, he turned so Jack could see the tongue and tail, and so Barnaby could see Jack's face.

"That's incredible," Jack said.

"Thank you. I've had it a long time. I sometimes forget it's there. Or that people don't know it's there, anyway." He shrugged.

"Why did you do it?"

Barnaby explained about Ryu, filling in the details he'd intentionally left out before. Jack listened, his gaze thoughtful as Barnaby spoke, eventually nudging him to spin so he could see Barnaby's back in the light of the bedside lamp while Barnaby answered his questions about how long it had taken.

"So, did it help?" Jack asked at last.

"Pardon?"

"With the grief," Jack clarified.

"Oh...I suppose it did. I spent a lot of time lying on that table, in terrible pain, honestly, and thinking about Ryu. I don't know if that's a magical combination, but it did help me process it, now that I consider it. I felt better when it was done."

He looked over his shoulder to see Jack nodding. "You carry it with you," Jack said.

"The tattoo?"

"Ryu. The grief."

"I do. But it's not *bad*. It's..."

"Beautiful."

Barnaby turned. "Thank you. I hadn't really thought of it like that before, but maybe that's why it's always been such a comfort to me."

Jack shrugged, his expression thoughtful.

Barnaby's thoughts, as always, returned to Travis. "Perhaps I should consider getting another."

Jack pursed his lips. "Not yet."

"What do you mean, *not yet*? Why not?"

Rather than answer, Jack toed off his shoes and dropped his coat on Barnaby's desk chair.

"What are you doing?"

"Staying a while. You got beer?"

As it happened, he did. He retrieved a couple of bottles from the little refrigerator beside his desk and passed one to Jack.

Jack surprised him by climbing onto the bed and propping himself against the headboard. Barnaby sat beside him, their legs stretched out side-by-side but not touching. For a long while, neither said anything.

"I'm in love with Travis."

"I know."

Barnaby made a frustrated noise. "I'm an idiot."

"You're not. He's a good man. He's just..."

"Fucked up."

Jack sighed and leaned his shoulder into Barnaby's. "Yeah. I'm sorry, B."

Barnaby didn't fight the tears this time. He put his head on Jack's shoulder and drank his beer. Jack, bless him, didn't say anything more until their bottles were empty and he put them both on the bedside table. "Come on. Let's get some sleep."

Barnaby wasn't sure what to make of that, so he went along when Jack pulled down the covers. Barnaby crawled into bed, and watched as Jack stripped off his jeans and jumper and crawled in from the other side wearing only his boxers and a t-shirt.

Barnaby was certain the younger version of himself, had he been in bed with a man as devastatingly handsome as Jack, would have had some idea of what the hell to do with him. Instead, he hesitated until Jack reached for him, encouraging him to lie close and rest his head on Jack's shoulder.

He cautiously put an arm around Jack's ribs and let out a long breath from deep inside his chest, easing some of the tension that had been knotted in him. "Thanks, Jack."

Jack nodded and curled his arm around Barnaby's back. Barnaby hoped, with all his heart, that there was some comfort given, along with the comfort he took.

He woke up the next morning feeling more rested than he had in a week and with Jack snoring softly beside him. Barnaby felt remarkably ready to face the day. Better than he had in a week.

He barely lifted his head and Jack's eyes snapped open and zeroed in on him.

"Good morning," he said, worried he'd frightened Jack.

Jack blinked a few times, attempted a smile. "Good morning."

With that bit of awkwardness accomplished, Barnaby rolled out of bed and ran his fingers through his hair, which he could tell was standing straight on end by the way Jack's smile became more genuine.

"You got time for dinner this week?" Jack asked as he got out of bed and pulled on his jeans.

"Sure."

"Tomorrow night? After the game?"

"That works," Barnaby said, hoping Jack would be okay with not actually talking about the game, or its participants.

"You okay if I invite Grady along? He'd like to see you."

Barnaby hesitated, turning to hunt for a fresh shirt to give himself a moment. He pulled it on and found Jack watching him with a frown.

"What?" Jack asked.

"Grady is really Travis's friend," Barnaby explained.

"Because I like you," Jack said, "I'm never going to tell Grady you said that. Grady is *your* friend, you dick. He's also friends with Travis, but that's not going to change how he feels about you."

"That's...I'm glad. You're right. He's a really great guy."

"He is." The smile on Jack's face was heartbreaking. "Will you be going to the game? Grady would probably love to sit with you."

"No. Not...not this season. And not any game Travis is playing in, ever," he said, hoping Jack would understand. "I just can't. What if...Well, I guess that's what this all boils down to. *What if.* Or, possibly even more grimly, *when.*"

Jack nodded. "I get it."

It mattered, a lot, that he did. Barnaby suspected Jack wouldn't be able to enjoy a game Travis played in much either, but he didn't ask. It felt too much like sticking a finger in a festering wound and swirling it around. Also, it was Jack's job to be at those games.

Barnaby finished getting dressed and walked Jack to the front door. Jack's ability to disguise his emotions didn't quite rise to the level required not to blush in the face of the shocked expressions on everyone's face when he walked out of Barnaby's bedroom at seven o'clock in the morning, wearing the same clothes as the night before.

"I'll explain," Barnaby murmured to Jack, holding the front door for him.

Jack nodded once and fled.

Barnaby locked up, then turned and almost laughed at the comical mix of expressions. Oliver, bless him, appeared confused. Christian outraged. Callum stunned, and Rupert amused.

Callum turned to Christian. "Can you please take Oliver downstairs? We need to speak with Barnaby."

"No way," Christian said.

Barnaby came over to the table and gratefully accepted the

plate Rupert passed him, taking his seat and loading it with eggs and toast. "It's okay if they stay. Jack was worried about me, so he spent the night to make me feel better."

Callum arched an eyebrow. "And just how much better did Jack make you feel?"

Barnaby choked on his eggs and was forced to cough them back out of his lungs. "We're *just friends*," he managed once he'd recovered.

"Like you're just friends with Travis?" Rupert asked mildly.

"No. I haven't fallen in love with Jack, more's the pity."

The family greeted that confession with silence, except Oliver. "So, it was a sleepover?"

Barnaby smiled. "Yes. I had a sleepover with my friend Jack."

"Can I have a sleepover with my friend Austin?" Christian asked.

"No," his fathers said in unison.

Barnaby made a mental note to ask Christian about this Austin later.

Christian sighed mightily. "Fine." He stood from the table and chugged the last of his juice. "Come on, Oliver. Let's go downstairs and leave the grownups to talk about things I'm not too young to hear about."

The grownups in question smiled at one another while the boys marched down the hallway.

Barnaby slid into Christian's spot next to Rupert and Callum, which put a vase full of daffodils, of all things, in front of him. He'd been so busy feeling sorry for himself this week, he'd barely noticed how the long-awaited spring was finally taking hold in Moncton.

He promised himself he'd pick up his head today and really enjoy the warmer weather. Reaching out, he drew a finger over the silky trumpet of one of the flowers. He might not be able to dig up much hope, but he certainly could cling to the notion of resilience right then.

"Thanks for giving me some time," he said.

"You okay?" Callum asked.

"I am. Or, I will be. I've gone and broken my heart, is all." He rubbed his sternum where the ache was easing, but still present. It would be for a long time, he suspected.

"Can we ask what happened?" Rupert asked.

Barnaby considered it, tempted to say no. He didn't really want to go over it, let alone cry *again*, which he knew he would do.

He jumped when Callum's hand slid over his. "Hey. You don't have to tell us anything, but we're worried about you. You're a member of this family, and we want to know how to take care of you."

And well, *damn them,* if he was going to get all teary anyway, he might as well lay it all out.

So, he did. Including, after a long hesitation where he tried to figure out how not to mention it, Travis's concussion history.

It was clear, as Barnaby had suspected, that Rupert and Callum hadn't known the extent of that history. It was a relief that they were obviously dismayed, but it also made him feel more guilty.

"Will you kick him off the team?" he asked, afraid the answer would be yes. More afraid the answer would be no.

"I can't," Rupert said with a frown. "The contract protects both parties. I can warn the medical staff to take a closer look before they clear him to play, but they're already incredibly thorough and conscientious, so if Travis isn't upfront with them, there's only so much they can do. The good news," he added, "is that they *are* incredibly thorough and conscientious, so when they cleared him last time, he was completely healed by their measure."

Barnaby nodded. "That's good." He thought about it, picking at his breakfast for a long while. "Is he getting better?"

Rupert smiled sadly. "I can't tell you what the doctors say, but yes, he's getting better."

Barnaby nodded, his stomach going sour. He regretted

having dug into his breakfast so enthusiastically. "Okay."

"Barnaby, I know this is hard, but Travis—"

"No," Barnaby said, cutting Rupert off. "I don't want to know anything else. I'd prefer it if we didn't talk about him again."

Ever.

Travis was healing. That was all Barnaby needed to know.

"I can't be with Travis," he said, trying to explain something he hadn't been able to put into words to this point. "Not like this. He may have been the one to send me away, but I can see it's for the best."

Callum watched him. "Why is that?"

"Because I'm a romantic," Barnaby said with a self-deprecating smile. "And for the first time in a long time, I can see that's not a bad thing. I've been beating myself up for my penchant for grand gestures, for wearing my heart on my sleeve, and have only realized this week that there's nothing wrong with those things. I don't regret those gestures, or being honest about who I love. I don't regret having Ryu more or less tattooed on my back. And I don't regret helping Robert launch his career. Ryu may never know what I did, but I do, and it's allowed me to carry my friend, and my love for him, with me. It gives me strength." Something he hadn't really recognized until Jack pointed it out, for which he would be eternally grateful. "And my mistake with Robert was that he didn't deserve the gesture. But that's his failing, not mine."

He took a sip of his tea to clear the scratch from his throat, not sure what to do with the expressions on Callum and Rupert's faces. They looked *proud*.

"For me, being in love means going all-in," Barnaby admitted, working it out as he spoke the words aloud. "It means building a life together, and looking to the future, and figuring out what makes you and the person you love happy. Travis can't do that. He can't see the future at all, let alone what will make him happy, so he is, by definition, not able to do the same for me." He shrugged, some of the defeat seeping back in, his chest tight. "So, he's not for me. And I'm not for him."

Barnaby didn't know what he expected in response to all that, but it wasn't for Callum to haul him out of his chair and into a rib-crushing hug. Perhaps more shocking was that as soon as he was released, Rupert did the same.

Barnaby sagged again his cousin. "We never used to do this hugging thing back home."

"No," Rupert agreed, thankfully still holding on tight. "Not in England. But this is your home now."

"Yes," Barnaby said, taking a deep breath and letting his family bolster him. "It is."

Travis sat in his living room watching the Toronto game on TV, telling himself it wasn't the beginnings of a headache blooming behind his eyeballs.

It had been over a week, and he was getting better. The nausea had passed quickly, thank Christ, and the headaches and light sensitivity had improved incrementally each day. He'd been cleared for some limited screens and decided he wanted to use it to watch hockey, of course. He'd even convinced Grady and Jack to join him.

They were stretched out on the couch, beers in hand, popcorn within reach. Travis took a sip of his water and refused to be jealous. The last time he'd been recovering, no one had eaten or drunk anything in front of him that he couldn't have, too. Barnaby's influence, no doubt.

Don't think about that.

It was also quite possible they'd agreed to it last time, but this time figured he didn't deserve the courtesy. He probably didn't.

He was trying to be less of a massive dick, though. Trying to find his feet and get back to the normal routines of life. He'd even attempted some homework today, but had given up almost immediately. School had always sucked, but now it *hurt*. And not his head. God, he could probably learn fucking poetry better with a headache than he could reading stirring words about love and loss while thinking about Barnaby.

It was remarkable, really. He'd somehow made the learning process even *more* painful. That was some real A+ work right there.

He was startled when the front door buzzer sounded, then his heart leaped.

Only so many people in Moncton knew where he lived and might stop by this late at night.

Grady sat up and arched an eyebrow. Travis tried so damn hard not to look hopeful. He forced himself to stay in what he'd started to think of as his Lonely Boy Chair and wait for Grady to murmur something into the speaker. Travis strained his ears to hear the response but couldn't quite make it out over the TV. He didn't look to see what the crowd was roaring about. He didn't care.

He couldn't tear his eyes off the door.

His heart fell to his feet when Callum stepped into the apartment.

Jack stood. "Hey. What's up?"

Callum gave Jack a nod, then treated Travis to the least friendly once-over he'd ever receive. "You guys mind watching the rest of the game somewhere else?"

"Nope," Grady said, taking their beer bottles and tossing them in the recycling.

They left without another word. Travis tried not to feel betrayed.

He eyed Callum warily as he crossed the room, bypassed the couch, and sat on the coffee table directly in front of Travis.

"I'm supposed to read you poetry by some dude named Percy Shelley." Callum sounded angry about it.

"You don't have to do that," Travis said dully. He couldn't manage better, and not just because his head fucking hurt for sure now.

"No, I don't. But I'm going to. There's some good shit in here. Want to hear it?"

He really didn't. "Sure."

Like a poet hidden
In the light of thought,
Singing hymns unbidden,
Till the world is wrought
To sympathy with hopes and fears it heeded not...

Travis tried to keep his face blank, but it wasn't working. Callum might as well have stabbed him in the chest. "What's the name of that one?" he croaked.

"To a Skylark."

He swallowed, holding onto his composure by a thread. "Sounds cheerful."

Callum snorted, his gaze still on Travis's face, like he was a puzzle Callum could figure out.

Good fucking luck.

Travis was tired, and so, so ready to be done with this farce. "Is this where you give me the retroactive shovel talk about hurting Barnaby? Because, at this point, death would just be a fucking relief."

Callum sighed and looked...maybe disappointed. Maybe just sad. "I'm here to talk about options."

"Shouldn't Rupert be the one to boot me off the team? He send you instead?"

"Neither of us deserve that."

Travis took a deep breath. "You're right. I'm sorry."

Callum nodded, accepting his apology with more grace than Travis deserved. "I know you don't want to hear what I have to say, but are you ready to listen?"

It wasn't like this conversation was avoidable. Travis had been terrified of it for years, so he couldn't quite figure out how it had snuck up on him.

Worse, he couldn't figure out if the sacrifices he'd made to come this far had been worth it.

Hindsight was a bitch.

"Yeah, I'm listening."

Chapter Twenty-Two

Travis stood in the hallway outside Rupert and Callum's home and waited for the door to open. He was terrified.

It had been four long, horrible weeks since he'd last laid eyes on Barnaby, and he was afraid he was going to embarrass himself when he finally did. He'd spent most of the last three weeks since his talk with Callum thinking about texting Barnaby. Or calling him. Facetime, maybe.

Mostly he'd thought about falling to his knees and begging Barnaby to forgive him.

That was on the agenda for today. And not one part of Travis was scared of that. It was what he needed to do. It would be a *relief.*

What scared the ever-loving shit out of him was that Barnaby had no idea he was coming, and he had no idea what Barnaby's reaction to seeing him would be.

He jumped when the door finally popped open and Callum appeared, his broad shoulders blocking the view from the hallway—*of* the hallway—as he called back into the house, "We'll be out for a couple hours at least. Unless you need us."

"Why would I need you?" Barnaby asked.

Travis's heart stopped at the sound of his voice. That achingly familiar voice.

He hadn't allowed himself any contact, but he'd listened to Barnaby read him poetry, over and over, until he had every single word memorized. He had an appreciation for poetry, now, that he was certain far exceeded his professor's wildest hopes. She'd been happy to give him a solid B+ in her class, a grade that had only been possible thanks to Rupert and Callum helping him limp across the finish line.

He wanted to tell Barnaby about that—about everything he'd done since they'd last seen one another—but first he had to apologize. First, he had things he needed to say.

Regardless of how supportive they'd been of him, he'd been surprised when Callum and Rupert had agreed to help him today. He'd explained what he wanted to do, and when Callum asked him why, he'd admitted he wanted to make a grand romantic gesture.

Callum had immediately agreed, and refused to explain his big smile. That he and Rupert were rooting for Travis went a long way toward boosting his confidence.

Christian called goodbye to Barnaby and stepped into the hallway. His mouth dropped open, his eyes bulging, when he saw Travis. Rupert slipped into the hallway in time to clap a hand over Christian's mouth.

"Not a word," Rupert whispered, nudging Christian toward the elevator. "We know what we're about."

"Busybodying is what you're about," Christian muttered in an uncanny impersonation of Rupert's accent. He climbed aboard the rickety old lift and held the door for Oliver, who was getting the same warning from Rupert as he was towed along.

Christian wasn't wrong, was the thing.

Callum stepped into the hallway backwards, with Eleanor on his hip. He left the door ajar, whispered, "Good luck," and practically ran to the elevator.

Travis took a deep breath, stepped through the door, and closed it behind him.

"Did you forget something?" Barnaby asked from where he was bent over some papers at the table.

Travis opened his mouth to answer, to say *something*, but he had lost his voice. All he could do was drink in the sight of Barnaby. His brown curls were shorter, presumably in deference to the rising summer temperatures, but his skin was still winter pale. Travis's fingers ached to touch a smooth cheek. His lips burned to taste the spot behind Barnaby's ear, at the top of the long, strong column of his neck. His heart beat so hard he could barely breathe.

Unfortunately, his knees had also gone to water, so he was

stuck, gaping at the man he loved from across the room.

He licked his lips and swallowed hard. "Hi."

As entrances went, it left something to be desired, but it worked.

Barnaby's head snapped up. "Travis? What are you doing here? How—"

"Callum let me in."

Barnaby's frown did not bode well for Travis *or* Callum. "Did he." His eyes dipped and his eyebrows went up. The color on his cheeks deepened to red as he took in the huge bouquet of bright yellow daffodils and dark red roses Travis carried in his arms.

It was a weird combination, which the florist had told him at least eight times, but Travis knew what he was doing.

Mostly.

He reminded himself he was an athlete and that his legs fucking worked. He made it to the corner of the table before he drew up short.

Barnaby rose slowly, less than a dozen feet away. Travis's heart broke all over again when he saw how Barnaby's hands shook before he shoved them behind his back.

"These are for you," Travis said, holding the flowers out.

When Barnaby didn't move to take them, Travis laid them gently on the table and told himself it was okay. Flowers shouldn't be enough. Not even close.

The grand romantic gesture would wait. First, he needed to talk.

"I'd like to tell you what I've been doing these three weeks," he began. "If you'd be willing to listen?" he added.

Barnaby thought about it for a moment, his eyes straying to the flowers. He nodded.

Travis squelched the surge of hope that made his heart feel too big, his head light. He needed to get this done.

"It took me about a week to figure out you were right," he admitted, his voice so gravelly he had to pause to clear it.

Barnaby's big blue eyes were pinned on Travis's face, and he swore to himself he'd do whatever it took to make sure he never had to go so long without seeing them again.

He took a breath and continued. "I'd like to take all the credit for finally waking up, but it was Callum and Rupert who really kicked my ass."

Barnaby frowned. "I'm sorry. I didn't send them—"

"No. I know you didn't. You told them what happened, though, and why."

"I betrayed your trust."

"You helped me. No, don't shake your head. I'm not mad. I'm glad you told them. It was the right thing to do. I should have done it when I started on the Ice Cats, and certainly after the first concussion here. But more than that, I should have talked to someone, *anyone*, in the hockey world about what was going on with me. In hindsight, I can see that was a huge and really stupid oversight on my part. I didn't tell anyone, and when I did, I dumped it on you and Grady and Jack, and not someone who understood what it was to play hockey, like Callum. Or someone who understood how the hockey world works, like Rupert. In the end, you kind of told the two most ideal people, really."

"I told them because they were worried about me. Not because I was worried about you."

That hurt, but it was no less than Travis had expected. "I get that."

Barnaby looked at his feet, his frown deepening.

Travis wondered if he'd ever been able to read someone as well as he could Barnaby. If he'd ever been so connected to someone. Not even Martin. But then, he'd never felt like this about anyone before.

"Don't feel bad about that," he said. Barnaby's head came up and he looked surprised. "You have nothing to feel guilty about. Not for not telling Rupert sooner about my head, or for telling him when you did and why, okay?"

Barnaby studied his face, then nodded.

Travis let out a breath. One hurdle crossed, three hundred to go.

He took a chance and moved a step closer to Barnaby. His entire body ached to reach out and touch. To pull Barnaby into his arms. He had to settle for viewing it as a win when Barnaby didn't step back.

"I retired from playing hockey," Travis said, needing to get it out. It still hurt, but not like it used to. The fear of it was gone. And ultimately, that hadn't been nearly as scary as what he'd done next. "Then I went to a clinic in the States that specializes in rehabilitating head trauma. I stayed as long as I could, this go-round. A couple weeks. And I have to go back, maybe a few times." He smiled a little. "I blew a good chunk of my savings, but it was worth it."

His heart leaped when Barnaby took a step closer to him. "Was it? Did...did it help?"

"I think so. It was..." He considered prettying it up, but discarded the idea. "It was awful, actually. Nauseating and terrifying. They put you through all these tests and challenges. Fuck with your eyes, your balance." He shook his head, forcing himself to push the worst of it away. "It was bad. I mean, it was *good* because I know those doctors were helping me, but it was...yeah, it was bad."

And lonely. God, he'd never been so alone in his life.

He swallowed hard. "I listened to your voice. A lot. Every night. Reading me poems."

It had been the only thing he could cling to.

He held perfectly still as Barnaby took another step.

"I'm sorry. I'm sorry you had to go through that alone."

"It's okay. I kind of had to do it alone, you know? I had to pay the price for being stubborn. And stupid."

"I wasn't trying to punish you, I—"

Travis dared to press a finger to Barnaby's full, pink lips, pulling it away again before he could give into the consuming need to touch more.

"It helped to know you were here, in Moncton, finishing your semester and working toward your degree. I needed to know you were at home and safe when I...wasn't."

Barnaby looked bewildered.

Travis smiled sadly. "It was okay. Grady and Jack let me vent, and Rupert and Callum were always checking in. They made me finish my class while I was there," he added with a wry smile. "It was brutal. Callum does *not* have your gift for reading poetry. Like, *at all*."

Barnaby laughed, just a little, and Travis ached. God, he was so beautiful.

He still wasn't sure what he'd ever done to make this man, this perfect, brilliant, beautiful man, fall in love with him.

He could only hope he hadn't killed it too thoroughly to fix it.

Barnaby hovered by the table, his hands useless at his sides, and drank in the sight of Travis. He looked so much better than he had a month ago. Healthier. Happier.

Though no less worried. No less sad.

Barnaby understood. Just thinking of that moment hurt. A constant ache he hadn't been able to shake for a minute. It had become more about learning to live with it. Learning to accept he'd been immutably changed by loving Travis.

He'd spent a great deal of the last two weeks in a tattoo parlor with Jack, watching him adopt the process Barnaby had gone through for Ryu and turn it into a tool he could apply to his own body. His own grief. Barnaby had sat silently and held his hand as much as possible because Jack seemed to want a witness. It was a role Barnaby had taken gladly, a task he was honored to have been offered.

Even if he did think Jack had lost his mind for getting those particular bits of himself tattooed.

But while he'd sat there, he'd spent a lot of time trying to work out how to process his feelings for Travis. The only conclusion he'd come to was that there wasn't a mark he could make on his body, at least, that would be able to contain them.

He looked at the flowers on the table again. Daffodils and roses.

Travis stepped closer. "Wordsworth and Burns."

Barnaby looked into those familiar, beloved caramel-brown eyes. "What?"

"Wordsworth and his daffodils. Resilience, right? Spring. A fresh start. Hope. I thought maybe we could use some of that."

Barnaby nodded, certain Travis hadn't come for another lecture on metaphor in poetry but unable to truly believe what the frantic beat of his heart was trying to tell him. "And the roses?" he asked, his voice little more than a scratch.

Travis picked up the bundle of flowers and pressed them into Barnaby's trembling hands. "Love."

"Love?" he whispered, his chest painfully tight. His breath shallow. Because he'd gone over that night in his head, so many times. He'd talked about love, shouted it at Travis, when all Travis had ever said was *boyfriends*.

He shuddered when Travis drew the back of his hand, his scarred and calloused knuckles, down Barnaby's cheek. They stood close enough that the flowers were pressed between them, and Barnaby could not tear his eyes from Travis's gaze.

Barnaby leaned into Travis's touch.

"Elizabeth Barrett Browning," Travis asked.

"What?" Barnaby's heart stuttered, then fell to his feet, because Travis couldn't possibly mean—

Then Travis was speaking, the words spilling over Barnaby like a summer rain. Like a dream.

How do I love thee? Let me count the ways.
I love thee to the depth and breadth and height
My soul can reach, when feeling out of sight
For the ends of Being and ideal Grace.
I love thee to the level of everyday's
Most quiet need, by sun and candlelight.

I love thee freely, as men strive for Right;
I love thee purely, as they turn from Praise.
I love thee with the passion put to use
In my old griefs, and with my childhood's faith.
I love thee with a love I seemed to lose
With my lost Saints—I love thee with the breath,
Smile, tears, of all my love!—and, if God choose,
I shall but love thee better after death.

The sound that tore out of Barnaby was more animal than human, primal from where it had come right up out of his soul. He had no words, knew none could ever be found to do better than Browning had done, so he kissed Travis instead.

Travis cupped his face and kissed him back, his thumbs tracing through the wet streaks on Barnaby's face.

"I'm sorry," he murmured, over and over as he pressed endless kisses to Barnaby's lips. "I'm so, so sorry."

"No. Travis, no. Don't be sorry. I love you, too. I shouldn't have—"

Travis stopped his words with another kiss, this one longer, his tongue slipping between Barnaby's lips and stealing his every thought.

When the kiss ended, Travis stepped back, leaving Barnaby standing there with his eyes closed and his head spinning. Travis's chuckle brought him back to the present.

"I'll buy you more flowers," Travis said with a rueful smile.

Barnaby looked down and laughed. "Oh, dear." The roses, not quite open yet, had managed to survive being pressed between their bodies. The delicate trumpets and frills of the daffodils, not so much.

He looked back up at Travis consideringly. "Not that I'd say no to more flowers," he began, picking his way carefully, "but what does all this mean?"

"It means I love you," Travis said.

Barnaby smiled. "I got that bit, but..."

"Oh," Travis said, and Barnaby could see how his nerves

came back. "That's up to you, I guess. I'm too old to be called a boyfriend, but if that's what you want, then I'll take it. I'm ready for more, though. Whatever you want. I want you with me all the time. When you're ready to move in together, I'm ready, too. I'm ready for anything."

Barnaby's heart was pounding again. "Anything?"

"I can apply for a marriage certificate this afternoon."

Barnaby's heart stopped and he swayed precariously on his feet before Travis caught him.

"Or not!" Travis yelped. "Too soon. I'm sorry. I'm just..." Travis took a deep breath and let it out fast. "Barnaby Birtwistle, I am in love with you, and I have been for a long time. I didn't know what it was, and it was too tied up in the constant panic I've been living with for years. The panic is gone, now, and I can see clearly, *feel* clearly, for the first time in ages. And what I see is you. I guess I should tell you that this is what being in love means to me. It's going all-in. I want it all. I want to build a life with you."

Something on Barnaby's face must have alarmed him because he gripped his arms tighter and kept talking.

"But you don't have to be on the same page. I just wanted you to know what page I'm on. It's okay if you're not there yet. Jesus, I'm screwing this up."

"You're not," Barnaby said, half laugh, half gasp. "You're not screwing this up at all."

"I'm not?" The hope on Travis's face was almost painful to look at.

"I'd love to move in with you, to start."

Travis's smile grew while his shoulders came down from around his ears. "Yeah?"

"We'll need to figure out how the two of us are going to pay the rent, given I'm a student with massive debt and you're figuring out your next steps."

"Oh! Oh, wait. I forgot to tell you stuff. I enrolled in two classes for next semester. And I have a job."

"You did? You *do*?" Barnaby asked.

"You're looking at the new talent scout for the Moncton Ice Cats. Apparently, I've been doing part of the job for free for Rupert all season." Travis laughed. "I just thought all those times Rupert sat next to me were his way of harassing me because you and I were boinking, but it turns out he actually liked listening to me break down the players on other teams."

Barnaby laughed, enchanted by how Travis's entire face was lit up. "Really?"

"Yes. It's a cool job. I'll also be doing some player development stuff with the guys on the team." Travis frowned. "But it does mean I'll be traveling a lot to check out prospects. Is that okay?"

"Versus all the traveling you did when you were playing and I fell in love with you?" Barnaby teased. "Of course that's okay. I'm more concerned that you still work for my family."

"Does that bother you?"

"Not if it doesn't bother you. Will it bother you if we spend a lot of time here? I'll be happy living with you, wherever that is, but I want to stay close to them, too."

"Of course. I kind of figured we'd move into my place, but we can move closer if you want."

Barnaby smiled. "I'd love to have Grady as my neighbor."

"Feeling's mutual, you know. He and Jack did not pull any punches when I fucked things up. I was pretty sure I would have lost the both of them as friends out of loyalty to you if I hadn't pulled my head out of my ass."

That should have made him sad for Travis, but Barnaby was so warmed by the idea, he wanted to find Jack and Grady and hug them. God, Callum and Rupert were rubbing off on him in the most appalling ways.

He wrapped his arms around Travis, as consolation to them both, and kissed him again. It wasn't long before he started to lose track of time, the buzz of his phone in his pocket the only reason he stopped.

He checked the screen and smiled, unlocking his phone just long enough to send a heart back to Rupert. They'd get the idea.

He recalled, suddenly, Callum's emphatic promise not to be back for hours. He smiled at Travis.

"You got anywhere to be this afternoon?"

"Not unless I'm going to city hall."

Barnaby's chest felt like it was exploding with happiness. "And I'm not saying no to that marriage certificate, but let's at least hold off until one of us can ask the other properly." He poked Travis in the stomach.

Travis grinned. "That seems fair. So, what did you want to do instead?"

Barnaby pressed his body the full length of Travis's and slid his hands down the back of Travis's jeans. He laughed when his fingers curled around the elastic of a jockstrap. "Feeling pretty confident, weren't you?"

"It's the first time I've put one on in a month," Travis admitted, his smile sly.

Barnaby tucked his lips behind Travis's ear, nuzzling him just there while he told him *exactly* what he wanted to do with their afternoon.

He could tell Travis liked the idea when he threw Barnaby over his shoulder and ran down the hallway to Barnaby's room.

Author's Note

All of the poems in this book were ones I studied in Poetry 101 my freshman year in college. My textbook for that course was the Norton Anthology of Poetry (3rd ed.), the source from which I drew a great deal of the poems contained in this book. I have presented all of these poems in chronological order, and mentioned the titles and authors in all cases. These works are all in the public domain, though, and can be found any number of places.

To that end, I found *His Coy Mistress*, by Andrew Marvel, and *The Tally*, by Hafiz, on a number of websites/online resources while searching and researching various poems.

The haiku to a jockstrap was written by me, and the limerick to a jockstrap was penned by a friend, Claire, who has chosen to remain otherwise anonymous, but has been kind enough to grant me use of her opus.

The greeting card (*the honor of your presence is requested in my pants*) is by Emily McDowell, who had a number of amazing cards for all different occasions. Her work can be found HERE.

The *Hockey is Importanter* shirt can be found any number of places online.

About the Author

Samantha Wayland has three great loves in life; her family, writing books, and hockey. She is often found apologizing to the first for how much time and attention is taken up by the latter two, but they forgive her because they are awesome and she clearly doesn't deserve them.

Sam lives with her family—of both the two and four-legged variety—outside of Boston. She is a wicked passionate New Englander (born and raised) who has been known to wax rhapsodic about the Maine Coast, the mountains of New Hampshire and Vermont, and the sensible way in which her local brethren don't see a need for directional signals (blinkahs!). When she's not locked away in her home office, she can generally be found tucked in the corner of the local Thai place with other socially-starved authors and an adult beverage.

Her favorite things include mango martinis, tiny Chihuahuas with big attitude problems, and the Oxford comma.

Sam loves to hear from readers. Email her at samantha@samanthawayland.com, visit her website at www.samanthawayland.com, or find her on Facebook (Samantha Wayland), Twitter (@samwayland), or Instagram (SamWayRomance).

www.ingramcontent.com/pod-product-compliance
Lightning Source LLC
Chambersburg PA
CBHW021324250626
47155CB00002B/611